W.

Ella Reeve Bloor. Sculpture by A. Cortizas

WE ARE MANY

AN AUTOBIOGRAPHY BY *Ella Reeve Bloor*

FOREWORD BY CHAUNCEY ROBINSON

Rise like lions after slumber
In unvanquishable number!
Shake your chains to earth, like dew
Which in sleep had fallen on you—
Ye are many, they are few.

—PERCY BYSSHE SHELLEY

INTERNATIONAL PUBLISHERS, NEW YORK

ISBN10: 0717808807   ISBN13: 9780717808809

CONTENTS

LIST OF ILLUSTRATIONS

The Practical Lessons of Mother Bloor's Life

By Chauncey Robinson

ELLA Reeve Bloor, also affectionately known as Mother Bloor, is an American icon. The work she did in the early days of the labor movement in the United States was a key piece to the great picture that shapes our present day victories and struggles.

As the famous Black American writer James Baldwin noted, "Know from whence you came. If you know whence you came, there are absolutely no limitations to where you can go." That's what I think of when it comes to Mother Bloor. History is not stagnant; it is part of an ever changing and evolving landscape of the reality we all find ourselves. Mother Bloor's story is not only her own individual tale, but the story of a movement—of a people, the working class. To read of the struggles, defeats, and triumphs she lived through, is to have the privilege to get a glimpse of what we achieved, and what can be achieved now and in the future.

I call Ella Reeve Bloor my comrade, even though I never had the chance to personally meet her, because she was a fellow fighter for a better world for the masses of people that build and shape our society. And I guarantee that by the end of *We Are Many*, you will consider her a comrade as well.

What she left for those of us who still battle for true democracy, equality, and empowerment, is a colorful memoir that easily serves as a guide for the world we live in today. You will read about stories concerning women's rights, racial equality, better working conditions, and aims for an overhaul of an exploitative system. Readers will gain insight on useful methods of discerning what should be priorities when building a worker's movement, along with the trials and tribulations of forming organizations that serve in such an endeavor.

Bloor's sharp wit and no nonsense truth-telling comes through clearly in this book as the day it was originally published in 1940. By this time, she was 78 years old with decades of experience. Even at a young age, born in Staten Island and raised in New Jersey, Bloor began questioning the status quo. It began with the ideas surrounding religion and evolved to a passion for empower working people. When Bloor began her journey, things workers have now—the eight-hour workday and child labor laws—did not exist. Women were still fighting for the right to vote. The unions of today, were either in their infancy or non-existent. She was a trailblazer.

Names will surface in this book that have been referred to often in history, such as the famous socialist Eugene V. Debs and famous writer Upton Sinclair. Bloor worked closely with both men and considered them friends. In addition, you may read about people that are new to you or have been lost to the pages of mainstream history. I implore readers to take some time to dig further into who they were and the roles they played. Bloor devotes a good number of pages to the people and family members who came before her, and who she grew up around. She too understood the importance of connecting the past to the present. Let her book serve as a gateway to digging deeper into that living history.

There are a number of lessons to be learned from *We Are Many*. Decades before the phrase "the personal is political" was coined during the period of second-wave feminism in the 1960s, Ella Reeve Bloor was already living this truth. Like many women of her time, Bloor was married young and began having children early. While juggling motherhood, and at times lack of funds, she fought to secure an education. She also had to grapple with her emerging political consciousness in connection to the relationships she had and the way she lived her life. Bloor doesn't hold back when discussing what her calling to politics meant for her marriages, her family life, and her sense of self. She talks about her experiences in the suffrage movement and all the progress and setbacks that came with it. Bloor talks about the internal divide at times between working women and those that came from wealth within that movement. These are sobering accounts that will sound all too familiar to women today.

In 1973, years after Mother Bloor's death, the Supreme Court ruled that a woman's right to an abortion was implicit in the right to privacy protected by the 14th Amendment in the Constitution. *Roe v Wade* was a landmark decision in a long history of battles for gender equality. At the time of this writing, August 2022, an ultra-conservative Supreme Court has done away with this historic ruling. This devastating setback foreshadows other rights for women and marginalized groups being stripped away. Reading Mother Bloor's account of the fight for equal wages for women (something we still deal with) and the overall empowerment of women leaders in these struggles, shows us that progress is not always a straight line.

Bloor was also a woman who believed in science; she was practical. She studied botany and biology closely, to the point where she at one time thought her studies would take her in a different direction. Yet, she continued to use her application of theory, hypothesis, and concrete results in relation to her political activism. This fact is critically important in a number of ways.

Mother Bloor took some time before she called herself a socialist and then a communist. It wasn't instantaneous with her political work. It was through her lived experiences and lessons that she arrived at that point. The list of organizations she belonged to serve as a roadmap to her destination for what she described as a search "for that group which really understood the class struggle, which saw clearly the need of organizing the workers, with the greatest of all aims—that of taking over for the workers and farmers the means of production, the means of life." The reason why her background in science is so fascinating here is because every time she joined or left a group it was with a constant theme of what that group was doing effectively for and with the working class. It wasn't about empty platitudes of socialist utopias and disassociated talk of revolution for Bloor. She always understood that the results of progress and victory rested with the masses.

We see an example of this when she challenges the idea of Debs and the Socialist Democratic Party (SDP) at the time when they were talking about forming a socialist colony. Bloor considered this to be an unscientific approach and left that organization because she couldn't, in good conscience, support it. Some years later, Debs would come to realize the error in his socialist colony method as well. This is one example of many where Mother Bloor was ahead of the curve.

And where the masses were was where Bloor firmly had her politics rooted. The quote, "Politics begin[s] where the masses are, not where there are thousands, but where there are millions, that is where serious politics begin," is from the Russian revolutionary Vladimir Lenin (who Mother Bloor was able to see speak in person after the 1917 Russian Revolution). Yet, it should be noted that Bloor was implementing this fact of life already in the late 1890s. As Elizabeth Gurley Flynn rightfully points out in the first Foreword to this book, Mother Bloor was "preaching socialism" when Lenin was finishing his law exams and later dealing with exile. This is no slight to Lenin. It serves to put into perspective just how influential and pioneering Bloor was.

In honoring her pioneering spirit, we can take a lesson from her insistence of being part of the people and not separate and apart from their struggles. An organization that aims to serve the working class is one that must first listen to the working class. This is in order to understand the immediate wants and needs of the people. That means not dismissing those fights as short-sighted or short of a systemic revolution. It's understanding that there can be no significant change in society without the people who society is built on the backs of. Bloor knew this. As she remarked, she learned more from workers and farmers than she taught them. Of course, she was likely being humble. She had a lot to teach, but it exemplifies her understanding of being a piece in a much larger puzzle of progress.

And in her 89 years she witnessed the many ebbs and flows of human history, particularly some of the most historic of the late-19th and early-20th centuries. To put it into perspective: Mother Bloor notes that one of her first memories was the assassination of President Abraham Lincoln. As she came of age she was growing up in a time that working class culture was truly taking shape in the United States. Millions of people were becoming wage workers as a result of a number of factors.

One of those factors being what historians often refer to as the Second Industrial Revolution. The Industrial Revolution of the 18th century was a period of scientific and technological development. It made it so largely rural societies—particularly in Europe and North America—were being transformed into more industrialized, urban ones. Yet, it was the Second Industrial Revolution, that began in the mid-19th century, that ramped this transition up with advancements taking place in automobile, electric, and steel industries. Coupled with the emancipation of Black Americans from slavery after the Civil War, and with millions of immigrants coming to the U.S. in search for the ever elusive American Dream, and you had a melting pot of working class vibrancy.

Yet, with this growth and centralization of working people, came the emergence of industrial bosses, who—in their want for more wealth—often forced workers into horrid conditions for abysmal pay. As capitalist wealth was booming due to the labor of the masse, workers were seeing none of the benefits. In response, labor activism began to grow. Organizations and unions began to take shape, demanding better wages for workers. Mother Bloor bore witness to the dawn of a new age of worker empowerment. In her time a number of victories and tragedies took place.

She witnessed the Ludlow Massacre of 1914. It all began when the United Mine Workers of America (UMWA) went on strike against abysmal working conditions in the John Davison Rockefeller Jr. owned Colorado Fuel and Iron (CF&I) company. The workers were fighting for a number of demands, such as recognition of their union and enforcement of the eight-hour workday.

The anti-strike militia attacked a tent colony of nearly 1,200 coal miners and their families. Twenty-one people—including 13 children—were killed. This moment became influential in pushing the government towards implementing child labor laws and the enforcement of the eight-hour workday. You could read about this in a number of other history books in a distant third-person narrative, but you'll get to read a firsthand account of it through Mother Bloor. She was there, with other socialists, activists, union members, and communists helping the miners in their war with CF&I.

A story you most likely won't read about in most history textbooks is the Italian Hall Disaster of 1913 in Calumet, Michigan.

It happened in December, during a holiday party. Striking miners and their families gathered. Hundreds of them, including Mother Bloor, were in the hall that night. Someone, speculation points to anti-strike thugs looking to cause chaos, came into the hall yelling "fire." This deliberate false alarm caused nearly 100 attendees to run down the steep and narrow staircase. Tragically, someone had closed the door to the outside, and the staircase became a suffocating coffin for dozens of men, women, and children who tumbled on top of one another down the stairs. In the end, it was reported that 74 people were crushed and suffocated. Of that number, 59 were children.

This tragedy was a culmination of intimidation tactics by the coal company bosses and their supporters. What you will read about in this book is how a small company town of workers continued to stand strong and united despite violence and harassment. Years after this disaster, there was a push to paint the ordeal as a mixture of "conflicting accounts" so as to not put the onus on the company that facilitated such an atmosphere. But, dear reader, Mother Bloor has got you covered. She gives a firsthand description of the emotional turmoil and resilience of that fateful night and the weeks that followed. She'll even introduce you to another brave woman named Anna Klobuchar Clemenc (Bloor calls her Annie Clemenc in her account). Years after Mother Bloor's time, Clemenc—who died in 1968—would get the recognition that she deserved through the Michigan House of Representatives; June 17th was posthumously declared "Anna Clemenc Day" in 1980.

It was Mother Bloor, through her autobiography, who gave the sobering account of a tragedy that those in power were all too eager to sweep under the rug. Bloor's story would go on to inspire American folk music legend Woody Guthrie to write the classic song "1913 Massacre," after reading *We Are Many*. This movement's roots run deep.

Mother Bloor was around for both World War I and World War II. She experienced the joy of seeing workers take power from the oppressive tsar after in the Russian Revolution of 1917. She continued this political trajectory despite the red-baiting and repression that followed after the Bolshevik's came to power in Russia.

And this is where it is important to expound on Bloor's politics and activism. She was a proud Communist. She was one of the founding members of the Communist Labor Party of America and served on the Central Committee of the Communist Party, USA (CPUSA) for nearly 16 years. Although Bloor was inspired by the Russian Revolution, she had come to support the ideas of Marxism and communism from her own lived experiences. She saw that working people, under capitalism, would never truly be free from exploitation as long as there were those in power who benefited from their subjugation. You'll read how, through scientific observation, she saw socialism as the only viable future possible for the U.S. She loved this country and the people who inhabited it. That love shows through in this book. Her actions for a better and more democratic society shows through in her words. Bloor's work flies in the face of McCarthy era and Red Scare-like tactics that try to paint Communists as people to be feared and condemned. No, Communists are not a monolith. At the heart and origin of communism is a desire to empower working people—the people who create the wealth.

Bloor was an American working class woman who saw the inequality of the capitalist system and fought to change it. Workers, many who didn't get bogged down with the labels and anti-communist propaganda, saw that and loved her for it. It serves as a lesson that actions and deeds can hold more weight than slander and misinformation. There were times when she was pursued by law enforcement for preaching socialism, but it wasn't because what she was saying was wrong. It was because those in power were (and remain) scared of what would happen if millions of working people banded together to demand something better.

As of this writing, there have been a number of polls and surveys published showing that a growing number youth have become disillusioned with capitalism, while growing curious—and at times supportive—of socialism. I would argue that there are millions of workers in the U.S. who support socialist ideas and may not even know it. Ideas such as universal healthcare, worker representation, free public education, and higher wages cannot be claimed by capitalism. If capitalist bosses had their way, as we saw in Mother

Bloor's time, none of these gains would be given any consideration. These objectives were being pushed forward by progressive forces, and those progressive forces included socialists and Communists.

Bloor's testimony, the reprinting of this book at a time when right-wing forces are pushing fear to distract from their fascist leanings, is an important tool in the battle against misinformation. What her life demonstrates for those who consider themselves Communists, is that your political work must always be connected to working people and the class struggle. The class struggle isn't just economics. It's about gender equality, anti-racism, and civil rights. Organizations that claim to be for working people cannot afford to be on the sidelines, pontificating from afar. She helps us understand that progress is important, and even so-called "small victories" are victories all the same. And that any space where workers have the chance to have their voices heard, and gain a little bit more power, should be utilized.

This book will hopefully show those who are curious about the Communist movement in America that it is greatly intertwined with the labor movement. They were born together. They struggled together. And although some have gone to great lengths to make the words "communism" and "socialism" dirty four-letter words, history tells a different story. Bloor is part of a long line of American Communists that plenty of people know and love, but whose stories have been nitpicked to "coincidently" leave out their politics. Mother Bloor is part of a political legacy. Figures such as W.E.B. Du Bois, Paul Robeson, John Reed, and the aforementioned Woody Guthrie are also part of this legacy. The idea of communism—worker empowerment and true democracy—is as American as apple pie!

And under a true democracy everyone has the right to vote. Mother Bloor was a strong advocate for electoral work and its connection to socialism. This is another lesson to take from her writing. Bloor explains how everything is connected when it comes to empowering workers. When she fought in the suffrage movement, for women to have the right to vote, it was also understood that when working women had the right to vote they could help bring about candidates and legislation that would improve labor conditions for workers on the job. Even in those days, some within left political circles could not see the power of the vote. Mother Blood did. She recognized wherever there was space for workers to gain leverage was where organizing should take place. That included the emerging labor unions and the electoral sphere. This is a concept some still grappled with today.

Years of struggle have resulted in not only giving women and people of color the right to vote, but legislation to protect that right. The Voting Rights Act (VRA) of 1965 was landmark legislation that prohibited racial discrimination in voting. It combated years of violence and harassment Black voters dealt with in many parts of the country. I'm sure Mother Bloor would have been proud. Unfortunately, the rights of voters have been under attack since the removal of a major provision in the VRA by the Supreme Court in 2013. This provision required that lawmakers in states with a history of discrimination against minority voters had to get federal permission before changing voting rules. Since this change to the VRA, many of these same states have implemented stricter voter registration rules, often targeting voters of color. Couple this with rampant racist gerrymandering from the right-wing to weaken the impact of Black and working class voters, it is clear that voter suppression is a major threat to democracy.

If voting didn't matter, and never changed anything, why do those in power work so hard to discourage working people from participating? That's because it does matter. Electoral activism goes hand in hand with labor strikes and protests. In fact, it is essential to combine all of these methods to truly make an impact. Choosing to not engage in the electoral process only serves to put workers at a disadvantage. Mother Bloor knew this well.

Finally, this autobiography serves as Bloor's continued contribution to a truthful narrative of working class struggle. As a journalist, I believe narrative is one of the most important parts of advocacy work. History happens every day, and the way that history is told to others can shape the present and the future. As I write this, right-wing individuals and organizations throw around terms such as "fake news," while attacking freedom of the press. History has taught us one of the first things to be targeted under fascism and authoritarianism is the press. That's because, when done correctly, journalism holds those in power accountable. You'll read about how Mother Bloor did just that while writing for the *Daily Worker*, the predecessor to the news publication I write for—*People's World*.

On the front page of its first edition the *Daily Worker* declared, "big business interests, bankers, merchant princes, landlords, and other profiteers" should fear the *Daily Worker*. It pledged to "raise the standards of struggle against the few who rob and plunder the many." This book has the same purpose. Mother Bloor set a standard with her dedication and passion in striving for a better world that we all should be inspired by.

This is a feel-good book. Really, I mean that. You're going to read about defeats and sorrow, but above all you will read about hope and perseverance. Not only of Mother Bloor, but of the people around her who she pays tribute to. From the miners she spoke with to the politicians she worked with.

Book burnings have re-emerged in 2022 to go along with an effort by extremists to erase parts of history that don't align with their conservative ideology. There is a mounting effort to eradicate the stories of women, people of color, and other marginalized groups in the name of thinly veiled white supremacy. There is a concerted effort to push back the progress won by earlier generations. Too many lives have been lost, and sacrifices made. We cannot stand aside and accept defeat.

By reading this book, you're taking a stand against the right-wing, against creeping fascism. You're reclaiming our radical history. It is essential that we make connections between the struggles of the past and the trials and tribulations of today. This is true not only as individuals, but as a movement of peoples, cultures, and histories, intertwining towards what is hopefully a brighter and better future together. None of this today would be possible if not for the fights of our past. Mother Bloor was a key player in American history. Stories like hers influence our present. How we learn from them shall determine our future.

1. My Pioneer Forefathers

IT has been said, I know, that when one begins to write an autobiography it is time to send for the undertaker. I hasten to say, however, that never have I felt so far from the end of life as I do today, as I begin this story. I am strong and vigorous at the age of 78 and I would really much rather talk about plans and dreams for the future than to delve back into the past. But my life has been a part of so many phases of the workers' and farmers' struggle for freedom in this country that my experiences really do not belong to me alone. And for the sake of those who are younger than I, I realize I must make some kind of record of my work, my joys, my sorrows, and my mistakes so that others may learn through my experiences how to do better work for the labor movement in the great days that will come.

But before I begin to talk of myself, I should like to introduce my family.

My father, Charles Reeve, moved to New York City in 1860, from Bridgeton, New Jersey, where he was born, and began working with a large firm of tailors on Broadway. A year later, when the Civil War began, he enlisted in the 7th Regiment of New York, made his own uniform and started off. Father was very proud in later years that he had enlisted, and always went faithfully to the reunions of his regiment.

Before the war father married my mother, Harriet Amanda

Disbrow, in the old Presbyterian Church on 14th Street and Second Avenue, New York City. The church is no longer there, but I have spoken many times in the Labor Temple which stands in its place. They made their home on Staten Island. I arrived on July 8, 1862.

My earliest memory was of the assassination of Abraham Lincoln, and the day of his funeral, when all the shutters of the neighborhood were closed and tied with black streamers.

Our house was in Sailors' Snug Harbor, on the bay, which I loved. I often visited my maternal great-grandmother, Betsy Stevens Weed, descended from seventeenth century settlers in Connecticut.

My great-grandmother often read me stories from her diary told her by her pioneer husband, Jonathan Weed. He had a wandering, adventurous spirit and every now and then went off to see the new settlements beyond the Alleghenies. During the Revolutionary war he would take part in a battle, then come home unexpectedly, tell her about it, and be off again. One day he wandered away for the last time. She never heard from him again, but learned long after he had died fighting for his country's freedom. My other great-grandfathers also carried arms in the forces of George Washington.

Jonathan and Betsy had three children, one of them my grandmother, Emmeline Weed. My two great-uncles, Hamilton and Levi Weed were tall men, with large, handsome heads. The latter was pastor of the Old John Street Methodist Church in New York. He was a remarkable looking man, with thick, unusually black hair, suggesting that our family might have some Indian blood in its veins.

Hamilton Weed built a fine home on DeKalb Avenue in Brooklyn, bought land and helped develop Flatbush. He owned an amusement park where I went often as a child. He had no children of his own, and made much of me. He died a very rich man and willed everything to his wife, an Englishwoman, who took the money back with her to England. Meantime my grandmother, Emmeline Weed, acquired property on Willoughby Avenue, Brooklyn, at that time a very fine residential neighborhood. She was a brisk and forceful woman—a great organizer. She ran the home, organized church and temperance societies, and subscribed to the *National Union Signal,* a temperance weekly, which she made me read. She impressed on me the horrors of drink, forming a prejudice which has lasted all my life. She considered going to the theater or playing cards immoral. Her children, however, soon transgressed and became devoted lovers of the theater.

One day in Bridgeton, where we lived during part of my childhood, our family read of a dreadful fire in a Brooklyn theater. We said to one another: "Well, there is one thing sure. We don't have to worry about Grandma being there."

But it so happened that my grandmother *had* been there. That night the *Two Orphans,* with Kate Claxton, which everyone considered a very proper play, was on. My uncle, Herman Gunnell Disbrow, teased my grandmother to accompany him. For once, though with misgivings, my grandmother consented to go.

When the fire broke out, she took command of the situation at once. Climbing on a seat, she beseeched the people to be calm, and led the audience to safety down burning stairs which collapsed behind them. When she arrived home, she ran up the stairs shouting: "Get up! Get up! Get up out of your beds, and thank the Lord!" Her family, awakened by her shouting, thought her first visit to the theater had unhinged her reason.

Her husband, Thomas Disbrow, descended from the French Huguenots, also came of a family that had settled in Connecticut in the early years. He had great charm and a wonderful disposition, placid and kindly. He was one of the sweetest men I ever knew.

I had delightful times with my grandmother and grandfather. They used to take me with them to a lonely beach that is now Coney Island. Sometimes my grandfather, when he should have been on his way to business, would say: "Come on, Ella, let's run away and go fishing at Canarsie. Grandma won't mind, so long as we bring home some nice fat flounder." We'd go and sit on the wharf and fish and bring a mess of fish home to Grandma who fried them for supper.

I am proud of the fact that some of my ancestors on my mother's side were pioneers of the anti-slavery movement and maintained stations on the underground railroad, sending escaped slaves to freedom in the North. But there were also Tories among my ancestors who tried to disown their more revolutionary relatives, and for that reason I never discovered until I was sixty years old the most distinguished of all my ancestors, for his name was never mentioned in the family.

On a hitch-hiking trip from San Francisco to New York, in the summer of 1927, I found myself in Pennsylvania, almost home, but unable to get a ride for the last lap of the journey. Along the road between Lancaster and Philadelphia I saw a fine old mansion which had been turned into a summer boarding house, and decided to spend the night there. Sitting in the huge living room, I noticed on the opposite wall, over a big old-fashioned fireplace, a portrait to which my eyes were drawn by some compelling sense of familiarity. I felt sure this was a member of my own family. That firm mouth, those dark, intense eyes, were the mouth and eyes of my grandmother, Emmeline Weed, and her son Levi. No people could possibly look so much alike and not be related. I went over to the portrait and read the name on the plate below— THADDEUS STEVENS. I knew I had found a new ancestor. I investigated after I got home, and sure enough, Thaddeus Stevens was a first cousin of my great-grandmother, Betsy Stevens Weed.

Thaddeus Stevens, that great fighter for human freedom, was an uncompromising Abolitionist. The slaveowners and bankers of his time called him a revolutionist. Deeply interested in education, he started the first vocational training school for boys, in Lancaster, Pennsylvania. He helped establish the free public school system in Pennsylvania, and fought for equal educational opportunities for the Negro people. His championship of social as well as political equality for Negroes was the real reason for the family's disapproval of him.

As Congressman, Stevens encouraged Lincoln to issue the

Emancipation Proclamation, and introduced the 14th Amendment. After the Civil War, as chairman of the committee on reconstruction, he worked to have southern state constitutions grant Negro suffrage. Before he died he made arrangements to be buried in a small graveyard in Lancaster that was not closed to Negroes. A large mausoleum stands there, bearing this epitaph, which he wrote himself:

"I repose in this quiet and secluded spot, not from any natural preference for solitude, but finding other cemeteries limited as to race, by charter rules, I have chosen this that I might illustrate in my death the principles which I advocated through a long life: Equality of Man before his Creator."

The store of energy which has stood me in such good stead all my life came from both sides of the family. I remember seeing my father's great-uncle, Samuel Reeve, run for a horse-car when he was 90. He lived on 7th Street in New York in a beautiful old house, now gone. He worshiped Horace Greeley, and talked to me about Greeley's dreams of a new life for young people through homesteading in the West. It was like meeting an old friend when I first saw Horace Greeley's statue in front of the Tribune Building in New York. My great-uncle was also devoted to Peter Cooper, that pioneer of vocational education, who founded Cooper Institute, "devoted forever to the union of art and science in their application to the useful purposes of life."

My mother was a beautiful woman both in appearance and character. Our family was a large one. There were twelve children altogether, seven boys, one of them blind, and five girls. In spite of all her responsibilities at home, Mother always managed to take part in community affairs.

We had just moved to a new house in Bridgeton in a fashionable neighborhood, near my father's five sisters—stiff and proper ladies who sometimes found my mother's unconventional behavior shocking. My mother, needing help with her large household, had brought the daughter of a former neighbor, a pleasant girl, to live with us. One day one of Papa's sisters saw this young girl eating with us, and remarked disapprovingly: "Why, Hattie—now that you have moved up here on the hill—you mustn't have your 'help' eat with you!"

I can remember the way my mother looked at her. "Lucy Ware," she said, "I have not changed my identity since I've moved up on the hill. I am still the same Hattie Reeve!"

I remember, too, how my mother befriended Lottie, a pretty young girl living next door to us who had an illegitimate baby. She was, of course, considered a damned soul by the community. This girl lost her own mother when she was quite young. Her stepmother, a vicious, cruel woman treated Lottie like a slavey. On a visit, she met a young cousin who made love to her. Hungry for affection and totally ignorant of life, she came home pregnant. After the baby was born, Lottie seemed doomed to the kitchen for life, hidden away with her baby.

But my mother planned otherwise. When she saw Lottie hanging up clothes she would also get some clothes to hang up, so she could talk to the girl and get her to hold up her head. I can remember Lottie's first visit after that, and how she sat on the edge of a chair in our kitchen, frightened to death somebody might come in and see her.

My mother finally induced her to go to prayer meeting with her one night. Since my mother set the pace in the community, others followed her lead. My mother really saved the life of that woman and her son.

I was brought up in the Second Presbyterian Church. My father's sisters were determined to make their father join the church before he died. My mother and I were the only ones Grandfather Reeve really liked to talk to. Mamma used to sit on the arm of his chair and put her arms around him. My aunts thought that was terrible but she didn't care. I thought he was a lovely old man, and when I heard unkind stories about him, I used to defend him vigorously.

Finally my aunts prevailed and I remember the Sunday he walked up the aisle and joined the church. My aunts rejoiced—I guess they calculated that if he didn't go to church he would certainly go to hell, and, indeed, he was pretty well qualified. He actually was an old usurer, who made a lot of money by demanding not only a high rate of interest, but a bonus besides on the loans he made. He invested heavily with the Jay Cooke interests, financiers of the Civil War, who fleeced so many Americans. The family lost most of the money in subsequent crashes. On my tenth birthday, my grandfather was stricken with paralysis, and died the next day.

My father ran a drugstore in Bridgeton, one of the first to sell other articles besides druggist goods. After my grandfather died we had more money and my father enlarged his stock, especially of books, which he brought home to me. In this way I became acquainted with Scott, Eliot, Dickens, and others. My father loved Dickens especially, and we talked about Micawber and David Copperfield and other beloved Dickens characters as though they were members of the family. Papa often had me read aloud. He taught me to enunciate clearly, and mimicked me whenever I read without expression. This helped later on to make me unafraid to hear my own voice in public.

When I was about twelve years old, Papa often took me with him to visit his sister, Hannah, who lived on Mickle Street in Camden, where Walt Whitman lived. I took my place among the children of the neighborhood who loved him, and gathered around the marble steps where he came to sit in the evening. He wore a gray plaid shawl around his shoulders and a big soft hat on his head. The house still stands there, exactly as he left it. Only the other day I went to visit it, and saw the little frame house standing as always, the low stone steps where we gathered in the evening. "Here lived the Good Gray Poet," reads the plaque on the front of the house. But it did not need this to bring back my own memories of him, clear and bright.

When Papa went on his shopping trips to Philadelphia, he would leave me in the Camden ferry house. When I thought he was going to be gone for a long time I'd go aboard the ferry-boat and go back and forth without paying. After a while I found out that Walt Whitman did the same thing. He recognized me and we would sit together.

I wondered why nobody stopped either of us. I found out later that he was the honored guest of all the ferry hands. On the ferry-boat I felt I was a partner in a great adventure. That was the height of happiness, watching the people with him, watching the water. As I remember, he did not talk very much, but I felt we had a deep understanding between us.

And so began for me what has been one of the greatest joys of my life, the joy of watching people, the joy of being with people. I have always loved to sit in ferry and railroad stations and watch the people, to walk on crowded streets, just walk along among the people, and see their faces, to be among people on street cars and trains and boats. Perhaps it was on those ferry-boat rides that the course of my life was determined, and that Whitman somehow transferred to me, without words, his own great long-ing to establish everywhere on earth "the institution of the dear love of comrades."

As Whitman grew to look more frail, we children realized that we must not bother him so much. He had to have a man to take care of him, to help him up the low stone steps, back into the little frame house when the evening grew too chilly. And there was a young man named Horace Traubel who came every night to see him. In later years when I was searching for something to believe in with all my heart and mind, I met Horace Traubel in the Ethi-cal Culture Society in Philadelphia, and we were fast friends, until he died. Horace wrote a day by day story of Walt Whitman's life, *Walt Whitman in Camden*. I have a copy which belonged to Horace, bearing the penciled inscription, in Walt Whitman's own hand: "To Horace Traubel—You will be speaking long after I am gone. Be sure and always tell the truth, Walt Whitman." Underneath is another inscription, from one of my friends who had the book in his possession. It reads: "We now pass this book of Horace's on to our beloved Ella Reeve Bloor, Percival Wixsell." The signer is a member of the Walt Whitman group of Los Angeles. Every year I receive an invitation to celebrate Walt

Whitman's birthday with this group, and I have many rich memories of the occasions when I could be with them.

The poem of Whitman's I love best, *The Mystic Trumpeter,* always seemed to me to be a prophecy of the coming of the new world which so many of us have dreamed about and worked for and seen come into being with the success of the Russian Revolution. Because this poem is less well known than some of the others, I want to quote the last part of it here:

Blow again, trumpeter! and for thy theme,
Take now the enclosing theme of all—the solvent and the setting;
Love, that is pulse of all—the sustenance and the pang;
The heart of man and woman all for love;
No other theme but love—knitting, enclosing, all-diffusing love. . . .

Blow again, trumpeter—conjure war's wild alarums.
Swift to thy spell, a shuddering hum like distant thunder rolls;
Lo! where the arm'd men hasten—Lo! mid the clouds of dust, the glint of bayonets;
I see the grime-faced cannoniers—I mark the rosy flash amid the smoke—I hear the cracking of the guns:
—Nor war alone—thy fearful music-song, wild player, brings every sight of fear,
The deeds of ruthless brigands—rapine, murder—I hear the cries for help!
I see ships foundering at sea—I behold on deck, and below deck, the terrible tableaux.

Oh Trumpeter! methinks I am myself the instrument thou playest!
Thou melt'st my heart, my brain—thou movest, drawest, changest them, at will:
And now thy sullen notes send darkness through me;
Thou takest away all cheering light—all hope:
I see the enslaved, the overthrown, the hurt, the opprest of the whole earth;

I feel the measureless shame and humiliation of my race—it
    becomes all mine;
Mine too the revenges of humanity—the wrongs of ages—baf-
    fled feuds and hatreds;
Utter defeat upon me weighs—all lost! the foe victorious!
(Yet 'mid the ruins Pride colossal stands, unshaken to the last;
Endurance, resolution, to the last.)

Now, trumpeter, for thy close,
Vouchsafe a higher strain than any yet;
Sing to my soul—renew its languishing faith and hope;
Rouse up my slow belief—give me some vision of the future;
Give me, for once, its prophecy and joy.

O glad, exulting, culminating song!
A vigor more than earth's is in thy notes!
Marches of victory—man disenthrall'd—the conqueror at last!
Hymns to the universal God, from universal Man—all joy!
A reborn race appears—a perfect World, all joy!
Women and Men, in wisdom, innocence and health—all joy!
Riotous, laughing bacchanals, fill'd with joy!

War, sorrow, suffering gone—The rank earth purged—nothing
    but joy left!
The ocean fill'd with joy—the atmosphere all joy!
Joy! Joy! in freedom, worship, love! Joy in the ecstasy of life!
Enough to merely be! Enough to breathe!
Joy! Joy! all over Joy!

I think Whitman more than any other poet possessed the gift
of revealing to others the beauty of everything around us, the
beauty of nature, the beauty of human beings. I feel so often these
things that he expresses—his closeness to nature, his great love
for mankind, his ecstatic joy in the beauty of the physical world—
things I cannot possibly put into words myself. Some of his own
closeness to nature, his great love for human beings, was passed
on by Whitman to all of us who knew and loved him.

We who had the privilege of knowing Whitman have a special understanding of each other. We have no inhibitions, no reserve. There is a kind of understanding among us that makes it impossible for us to offend one another, no matter what we say, and this has given me the most free and frank human relationships I have ever known. Nor is this rich heritage ours alone, it is there for all who know and love Whitman's poems to share.

Soon after meeting Whitman I met the great preacher Henry Ward Beecher, whom my father, then a member of a lecture committee of the Y.M.C.A., brought to Bridgeton. Beecher, brother of Harriet Beecher Stowe who wrote *Uncle Tom's Cabin,* had been a leader in the anti-slavery struggle before the Civil War, and had remained a leader in all progressive movements of the time. At that time Henry Ward Beecher was in the midst of a lawsuit brought against him in 1875 by a man named Tilton, a former friend who accused him of intimacy with his wife. It was a tremendous scandal, and everyone took sides. Old-time friends of Henry Ward Beecher fought for him valiantly. Those who did not know him, especially in such small towns as ours, were violently against him. So it took courage on the part of my father to bring him to the Bridgeton Y.M.C.A.

I was allowed to go to his lecture, although I was so young. I have no clear memory of his words, but I can remember how impressed I was by his magnetic personality, his distinguished bearing, his fresh healthy color and white hair, and his ringing voice.

At our house after the lecture, I remember asking him whether he prepared his lectures beforehand, and if he wrote them out.

"No, my child," he told me. "I sometimes have no idea at all what I am going to say until I look over my audience, and then I draw my inspiration from them. Other times I prepare a lecture in my mind beforehand, carefully working out points one, two and three and then something I see in my audience will change my whole train of thought, and I will make an entirely different speech from the one I had in mind."

I have often remembered this, and later when I began to speak

myself, I too found that my greatest inspiration always came from
the people to whom I was talking.

When the time came for me to go to high school, my father
insisted on my going to the Ivy Hall Seminary, a "finishing
school" where I could associate with young ladies of good family,
although I wanted to continue in the public schools. I hated Ivy
Hall, except for one teacher, Miss Miriam Shephard, who made
history very exciting because she told about events other than the
dreary succession of births and deaths of kings that made up the
text-books of those days. She told us about the real makers of history, the people, and history became my favorite study.

My mother took me out of Ivy Hall when I was fourteen. I
stayed at home with her after that, and helped her with the children. My mother was an excellent mathematician and she taught
me. Since I read so much at home, I really had a better education
than most of the children around me.

At this period I became interested in biographies of great women.
I had always loved George Eliot's novels, and was enthralled
with the story of her life written by George Henry Lewes. The
life of James and Lucretia Mott gave me my first glimpse of the
great struggle for woman suffrage. The story of Harriet Beecher
Stowe's life was also an inspiration to me. I was very much impressed, too, with the essays of Lydia Maria Child, an American
writer about whom little is written these days. She had to write
in the kitchen. "Neither God nor man" she wrote "can keep my
soul here among the pots and pans if I choose to soar among
the lovely fields and woods and enjoy the beautiful things of
life. . . ." Like all girls of that period, I loved Louisa May Alcott.
As I grew a little older I was greatly drawn to Emerson and read
his essays on *Self-Reliance, Compensation, Friendship.*

In my early teens I saw much of Reverend Heber Beadle, minister of our church. Reverend Beadle must have been about forty
years old at this time. He used to tell me "If I were younger and
you were older, I would marry you." He was the son of a famous
Presbyterian missionary who was also a fine mineralogist. He had

his father's collection and taught me a great deal about geology.

Reverend Beadle used to take me with him on visits to his parishioners when they were in trouble and counted on me to help comfort grief-stricken families. He felt that I sometimes found the right words to say to these people when he could not. These visits, and my own observations of the life around me, set me to wondering why there had to be so much suffering and poverty in the world.

I used to ask my father and the Reverend Beadle why it was that we lived in a nice place on the hill, with a beautiful lawn around our home, while down in the town, where the glass factories were, the homes were so poor. And why was it that the owners of those factories lived on the hill with us, while the workers lived down below? "The poor will always be with us" was the only answer I could get.

At this period I used to go often to Woodstown, New Jersey, to see my paternal great-uncle, Dan Ware, a wonderful looking old man with fine, tender eyes and a long white beard. Uncle Dan and his wife, Cornelia, lived in a beautiful old home. There were always young people about, and the air was full of music. He himself was a good musician, as was his daughter, Belle, who was my close friend, and they were always bringing stray musicians into the house. His son, Lucien, whom I afterward married, was a fine pianist and played the violin too. A leg injury had prevented his taking part in sports, so he spent a lot of time on his music. His teacher was Felix Schelling (father of Ernest Schelling) who was a sort of family institution. Mrs. Schelling was blind, and a spiritualist medium. Her husband believed everything she told him. I can remember one time he said to Uncle Dan: "What would you think if you were to see that piano rising slowly from the ground?" and Uncle Dan answered characteristically, "I'd go straight to the oculist to see what was wrong with my eyes!"

In Uncle Dan's household I was very happy, especially as I found that Uncle Dan would answer my questions. "Don't listen to your Uncle Dan," Father used to say to me, "he is a terrible atheist." But I did listen to him. He saw I was earnestly trying to understand the world around me. He used to talk to me in his shop in a building on his grounds, which he used for a study as well. By trade he was a house-painter and decorator, but in his shop, for his own pleasure, he made beautiful rush-bottom chairs, a craft which had been in the family for generations. The Ware chairs are famous in antique shops everywhere, and our family has some that are 150 years old. Uncle Dan gathered the rushes in the swamps and treated them in a room on the third floor. On the second floor, he made his chairs. His library was on the first floor.

An ardent Abolitionist, Uncle Dan had been in charge of one of the underground railroads through which he had saved many Negroes before the Civil War. He used to tell me stories of how the slaves narrowly escaped capture even when, as in one instance, they had been brought as far north as Salem County, New Jersey. He was still fighting for education and social rights for Negroes, and the Negroes from miles around came to visit and consult him. For this the neighbors encouraged their children to insult him, and the boys of the neighborhood used to write "nigger" in big letters on his shop.

Uncle Dan's stately wife was really a white chauvinist; while she believed that Negroes should have the right to vote, she did not believe in social equality for them. Years afterward, when I married Uncle Dan's son and lived across the street, he would send for me to help him entertain prominent Negroes in his home, since his wife refused to sit at the table with them.

Uncle Dan was a Greenbacker, which was considered very radical at the time. The panic of 1873 had left many thousands of people in desperate poverty. Labor organizations were now joining with the Greenbackers in a demand for more currency, as an effort to meet the debt load burdening the people. Greenbacks were the legal tender notes first issued by the U. S. Government in the Civil War period as a war revenue measure. On the mistaken theory that a currency increase would help lift the burden of debt, the Greenback Party had been organized in 1875 to support such measures. By 1878 in the congressional elections of that year, the Greenback-Labor Party polled over 1,000,000 votes and sent 14 representatives to Congress. Labor's success in this election was partly because the great strikes of 1877 had strengthened trade union organizations all over the country.

Whatever the weaknesses of the Greenback movement, Uncle Dan sincerely believed in it as a way of breaking the grip of the money interests and opening up a better life for the people. In later years he used to take me with him to hear William Jennings Bryan whose turbulent oratory made more impression on me than his words. I noticed especially how he sensed and played on the mood of the crowd.

Uncle Dan had become a Unitarian, and I heard many religious discussions at his home. Unitarianism appealed to me much more than the hidebound Presbyterian faith in which I had been raised. Concern with the life of people on earth today made more sense than teachings of hell fire and damnation. Unitarians in those days were usually liberal on social as well as religious questions, though today many Unitarians are reactionary in their political thinking. Uncle Dan used to subscribe to the sermons of the great Unitarian preacher, Rev. Minot Savage, and we read them together on Sunday afternoons. Others came too, and the neighbors grew curious about what was going on. An old Irishwoman who lived across the street would drop in and ask, "Mr. Ware, what do you do at those meetings—you don't pray, do you?" And Uncle Dan would answer, "Oh no, Mrs. Carey, we behave ourselves so well during the week, we don't have to fall on our knees and ask God to forgive us." And he would add, "Don't worry, Mrs. Carey, when I die I'll be flying around among the stars with the best of them—I always wanted to see what the stars were made of."

It was Uncle Dan who first broke down my faith in the Bible stories, by reading Robert Ingersoll to me.

"What a poor idea Noah must have had of ventilation!" I can remember him saying. "How could all those people and animals possibly have stayed alive in the Ark if the only time they had any air was when the one window was opened for the dove to fly out!"

I was so fascinated both by Ingersoll's flowing beautiful language and his ideas, that I began to read everything of his I could lay my hands on. Ingersoll, known as "the great agnostic," was attacked by orthodox ministers all over the country. He had been a colonel in the Civil War and as a leading Republican lawyer could have held high political office. But his fearless agnostic lectures made this impossible. His writings were widely read for a generation and greatly influenced American thinking.

No other orator except Debs has ever appealed to me as did Ingersoll. Deb's analogies and imagery were so like those of Ingersoll that people sometimes said he copied Ingersoll. This, of course, was not true, but Debs did soak himself in Ingersoll's writings before speaking and quoted Ingersoll frequently. Ingersoll, to be sure, knew nothing of the class struggle. His chief concern was to free people's minds of superstition—he was a revolutionary in religion only.

Uncle Dan was not content with simply tearing down the old superstitious doctrines, but he also took pains to build up my interest in biology and the processes of evolution, by reading to me the works of Darwin. First, *The Origin of the Species* and then *The Descent of Man,* and other books on evolution. It was then considered just as radical to be an evolutionist as it is to be a revolutionist today.

After these visits I went home and asked my family how they could possibly believe in the "Bible miracles." Their answer was "All things are possible with God." My mother was sympathetic, although sometimes fearing I was going a little too far, but it seemed to me that my father really did not believe the things he professed, but was simply afraid of public opinion. I asked Mr. Beadle whether he really believed that people were damned at birth, no matter how good a life they might lead. "You do not have to believe that," he told me. "It is not what you believe; it is what you *do* that matters." I said quickly, "Oh! then you don't believe it, either, do you?"

He only looked at me soberly in reply, and I came to a sudden decision. Up until then I had been teaching a Sunday school class and had gone to church regularly with my family. Now I knew that I could no longer stay in the church, and I asked him to take my name off the church membership roll.

"What will your father say?" he asked me.

"I don't care," I told him.

He said nothing of this talk to my father, who did not know what I had done until one Sunday soon after when the Communion Plate was passed, I did not touch the bread and wine. When we got home Father asked me why. I was the only one in the family who wasn't scared of my father and I did not hesitate to speak up and tell him I was leaving the church.

I had not been a very docile child at prayer meetings. I laughed at some of the old codgers who got up to pray. There was one old fellow who used to stamp his foot noisily at the end of every sentence of his prayer. At the next prayer meeting, when he got up to pray, my cousin and I stamped with him. My father got so he did not much care whether I went to prayer meetings or not. He never knew what I might do next. His reaction about my leaving the church was of course very different. He never forgave me.

Meantime, I had found new interests. One of the frequent visitors at our house was a fine old maid friend of my mother's, Martha Garrison. She taught the boys who worked in the glass factories how to read and write. The boys worked all night and had to sleep by day. They started working at 13 or 14. Miss Garrison set up a school for them, through contributions. And when she asked me to help her, I agreed willingly. Some of the boys were bigger than I. I did not tell my father about this, as I knew he would not approve.

About this time I decided I wanted to be a foreign missionary. This may seem inconsistent with other ideas I was developing, but I thought of it as social work rather than as religious work. One of my young friends in that period (my first boy-friend, as a matter of fact!) was the son of a well known Presbyterian missionary to India. The name of my friend was Caesar Augustus Rodney Janvier. He was going to Princeton, and I looked up to him as a great oracle. He told me about his father's experiences and the great sacrifices he had made to take the teachings of Christ to India. My feelings about the Presbyterian church did not mean that I had lost my respect for the teachings of Christ as they are given in many parts of the New Testament. I have never lost that respect, any more than I have for the teachings of Buddha or other great religious teachers of whom I learned later.

Uncle Dan gave me Ernest Renan's *Life of Christ*, which sets forth so well the underlying principles of Christ's teachings. That book helped me much in later years, in expressing the respect I felt for those teachings, not to be worshiped of course, but to be considered as one of the great forces of history.

I had always wanted to travel in foreign lands, and now I was very anxious to get away from Bridgeton, and I thought it would be a wonderful thing to go to a far country and help people lead better and happier lives. So I went to Mr. Beadle and told him of my plans, for he remained a good friend to me even after I left the church. He told me I was already doing missionary work at home.

My father's family cared terribly about public opinion. I can remember my Aunt Hannah objecting to my clothes and saying "Why don't you wear that nice new dress?" "I don't think it's suitable," I would answer. "I have work to do." "But," she would say, "you really ought to let people know you have a good dress!" I couldn't stand this attitude. I was beginning even in those days to feel a contempt for the false standards set by the upper classes. This has helped me to bear all kinds of slander throughout my life, and I have always felt stronger and freer because this feeling is so deeply rooted in me.

My aunts and my father disapproved of the friends I made and used to insist that I go out with the boys in my cousin's "set." When I refused to go out with the banker's son who used to drive up with a spanking team of horses my father was furious.

Harriet Amanda Disbrow Reeve, and Charles Reeve, mother and father of Ella Reeve Bloor

Daniel Ware (Uncle Dan)

I enjoyed much more the company of an old German Jew who moved to Bridgeton and lived near us, and used to talk to him by the hour. Then one day at a party I met a young Jewish boy named Philip Goldsmith, who seemed to me to be the most interesting young person I had ever met. My father sneered, "If there were a Jew anywhere in the state you would find him, wouldn't you?" and he treated this young man terribly when he came to the house. (The Goldsmith family happened to be the only Jewish people in Bridgeton.)

My mother, on the other hand, hated all intolerance. Her attitude made me feel while I was still very young that since all human beings everywhere were of one blood there should be no social or racial distinctions. As I think over the past it was really remarkable that she had so much understanding. She was brought up in New York, and surrounded by sectarian influences. My uncle Hamilton who did not approve of my opinions at all always said that if only my mother had lived, I would have been different. But I think she would have been way ahead of me! She gave me a very good start by always talking to me freely and frankly about the "facts of life." She gave me good training as a housekeeper, and taught me to cook and bake bread, which stood me in good stead when I had my own large family later.

I remember her as a woman of great courage. In spite of her family responsibilities, she always managed to keep our home bright and cheerful. She did her best to live up to my father's expectations and always managed to dress for dinner, no matter how hard she had worked all day. Father had a good team of horses and loved to go driving after dinner. Mother always arranged to have the children taken care of so she could go with him. She loved young people, always had a lot of them around, and was young in spirit herself.

My mother died suddenly, giving premature birth, when I was seventeen. She herself was only thirty-eight. Her mother had come to visit us, and was completely unnerved by her daughter's sudden illness, so I had to take the helm. The doctor needed help, and I had to keep my head. Just before Mother died she said to me between painful breaths, "Oh, Ella, I am leaving you such a heavy burden!" I couldn't understand the collapse of my strong-minded grandmother at this time, but I learned a little later that she herself was ill with an organic trouble that caused her own death the following spring. I had been with her so much that it was like losing two mothers.

When the notice of my mother's funeral was read in church, the minister broke down and the whole church wept. She had been a great friend to the whole community. Many Negro women came to the funeral.

Mother died in December when the daylight went early. As the day was ending, just at dusk when it seemed the very hardest, Mr. Beadle would come over and play with the children to comfort me. He never missed a day, although it meant walking a mile and a half up a steep hill to reach our house.

After Mother's death, my father became bitter and retired within himself. He seemed to have lost all regard for me and the younger children who were now my responsibility. Two of my brothers were five and seven. One sister was four years old and the youngest eighteen months. Papa would come home and say, "Can't you keep those children still?" He also expected me to cook his favorite dishes for him.

At the end of two years, he built a big house and married one of the richest women in Bridgeton. My stepmother had never done a stroke of work all her life. She did not even mend her own stockings.

I was lonely and unhappy in this household. Only my visits to Uncle Dan's household brightened my life. Uncle Dan's son, Lucien, had been away from home a great deal, so that I never met him until just about the time of my father's re-marriage. Lucien was a court stenographer, and had covered the Molly Maguire trials. From him I heard of the terrible frame-up of these brave Irish miners who were forced to form a secret organization because of the ferocious oppression visited on them by the mine owners after their long strike of 1875 was crushed. Pinkerton's had been brought into the anthracite field in 1873—the first recorded use of spies against labor. The mine owners had sent these provocateurs into the miners' organization to commit murders and other crimes for which the Molly Maguires were held responsible. The spies and provocateurs were the only witnesses against the miners, who were given no chance to defend themselves. Lucien knew that the twenty-four men who were convicted, nineteen of them to be hanged, were innocent, and he was outraged at this horrible injustice. He was invited to witness the hangings, which made a terrible impression on him. Lucien was a freethinker and very progressive for those days. Drawn together at once through our mutual interests and close family association, we were married within a few months after our first meeting.

We lived first in Camden, New Jersey. Hoping to qualify for law without going to college, Lucien went to work every night in a lawyer's office. I was only nineteen and although I had known spiritual loneliness at home, there had always been a lot of people around. But I did not know anyone in Camden, and I was very lonely.

Then Lucien's work took us to Haddonfield, New Jersey, for a time. Inside of two years and nine months I had three children. The older of my children, Pauline, became seriously ill. The anxious months of going from one doctor to another were eased by the happiness and health of my baby boy, Charlie. Two days after my third child, Grace, was born, Pauline died. That very night my happy baby, Charlie, was taken suddenly with spinal meningitis, and died. There was a double funeral in my bedroom. At that time my father was moved to say: "You will have your joys later on in life, Ella."

After all this trouble we moved to Woodstown, New Jersey, where Uncle Dan Ware built us a house across from his own. Later we went to Woodbury, New Jersey, where Hal and Helen were born. A woman who had been a cook in my father's house came to help me with my three children but since she had to go home nights I was tied to the house. One day I suddenly realized that in spite of all the things I had planned to do I was well on the way to become just a household drudge. The world was outside my door, and there was much I wanted to learn about it. Since I had been taken out of school when I was fourteen, I needed more education if I wanted to go on to other activities. I did some writing for local periodicals, earning enough to have professors come and teach me at home. I studied principally the works of Herbert Spencer, and the philosophy of religion.

There were many Quakers in Woodbury, and I became acquainted with a number of Hicksite Friends. My children went to the Quaker "First-Day School" where they were taught character development and neighborliness. It was a Friend, a woman doctor named Dr. Mary Branson, one of the first women physicians in this country, who attended me when Hal was born on August 19, 1890. From her I learned what the women were up against who were pioneering in this profession.

Through the Quakers, who believed in equality for women, I first came into touch with the woman suffrage movement. I began to be very much interested in the question, especially after reading about Lucy Stone, one of the earliest fighters against Negro slavery, and a leader for many years in the struggle for woman's suffrage. When she married the Abolitionist, Henry Brown Blackwell, she continued as a matter of principle to use her own name. His championship of higher education for women opened the way for women in the professions and his sister Elizabeth Blackwell was the first woman in this country to get a medical degree.

Lucy Stone had founded in 1870 the *Woman's Journal,* for nearly 50 years official organ of the American Woman Suffrage Association. After her death in 1893 it was edited by her daughter, Alice Stone Blackwell, who naturally became a champion for woman's political and legal freedom and for the equality of the Negro people. These interests led her to an understanding of socialism. Today, at eighty-three, she is still a vigorous champion of human rights. Just last year I had a wonderful visit with her at her home in Boston, discussing our precious heritage of great American women.

While visiting Uncle Dan at Woodstown, I tried my hand at an article on suffrage. Uncle Dan looked it over and approved.

This encouraged me to send it to the Woodstown *Register,* and it was printed.

I then discovered that women could vote in New Jersey for school trustees, although they had never availed themselves of this right. So at the next election, I attempted to get the women to come with me to vote. Only one Quaker lady, whose husband was very critical, came. As we stood in line at the polls with people staring and jeering at us, her husband came up and said sarcastically, "I hope you are enjoying this." "Not exactly enjoying this," I told him, nodding toward the jeering crowd, "but enjoying the right to vote."

At the next elections I was able to marshal a large group of women and after that the politicians of the town began to show an interest in the women, and around election time the candidates all told us how wonderful we were.

In the 1880's and '90's Susan B. Anthony's influence on the women of the country—and on the men, too—was still strong. She was over sixty, but still fighting for women's right to vote as earlier she had fought against slavery. Ridiculed and denounced as a "revolutionary firebrand" she kept right on. She and other women pioneers such as Lucretia Mott and Elizabeth Cady Stanton traveled and lectured throughout the United States making woman suffrage a national issue.

A Unitarian minister by the name of William Gilbert first taught me to express my thoughts while standing on my feet. An old millionaire by the name of Green, who had become wealthy making a patent medicine which he called *Green's August Flower,* induced Rev. Gilbert to start a Unitarian Church in Woodbury. Green's wife was a dyed-in-the-wool Methodist, spouting hell-fire and damnation. No wonder the old man was attracted by the Unitarian idea of one God, no hell and no damnation.

My husband, Uncle Dan and I went to hear Rev. Gilbert, and found him a most gifted and tolerant man, and a very fine speaker. In time I became one of the trustees of his church.

One day he sent word that he would not be able to preach the following Sunday, and requested me to take over the meeting. I had written an article for Jenkin Lloyd Jones' paper *Unity*, "Is Marriage a Bondage," advocating real equality for women and freedom to pursue their own interests in the marriage relationship, which I felt could be stable and enduring only if built on love, mutual interests and equality. It was this that gave Rev. Gilbert the idea that I might be able to speak. For the subject of my first "sermon" I chose prayer, since there was a lively controversy at that time about the efficacy of prayer. I took the stand that just to address one's self formally to God was meaningless; that prayer was simply the soul's sincere desire, whether uttered or unexpressed, and more important than prayer was the will to carry out the desire.

After that Rev. Gilbert gave me pointers about the technique of speaking. He stressed the importance of enunciation and told me how he had enlarged his vocabulary by never failing to look up a word he was doubtful about. He advised me never to write speeches, just to think about them, and not to be afraid to repeat the things I wanted to emphasize. Ever since, my preparation for a speech has been to read all I could, if it were a new subject, then perhaps to take a long walk and think about it—but never to write it out.

As for Mr. Green, when the old man died, his relatives and his wife got even with him, and gave him a real *Methodist funeral*.

2. Marriage, Motherhood and a Cause

IN time Uncle Dan Ware became a Prohibitionist. I followed right along and often went with him to meetings of the Prohibition Party. General Clinton B. Fisk was their nominee for Governor of New Jersey. As their candidate for President in 1888, he had polled about 250,000 votes. One night when I was at a meeting with Uncle Dan, the saloon-keepers of the town ganged up against us, and broke up our meeting. Frankly, I felt that I was a martyr to my principles.

The Prohibition Party, formed to fight the use of alcohol as a beverage, also stood for woman suffrage and direct election of United States Senators. Becoming a member of the Prohibition Party made me very much alive to state politics. I got to know some of the women who were organizing the Woman's Christian Temperance Union, and became deeply interested in the important educational work they were doing. I met Frances Willard, whose statue is now in the Hall of Fame. She had been a professor, then president and dean of the Woman's College, which became part of Northwestern University. Always an ardent advocate of woman suffrage, she devoted most of her life to organizing women against the evils of liquor. For more than twenty years, until her death in 1898, she was president of the National W.C.T.U. and for many years was president of the World W.C.T.U. as well. She was far in advance of the usual temperance advocate, pointing out that poverty was a fundamental cause of intemperance. She was also a member of the Knights of Labor, which I heard about for the first time from her.

The program of Uriah Stephens, who founded the Knights of Labor in 1869, was the first approach to socialism I had seen, although of course it was not called that. Stephens believed that the workers should receive the full value of their labor. His honesty and sincerity and singleness of purpose made him an outstanding leader.

The Noble Order of the Knights of Labor became important in the American labor movement after 1873. A secret order at first, it later organized openly in an effort to unite isolated craft unions and labor sympathizers in "one big union" with "solidarity" as its watchword. After winning important railroad strikes in 1884 and 1885, it gradually lost influence as it came under the domination of men like Terence V. Powderly who developed a bureaucracy similar to what later developed in the A.F. of L. The later leaders of the Knights of Labor completely betrayed the purposes of its founder, and the workers. At the time I did not at all comprehend the issues involved. But I had already begun to feel that I belonged in the labor movement and a little later I joined a "mixed local" of this historical union, an educational group whose members in the main were sympathizers with the labor movement rather than actual workers.

I also helped to organize and served as president of a branch of the W.C.T.U. in Woodbury. The state president was Sarah Downs, a remarkable woman of sixty. A fine speaker herself, she used to implore us: "Sisters, place your voices on the altar of your cause." She tried to make us all speak with strong, full voices. Her imitations of the high squeaky way women spoke in public had a lot to do with the development of my speaking voice. Amy Ames, the secretary, also a member of Dr. Gilbert's Unitarian Church, and I, were bitterly attacked by one of the town's Methodist ministers, who claimed that neither of us had a right to be officers of the W.C.T.U. because we were not Christians at all, but Unitarians. Sarah Downs was herself the widow of a Methodist minister. She wired us from Atlantic City where she was attending a convention, "Hold the fort! Don't be moved!" A few months afterward when our attacker died, I spoke at memorial services for him upon invitation from his own church.

Later on, here and there, in the labor movement, certain isolated incidents crystallized those early ideas about drink in my mind. I have always been deeply distressed to see the degrading effects of too much drinking on otherwise fine people.

On Sundays I went to a meeting in Philadelphia at the Society for Ethical Culture on the *History of Religions,* a topic in which I had always been interested, and took part in the discussion that followed. I was wearing a demure, gray dress, and thinking me a Quaker, one of the Society's officers asked me to prepare a paper on the history of the Quakers. I went into the subject energetically and they were so well satisfied they asked me to write another on the history of Buddhism.

This led to my joining both the Reform Section of the Ethical Culture Society, which dealt with the problems of labor, and its Philosophical Section, which discussed the widest variety of questions.

About this time I made the acquaintance of a remarkable Russian woman, Mme. Ragozin, a writer and translator of books from French and Russian. Arthritis confined her to a wheel chair, but she did not let this deter her from getting about. It was through her I first became acquainted with Russian literature, the beginnings of the Russian revolutionary movement, and the problems of the Russian people. She gave me the novel *What Is To Be Done?* by Chernyshevsky, the great nineteenth-century Russian revolutionary writer, critic and materialist philosopher. Mme. Ragozin told me this challenging book had swept like a wave over Russia and had a tremendous effect in developing revolutionary ideas among the younger people especially. She told me about Chernyshevsky himself, his leadership in the revolutionary movement of the 'sixties, his long years of exile and imprisonment. This book made a powerful impression on me at the time, and came back to me vividly in later years when I read Lenin's comments on Chernyshevsky. In Krupskaya's *Memories of Lenin,* discussing Lenin's taste in literature, she wrote: "... But he not only valued good style. For example, he liked Chernyshevsky's novel, *What Is To Be Done?* in spite of its not being a great example of literary art, and its naïve form. I was surprised to see how attentively he read that novel, and how he took note of all the very fine nuances that are to be found in it." Lenin used the same title for one of his own most important books.

My first experience in a strike occurred about this time. The street car men of Philadelphia, who had a strong union for those days, struck against the long hours and short wages. It was about Christmas time, in the early 1890's. The strike was bitterly fought, scabs being recruited from organized gangs. There was one neighborhood, however, whose gang, the "Bulldogs," furnished no recruits. They wrecked every scab-manned, police-protected car that passed through. It was not until I read *Pages from a Worker's Life* that I learned this was young Bill Foster's gang. John Wanamaker was desperate because the strike interfered with his Christmas trade. In the end, he helped to break the strike by buying off some of the leaders. Our committee from the Reform Section of the Ethical Society attended strike meetings, and learned to discriminate between the real labor leaders and the fakers, and to spot the spies in the union, the Amalgamated Association of Street and Electric Railway Employees. After the strike the honest leaders were discharged.

Dr. William Salter, head of the Ethical Culture Society, ran a Sunday evening forum in Kensington. He asked me to go there with him, because the forum was not doing well. I saw at once what was wrong. The audience was composed largely of Scotch and English weavers who were used to speaking their minds. Here they were "talked down to" and the subjects were far away from their everyday lives. The week before my first visit, the subject was Greek Art.

I told Dr. Salter there should be many types of speakers, discussing daily problems of the workers, who should be encouraged to take part in the discussions. Dr. Salter then asked me to become director of the forum. The first man I got to speak was Henry Hetzel, Single Taxer and Democrat. He knew just how to talk to workers and they packed the place. I also invited a fine Socialist speaker by the name of Fred Long, a printer, who was responsible for the conversion to socialism of another printer, Ben Hanford, who was to become Debs' closest associate, and who was the creator of that wonderful character "Jimmie Higgins" who personifies the devotion of the rank and file in our movement.

Through Uncle Dan and other early influences I had become deeply interested in the natural sciences and at this time was taking courses in biology and botany at the University of Pennsylvania. But my contacts with the labor movement and the vital currents of political life exerted a stronger pull and I was going through a period of intense conflict as to what direction my life should take. The conflict was more intense because Lucien's interests had not followed a political trend, as had mine, and we were drawing apart.

Horace Traubel edited the little paper of the Ethical Culture Society in Philadelphia with Dr. Salter. When Salter left the city, Horace had to write most of the paper himself. On one of these occasions a book review was published which, to the consternation of the members, made the Ethical Culture Society appear to be advocating radical (for those days), or at least rather liberal marriage relations and laws. Horace was assailed from all sides, and when Dr. Salter returned he wrote an editorial attacking Horace's views. Factions developed and it ended with Horace starting another society called the Ethical Research Society, whose principles more nearly approached my own thinking than the older group's.

Horace Traubel, a devoted friend and disciple of Whitman, had been discharged from a bank where he was an accountant because of his advanced ideas and thereafter devoted his life to writing. For thirty-eight years he published a paper called *The Conservator,* editing it, printing it, and even setting the type himself. Some of the people who loved Whitman and had formed Whitman groups provided money to keep it going.

When we wanted to see Horace we knew that if we could not find him at his office, he would be at McKay's restaurant on Market Street. Horace's printing office was in the garret of a big building owned by William Price, architect and single taxer. We would stand sometimes at the corner of 16th and Walnut, whistle and throw stones against the window where Horace was putting his paper to press. Presently his old gray head appeared at the window, and then we would all go on to McKay's. Night after night he sat there at a big round table with writers, actors, workers, radicals of all types, discussing the affairs of the universe until morning. One of the group was H. L. Mencken, who was very individualistic, and whom we all looked upon as an anarchist. His hatred of hypocrisy, which was his outstanding characteristic in those days, made him welcome in the group, and he was devoted to Horace. "Round table" groups like this grew up around Horace in every city he lived in. Horace gradually outgrew his anarchistic and individualistic ideas, and developed a socialist philosophy. He loved Debs and they used to talk together for hours. When the Russian Revolution came, he rejoiced.

In Boston, Horace had his first paralytic stroke, in 1919 or 1920. After he recovered, he went to Canada with Frank and Mildred Bain, ardent Whitmanites. I went to see him there, taking him messages from his beloved Debs. While we were sitting around the table discussing Debs, he began to cry, saying, "Debs and you are doing all the work and I am doing nothing." He was still partially paralyzed and almost completely helpless. That was the last time I saw him. He died in Canada and they brought his body to New York. I was away in Kansas, but my daughter Helen attended the funeral and played a violin solo. Horace had encouraged her in her music, and had been very fond of her.

Horace's friends did not know where to hold the services. He had hardly ever been in a church. But they knew he had admired the writings of Dr. John Haynes Holmes so they thought the auditorium of his church might be a fitting place.

Art Young told me afterwards how Horace's friends accompanied the body there from the railroad station. Just as they reached the church, engines came roaring down the street and firemen blocked the way—the place was on fire. So they took him to the Rand School, then the center of socialist activities in New York, as the only place available.

Art told me that one of his friends remarked: "How Horace must be laughing at us! He would never have let us take him into a church when he was alive—and now we have not been able to get him in even though he is dead."

Back in 1894 and 1895 in Philadelphia, I had begun to learn about socialism from a dear friend who is still living, Dr. M. V. Ball. He was well grounded in theoretical socialism, discussed it with me and gave me books by Marx and Engels. But I was not yet able to apply the socialist theories he discussed to the actual conditions of the time.

It was during the time of William Jennings Bryan's "free silver" campaign with the slogan "16 to 1." Debates were being held all over the country. At Kensington I was chairman at some of these debates, where the merits of gold versus silver were vigorously argued. I had begun to be aware of the growing power of the trusts, and the free coinage of silver seemed to me a real step toward breaking up the power of the rich and helping the position of the workers and farmers, who were suffering from the terrible economic crisis and depression beginning in 1893. Grover Cleveland, a Democrat, was President for the second time but had lost his popularity because he did nothing for the farmers or for the workers. The Populists were demanding free silver as a way of helping those who were in debt. But the Republicans, representing big business, had the gold, and their candidate, William McKinley, won the election of 1896.

One Sunday night when I was chairing a political debate at Kensington, Dr. Ball brought with him to the forum a young man whom he introduced as a "Socialist from New York." During the discussion period the young man got up and said, "You mill workers haven't got a dollar amongst you—right now you are suffering from the effects of a lockout. Why are you so interested in what *kind* of dollars you have, whether they are gold or silver when you have *no dollars* at all?"

Then he showed how little the subject of the forum had to do with their everyday lives. He told them cheap money could not help them—it would only send prices up and leave them worse off than before. Now, he said, the weavers worked the machines and wove the cloth but had nothing. They were slaves to the boss who owned the machines. But the machines might become their slaves if they owned them collectively as well as used them collectively. Only with the tools of production in their own hands could the workers ever hope to control their own lives and receive the fruits of their labor. He put it so simply and directly that all I had been hearing and reading about Marx's teachings suddenly clicked. *To unite and organize the workers so they could achieve the power they needed to own the machines themselves.* Here at last was something real to work for.

The young man's talk hit the mark because new modern machinery had recently been installed in the Kensington textile factories. These machines were lighter than the old. So the mill owners discharged the men, and used women to run the looms, paying them $6 a week for work for which the men had been receiving $18 and over.

The Kensington mills manufactured chiefly heavy carpets and rugs, and the owners drove the women cruelly, expecting them to run several looms at a time. The men protested at being replaced by women, and tried to arouse the women to demand higher wages. The textile workers in Kensington, seeing my interest in their problems, asked me to join their union, especially to help bring the women in. So I joined my first union. Although I had four children to care for at home, I did everything I could to help. The owners, in their drive to intimidate the workers and keep wages down, shut down several of the mills, and the people were on the verge of starvation. The families in Kensington and other mill towns near by lived huddled together in old rickety houses with no sanitation. The old stone mills were damp and gloomy. Modern machinery was introduced, but no corresponding improvements were made in the lives of the workers. There was no hospitalization, no provision for maternity care. A few individuals from the churches and other groups made futile efforts to alleviate conditions through *The Lighthouse* organization.

And now when I heard the young man from New York speak at the Kensington forum on socialism, I understood at last that there was no other way but to work together for the ownership of the machines. After that meeting I sought out Dr. Ball who had labored so long with me.

"I am a Socialist now," I said. He looked at me soberly and said, "Do not be in such a hurry. Wait until you are sure."

"Give me one of the Socialist buttons," I answered him, "I *am* sure." He gave me a Socialist Labor Party button but it so happened that it was not the S.L.P. I first joined.

I was then living in West Philadelphia, a short distance from the University of Pennsylvania where I was taking courses in histological botany, biology and chemistry. While my four children (the youngest, "Buzz," was then six), were at school I bicycled to the university. A nice colored woman did the cooking, and I came home to have lunch with the children. I always tried to be at home in the evenings to put the children to bed. My life at the university was rich and full. A number of the professors were active in the Ethical Culture Society, and several of the economics professors lectured at our Kensington forum. Simon Patten was teaching economics at the university at that time. Among the people he influenced was Scott Nearing who became a Socialist.

The university at that time offered women only special courses. In addition to my scientific courses I worked in courses on Medieval Architecture, Medieval History and a course in Medieval Philosophy given by a Catholic priest from Washington University, whose lectures were enriched with material from his own research work in the Vatican. I also took summer courses with weekly round tables conducted by noted men. The most remarkable session that I remember was conducted by Edward Everett Hale.

I also managed to do a lot of outside reading, and was laying a foundation for my future work. I pored over American history and English and American literature, thinking over what I read as I went about my housework.

During this period my personal struggle was reaching a climax. My interests and activities were more and more leading me away from my husband. He was a wonderful character, one of the best friends I have ever had, but although a free-thinker, he was politically conservative in those days. I knew by this time that my place was in the labor movement and that Lucien was not prepared to go on with me in this field. For us to stay together would force him into a false position. At the same time, I knew how much the children needed him. My problem was to arrange a separation, and at the same time keep his friendship and maintain his relation with the children. The struggle was so severe I had a nervous breakdown and was in bed two months. I had not confided my troubles to anyone except Dr. Ball, who was my physician. He felt things could be worked out as I hoped, and a separation was decided on. Later I moved to New York and Mr. Ware secured a divorce. We have always remained the best of friends, and he has always helped support and kept in close touch with his children, who all love him dearly. In later years, largely through the influence of our son Hal, Mr. Ware himself grew much more radical in his thinking.

In the Ethical Culture Society in Philadelphia, I met a brilliant woman who had several little children. We became very fond of one another and used to take long bicycle rides with the children through Wissahickon Park. Together we started a Sunday School in the Society. I taught nature studies, using the fine series of children's books by Katherine Dopps of the University of Chicago (*Cave Dwellers, Tree Dwellers,* etc.); my friend, a fine musician herself, taught music. Both of us were very much interested in a theatrical group that met at the home of Frank Stephens, the ardent Single Taxer. He had a big stage in his home, and we had delightful times putting on Shakespeare's

Ella Reeve Bloor in 1910

Ella Reeve Bloor addressing an open air meeting in Wall Street at the turn of the century

plays. I can remember playing the wife of Brutus, in *Julius Caesar,* and Jessica in the *Merchant of Venice.*

My knowledge of botany and biology had been helpful in teaching my own children freely and frankly about the processes of life about which the schools were so reticent in those days. I had a microscope at home, and taught them a great deal by direct observation. I wrote several articles on the use of the microscope in teaching children, and this led me to write a textbook, *Three Little Lovers of Nature,* which was published in 1895, and widely used in the schools. Later I wrote another book, *Talks About Authors and Their Works.* I enjoyed doing this and it added to the slender family income.

I have already mentioned writing articles for Dr. Jenkin Lloyd Jones, for whom I had the greatest admiration. When he came to Philadelphia to lecture for the Ethical Culture Society, I was in the seventh heaven. He made a magnificent address on the need of tolerance for all religions and for all races, because of the underlying unity of all real religious feeling, the underlying brotherhood of all men. I was deeply moved. When he had finished and just as I was diving under the seat for my rubbers, I heard Dr. Jones saying: "Can anyone tell me whether Mrs. Ware is here? I particularly hoped to see her." I straightened up and said very meekly, "Here I am."

Since Dr. Jones had a dinner engagement out past West Philadelphia where I lived, we rode on the street car together. He got me to tell him about my problems. I told him I had been a Unitarian for a while, and then had joined the Ethical Culture Society; but now it seemed to me I did not belong there either, since their philosophy was never to take sides on anything, and I had already taken sides, for I had become a convinced Socialist. I told him I felt quite out in the cold, and didn't seem to belong anywhere. Dr. Jones refused to consider this a catastrophe. "Keep right on growing," he told me. "Keep right on *going*—no matter where it takes you. Of course seek guidance along the road."

I have never forgotten that advice, and have tried to keep on growing and going all my life.

3. First Tidings of Socialism

MY courses in biology had so deepened my interest in scientific problems that I began to consider seriously the idea of becoming a doctor. I had seen so much disease and physical suffering among the workers of Kensington that it seemed to me here was a profession which would enable me to combine science with work in the labor movement. But just about this time my four children came down with measles, one after the other. I myself was quarantined, and I had to look after the children for a long period, which ended my work at the university. By this time, too, a definite decision had been reached about a divorce, and soon after I had to move to New York.

I was urged by my Ethical Culture Society friends to join Felix Adler in the Society's work in New York. But I had become fed up with their "Look on both sides! Don't take a positive position on anything!"

And then I met Debs. This was not long after his release in 1895 from a six months' sentence in Woodstock County jail for his part in the Pullman strike. Debs had become a Socialist in jail after reading Marx's *Capital* and other socialist classics brought to him by Victor Berger, later the first Socialist Congressman.

The work of Eugene Victor Debs was already well known to me. Debs had gone into railroading as a boy of fourteen. By the time he was twenty he was a charter member of the Brotherhood of Locomotive Firemen and secretary of his Terre Haute local.

Five years later he had become grand secretary-treasurer of the national union. In 1885, at the age of 30, he was elected to the Indiana state legislature. His experiences in organizing the separate railroad crafts led him to a burning belief in industrial unionism and in 1893 he organized the American Railway Union, for the unification of all railroad workers. He gave up a $4,000 a year job to work for the new organization at $900 a year. The first year of its existence, he led the A.R.U. to a victorious struggle for higher wages with the Great Northern Railroad. In 1894 the A.R.U., now 150,000 members strong, engaged in a sympathetic strike in defense of the striking Pullman Company shop workers who had joined the A.R.U. It was bitterly fought, tying up all the railroads west of Chicago. President Cleveland sent federal troops to break the strike over the protest of Governor Altgeld of Illinois. Sweeping injunctions were issued, and Debs and other strike leaders were sent to jail.

I heard Debs speak for the first time at a big mass meeting in New York. With his matchless oratory he described the unspeakable conditions of paternalism under which the Pullman workers had been forced to live: the nice houses the company had built, and for which they deducted rent, leaving the workers less than a dollar a week on which to live, while declaring high dividends for stockholders. He described the strike, actually won by the courage and determination of the workers, but crushed when the thugs and murderers were turned loose, federal troops sent to smash the union headquarters and injunctions issued and arrests made. At this meeting Debs, who had said at his trial, "I was baptized in socialism in the roar of the conflict," talked in clear terms of the class struggle.

"The only way out," he said, "is for the workers to unite together and abolish the cause of the struggle—the private ownership of the railroads and the machines."

Deeply impressed by Debs, I became a member of a group called "The Social Democracy of America" organized by him in 1897. Since Debs was himself a railroad man and had just come through the great railroad strikes, he naturally appealed particularly to railroad men, and in the branch in Brooklyn which I joined, I was the only member who did not belong to the railwaymen's union. I became very active in this branch and was elected secretary.

Debs was still a comparatively young man then—about forty. He had all the enthusiasm of a new convert. After many struggles, he felt he had just learned the real remedy for the evils of the world. He was sure and happy and full of life. Debs had wonderful personal magnetism. In speaking he used powerful similes and illustrations. He spoke like an evangelist, using his whole body to drive his points home, leaning far over the platform, and stretching out his long lean arm toward his audience.

Referring to the growing power of the capitalists and financial heads of the fast developing trusts of America, I heard him say: "Remember John D. Rockefeller—I say to you 'shrouds have no pockets!' "

Once, I was on a committee in Philadelphia that had arranged several Socialist meetings for Debs. He was coming in from Wilkes-Barre, and I went to the station to meet him. He looked drawn and tired.

"I'll bet you have been staying up every night talking to the miners," I said.

"Yes, I have," he admitted. "Aren't they great fellows? Last night they were talking to me until pretty nearly morning and then when I was going to bed, a fellow timidly knocked on my door. 'I thought,' he said, 'since you have to get up at five anyway, we might as well spend the rest of the night talking.' "

Then, his tired face alight with warmth and love, Debs exclaimed, "Now, aren't they wonderful fellows?—Ella, I know you would do the very same thing!"

When Debs came to our house the children followed him wherever he went, even tagging after him to the railroad station, not wanting to miss a moment of his company.

When I joined the Social Democracy I was living in Brooklyn and had married for the second time. My husband, Louis Cohen, was a Socialist. I was pregnant with the first of the two children of that marriage. The railroad men came to my house so I could continue to act as secretary.

But a new disappointment was in store for me. The Social Democracy, I soon discovered, was a utopian scheme. Debs' plan was to form an ideal colony out West to show by example that socialism could work. From the outset I told the members of my group that this colonization scheme was unsound, not real socialism at all. I stayed with it for a while because of my loyalty to Debs, and because this was the nearest thing I had yet found to a socialist movement.

Debs set up a paper in Chicago called the *Social-Democrat*. At his request I wrote a children's column for it. The children answered the appeals of Debs and his colonization committee by sending me money. I felt it was unfair to collect money for something that did not yet exist. People were already selling out businesses to join the colony. A national convention was held in Chicago and our local sent delegates. Among them was my husband who still felt that anything Debs was in must be all right. I agreed to withhold final judgment until the delegates returned. When they came back and reported that plans to establish the colony would continue, I resigned. I simply could not stay with anything so unscientific.

Debs himself soon came to see the fallacy of it, and at the convention of the Social Democracy in June 1898, he joined with Victor Berger in splitting away and forming the Social-Democratic Party of America, which was to be a political party built on the lines of the European Socialist parties. In 1900 this party joined forces with a large group that had split off from the Socialist Labor Party and in 1901 formed the Socialist Party of America.

Once again I felt quite an outcast. Not long after these events, I attended a meeting of the Socialist Labor Party with Daniel DeLeon as the speaker. He was small and slight and prematurely gray, and spoke very deliberately and convincingly.

The Socialist Labor Party was a revolutionary party in those days and DeLeon, its leader, was a brilliant theoretician and speaker, a courageous fighter against capitalism. My own grounding in Marxism was not yet sufficiently solid for me to detect DeLeon's sectarianism. It was, in fact, only in the development of a practical program that DeLeon's errors became apparent. I was impressed with his analysis of the evils of the capitalist system, and of the fallacy of isolated socialist colonies as a way of achieving socialism. I felt that at last here was scientific socialism, and joined the S.L.P.

Daniel DeLeon and I became friends. We were both determined that the Socialist classics of France and Germany should be translated into English, so that the American movement could get the much-needed theoretical groundwork to be found in these works. DeLeon translated Kautsky's pamphlets before Kautsky departed from the line of Marx. I became very much interested in the New York Labor News Company—the first organization that published revolutionary books and pamphlets in English on a large scale. Its manager was Julien Pierce. Together we proof-read the pamphlets translated by DeLeon, often having to reconstruct the English, a greater task than we ever let him know. DeLeon had been born on the island of Curaçao, Dutch West Indies; his native language was Spanish, and he had received his education in universities in Holland and Germany.

DeLeon was a very finicky man, revolted by coarseness of any kind. Whenever he sent a young organizer out into the field he would call him into his office and say, "The shores of the labor movement are strewn with the wrecks made by drink."

The growing conservatism of Gompers and the A.F. of L., and the failure of the Socialists to capture the Knights of Labor, had led DeLeon into a typical "dual union" adventure. In December, 1895, he had organized a conference to set up a strictly Socialist trade union group, with delegates from the New York, Brooklyn and Newark Central Labor Federations and the United Hebrew Trades. The Socialist Trade and Labor Alliance emerged.

The S.T.L.A. stood for industrial unionism, and issued a call for all radicals to come out of the A.F. of L. and build a dual Socialist organization nationally. DeLeon believed these Socialist unions would gradually win over the majority of the workers, and the unions would then take over the management of society. Since DeLeon and the S.L.P. neglected the immediate struggles of the workers in favor of abstract propaganda for socialism, none of their attempts at dualism resulted in strong permanent unions.

"Not sops," said DeLeon, "but unconditional surrender of capitalism." Neither he, nor the S.L.P. however, could see that you had to win the "sops" for the workers at the same time that you made it clear that the sops weren't all.

DeLeon's positive contribution to trade union thought was his insistent and brilliant exposure of right wing opportunism, and the A.F. of L. bureaucracy for whom he used the term "labor fakers." His analyses of how the capitalists buy off the leaders of the workers, making them what Lenin later called "agents of the bourgeoisie in the ranks of the working class," were incorporated in some of the finest pamphleteering produced by the socialist movement.

I helped in the organization of a national Socialist Labor Party convention held in New York in 1900. The S.L.P. then had a large membership. The convention was attended by such leaders as Lucien Sanial, a survivor of the Paris Commune, Hugo Vogt, Arthur Keep—a young English Socialist, Val Remmel, later S.L.P. candidate for vice-president, and many others. I was on the constitution committee, with Lucien Sanial, and was appointed to the General Executive Board of the S.T.L.A. I served on the board for some time and became an organizer.

One day an urgent letter came to me in Brooklyn where I was keeping house, and taking care of several of my husband's small brothers besides my own five children.

The letter was from one of the leaders of the S.T.L.A. in Providence, R. I. He wrote that a man had been discharged from the Slatersville textile mill because he was a Socialist. The whole mill had rebelled by going out on strike. The priests had been going around to the houses telling the men and women they would all be damned if they stood for socialism. He urged me to come at once to help.

There I was, with a nursing baby, but I felt I must go. I strapped a collapsible go-cart to my bag, and off I went with my baby in arms, my oldest, Helen, twelve years old, tagging along. I stopped at Providence to see the S.T.L.A. leaders. The next day I went to Woonsocket, left my things at a hotel and took Helen and the baby on a short line train down to Slatersville. I wheeled the baby to the public square, where a tremendous mass meeting was going on. It looked as though everybody in town had gathered to meet me. Before the crowd discovered me, I managed to nurse the baby and put him to sleep. Helen sat on a doorstep holding on to the go-cart. The applause when I got up to speak woke the baby and as the crowd grew quiet, Dick let out a loud wail. I saw Helen rocking the go-cart and went right on speaking, but he gave me plenty of competition during that meeting.

The strikers asked me to go on to Boston to raise money. I went with my retinue—my daughter, my son, my baby carriage. I held a big meeting on Boston Common while Helen and some of the comrades played with the baby in his carriage. We raised enough money to move all the strikers out of Slatersville and get them work in other places.

The baby was none the worse for the trip.

A little more than two years after I joined the Socialist Labor Party my youngest son, Carl, was born (October 12, 1900). I was then writing a full page story on the Trade Unions in America for the *Weekly People,* the Sunday edition of the official organ of the S.L.P.

At this time, though my husband and I were living in East Orange, I went to the fortnightly meetings of the General Executive Board in New York. At night when we met, there was no elevator running, and I walked up seven flights of stairs, every two weeks, until just before Carl was born.

There was a very large Socialist Labor Party membership in East Orange. Soon after my baby was born, I went down to the county office, which was in Newark, back of a beer garden, to offer my services. The party officials looked at me as if to say, "What are you, a woman, doing here? You should be attending to your home!"

I made up my mind that I would be their organizer before I got through with them. Sure enough I was elected county organizer for Essex County within a few months. We organized the Ampere Shop in East Orange, where a great many Scandinavians who were skilled machinists worked. Our house was practically next door to a big boarding house where many of them lived.

Then the party sent me on a trip to Philadelphia to organize the street car men in the S.T.L.A. Though it had to be done secretly, it was easy to organize the car men since they were discouraged with their leadership, which had sold them out in previous years. We organized a "Round Robin" system. Each man taken into the organization would sign up ten more who, of course, would not know the members of other groups outside their own.

During one of our secret meetings I recognized a man who had helped break the strike of the 1890's. Every proposition he made was destructive. I finally got up and exposed his role in the strike. William Bowers, national S.T.L.A. secretary was present. He told me I should not talk against the man before the workers. I indignantly retorted that I would expose a stool pigeon wherever I saw one. This and other incidents illustrated the bureaucratic attitude creeping into the S.T.L.A., which preferred not to take the workers, or even its own organizers into its confidence, but acted behind closed doors. Then I discovered that Bowers was hand in glove with some of the very A.F. of L. organizers we were fighting and I felt we could not keep him as secretary. But DeLeon supported his retention in office, although admitting he "wasn't fit to run a dog house."

Gradually the defects of the S.L.P. were brought home to me. I found many workers antagonistic because I was organizing a rival union. The S.T.L.A. was weakening the A.F. of L. by drawing off its more radical elements and leaving the reactionaries in control, and was itself organized on too narrow and sectarian a basis to accomplish anything. Furthermore, the S.L.P. as a political party had little real influence because DeLeon was against taking part in the immediate struggles of the workers. His idea was that the party's role should be educational and that capitalism could just be talked into surrender. I was beginning to see the harm of this divorce of theory and practice, this separation of the political party from economic struggles, and the isolation of the revolutionary workers into a sectarian group. (Witness the degeneration of the S.L.P. into a small counter-revolutionary group today.) I began very early to see the importance of a united trade union movement, and felt that Socialists should work within the A.F. of L. I felt DeLeon understood Marx very well abstractly but knew little about the practical needs of the labor movement.

The last time I talked with DeLeon I told him I was moving to Philadelphia and was willing to accept the secretaryship of the S.L.P. local there, which had been offered me, but that I could not go along with their principles wholeheartedly. As a good friend of mine, DeLeon accepted what I said without anger, but would not change his methods.

Soon after I moved to Philadelphia the S.L.P. leaders in Pennsylvania voted at a state convention to leave the party in a body. I opposed this move, feeling it would be an easy matter to change the policy of our organization on trade unionism if we had the membership behind us, since most of the errors had been committed not by the movement as a whole but by a few leaders.

The Pennsylvania group, joined by some New York members, formed a "third party," called "The Logical Center." Lucien Sanial, who with DeLeon and Vogt had constituted the dominant triumvirate in the S.L.P., was one of the founders, as well as Frank MacDonald who had been working on the *Weekly People*. Sanial and several others spent an evening at my home urging me to join them. I had been watching with interest the Socialist Party, formed in 1901 by another split-off from the S.L.P. and the Social-Democratic Party of Debs.

My friends insisted that the Socialist Party was weak and was formed mainly of preachers and professionals. "To us," they said, "is given the task of educating the socialist movement of America —like the *Partie Ouvrier* of France."

That decided me. I told Sanial this was outright impudence—

to stand outside a party to educate those inside who were working to put their ideas into practice. I announced that whatever the imperfections of the Socialist Party, it was a growing party, closely allied with the labor movement and I wanted to go where the labor movement was. On this I stood alone with an old Scotchman, Sam Clarke, a weaver from Kensington. Even my husband laughed at me. But I told him "You will join too before long!"

When, in 1902, I joined the Socialist Party, many of my old S.L.P. friends sent me insulting letters, and showered me with rosaries, charms, crucifixes, prayer books, as though I had joined the Catholic Church. People I had entertained in my home would not speak to me.

In the Socialist Party I met Debs again. At that time the face of the party was truly turned towards the labor movement and from the first both Debs and I found our place mainly among the workers. We were always associated in the left wing of the party and both of us struggled constantly against the opportunistic, petty-bourgeois tendencies in the right wing of the party, led by the old-guard lawyer, Morris Hillquit.

Hillquit had been the leader of the right wing Socialists since their split off from the Socialist Labor Party. As chairman of the Socialist Party's national executive committee, he represented the American party in the Second International. At the same time, he was a lawyer who served corporations as well as unions. He was several times Socialist candidate for Congress and ran for Mayor of New York in 1917 and in 1932. In 1924 he led all the Socialists who would follow into Robert La Follette's Progressive Party.

The rank and file of the Socialist Party were constantly electing committees to meet with S.L.P. delegates to work out some basis for unity. Debs was independent and courageous enough to speak from the same platform as DeLeon, whom the S.P. leaders hated. Debs and I organized, with DeLeon, a great unity meeting in the old Crystal Palace, down below Fourteenth Street. The state secretary of the Socialist Party at that time was John Chase, a "Yes-man" to Hillquit. Both Chase and Hillquit used all their influence to keep me from taking part in the meeting. But we held a huge, spirited meeting, with Debs, DeLeon and an I.W.W. speaking on the same platform. DeLeon made a good speech for unity and for industrial unionism, but Debs got the biggest hand.

While aware even then of weaknesses in the Socialist Party, I knew I had made the only decision possible. In my political development my study of science stood me in good stead. I knew that in all evolution, whether industrial or biological, there were some forces that accelerated development, others that set it back. So it became a question of always seeking out the forces of growth and progress and working with those forces, against the forces that dragged life backward. Capitalism meant death and decay. The profit system held back progress, prevented the development of a fuller life for all the people. There were elements in the socialist movement who upheld capitalism, who were perhaps even greater enemies of the people than the capitalists themselves, because they fooled the workers with their revolutionary phraseology. Therefore my search was always for that group which really understood the class struggle, which saw clearly the need of organizing the workers, with the greatest of all aims—that of taking over for the workers and farmers the means of production, the means of life. I knew that the fullest development for all human beings could only come about under those conditions.

4. Suffer, Little Children—

NOT long after I joined the Socialist Party, Louis, my husband, also joined, as I had predicted he would. He became secretary of the Philadelphia organization, while I was state organizer in Pennsylvania. We lived in a first floor apartment on North 7th Street in Philadelphia. Because of the big anthracite miners' strike, there was little coal. I kept the children in bed until 11 o'clock in the morning so they could keep warm. One of our Socialist organizers, Frank Jordan, who had contracted tuberculosis while organizing in the coal strike, was staying at our apartment until we could raise money to send him to California. I used to buy meat for him and for Louis, but never ate a bit myself, because we had too little money. My daughter Helen used to insist that I take her weekly allowance from her father and I often had to. In spite of the pinching it meant, we loved to have Frank with us. He was a great student of philosophy, and was always reading Hegel and Marx and Engels, and guided my study of dialectical materialism.

Carl and Dick were too young for me to go away on long trips, but I went to the strike area for a day or two at a time, working around Lucerne County and east of Wilkes-Barre. I had organized Socialist locals among the miners, and my function was to strengthen and inspire the party members in the strike. I stayed at the miners' houses to talk to their wives, who were wonderfully brave and never complained although they were almost starving. It gave them new courage to know that I was doing everything possible to raise money for their relief. There was usually only one bed in the house where the whole family slept crosswise, keeping their clothes on for warmth. They gave me a place in the bed with the wife and children, while the poor miner slept on the floor.

As far back as 1890, the productive capacity of the large anthracite mine industry was 12 to 15 million tons greater than the market would take at satisfactory prices—that is, satisfactory to the companies. From that period on, there had been great unrest among the miners. Right after the Civil War, three organizations tried to organize the miners: the Miners' and Laborers' Benevolent Association, crushed in 1875, after an attempted general strike, the Knights of Labor, and the Miners' National Progressive Union. Then came a great influx of workers from other countries: Russians, Poles and other Slavic peoples, Hungarians and Italians. These people, seeking the promised land, were bitterly exploited. In 1902, two years after the organization of the United Mine Workers of America, the average wage through the entire coal field was only $22.00 a month. The miners had to buy all their food, clothing, household goods and tools from the company store at exorbitant prices and often had not a cent left over—frequently owing the company money, as their rent was also taken out of their pay checks.

The mine-owners ignored Pennsylvania laws prohibiting employment of children under fourteen inside and under twelve outside the mine. Many boys under twelve worked on the breakers—huge slanting screens where the slate and slag were picked out of the coal. They would work there until their tender little fingers bled, getting an average of 35¢ for a ten-hour day. Other boys under the legal age worked inside the mines, never seeing daylight, getting only 67½¢ for a ten-hour day.

On May 12, 1902, the hard coal miners struck for a state-wide contract—a decent wage, enforcement of the eight-hour day, and union checkweighmen. George F. Baer, president of the Reading Railroad, was spokesman for the operators and the toughest of them all. His company, controlling about 70 per cent of the nation's anthracite output, was dominated by Morgan.

The strike, with 150,000 men out, continued 100 per cent effective until October 23. It was supported not only by the Socialists, but by the working class throughout the country. The bituminous miners contributed large sums to the strike fund through weekly assessments of $1.00 each.

Every colliery was enclosed in barbed wire fences. Four thousand armed coal and iron police patrolled the towns. The miners countered with a widespread boycott. Strikers' children stayed away from schools where children of scabs went; stores which sold to scabs and imported strikebreakers lost their trade. Though a Citizens' Alliance was organized in Wilkes-Barre which offered rewards for the arrest and conviction of those engaged in the boycott, it was not weakened.

The mine owners brought in the national guard and General John M. Wilson gave orders "shoot to kill." Priests were used to fight the strike. In the Church of the Annunciation at Shenandoah, Pa., Father O'Reilly told the miners: "You should have the manhood to go back to work and defy the United Mine Workers of America. It is a bloodstained organization and will be bloodstained until it ceases to exist. It was formed to promote crime and protect criminals. Everybody was happy and contented here until Mitchell and Fahy came."

Actually John Mitchell, national president of the U.M.W.A., did things that were open to question by the miners. He had been hailed as a great labor leader two years before when he had led the miners to a great victory. October 29, the date of the settlement of that successful strike, is still celebrated in the anthracite fields as "Mitchell Day." But by 1902 Mitchell was beginning to take the compromiser's course. He stalled a long time on the miners' demands to call a national convention to discuss a general strike, and finally considered a proposal from the National Civic Federation to use its "good offices" to find a solution in the interests of both miners and mine owners. The National Civic Federation, dominated by anti-union employers, with that arch foe of labor

Mark Hanna, boss of the Republican Party, as chairman, included in its membership reactionary trade union leaders bought out and used to serve the interests of the capitalist class. When Mitchell became chairman of the trade agreement department of the National Civic Federation, the miners said, "John, if you stay in that anti-union organization, you will be put out of the miners' union— you can take your choice between the Civic Federation and us." Mitchell stayed in the miners' union. But when he died in 1919 he is reported to have left $250,000, most of it in coal, railroad and steel stocks.

President Roosevelt, on the suggestion of Morgan and with the acquiescence of Mitchell, appointed an Anthracite Coal Commission. The chairman, Judge Gray of Delaware, was at that very time fighting to get a bill through the Delaware legislature disfranchising Negroes and many poor whites through the device of a "literacy" qualification. Roosevelt answered Mitchell's request for a Catholic priest on the commission, since most of the miners were Catholic, by appointing Bishop Spalding, who sided with the mine owners. Other members were the army officer, General Wilson, and E. E. Clark, Chief of the Order of Railroad Conductors, who had helped break the Pullman strike.

The miners convening at Wilkes-Barre, in October, raised vigorous objections because there was no representative of labor on the commission. They naturally considered Clark a strikebreaker. But the leaders told the miners to keep quiet until the commission issued its report, and the strike was called off.

I attended the commission hearings in Philadelphia at the Federal Court Building, where it remained in session for many days; 558 witnesses were examined. One of the outstanding lawyers present was Henry Demarest Lloyd, whose *Wealth and Commonwealth* was such a powerful indictment of monopoly capitalism and who gave his services freely to the miners during the entire strike. Many utterances at that time have become legends in the history of labor. One was Harvard's President Eliot's declaration that the scab was a "good type of American hero." Henry Demarest Lloyd answered:

"The strikebreaker or scab is in our day precisely the same kind of 'good type of American hero' as the New England loyalist was in his day when he did his best to ruin the struggle of his fellow-colonists for independence."

Counsel for the miners, with Lloyd, was Clarence Darrow, who made one of the most striking orations of all. He talked for nine hours. Coming right up to where the commission was sitting and thrusting his great rugged head forward, he declared:

"Gentlemen of the board, I might stand here for hours and try to change your views, but I am convinced that no matter what I say, you have decided what you may or may not do for these miners, but I wish to say to you, that the day will come when not one man nor 400 shall say whether we shall have coal or not. The time will come when the people themselves will own the coal!"

Judge Gray tried to silence the applause although he had not silenced the mine owners' friends when they had applauded Baer's statement that "God had given the mine owners the divine right to control the workers in the great task of building up the country."

"Divine Right Baer," as he was nicknamed, was full of religious cant. In the biography of Henry Demarest Lloyd by his sister Caro Lloyd Strobell, she quotes one of Baer's letters which contains the following paragraph: "The rights and interests of the laboring man will be protected and cared for—not by the labor agitators, but by the Christian men to whom God in His infinite wisdom has given the control of the property interests of the country, and upon the successful management of which so much depends."

The board made a miserable settlement, binding for three years, the miners receiving a 10 per cent instead of the 20 per cent wage increase they had asked, and the eight-hour day only for the engineers, pumpmen and firemen, the rest getting the nine-hour day. Their chief demand, union recognition, was refused. In a few years the miners struck again. But although the miners did not gain their demands, the long struggle lifted them many rungs up the ladder of progress. They had demonstrated their strength and learned the power of organization.

Frank Stephens, Philadelphia sculptor, Will Price, a Philadelphia architect who afterward founded Rose Valley, and others had conceived the idea of starting a single tax colony. Joseph Fels offered to help finance it.

Fels, who had made a fortune from naphtha soap, had announced his conversion to single tax in a Chicago speech: "We cannot get rich under present conditions without robbing somebody. I have done it; you are doing it now, and I am still doing it, but I am proposing to spend the money to wipe out the system by which I made it."

The group bought about 200 acres of land in Delaware, six miles from Wilmington, where they founded the single tax colony, Arden. The land was held in common by a town committee, and could be rented, but not sold. The people in the colony only had to pay taxes and interest on the mortgage. Every resident, including children, had a vote in the town committee. The rent was fifty cents a month per acre. Members of the colony could build any kind of house they wished and could lease the land for ninety-nine years. If they wanted to move, they could turn the lease over to the community or sell it.

When I was approached about living there I said: "I don't believe in the single tax as a remedy for anything but I do think it would be a nice place to take the children." Carl at the time was almost two, Dick four, and I had Buzz, Hal, Helen and Grace to care for. The committee replied that while members of the colony would for the most part be single taxers, they would also welcome people of other political beliefs. So I decided to join the colony.

I built an $80 shack where we spent our summers. Gradually people began to move in. Lucien Ware moved in from Philadelphia, and still lives there today.

One winter when Hal was 15 years old, measles left him with a spot on his lung. The doctor said he must live in the country, eat well and rest. So I moved to Arden for the winter, living in a little red house called Assembly Place. It had a good wood stove and a big fireplace. I had plenty of books. We had a big Scotch collie called Nellie, a toothless fox hound who could make a noise that would scare anybody away, and a little fox terrier which guarded the front door. Hal, Carl and Dick were with me all the time. The other children went to school in Philadelphia, staying with their father during the week, and came down every weekend. The town pump froze up and I carried water for washing clear from the creek across the next farm. But it was well worth it. Hal grew strong and went back to school the next year.

I was then state organizer of the Socialist Party of Delaware and raced to Wilmington once a week to get there before Frank Stephens, or else he would occupy my street-meeting corner for a speech on single tax. One of the Du Ponts was also a single taxer. When he ran for the legislature, I stood on a corner opposite him and talked on socialism while he was talking single tax.

In the wintertime I organized the sale of the *Appeal to Reason,* a Socialist weekly paper published in Girard, Kansas, which at that time had a 500,000 circulation, largest of any socialist paper before or since. Even today I find people in the most remote places who used to read the *Appeal.* Its editor, S. A. Wayland, who aimed to "Yankeefy" the socialist movement, started the weekly *Appeal* in 1894 to spread socialist ideas in the farm areas. The subscription price was low, bundle orders cheap. Its chief influence was in the Middle West and Southwest, and it did more to popularize socialism than a dozen of the doctrinaire papers like the S.L.P.'s *Weekly People.*

I also held meetings against lynching, after a half-witted young Negro who had murdered a white girl was burned at the stake right in Wilmington. I took the occasion not only to denounce the horrors of lynching, but to expose the terrible child labor conditions in the city.

"You men of Wilmington," I told my street corner audience, "were so incensed about the brutal murder of one white girl that you lawlessly burned a young Negro, who should have been in an institution, but you have never raised a finger to prevent the death of hundreds of girls who die from phossy jaw from working in your match factories, even though they are your own children. . . ."

The crowd stood in shocked silence as I described the wholesale child murder going on in Wilmington where children of twelve and fourteen were exposed to sulphur fumes to make profits for the owners.

When my butcher came to the house for orders, he regaled me with tales of the lynching. One day he said meaningfully, "Pretty lonesome for you around here, isn't it?" Then looking up over my bookcase, "Oh, but I see you've got a gun." "Sure," I said, "and I know how to use it, too!" I didn't tell him that it was a rusty old blunderbuss that didn't work. He spread the tale around that I was a good shot.

My husband Louis had been much away from home, traveling for Fels Naphtha soap. Our interests began to diverge. Louis turned away from the socialist movement, became involved in business and got interested in mystical ideas. We eventually separated, and I had to face the problem of supporting the two younger boys. I got a position at the University of Pennsylvania teaching foreign students English. I went to Philadelphia every other day teaching students from South America, Turkey, Armenia, Russia, Germany, and even one from Japan, all day and all evening.

I would get to Arden late at night on the last train and walk home. The conductor seeing I was very tired used to say, "Now you go to sleep. Don't worry. I'll wake you up." And I slept till we came to Arden. When I got home the children would all be asleep. The next morning I would get up very early and bake enough for two days. In those days we could not get many things ready-made, and much of the children's clothing had to be made at home. One pair of their father's trousers made two or three pairs for the little boys. I had to do all of that sewing.

No matter where they were or how much I was away from home, the children were always a very close part of my life. They always had the utmost faith and confidence in me; and we had a wonderfully close relationship. We always seemed to pack more talk and real comradeship into a few hours together than occurs in many other families in weeks or months. One reason was that nothing was hidden between us. I had always talked to the children very naturally and they had no reticence, ever, in discussing the most intimate things with me. Another thing my children always appreciated was that, however irritating they might be, I never corrected or punished them before strangers. If they behaved badly, I made a point to talk to them long and earnestly in private. Whatever my own activities and interests, I always shared them with the children, told them what I was doing and why, and made them feel a part of it. During free speech fights in Philadelphia they got used to the clang of patrol wagons carrying off their mother, and Dick was once arrested with me. They used to meet me often on picket lines. None of them ever resented my work as something that took me away from them, and I think this free and frank attitude between us is the reason so many of my family have themselves taken part in the radical movement, and even those who have not maintained the closest and warmest relationship both with me and with each other, always.

Grace, my oldest daughter, had wanted to be an artist, and went for three years to the Academy of Fine Arts in Philadelphia. She brought her student friends to our place in Arden, where they had gay times. Then she became engaged to a rascally minister's son, whom we all knew it would be a disaster for her to marry. She herself soon found out his worthlessness through bitter experience. She was in a terrible state when their affair broke up, but came to me with the whole story, so I was able to help her. I had to take her away from everything for a while. Grace got interested in nursing and gave up her art work to become a trained nurse. She has done fine work in her profession, specializing in nervous and surgical cases. With her patients she has traveled all over the world. Now with her hair growing white, she is still nursing, but has turned back to her art and works seriously at it during the summer months.

Next to Grace was Hal, of whose life and fine work in the movement I shall write more fully later. Hal and I were always very close, and I remember his saying to me before he went away to college, "You don't know what you've done for me, Mom, by always talking to me so frankly about everything."

Helen showed her musical talent very early and her father helped her with the violin. Once when Ernest Schelling came to visit us, the whole house rocked with his music, and Helen was enthralled. Then she played for him, and when the great musician told her she was very gifted, her career was determined. She practiced with the greatest persistence and devotion. While Helen's whole life was bound up in her music, she had a very sympathetic attitude toward all my activities, and helped greatly with the littler children. Helen became engaged while she was very young to a Southern fellow. It seemed an unwise match, but I did not interfere, hoping it would work out. They were both musicians and both temperamental, and both came to me constantly to talk about their difficulties. Realizing at last that it wouldn't work, they came to me together to tell me, and gave me their engagement ring.

Buzz, easy-going and full of dry humor, showed his bent for drawing very early. He went to the Manual High in Philadelphia while we were living in Arden, and during that period made a mural for the "Red House," the Arden ice cream parlor and general gathering place. The mural won so much acclaim that Buzz's career was decided on. He became a successful commercial artist. Dick and Carl, the two youngest boys, both showed literary tastes quite early. Dick eventually became a Professor of English; while Carl turned to labor journalism, which led him to party work. My close relationship with my children has always endured. No matter how far we are away from each other, or for how long, we always pick up the threads where we left off, and display a "clannishness" which others find amazing.

As the younger children grew more self-reliant, and went to school, I boarded them with a comrade, a Mrs. Newcombe, who kept the Arden Inn. In that Inn, when Carl was about thirteen, many were the learned discussions he held trying to convert Scott Nearing, who was a neighbor, to socialism. Scott at that time refused to be labeled. Later he was expelled from the University of Pennsylvania as a dangerous Socialist.

While I am discussing the Arden days (which have carried me way ahead of the rest of my story) I want to recount an incident that happened much later when Hal had a little farm of his own in Arden, out on the edge of the town. I took a place of my own for the two younger boys nearby and Hal used to look after the boys when I went away. Sometimes after a tour, I would come home unexpectedly in the middle of the night. On this occasion I came home on the midnight train from Mechanicsville, New York, where I had just helped to lead a big successful, but strenuous, strike of brickmakers.

As I walked up the country road at midnight and cut across the fields toward home, I fell into a deep irrigation ditch. I picked myself up and stumbled on in the dark. When I got to the house, I found the front room where my bed was full of boys—seven of them. My boys had evidently had a party. There were boys asleep all over the place, on the couch, on my bed, on the floor. I had to take them off the bed and put them in rows on the floor so I could sleep. I was very tired and miserable. Then on the table I saw my mail. On top was a letter from the brickmakers, with a long list of names of workers, followed by the amounts of contributions for me which they had taken up among themselves. They knew I was working for nothing. Many of them were French and Italian workers, and in broken English, at the top of the page, was written their appreciation of what I had done for them. The list below read:

Tony	5¢
Bill	10¢
Louis	5¢ etc.

They had collected eleven dollars in nickels and dimes. Deeply touched, I tumbled into bed, reproaching myself for having felt discouraged for even a moment.

The year following our winter in Arden I moved back to Philadelphia.

The unions in Pennsylvania, led by those in the hosiery and textile districts, were making a well-organized fight for better child labor laws. Church organizations, women's clubs and other groups participated.

The laws permitted children as young as 11 and 12 years to work on the anthracite breakers. A story about these "breaker boys," written by Clarence Darrow at that time, did a lot to arouse public opinion to the horror of what was going on. Sisters in misery of these "breaker boys" were the little girls in the silk mills of Bethlehem, who sometimes worked through the night.

A state convention of women was called in Philadelphia, presided over by Mrs. Mary Mumford, a well-known authority on modern education. I took with me a little Russian-Jewish girl who was in the Socialist Party. She had worked as a child herself in tobacco factories. Seeing that she believed these philanthropic women were doing great things, I thought it would be a good idea for her to hear them talk.

Mrs. Mumford opened the convention by saying, "It seems to me that the reason children go to work in the mills and factories is because they are tired of the present methods of education."

My young friend who was seventeen and looked younger sat there with her mouth open and finally whispered to me, "Can I speak?"

"Yes, there will be discussion now, of course you can speak. Stand out in the aisle and speak very slowly and distinctly and tell them just what you think!"

So she stood up and said timidly: "Ladies, may I speak?"

Highly gratified that this young girl should take such an interest, they encouraged her. She began:

"Ladies, I think you are talking about something that you do not know anything about."

The ladies gasped. She went on:

"I worked stripping tobacco when I was only 12 years old. I did not go to the factory because I was tired of the methods of education. I never had a chance to go to school at all. When I saw other children going to school my heart bled—not because of the methods of education but because I had to help my father and mother make a living for their eight children."

She gave it to them straight.

"Did you ever see little girls strip tobacco? Did you ever see little girls bending their backs all day over their work? Did you ever see tired, pale children dragging themselves home after a day's or perhaps a night's work in the factory?"

Afterwards some of the women apologized to her. One of the women there was the wife of the president of a Bethlehem silk mill where little girls went to work at 9 o'clock at night so people would not see them go in. That woman did not open her mouth.

I hadn't expected to say much, because my young friend had done a good job. But one woman started me off. Said she:

"The point is that the children play in the streets and it's dangerous. So—since they do not want to go to school—their mothers let them go to the mills as a safer place for them than the streets."

"A safer place!" I cried. "When more men are killed in Pennsylvania because of industrial hazards than any place else in the country! A safer place—tell me, ladies, would you like your own daughters to go to work in the factories?"

They thought the revolution had come when I got through with them.

There, as always, I was able to speak from direct investigation. Always, in my work, I felt no one was interested in just having me tell them what I had read in a book. I looked into things carefully myself so that I could speak from first hand knowledge.

Once Upton Sinclair, then also a member of the Arden Colony, was doing an article for *Everybody's* on child labor and asked me to help him find out whether the glass factories of New Jersey were observing the law prohibiting night work for children. On my suggestion he went with me to Bridgeton, New Jersey, to see the "tender boys" in the glass factories working all night as helpers to the glass blowers. Our story was that I was his widowed stepmother, and that he had two little brothers the right age for this work. We went to the biggest factory there and asked the manager whether they had any company houses for rent. They were very eager indeed to get hold of the boys. They gave us the prices of food at the company store, and many other facts, and tried to induce us to come there.

As I was crossing the yard with Sinclair whom should I see but the owner of the factory, an old friend and neighbor of my father. I lowered my head and hurried by. Fortunately he did not recognize me.

I visited a glass blower whom I knew and persuaded him to get me into the factory as one of his family. I wore an old dress, and took his dinner to him. The owner of the glass factory was a great "Christian"—one of the town's leading citizens. Most of the boys I saw were ten or twelve years old. It was the children's job to hold bottles at the end of long iron rods in the blazing furnace for a certain length of time, then hand them to the blowers. The heat was intense but they dared not move the bottle even a hair's breadth. It was terrible work for children.

Another time Scott Nearing, then state secretary of the Pennsylvania Child Labor Committee, called me in and told me:

"There is an ugly story about child labor in Downington, Pennsylvania. It is rumored that the Catholic Orphan Asylum there is renting out boys to the glass factory. I think you should go and find out if it is true."

I made myself look as old as I could and took a train to Downington and went to a little restaurant nearby the factory. I saw no sign of the Catholic boys. Most of the boys who came out were Negroes, ten to thirteen years of age. This was queer because there were no Negro families living nearby.

I asked the manager of the restaurant: "Have they always had colored boys working here?" "No," he told me, "this is a kind of emergency. They had a lot of little boys from the Catholic Orphan Asylum but that didn't work, so they had to bring these boys in." He talked about children working in the factory as a matter of course. "They rented a big house for the orphans and had a matron to take care of them and they worked in the factory at night. But the matron could not manage the boys. During the day they ran wild."

I went back and told Scott the story. "You know," I told him, "the strangest thing about the whole matter is that the owner of this mill is a man who lived in Bridgeton. He was a cousin of my rich stepmother, and an elder in the Presbyterian Church!"

Scott answered, "I'll tell you something stranger than that. That man is a member of our State Child Labor Committee!"

Later I investigated the trapper boys, who worked in the soft coal fields of Pennsylvania, before they had electricity in the mines or much machinery. They used to have what they called "air-chambers," fresh-air traps which were only opened to let the mule drivers through with their cars. These little trapper boys had to sit underground all day long and open and close these trap-doors. They went to the mine early in the morning, and came out with the men at night. They never saw the sunlight. The trapper boys had no color at all. They looked like little old men.

One day I saw a couple of boys about 12 and 14, coming out of a mine, carrying heavy miner's tools. I talked to them and found that they had taken their father's place because he was home sick with miners' asthma.

Once at a mining camp near Johnstown, Pennsylvania, I saw a little trapper boy being carried out of the mine. He had climbed on a coal car to get a ride out of the mine and had fallen off and crushed his arm. The miners' families came running up, and stood around offering help.

"Hurry," I said, "we must get a doctor here at once." They explained that the nearest doctor was in Johnstown—a twelve hours' journey. There was no train, no automobile, no way of getting the boy to Johnstown until the next morning.

I sat with him through the night. We used all the remedies possible to keep down his fever and ease his pain. His mother could not go to the hospital because she had little babies to care for at home. The miners tried to carry him to the train, but he insisted on walking. We could see the broken bones sticking through his skin. Getting on the train, he said to me: "Tell mother I didn't cry."

Our struggle through the organized labor movement succeeded in getting the Pennsylvania laws revised and the ages at which children were permitted to work raised. But there are frequent evasions and the struggle to enforce those laws continues.

The National Child Labor Committee took up the fight more than thirty years ago and is still working for the federal amendment. To America's shame, the Child Labor Amendment to the Constitution proposed twenty years ago has not yet been ratified by the required number of states. The Fair Labor Standards Act, passed in 1938, prohibits child labor in interstate industries, but does not apply to retail and service trades in which most of the children in industry are employed today. Thus the fight to abolish the exploitation of children in industry continues as a major issue.

On one of my trips to Connecticut during 1905, I found the Socialist Party organization in bad shape, without a regular state organizer. After I held several successful open air meetings in New Haven, the comrades asked me to come there as state organizer. I was comfortably established in Philadelphia, and was not eager to move. But after consultation with the Philadelphia comrades, we reached the decision that I was needed in Connecticut so I wired my acceptance.

The following Sunday when the Connecticut State Committee met in New Haven, two Catholic members insisted on a referendum vote as to whether I should become state organizer, on the ground that I was a divorced woman. I was informed of this decision by a special delivery letter.

I wired back that I would not be their organizer under such conditions. I proposed that instead I should move to New Haven and work there in an unofficial capacity. I chose New Haven because one of the Catholic members of the committee lived there, and I was determined to teach him a lesson.

So I moved to New Haven, with four of the children, the two oldest boys and the two youngest. The change in school was of course rather difficult for the older boys and was hardest on Buzz who hated school even under the best conditions.

One day my work took me to the reference room of the library and there sat Mr. Buzz reading away. He looked very sheepish when he saw me.

I went up to the librarian and asked whether he had been there often.

"But I thought you knew he was coming here!" she exclaimed. It turned out that that boy had never set foot inside the school once.

I felt very badly about it. I talked to a friend who was very much interested in boys and he advised: "Have him go to work at some small job and he'll soon want to go back to school."

Buzz went to work and by Christmas he told me that if I would let him go back to Philadelphia, he would promise to attend his old school faithfully. So it was arranged that he should live with his father in Philadelphia and return to his old school with the understanding that the teacher would report daily how he was doing . . . and that is how my son, Buzz, finally got started on his education.

I was elected to the educational committee of the party and we soon developed a fine forum, with speakers from the Yale faculty whom no one had been able to get before. Then when the New Haven comrades, including my Catholic opponent, seemed convinced that I could be of use to the Socialist Party, I moved to Waterbury where Henry Lazotte, the other Catholic member who had opposed me, lived.

I had already been supporting myself writing for the *Waterbury American* and now wrote a column called "Facts and Fancies about Fashions."

One night after a full day on my newspaper job and the evening on my educational committee work, I remarked to Henry Lazotte: "I must be getting home now to see if the children are all right."

He looked at me for a moment and then said earnestly: "You know, comrade, a woman who works like you for those two little children—and doing all the work you do for the party—and your writing besides, cannot be a bad woman!"

"Then I guess my work here is done. I moved to Waterbury mainly to make you realize that!"

"So you knew I opposed you? Well, you have taught me a lesson!"

"I hope so," I rejoined, "for the sake of other women."

Two years later, in 1908, I had the gratification of being elected state organizer of Connecticut by a large majority. I was also nominated for secretary of state on the Socialist ticket—the first time any woman was nominated for public office in Connecticut.

The opposing parties contested my right to run for office, since women did not even have the vote, and the idea of a woman running for office was indeed a shock to the conservative politicians. The Attorney General ruled that if the voters of the state wanted to vote for me at the ballot box, they had a right to do so—there was nothing in the law to prevent them.

One day I made a speech near our newspaper office on "The Cause and Cure of Child Labor." The editor of the *Waterbury American* sent for me soon after. "I am very sorry but we shall have to let you go," he said. "You are one of our best workers. I want to tell you that there will always be a place open on the editorial staff for you—on condition that you renounce your political faith."

Hearing I had lost my newspaper job, Mr. Saro, the local orchestra conductor and others offered me the editorship of a monthly magazine, *Musical Waterbury,* which I gladly accepted. Saro was a fine musician and considered my daughter, Helen, for whom he arranged an extremely successful recital in Waterbury, a great violinist.

There was at that time a group in Connecticut called the Unitarian Universalist Congress, which tried to unite all the more progressive religions into a single body. Through one of our Socialist members active in this group I was frequently asked to speak at their large church in Meriden. I used to take such texts as "Suffer the little children to come unto me" in order to talk about child labor, and used the story of driving the money changers from the temple to attack capitalism. The suggestion was made that I obtain a license to preach, which I did at one of the church conferences, although of course I was not ordained. Thus I was able to carry the campaign against child labor and other socialist issues right into the churches, speaking not as an outsider, but as a preacher.

At this point I want to speak of Florence Kelley, whom I knew in this period and who was one of the first American women Socialists who influenced me greatly. Florence Kelley made an important contribution to the literature of socialism in this country by her translation of Engels' *Conditions of the Working Class in England in 1844,* and her own writings. She was for many years secretary of the National Consumers' League of America and a leading member of the National Child Labor Committee. Her influence was great among working class women and her death in 1932 was a terrible loss.

In those days the Intercollegiate Socialist Society was a vigorous organization. I remember one occasion when the I.S.S. was giving a dinner in New Haven at which Florence Kelley was the main speaker. The chairman, Graham Phelps Stokes, was called away at the last moment, and Upton Sinclair, one of the vice-presidents, was called upon to preside. In introducing Mrs. Kelley he explained the purposes of the I.S.S. and how people were drawn into the socialist movement through its activities, attracting even such nationally known persons as Mrs. Kelley. Mrs. Kelley got up and told him that she had been a Socialist before he was dry behind the ears.

In the period between 1906-08, I had to leave Connecticut and go to New York. The Socialist Party could not pay wages and in New York I could do newspaper work and place articles with magazines like *Wilshire's* and *Pearson's.*

Gaylord Wilshire was a picturesque character. His schemes for cooperative gold mines induced some comrades to invest (and lose) their life savings in them. He moved to California and made money in real estate there, leaving as monuments "Gaylord Boulevard" and "Great Wilshire Boulevard." Before he went West he got together a number of budding liberals and Socialists, and established *Wilshire's Magazine*. It helped a lot of us to earn our living in those days, and along with *Pearson's Magazine* published much interesting and valuable material.

I remember writing one article for Wilshire's called "Rational Housekeeping," a subject very close to my heart. Women had to fight hard to have careers in those days, and many of the women comrades felt that they had to sacrifice their family life for the movement. I had always contended that it was possible to do both. But I had the help of my family and friends who in themselves constituted a sort of cooperative group, with a home base in Arden. So many struggling young people who had not these facilities came to me with their problems that I proposed a plan for groups of families to live together cooperatively, pooling their basic housekeeping expenses so that they could have a common dining room, a well run household, and a great sunny play room on the top floor for the children and expert care for them. I worked out detailed budgets for families with an average income of $30 a week, or less.

When I discussed this plan the objection was always raised that it did not allow for sufficient privacy, so I ended my article:

"...We know that the struggle of motherly, good women to maintain a good spirit in the home is growing harder every year. The energy expended to keep up the outward form of the household, just the necessary details of living, uses up the vital force to such a degree that there is none left for the cultivation of the true spirit of home life—helpfulness, comradeship and congenial work. Given the leisure that comes even to a business woman, if free from domestic cares, the mother will then bring to her children the best of her intellect—the vigor of a fully developed individuality. Privacy becomes, in the light of this new development, only a secondary consideration, and enough of it will always be secure where an intelligent, well-balanced woman reigns supreme.

"Is it worth while, then, for those of us who desire to preserve a true and highly developed motherhood and the perpetuation of the race, to endeavor to work out some of these problems?

"While the greater problems still clamor for solution, and the class war that may be more than a 'thirty years' war' rages around us, may we not, in all good faith, make our tents on the battlefield a little more comfortable and spend more time on the physical development of our soldiers?

"Surely our campaign will be more effective if we have better rations, more music, and occasional resting places along the weary march."

Naturally I had offered this co-operative scheme as no fundamental solution. However, small groups here and there tried out such plans as a temporary solution to their problems.

I was supporting myself by these articles and by research and newspaper work, when Upton Sinclair asked me to help in the stockyards investigation that followed the publication of *The Jungle*.

5. In the Chicago Stockyards

UPTON SINCLAIR wrote *The Jungle* at a time when Lincoln Steffens was writing about the political evils of the day and during the muckraking period of Ray Stannard Baker, and others. Sinclair was the only one of these muckrakers who drew the logical political conclusions. At the end of *The Jungle* he advocated socialism as the remedy for the terrible conditions in industry under private ownership. *The Jungle* had been translated into many languages. Foreign countries were horrified to learn the truth about their meat imports from America, and began protesting to President Roosevelt. Americans also wrote that if conditions in the Chicago packing-houses were as depicted by Sinclair, the Beef Trust was guilty of wholesale murder. President Roosevelt, as a gesture of appeasement, sent Wilson, Secretary of Agriculture, to the stockyards to investigate Sinclair's charges. Wilson brought back a complete white-wash.

But the book's sales and protests continued. Finally Roosevelt sent for Sinclair. He praised Sinclair's book to the skies and told him he had decided to send an investigating commission out to Chicago.

"Now," he said to Sinclair, "will you yourself go out there with this commission and prove that everything in this book is true?"

Sinclair should have insisted: "Every word in that book is true. Go ahead and try to disprove it!"

In the congressional investigations into the quality of canned meat furnished by the Chicago packers during the Spanish-American war, Roosevelt, then a colonel, had declared on the witness stand: "I would as soon eat my old hat as that meat." So now Upton Sinclair expected that President Theodore Roosevelt would really get something done about the stockyards.

I had just moved into an old stone house at Washington Crossing on the Delaware River which we rented for $4 a month, and was counting on a whole summer of writing and watching the children enjoy themselves.

Richard Bloor, a young comrade from the pottery works at Trenton, came over to help me to put up a stove. In the midst of our work, a telegram arrived from Upton. "Come to Princeton at once." I was at that time compiling some material for Sinclair, and he well knew I had no one to look after the children. I telegraphed back to him at his big farm near Princeton (bought with the proceeds of his book): "If you want to see me, come to Trenton."

A second telegram explaining that his mother was due on a train from the West that evening convinced me he really could not leave.

So I got Richard Bloor to stay with the children and took a trolley for Princeton. I arrived about 10 o'clock that night, and Sinclair met me with the announcement:

"Lady" (his name for me), "you have to go to Chicago to-morrow."

"Upton," I said, "I always thought you were crazy—now I am sure of it. . . . You know I have my hands full!"

"Well, after you hear my story you'll go."

Then he told me he had received a telegram from Roosevelt that day instructing him to come to Washington to report to the commission that was leaving to investigate the Chicago stockyards the following Monday.

"But I can't go!" he cried despairingly. "I have contracts for stories that have already been paid for. Go in my place, Ella—if you don't Roosevelt will think I can't prove the charges."

I laughed at Sinclair and said, "Roosevelt doesn't mean this the way you think he does. He is just playing to the galleries." Then Sinclair begged me to go for the sake of the Socialist Party.

I knew Congress was in session considering the Pure Food Bill. The Beef Trust lobby was fighting the bill tooth and nail, because while they didn't mind breaking the laws, they did not want any more of them cluttering up the statute books. Finally I telephoned Helen in Philadelphia and asked her if she could care for the other three boys, if I took Carl with me. She agreed to take the older boys and we arranged to meet in Philadelphia the next day. I realized that a woman could not do this job alone. I would be too conspicuous going about unescorted to saloons and other places where men gather and talk. So I dashed back to Trenton and persuaded Richard Bloor to go to Chicago with me. After that, in explaining the investigation to the public, Upton Sinclair thought it best to refer to us as Mr. and Mrs. Bloor, and the name has clung to me ever since. Richard Bloor was a Welsh immigrant, about half my age, and there was no romance connected with our association. He later went back to England, and was killed in the World War.

I was in Chicago by Saturday morning and immediately got in touch with Joseph Medill Patterson, the son of the owner of the Chicago *Tribune,* then a Socialist, now the conservative owner of the New York *Daily News.* He was very excited when I explained my mission. "We have to see that that story breaks big," he exclaimed.

"When the proper time comes," I told him, "and when it can be done without injuring the investigation, I will break the story. But you must promise me you won't release it until I say the word!"

The following day, I invited A. M. Simons, editor of the *International Socialist Review,* who knew the stockyards thoroughly, and William Bross Lloyd (son of Henry Demarest Lloyd), to dinner. The latter was to take care of the legal end. I also invited a doctor and his wife, who was the daughter of a superintendent in one of the packinghouses.

We planned our campaign as we sat around the table. I had already made numerous appointments for the commission. Most of the witnesses were men who worked in the yards who trusted our party and me. They risked their livelihood and, despite promises that they would be protected, many of them did lose their jobs.

As we were sitting around the hotel table, a telegram arrived from Charles P. Neill, national commissioner of labor who, with James B. Reynolds, then assistant Secretary of the Treasury, composed the commission. It said the commission was arriving at four o'clock Monday.

I had held up the story for fear the commission would not come. But now I realized that it would have to be released before the official story of the commission's arrival, to make sure the commission would be publicly committed to a real investigation.

As soon as we got the telegram, Patterson rushed off to the *Tribune* office to see whether Roosevelt had made any announcement to the press. He found a telegram from Loeb, the President's secretary, explaining apologetically that the investigation was only to please the over-critical. In other words, it informed the powers-that-be that they need not take the investigation seriously.

Patterson phoned me that there was a substitute editor on the shift who knew nothing about the policy of the paper. (The paper, of course, was the organ of the Beef Trust.) He was told to stand by for the biggest scoop of the year.

Arriving at the office I dictated the story. I quoted Roosevelt's explanations to Sinclair: that he was horrified at the disclosures in *The Jungle* and had authorized the commission to make a thorough investigation to corroborate them. I also announced the appointment I had arranged for the commission with Dr. Jacques, a famous bacteriologist and former commissioner of inspection, who had resigned because of the terrible inspection conditions. I stayed until the forms were closed. Then I went home literally exhausted.

The next day Mr. Neill and Mr. Reynolds appeared, and I

gave them the list of appointments. Just as they were leaving, Mr. Neill stepped back into the room and I quaked internally when he whispered: "I wonder how that story got into the papers?"

"I am sure I don't know, Mr. Neill, but I imagine the reporters found out about it before you left." Then taking a long shot, I asked, "Aren't you working with Dr. Bennett, chief inspector of the stockyards?"

"Oh, certainly. I have to work with him."

"Might it not have leaked out of his office?"

I showed the commission the actual formula calling for a high rate of saltpeter to preserve pork intended for export. I provided proof of frequent use of formaldehyde in "doping up" condemned beef to sell again. (One good result of the exposé was to stop that practice.)

But the commission avoided unpleasant facts—when it could. Mr. Reynolds tried to intimidate Dr. Jacques, and as we entered his office he said: "Well, doctor, before we came here we went to the best chemists in New York to determine whether the germs of trichinosis and tuberculosis are killed by the high temperature used in the rendering process." Dr. Jacques replied quietly: "Well, Mr. Reynolds, would you care to eat boiled trichinosis or tuberculosis? In the cooking of such diseased meat very poisonous toxins are set free, and it often smells like urine."

Bloor heard that a man had fallen into the lard vat at one packing plant. We found out later that they had shut down the room and sent everybody but one man and the foreman out, who tried to recover the body, but there was almost nothing left. The workers told us the lard tank was not emptied.

There was no record of this gruesome accident in the coroner's office. The rumor was that the man's widow was paid $2,500 to keep her quiet. Dick Bloor tried to see her. When the neighbors and the wife heard he was coming, they chased him off the block, fearing the money would be taken from her.

Workers testified before the commission that they went on the killing beds at five o'clock in the morning and worked on ancient wooden floors which soaked up blood all day.

As I expected, the commission did its best to tone down its reports. Roosevelt refused to let Sinclair testify before Congress on the Pure Food Bill. But the investigation could not be quashed. I was called to New York and did feature stories for the *Times* and the *World* and a series for the *Evening Journal* covering conditions in New York packing plants.

Roosevelt had hoped to put a new inspection bill through Congress without making the report of the commission public. But the bill was blocked by the packers, and finally the report was given out. Public indignation forced action and hearings were held before the House Agricultural Committee. Representatives of the Beef Trust were given full rein and treated with the greatest courtesy, while the members of the President's commission were treated like criminals when they tried to give even their mild testimony.

The great furore about Packingtown produced some good results; the plant walls were whitewashed, cement floors put in, a dozen manicurists got jobs. The Pure Food and Drug and Meat Inspection Acts of 1906 were passed. But the clamor of public indignation did not really change the workers' conditions and merely added new laws to be violated.

The muckraking era was the last big protest of the middle class. Each exposure of the trusts was thought to reveal an individual evil, not a symptom of the general corruption and exploitation inevitable under capitalism. The muckraking magazines became very popular, but an advertising boycott by the trusts soon brought them into conformity, most of their writers finding lucrative, safe pursuits. Only a couple turned toward socialism and the labor movement. Roosevelt himself typified the weaknesses of the middle class fight against trustifying capitalism.

After this investigation of the Meat Trust, it was clear that Theodore Roosevelt's talk about "trust-busting" was a mere gesture. He saw the popular demand for reform and took it up as a political maneuver. He played up to the small capitalists with a few prosecutions under the Sherman Anti-Trust Act. He was violent in denouncing Big Business and the "malefactors of great wealth," as he called them. But he did nothing to stop Morgan's U. S. Steel Corporation when it took over the Tennessee Coal & Iron Co. in the panic of 1907. No one took his anti-trust talk very seriously. He was an imperialist employing "dollar diplomacy" to build up American colonies.

During the administration of William Howard Taft, who followed Roosevelt, two of the leading trusts—Standard Oil Co. and American Tobacco Co.—were "broken up" by the U. S. Supreme Court into groups of smaller corporations. This was in 1911. But each group started its new career with the same stockholders it had before, and soon a new wave of mergers set in. The great trusts continued their stranglehold over the means of production in this rich country of ours.

About a year after the Roosevelt investigation, I grew tired of so much chasing around and wanted to settle down for awhile, and took a house in the suburbs of Philadelphia. I decided to spend more time with my children and was just getting settled when one night as I was giving my children their supper a man came to my door. He told me his name was Dan Ryan, and that he was political editor of the *Evening Telegram,* owned and published by the *New York Herald.* The editor of that paper was a Socialist—but very few people knew it—least of all the owner of the paper. Dan Ryan told me the editor had determined that I should go out to Chicago again, this time to get jobs in the stockyards and see if the packers were complying with the Pure Food Law of 1906. If they were not, I was to expose them.

"Do you realize what this means?" I asked him. "They know me now in Chicago. I have been there openly. Do you want me to come back from the stockyards made into sausages?"

The children began to bawl, "Mama, don't go back. You mustn't go back!"

But it ended with my agreeing to go with Dan Ryan the next

week. The plan was that we were both to get jobs. So Ryan donned old clothes and I wore an old black dress in my role of a "widow from Missouri," and we applied at Armour's.

I went into an old barn-like building and stood for over an hour with a lot of women, in blue calico dresses, with shawls over their heads, mostly Poles and Lithuanians, who waited patiently. Finally I went over to a man in the little office behind the window and asked: "I want to get a job in the sausage kitchen. Are there any?"

"Can't you cook?" he shouted at me.

"Of course."

"Then what do you want to come around here for? Look at the newspaper this morning—hundreds of jobs for cooks."

"I have a little boy home," I pleaded, "and I have to go home nights." True enough I did have four boys at home—though they were a long way off.

Then he growled: "Go up and see Mr. Pensil, the superintendent. Maybe he will give you a job."

I had visited Mr. Pensil with the Roosevelt Commission, so I made some excuse and went outside again. There was Mr. Ryan pushing a truck. I was glad to see he had a job that would take him through many departments.

I finally joined a long line of women in front of Nelson Morris' packinghouse where I knew conditions were very bad. A jaunty-looking individual dressed up like a policeman to intimidate the foreigners came up to me. "You need a job?" he asked.

"Yes, can I get one?"

"Oh, yes. A good looking woman like you can certainly get a job. You go on in and get a job and maybe some night you and I will go downtown and have a good time."

I went inside and got a job "inspecting" in Armour's "Veribest Beef" Department. I stood before a big table full of cans and was told to thump them hard before I wiped them off and if they sounded solid—they were good. If they sounded hollow, they were bad. I thumped them, and they all sounded alike to me so I passed them all. Presently a girl came along and pasted on bright new labels which said, "Inspected and passed according to the Pure Food Law of 1906."

The girls I worked with were very kind. At noontime they told me: "Everyone is supposed to chip in 15 cents for two weeks' coffee. But we'll pay for you this time, because you won't get paid for two weeks." The stuff was made in an old lard pail and tasted like anything in the world but coffee. But the women took the grounds home to make coffee for their families.

None of the girls could make over five dollars a week working ten hours a day. After working there for a few days, I got a job in the trimmed sausage meat department at Swift's. They had big chutes where the joints of meat slid down and fell into a trough which we women sat around. The temperature was kept at five degrees below freezing, to keep the meat from spoiling. We had to keep bundled up. We had sharp knives to cut the meat off the bone. For the coarse meat we got 25 cents a hundred pounds and for the fine, 60 cents. The foreman kept saying the pieces were not fine enough, and sweeping all the work we had piled up into a barrel so that we were not paid for it. I did not go back the next morning for fear I might get pneumonia.

In another department of Swift's, I filled cans with tongues. This was a showplace. Across the room we could see the company's guides escorting crowds of visitors past a group of girls being manicured. But the girls had to pay for this and they resented it.

At Swift's I saw what a fake their inspection was. In one department a huge turning wheel touched the pen where the pigs were huddled waiting to be killed. A man hitched each pig's leg to the wheel as it whirled by. It made half a revolution and then hit a trough, sending the pig down into a great tank of boiling water. Then by an electrical device, it slid along another trough to the inspector who slit open the throat to look for any sign of hog cholera, and passed it. The pigs shot down so fast it was humanly impossible to examine them properly. In another department, I saw an uncouth old man "inspecting" a row of "Star" hams, by sticking a long steel rod in and then smelling it. Whether he passed the hams or not depended on his sense of smell.

Mr. Ryan was having equally enlightening experiences. When he worked in the oleomargarine department he fished the most sickening objects out of the tanks.

One evening shortly before we left, I visited a former city inspector who had been discharged because he had condemned too much spoiled fish, earning the nick-name "Fish Murray." He had published an article in a Chicago journal that had been forced out of print because it told the truth about the stockyards. I wanted a copy of the journal because I knew it was full of facts about "lumpy jaw." The disease took the form of terrible abcesses on the jaw, and the report revealed the practice of simply cutting out these abcesses and then putting the animals on the market.

I told "Fish Murray" I was a newspaper writer and he showed me a copy of his article. When I asked him whether eating the meat of an animal with this lumpy jaw disease would affect human beings his answer was, "Woman, do you know this disease—actinomycosis—is a cancerous growth?" I asked him for a copy of his article to quote in my story, but he said this was his only one and would not give it up. But when I took some material out of my briefcase to show him, everything got quite mixed up on the table. When I got home I "found" his journal in my bag with the other papers. My conscience did not trouble me because I knew this valuable material would now get the publicity it deserved.

Back in New York we talked our story over with several of the editors of the paper. The staff decided the story must be seen by James Gordon Bennett, owner of the *Herald,* then in Bermuda. So the complete story written by Ryan and myself, with documents and photographs, was sent to Bennett. He had himself cabled authorization for our Chicago trip but when he saw this terrible indictment of the Beef Trust, he vetoed it. I wrote many stories for other papers, used the photographs we took, and lectured all over the country on our material.

6. Organizing for the Socialist Party

AFTER my investigations of 1906, 1907 and 1908, I returned again to Connecticut. While I continued my work in the Socialist Party there, I was now drawn into more active participation in the suffrage movement. I worked closely with Mrs. Hepburn, mother of Katherine, the actress. She was state president of the Woman's Suffrage Association and one of the most brilliant women I ever met. Her husband was the eminent social hygienist, Dr. Thomas Hepburn. They shared each other's interests, and I enjoyed my visits to their beautiful home in the Connecticut hills, full of pictures and books and good talk and warm companionship. Mrs. Hepburn spent a great deal of time with her children in spite of her varied interests, and they adored her, as we all did. Little Katherine was a gay and vivacious child, who always displayed deep interest in our conversations.

For many of the secure middle class ladies the suffrage movement was a mere feminist fad. I tried to make them see the really vital importance of suffrage to the working women, as a weapon against economic inequality. And I tried to make them see that not the vote alone was important, but its proper use in building a better society. Mrs. Hepburn understood these things better than the others, and it was through her insistence that the Department of Working Women, of which I became chairman, was established.

It was only through the participation of our Socialist women that the suffrage movement in general became awakened to the problems of working women. In 1908 the Socialist women in New York organized a mass demonstration of proletarian women for suffrage, which inaugurated the establishment of March 8 as Women's Day on a national scale. In 1910, on a motion of the great German Socialist leader, Clara Zetkin, the International Conference of Women Socialists in Copenhagen, made March 8 international. Thus International Women's Day is a contribution of the American workers to the world labor movement, as is May Day, which was originated in 1886 when the Knights of Labor, the Socialists and the A. F. of L. organized a great united walk-out on behalf of the eight hour day.

I helped Mrs. Hepburn get rid of the old-fashioned suffragists who had been in the office for forty years and were a dead weight on the movement. Together we brought in new elements. Mrs. Hepburn helped organize the National Woman's Party in Connecticut, and drew into it many of the more progressive suffragettes. This organization, which was quite militant and believed in the use of parades, demonstrations, and other active methods of agitation, was frowned on by the more conservative group.

The militant English suffrage leader, Emmeline Pankhurst, came to see me in Connecticut and scolded me soundly for lending my name, energy and work to a "man's party." She had the narrow feminist idea, which I never accepted, of working for women alone. She felt that women should not work for any political party until they got the vote.

Unfortunately the National Woman's Party which at one time carried on a splendidly militant fight has today degenerated into a narrow, anti-labor sect. Not long ago I had a stiff argument with one of my old Connecticut co-workers, the daughter of Ebenezer Hill, a Republican Congressman, who used to be mightily shocked by his daughter's socialistic views. She was attending the hearing on the equal rights bill backed by the Woman's Party, a bill that doesn't mean equal rights at all. If passed it would repeal all the protective laws for women in industry won by years of struggle to limit the exploitation of women —just because they are women. I was sorry to find old Ebenezer's daughter no longer on the side of progress.

In 1910 a national convention of the Socialist Party was held in Chicago. It was devoted to questions of policy, in contrast to those held in presidential election years which were largely nominating conventions. I won election, as one of the two Connecticut delegates, over the well known Robert Hunter who had been a candidate for governor, proof of my complete vindication in the Connecticut party. Jasper MacLevy was the other Connecticut delegate.

Among the subjects discussed at the convention was the I.W.W. The I.W.W.'s, although they were very militant, were opposed to political action, believing that industrial democracy could be secured through the struggles in the factories alone. Since many I.W.W.'s were also members of the Socialist Party, there was a great deal of friction over the question of whether the I.W.W. members should be permitted to continue their agitation against political action within the party.

It was a sign of the essential weakness and reformism of the Socialist Party that this internal conflict had become so fierce. The main trouble was that the Socialist Party, while declaring theoretically for the principle of industrial unionism, gave the workers no leadership at all in bringing it about. Vague right wing plans about amalgamation within the A. F. of L. always ended in compromises with the reactionary leaders. The left wing was driven to the other extreme, of dual unionism, of which the I.W.W. was the most striking example. The I.W.W. had the syndicalist idea that the whole struggle of the workers should be confined to trade union action, with the goal of setting up a trade union state. However fallacious their theories and methods, the I.W.W. carried on some grand fights, and won considerable following among the workers. I believed strongly in industrial unionism. But I also believed that even if the workers won control in the shops, they could not hold the shops or the means of production without a workers' state to back up their ownership.

Many of us felt there were not nearly enough workers present at the convention. The preachers, lawyers, professors, small business men seemed to overshadow the trade unionists and other labor delegates. I remember wishing there were more husky steel workers and miners to give life to the discussions. This middle class composition of the party's leadership was, of course, the main reason it never adopted a militant, class struggle policy.

We organized a National Committee of women at that convention to work with the National Executive Committee. This was a good step since the only woman at that time on the National Executive Committee was Kate Richards O'Hare, although many women were active in the party. I got to know some of these fine women of the Socialist Party. Among them was Anna Mailly, Socialist candidate for governor of the state of Washington; May Wood Simons, wife of A. M. Simons, herself also a talented writer and lecturer; Bertha Mailly, wife of William Mailly, national secretary of the Socialist Party and Caroline Lowe, a lawyer, of whom I shall write more later.

At the convention Charles E. Ruthenberg, then recording secretary of the Socialist Party in Ohio, informed me that the comrades there had voted to ask me to become state organizer of the party for Ohio. The transfer was arranged, and I moved to Ohio. I took an apartment in Columbus with my two youngest children, Dick and Carl, and put them in public school. An election campaign was then in progress. The Ohio Socialists at that time polled tremendous votes whenever there was an election of any kind. In 1910 we polled 90,000 votes for the Socialist Party candidates and elected thirteen Socialist mayors.

Ruthenberg, then a young and vigorous man, maintained the political character of the Socialist Party in spite of pressure from the ultra-leftists, and its revolutionary character in spite of pressure from the right opportunist elements, and built up a very good organization. Ruthenberg had joined the Socialist Party in 1909. Poised and capable, he later became the outstanding leader of the left wing of the party, particularly in the anti-war fight and in the founding of the Communist Party. Except for two years in prison, he was general secretary of the Communist Party from 1919 until his death in 1927.

From 1907 to 1912, the left wing exerted a strong influence on the party, and its class-struggle policy brought the greatest growth of the party's history. Membership rose from 23,000 in 1905 to 58,000 in 1910, and 118,000 in 1912, when the party polled its record 897,000 vote. Over a thousand of its members had been elected to public office. There were five Socialist daily papers in English, eight in foreign languages; and some 262 weekly magazines.

The growing influence of the Socialists in the labor movement of Columbus was answered by persecution. On the First of May, 1911, we held a parade in Cleveland. The police charged the marchers and shot down several comrades. During the police attack, Ruthenberg rode up and down the line of parade on horseback to give the marchers courage. Following their attack on the parade the police smashed the party office with pickaxes.

The city and county authorities refused the party a permit for the annual July 4 picnic, but a nice place was rented in the country. In asking me to speak Ruthenberg said, "Comrade, you will take your life in your hands—I really hesitate to ask you to go." I was in the prime of life then, fifty years old, feeling very young and vigorous, so I eagerly consented. I wrote all my children what I thought might be a farewell letter, although I did not tell them so.

We went to the picnic grounds in street cars. When we alighted we found hundreds of deputies who shoved us around roughly. A couple of them took off an old man's hat and peered inside of it. "Do you think I carry bombs in my hat to kill myself with?" he asked them. The deputies followed us into the picnic grounds, where thousands of workers had gathered around tables with their families.

Big autos kept driving up spilling more deputies—we counted about seventy cars.

"They think the meeting will start at two o'clock," Ruthenberg whispered to me. "But we won't start until four. They will buy all of our soft drinks!"

It was terribly hot. Perspiration was pouring from all of us. We joined the picnickers and had a good time. We waited until four before starting the meeting, and the deputies waited too. Sure enough, they did buy all our soft drinks, and so helped to swell the party coffers.

At four, Ruthenberg helped me up on a table, and started to introduce me.

The presence of so many deputies created a tension, and I felt a little uneasy. Then a wonderful thing happened. All over the picnic grounds about a thousand young huskies, Finnish and Hungarian workers mostly, rose up and surged toward the table and stood in solid ranks below me. The deputies, who were milling around, ready to go into action, stopped short in their tracks. Looking down into those strong, determined workers' faces, I knew our meeting was safe.

I began to recite the Declaration of Independence. A secret service man began hastily taking down what I was saying in short hand. Turning to him, I said:

"I am reciting the Declaration of Independence, as is customary at Fourth of July celebrations. So when you hear me talking about life, liberty and the pursuit of happiness don't you dare say that's sedition!"

I went on talking, and no one touched us. Again I saw illustrated on this occasion that the master class are more afraid of numbers than of anything else. It isn't so much what you say that counts, as how many you have organized.

While I was in Ohio, I often visited the mining camps of West Virginia, which with the Ohio Valley made up the Panhandle District.

One very hot Sunday I was to begin one of these tours in a mining camp called Winifred Creek. When the conductor saw my ticket, he said: "You can't go there on Sunday. This train only goes as far as the Junction. Only coal trains run into that town."

I thanked him and said I guessed I would keep on going. He told me he would hold the train to see if anybody met me since there was nothing but one tree to mark this stop.

At the Junction, a man wearing a Socialist badge was waiting. "We are having a big meeting for you at Winifred Creek," he announced.

"That's fine, but how am I going to get there?"

"I've got a bicycle."

"A bicycle!" I gasped, looking up at the perpendicular wall of rock rising alongside the track.

"Oh, I don't mean that kind of bicycle," he explained quickly, "I mean a train bicycle," and he pointed to a strange looking object. I climbed on behind him and off we pedalled down the track. He stopped at every house to tell them about the fine meeting we were going to have.

That night, 139 miners, their wives and children and their dogs came to the meeting in a big barn-like structure, lit by flickering kerosene lamps. These people hardly ever heard outside speakers, and to the women especially it meant a great deal to have a woman speak to them who was a mother herself and who understood their longings to educate their children, to have something beautiful in their lives. As I began to speak, children of all ages were crying in all keys. I had learned from experience to wait to give the heart of my speech until the children were quiet. Gradually they calmed down, and the mothers put them to sleep on benches around the walls. Then they gathered close around me, thrusting forward their hungry, eager faces, while I talked to them about socialism in terms of their everyday lives. Thirty-nine people joined the Socialist Party at that meeting. Because I knew how much these meetings meant to the miners and their families I was very troubled when toward the end of the meeting, having mentioned that I had to get up early and go to a place named "Sager" to speak the next night, I found no one there had ever heard of it.

The next morning I boarded the coal train that went up to get the miners at the Junction and bring them down to the mines. I asked the conductor on each car how to go to Sager camp, but no one knew. One man advised me to go farther south, get off at Fayette Junction and inquire there. The conductor went through the train asking all the miners if they knew where Sager was. None of them knew.

When I stepped off the train at the Junction a miner came up and greeted me. "We were afraid you would get lost! We posted one man at this junction and one at another, and others to watch the road. I'm going to take you to supper and then drive you to the meeting."

The Sager Camp turned out to be in an out-of-the-way spot. They were so afraid they would miss me that several of the men had actually given up a whole day's work to watch the trains and roads.

After supper at a miners' boarding house, my guide brought up the mule team and a big wagon and we rattled down the hill to Sager and drew up at the hall, erected by the miners' own hands. There were people at the meeting who had walked eight miles, carrying their children. And I thought it a hardship to ride all day on the train and come down with the mule team! We had a wonderful meeting which meant still more recruits for the Socialist Party.

Sometimes I went down into the mines to talk to the workers, and I always visited the miners in their homes when I could. They lived in forlorn and destitute company shacks, the sole decoration usually a marriage certificate surrounded by faded flowers. The miners' families lived on sow belly and corn bread, and they always owed the company money. On my tours now, I can see the results of some of that early work. Last spring at a meeting in a mining town called Scott's Run, the chairman was the son of an old Socialist, whom I had brought into the party in Huntington, West Virginia. The boy had recently returned from one of our Communist workers' schools.

In these tours of the Ohio minefields I often met Mother Jones. Our paths had crossed many times before, especially in the early

1900's in the Pennsylvania mining fields, and we were good friends. Mother Jones became interested in the labor movement after the death of her husband, who had been a soldier in the Civil War. She herself was born in Cork, Ireland, in 1830. She was an instinctive fighter against the capitalist class and spent her time organizing the miners into the U.M.W.A.

During the 1912 campaign for Debs, we were trying to get out a large vote in New York and flooded the city with speakers. One day the comrades informed me that Mother Jones, who had come to New York to speak, was lying sick in a furnished room, but would not let them help her. I went down to see her and found her in bed in a fever and wearing a coarse woolen undershirt. I got a new nightdress for her, made up the bed and got her something to eat.

"Don't fuss over me!" she expostulated. "I want you to write some letters for me while you are here. Do you suppose I'd want any Tom, Dick or Harry to write my letters?"

I told her I could do both. I fixed her all up and then wrote to her miners for her, letters that revealed how close she was to them. She wrote about their union problems, and their sick children. She told them they mustn't give in to wage reductions. She knew every petty mine boss by name.

The next day, Saturday, I went again to see her and was amazed to find her sitting by the bed with her funny little pancake bonnet on, the strings hanging loose.

"Mother," I cried, "what are you doing out of bed?"

"Do you think I am going to stay here and rot over Sunday?" she answered irritably. "I'm going over to Newark to the Goebel's and let Margaret take care of me." George and Margaret Goebel were Socialists, George a national organizer of the party for many years.

Going to Newark was a complicated trip in those days. I wasn't able to go with her since I had to speak that night and had to go home and look after the children first. I showed my anxiety by saying, "Mother, you can't go alone!" "You just put me on the trolley to the ferry," she snapped, "and I'll get there all right."

I put her on the trolley with fear and trembling. The next day was Sunday and I spoke at a mass meeting in the afternoon. There I heard that Mother Jones had gotten to Newark all right but had also come back. I went right up to her room after the meeting.

"Why, Mother—why in the world didn't you stay?" I asked her.

"Do you think I was going to stay and have George's mother talk to me about Jesus all the time?"

George's pious mother was a Home Missionary. She thought having Mother Jones right there in her home was too good an opportunity to miss, so she had at once set about converting her.

In later years Mother Jones came under the wrong influences, and was sometimes made use of to play a reactionary role. She always retained great prestige among the miners, who would do almost anything she asked. I can remember time after time when a caucus in the A. F. of L. prepared to make a demonstration of strength against Gompers, she would come in at the last moment and say, "Stick to your old Sammy, boys, stick to your old Sammy!" and they would vote for him again. But just the same Mother Jones was an historical figure, a fine woman and a fine courageous fighter.

I met this remarkable woman many more times, since a great deal of my work in the Socialist Party was spent among the miners, and we often held meetings together. Mother Jones died in December, 1930, at the age of 100. The last major strike in which she participated was the great steel strike of 1919, but she was in touch with things and spoke at meetings until 1923, when she was in her nineties. After that she went to stay with a Socialist family who took care of her until the end.

7. Face to Face with Europe's Social-Democrats

MY son, Carl, really began his career in the labor movement in Columbus. He was eleven and Dick thirteen when they joined the Young People's Socialist League there, much younger than the average membership age.

One night, arriving home from a mining camp in Ohio, I found my sons in a great state of excitement. They said, "Hurry up, Mom—we've all got to go to a Y.P.S.L. debate."

"Who's going to debate?" I asked. Dick announced: "Carl and I are going to debate with two lawyers from the Socialist Party on 'Resolved: trusts are beneficial for the people.'"

The boys, it seemed, were taking the affirmative. I asked them if they had prepared themselves. They said, "Oh, yes," and did not ask my advice at all.

I went to the debate with them and my two young men did very well. They took the position that if the trusts belonged to the people and were run collectively, they could be most useful and efficient.

Everyone took it for granted that I had coached the boys, and the lawyers, one of whom was the party's candidate for Congress, waxed quite eloquent because they thought they were really debating with me. But the boys, to their immense delight, were awarded the verdict.

At my meetings with miners and workers I was almost always received warmly, but sometimes in the larger towns, where my audiences were of a middle class type, I met with sneering remarks from people who thought I should be home "minding my own business" or taking care of my children. I often took Dick and Carlie along and at one meeting Carlie rose during the question period and asked me:

"Will you please tell the audience what you do with your children when you are out speaking? The lady next to me keeps talking about that."

Everyone giggled. I just smiled and said:

"A very fine question, young man, and very fitting that you, my son, should ask it." Then I addressed the discomfited woman sitting next to Carlie: "I take them along, that's what I do! I take them right with me."

At this time, early in 1912, letters I was receiving from my daughter Helen began to worry me. She was in Budapest, Hungary, studying the violin with Hubay. She was evidently in love and planning to get married. She was just about ready to make her concert debut in Europe. She was only twenty-one and looked even younger than her age, and all of us feared that someone might simply be trying to exploit her because of her talent. I did not see how I could leave my work, and at the same time I felt strongly I ought to go to her. Then one day I received a letter from Mr. Ware saying he was so worried about Helen that he had booked passage for me on the steamship "America."

I went, just as I was, to the East, taking Carl with me, and arranged for him to stay on the farm with Hal. I had received the wire from Helen's father on Sunday. On Thursday I was aboard ship, making my first crossing. My plans were to see Helen first, then stop at Vienna, Berlin and London, on my return. I especially looked forward to seeing Dr. Sudekum, Social-Democratic member of the German Reichstag, from Nuremburg. He had spoken for my campaign in Connecticut on the same platform with me, and had gotten my promise that if I ever went to Germany, I would stop and see him at the Reichstag.

About six in the morning on the day before the boat reached Plymouth we were all aroused early to come out and see the icebergs. From the deck we could see huge icebergs rising from the water. They made the air cold and terrible. All of us felt rather frightened. We wirelessed a warning to the "Titanic," which was crossing our path on its first sailing, but that same day, April 15, 1912, the "Titanic" was wrecked on those icebergs and over 1,500 people were lost. The captain delayed telling us about the accident the next morning, to prevent panic on our ship. Landing at Plymouth, we were surrounded by boys selling the Paris edition of the *Herald* with news of the disaster. Many of the members of the ship's crew and some of the passengers had relatives on the "Titanic," and fought for papers. It was a scene from which I was glad to escape.

Landing at Hamburg I took the train for Budapest at once. Crossing Germany I marvelled at the cleanliness and order and the superbly cultivated land I saw from the train window. My sons had cabled Helen about my arrival, but she had moved and had not received the cable, nor my telegram from Berlin. So no one met me at Budapest. I did not know a word of Hungarian, and I was completely at a loss. At last I found someone who spoke enough English to telephone for me to the impresario, Bela Mery, the uncle of the man Helen was planning to marry. From him I got Helen's new address.

A cab took me to a beautiful apartment house, built around an open court in which there was a little motion picture theatre. I had arrived but I could not get in. It was early in the morning and the elevator was not running. As I was standing there disconsolately amid my baggage, a messenger boy arrived. It occurred to me that he might be bringing my own telegram. "Helen Ware?" I asked. He nodded.

He helped me carry my baggage up four flights of stairs. At the top of the stairs we came out on a balcony. A window opened on the balcony and a breeze was blowing the curtains out. I stood there ringing and ringing the bell and talking excitedly but nobody answered. I was at my wits' end, not knowing that Helen was sleeping right behind those fluttering curtains.

Waking at last, Helen caught the sound of my voice, and suddenly jumped out of bed screaming, "Mama, mama, mama!" at the top of her lungs. She rushed out on the balcony in her night-gown and we stood there hugging each other, crying and laughing at the same time.

Helen sent for Laddie to come and meet me at once, and I soon saw that it was too late to break up the engagement. There was nothing for me to do but help them with the innumerable documents that had to be stamped and signed and countersigned before Hungarian law would let them be man and wife. They were married on the first of May. Helen gave a concert earlier the same day for the benefit of some charity in the city. She came to her wedding radiant and lovely, all in white, her arms full of flowers which they had given her at the concert. She had wanted a quiet wedding, without fuss, and was a little annoyed to look so much like a bride after all.

As the wedding party came out of the Burgomaster's office, we saw the May Day parade just starting, and we climbed on a big open cart to watch it. It was unusually large that year, as Parliament had just denied the workers the right to vote and they were demonstrating in protest. As they marched and sang, carrying banners of labor, singing the songs of labor, suddenly up through the strains of the music I heard sharp cries. "Why are they shouting so?" I asked the man beside me. He answered. "They are crying—'Give us the vote'—'On to Parliament'—'On to Parliament.'" Later, just after I left for America, street fighting broke out in the city, and hundreds of workers were shot down for demanding their rights.

Hungary was at this time one of the most intensely aristocratic and reactionary monarchies in the world. The Hapsburgs had ruled the country ever since the year 1526 and continued in power until 1918. But the republican and socialist movements were growing rapidly during the pre-war years. I saw their potential strength in these street demonstrations.

I made friends with the Socialists in Budapest, one of them an artist by the name of Biro, whose brother edited the Hungarian Socialist paper *Nepsava*. Biro had plastered the city with his strik-

ing posters calling the people out for the May First demonstration. While Helen was away concertizing, Biro took me to visit
the cooperative houses for workers and for artists, the cooperative bakeries and other cooperative enterprises. I saw the beauty
spots of the city—and its slums. At night we went to the coffee
houses where people sat talking endlessly while wonderful gypsy
orchestras played. I loved the city, with its broad avenues, the
graceful bridges across the Danube, its warm kindly people.

Helen persuaded me to go with her to visit some friends in
Vienna, so one night at five o'clock, Helen and I took the Danube
River boat, arriving at Vienna the next day. The horse-chestnuts
were all in bloom along the Ring. I had not dreamed cities could
be so lovely as were Budapest and Vienna that spring.

From Vienna I took a train for Berlin, and arrived on the
last day the Reichstag was in session that summer. I was happy
to find Sudekum, not dreaming that some years later I was to see
him with the Kaiser's Iron Cross on his breast. Sudekum was a
right wing reformist, one of the majority of the German Social-
Democratic Party who, as soon as war was declared, openly supported the Kaiser. Sudekum told me there would probably be a
demonstration that day against the military budget. There were
106 Socialists in the Reichstag, among them the young Karl Liebknecht, whom I saw for the first time, a dark young man with a
sensitive, scholarly face, and deep, burning eyes. He spoke with
ringing eloquence for two hours against the budget. Sudekum also
spoke against it, as did the Socialist leader, Ledebour.

At noon we all went down to the sumptuous dining room in
the Reichstag. I sat at a big table with about twenty of the leading
German Social-Democrats. Most of them were before long to become supporters of the war budget, bitter enemies of the workers,
and accomplices in the murder of Karl Liebknecht and Rosa
Luxemburg. I was not very favorably impressed with them. I
was introduced as a leading American Socialist. Talking to them
about America, I remarked to an old Socialist Deputy beside me:
"You who have so many representatives in the Reichstag must

think of us as being in the kindergarten of the movement in America."

In an arrogant manner he replied: "We do not think about America at all."

Later, a German nationalist made an impassioned speech for a greater German navy, ending up with "Hoch, hoch, hoch the Kaiser!" But the Socialist members had quietly left, and not a single one remained to join the final tribute.

Under Kaiser Wilhelm II, the German Government was carrying out a policy of *Weltpolitik,* the expansion of the empire in colonies and in trade. This brought Germany into conflict with other European powers, especially France and Great Britain. An agreement in 1911 had given Germany new colonies in the Congo (Central Africa) but gave Morocco to France.

The proposed expansion of the German navy disturbed Great Britain, and there was prolonged debate over a neutrality treaty between Germany and England. The Kaiser and Admiral Alfred von Tirpitz wanted a navy that would end Britain's domination of the seas. The German Chancellor, von Bethman-Hollweg, wanted a naval agreement with Great Britain.

The Balkan states, meanwhile, in coalition under the protectorate of Russia, decided to try to end Turkey's rule in that part of Europe. The Balkan wars started in October 1912, and continued for a year. All Europe was a powder keg ready to explode when a match was applied.

When the World War began, Sudekum supported the German Government, and the news was a shock to me. His name became a synonym for social-chauvinism, and in February 1915, Lenin wrote an article called "Russian Sudekums" attacking Plekhanov for his support of the war:

"The word Sudekum has acquired an appellative significance: It denotes a self-satisfied, unscrupulous opportunist and social chauvinist. It is a good indication that everyone speaks of the Sudekums with contempt. There is, however, only one way for us not to sink into chauvinism while doing this: We must help unmask the *Russian* Sudekums as far as it is in our power."

I went on to London where my daughter had told me I must stay with her friend Madame Tchaikowsky, niece of the great composer and daughter of a former Russian revolutionist, Nicholas Tchaikowsky, later to become head of the counter-revolutionary "Supreme Government of Northern Region" supported by the Allies during the intervention in Archangel, 1918-1919.

I arrived on a holiday, and everybody had gone to the country— or to a meeting. I rode by bus all over the city. I was surprised when I asked people on the bus questions to have them look at me blankly because I spoke to them without an introduction. I came to an open air meeting and got off, delighted to hear the English language spoken again. At one meeting held by the British Socialist Party, they were lambasting the Independent Labor Party. Too much like a Socialist Labor Party meeting, I thought and went on. At Hyde Park all kinds of meetings were going on. I was in my element! From the tenor of the speeches I realized that in England as on the continent people feared that war was coming.

Socialists of the Independent Labor Party in Great Britain were opposing the huge armament expenditures of the British government. Tom Mann had gone to prison that year for anti-militarist agitation. German imperialist aims were alarming Liberals as well as Conservatives. Viscount Haldane as secretary of state for war, having failed to negotiate a treaty of neutrality with Germany, was now active in building a larger and stronger army in Great Britain. British shipyards were busily turning out "dreadnaughts," more powerful—and more costly—than any fighting ships ever built. Left wing Socialists held that the vasts sums spent for army and navy should go for unemployment insurance and other benefits for the workers.

Next morning at the post office as I was looking through my mail, which bore the names and addresses of well known Socialists, a clerk came up to me and said, "Will you kindly step this way—the superintendent of mails wishes to speak to you." "Oh, my goodness!" I thought, "pinched in London!"

A dapper little Englishman appeared and said, "Well, comrade,

I see by this mail of yours that you are quite an active Socialist in America. I want to welcome you to London." At my look of astonishment, he went on, "I am organizer of my district in Leighton. We are holding an open air meeting tonight, and George Lansbury will speak. Will you come and tell us about the Socialist Party in America?"

I thanked him and told him I would be glad to come. Then I phoned Mme. Tchaikowsky, who immediately came to fetch me in a taxi, and took me back to her beautiful apartment. She accompanied me to Leighton and on the way, during a wait at one of the suburban stations, Mme. Tchaikowsky suggested a walk. At twilight we came to an old graveyard where an old verger seemed to be hovering around one particular spot. Investigating the grave the verger was watching so tenderly, we saw a memorial slab bearing the words, "This is the grave of William Morris." I was deeply moved to come upon his grave like this, for Morris had been among my earliest favorites and I had read and reread *News From Nowhere, The Dream of John Ball* and some of his songs.

At Leighton, I was introduced to George Lansbury, then a member of Parliament, and to his daughter and son. Lansbury made a fine socialist speech against the military budget. During my speech about America, someone in the audience wanted to know whether Theodore Roosevelt was a Socialist. Roosevelt and the progressive Republicans had just held the "Bull-Moose" convention and he had been nominated to run again for President on a moderately progressive, reformist platform. I told them about my stockyards experiences, and what kind of "Socialist" Teddy Roosevelt was.

The next day we had an appointment with Keir Hardie, whom I had met when he had visited America. James Keir Hardie was a Welsh miner. A fine, sincere fighter for the workers, he was bitterly against war. In 1893 he had founded the Independent Labor Party as a distinct organization to carry on socialist propaganda. For many years Hardie had been leader of the Labor Party in the House of Commons where in 1912 it had 42 members.

Hardie wanted us to see Parliament in session. At that time it was very hard for a woman to get into Parliament because of the activities of Emmeline Pankhurst, who was jailed for her militant efforts for woman suffrage. Only recently a woman had come into the gallery, which is fenced off by a kind of grill, and thrown down streamers demanding "Votes for Women." The M.P.'s were thrown into a panic at the mere sight of a woman.

Keir Hardie was to make a speech in Parliament that day in connection with the railwaymen's strike. Strikes of London dockers and of railwaymen all over the country had so alarmed Prime Minister Asquith that he informed the unions the government would "shoot the men down like dogs." In South Wales, many strikers had been killed and wounded.

Hardie took us right up to the door of Parliament where attendants went through my handbag to make sure I was not carrying any streamers. It seemed wonderful to me, with our small Socialist movement in America, that Socialists were functioning in the Reichstag and in Parliament. But Keir Hardie was maneuvered out of making his speech that day.

At Keir Hardie's invitation I went to a peace meeting that night with him and his wife and daughter. Bertha von Suttner, a noted German writer who had just finished writing a powerful book against war, was one of the speakers. Hardie spoke very strongly against the trend toward militarism. Later, when the Socialists forgot their internationalism and came out for the war, it broke Keir Hardie's heart.

Hardie was a very unassuming person. I never saw him wear anything but a sack coat, though he was called upon to speak to all kinds of audiences. He was a great and good man and his death, soon after the war broke out, was a serious loss to the socialist movement.

Since Mme. Tchaikowsky's apartment was the gathering place for many famous writers, I met Israel Zangwill, John Galsworthy, and others there. These people spent so much time talking and visiting around with each other, I wondered when they did their work. One day Mme. Tchaikowsky took me to tea at Lady

Gregory's house. I can still remember my surprise at seeing all the old ladies sitting around smoking cigarettes. I was interested in hearing Lady Gregory's ideas about bringing plays to the workers, ideas which she partly carried out through the Abbey players.

Mme. Tchaikowsky later, to my sorrow, became a counter-revolutionary like her father and delighted in giving teas to newspapermen in order to talk against Russia. Like so many of the old intellectuals, she turned against the revolution when it came because she had no faith in the working class. She and her kind did not want a workers' revolution or a workers' state—like their counterparts today, they were interested in revolution only for conversational purposes.

I left Europe in the late summer of 1912. The preparations I saw for a gigantic armed conflict to divide up the world had given me a new and deeper understanding of the importance of our socialist movement. I saw it happening before me, how capitalism inevitably leads to war. There was no other way out for the capitalist system. Refusing to give the workers the full product of their toil, the master class in each country could not find markets enough at home. Seeking undeveloped spheres of the world to exploit they came into conflict and sent their peoples to the slaughter. In Europe I saw the old world rushing to its destruction. But I had seen, too, that the whole socialist movement was further along than in America, and this made me more determined than ever to come back and build the party in America into a strong, mighty instrument to liberate the workers and build a new society.

While I was away that summer the conflict within the Socialist Party had come to a head. At the 1912 convention in Indianapolis, during May, Bill Haywood was forced out of the National Executive Committee. An amendment was passed to the Constitution which read, "Any member of the party who opposes political action or advocates crime, sabotage, or other methods of violence as a weapon of the working class to aid in its emancipation shall be expelled from membership in this party." Certainly

Haywood and the other I.W.W.'s were mistaken in their opposition to political action and in their dual union policy (as Haywood and many of their other best elements later recognized) but they had every reason to mistrust the opportunism of the party leaders, who would take no definite stand on the all-important issue of industrial unionism. They endorsed the principle, but failed to work out a program on which the right- and left-wing elements might have united to secure it. They didn't say whether it was to be achieved through the existing unions (boring-from-within), or through the I.W.W. and other dual union efforts.

The left wing came to the convention greatly strengthened among the masses by its aggressive work and by the nation-wide awakening of the workers. The right wingers, whose interest was vote-catching and maneuvering into positions where they could bargain and compromise with the reformists and trade union reactionaries, were afraid to face the issues presented by the militants. They selected the issue of sabotage as a device to fight the left wing. It was the greatest weakness in the left wing armor, and since the convention was packed with careerist professionals and intellectuals, the right wing consolidated its control of the party. After the convention sides were taken on political action and dual unionism, the militant elements began leaving in droves, and the decline of the party set in.

On the question of political action, it was not the simple matter many of us thought—of the Socialist Party for it and the I.W.W. against it. Haywood later pointed out just how political the I.W.W. was: "While there are some members who decry legislative action and who refuse to cast a ballot for any political party, yet the I.W.W. fought more political battles for the working class than any other labor organization—for free speech, against vagrancy laws and to establish the right of workers to organize. They have gone on strike for men in prison. It is to the ignominy of the Socialist Party and the Socialist Labor Party that they so seldom joined forces with the I.W.W. in these desperate political struggles."

When I came back I found very bitter feeling in the party. It was decided that I should visit party locals in Ohio, West Virginia and Southern Illinois, to try to restore unity and enthusiasm. While my sympathies were with the left elements in many respects, I knew that political action was essential, and felt it important to avoid a split if possible.

I came to Ohio again in the midst of a heated campaign for a referendum in that state on the women's suffrage amendment. I plunged in. At the same time there was a campaign for a new bill providing for a nine-hour day for women in industry. Women were then working ten hours a day and the bill was considered very radical. I attended a hearing on that bill during which a corporation lawyer struck a dramatic pose, and delivered himself of the following: "When I left home tonight, my dear old mother, 92 years old, said to me, 'Where are you going, my son?' and I answered, 'I am going to Columbus to fight against a nine-hour law for women.' And my mother said to me, 'That's right, my son. Women ought to work ten hours a day. Ten hours of useful work each day is what brought me to the ripe old age of 92!'"

In the audience was a fine woman who had dedicated her life to helping the working women—Mary McDowell. She arose and said, "Gentlemen, it is a far cry from the dear old mother of 92 who sits safely at home doing her sewing when she pleases, to the drudging girls in the sweatshops of America. It is a far cry from that dear old mother in her comfortable home, to the girls in the laundries, walking back and forth in the heat, running a mangle. . . ." In spite of Mary McDowell's moving speech, the nine-hour law for women was not passed until a year later.

While the referendum fight in Ohio was at its height, Governor James Cox was campaigning up and down the state for reelection. We made friends with his secretary and secured his itinerary. When he left for towns where he was scheduled to speak, often quite remote, I organized my retinue—a sympathizer who had a Ford, and some girls who distributed leaflets. The roads were bad and my head was often sore from bumping the top of the

car. We arranged to stay all night at the towns where Cox was
going to speak. Since he was already governor, both Republicans
and Democrats came out to hear him. The meetings were wonderfully well organized for our purpose. A huge stand was built
in the middle of the country road. People paraded to it. Then
Governor Cox came and spoke and hurried away to the next
place, where another stand was built and another parade held.

I'd come along just as he was ready to leave. I would go up to
him and shake hands before he left. The people thought I belonged with his crowd and hung around. I would say, "Wait a
minute, boys, we are going to have another meeting." Then I
held my meeting and finished in time to get on to the next place
just as Cox finished.

One time I over-stayed at one place and was a little late in
arriving at the next place. The politicians had gone, but the
crowd was still there. "Is another speaker coming?" I asked.

"We are waiting for you," they said. "They telephoned over
from the last place to hold the crowd, because the best speakers
were coming later!"

We also made it a point to have dinner wherever the Governor's party was eating, because a big chicken dinner was always
ready. At one place, the landlady thought there would not be
enough. She turned to the Governor and asked, "Is this part of
your party, Governor?" He winked at me and said, "Yes, sure
this is part of our party!"

In the evening he always had a mass meeting in some big hall.
Not wishing to interrupt the Governor while he was speaking, we
got there early and gave out leaflets until it was time for him to
start. Evenings we would often hold meetings in the lobby of our
hotel.

During that campaign, the president of the Women's Suffrage
Association of Ohio, Harriet T. Upton, said to me, "No matter
where you are or what's going on, if I send for you, you must
come, even if it's across the whole state!"

One day she wired asking me to go to a big teachers' convention at Gallipolis, on the border of Kentucky, where I was to debate on the suffrage amendment with a local lawyer.

At the hotel an old man asked, "Are you the lady who is going to debate with that lawyer?"

I said I was.

"Well," he said, "you will have a tough time. He is a mighty smart man."

"Good!" I answered, "I like to debate with somebody smart."

Arriving at the hall, I saw two men leading the lawyer gently down the steps. He had tried to prime his spirits a little and by this time could not stand up at all.

Inside the hall the teachers crowded around me and asked me what I proposed to do.

"At least I can give my side of the debate, and anyone who wishes may ask me questions." So I debated suffrage with the whole audience the entire afternoon.

Back at the hotel was a telegram from Mrs. Upton asking me to take the first train to Millersburg at the other end of the state. The train was packed with delegates from the teachers' convention, all continuing the afternoon debate.

Two men were going it hot and heavy. Finally one of them spying me, said, "Here she is—let her talk to you!" They took the conductor's step, put it between the two cars for me and keeping my balance as best I could, I talked all the way to Columbus, a trip of over a hundred miles. It was dusty and hot. The cars and vestibules were packed with people. I was sweating like a porpoise. At Columbus a new trainload of people got on and so I continued talking all the way to Millersburg.

I arrived at Millersburg at eight o'clock that night. The group of nicely dressed clubwomen who came to meet me took one look at me and one of them said, "I guess we won't have a meeting tonight." I was very tired and very angry.

"Indeed you will have a meeting," I stormed, "just because I haven't been able to wash, you repudiate me! I suppose you would repudiate Jesus Christ if he came along with a dirty face! If you don't want to sponsor my meeting, I shall hold it myself!"

I walked away, went to the hotel and registered, washed my face and combed my hair and left for the meeting without having supper. I felt fresh as a daisy. I took a chair from the hotel lobby and stood it up in the street and let my voice out. The clubwomen peered at me from across the street and did not come near at first. One by one the men began coming from the store doors and soon I had a crowd. After it was over the women came to tell me how proud they were of my success. I simply said, "Will you all come up to my room, please?" When they were in the room, I gave them a going over. The next day I spoke for the suffrage amendment in a state Prohibition convention meeting there.

All my suffrage speeches were class struggle speeches. I did not mention the word "socialism" but I handed out good, strong socialist doses. I always tried to make clear that the object of our campaign was not alone to get the vote but to prepare women to use the power of the ballot to get decent pay and decent working conditions for women and so to strengthen the position of the whole working class.

Our meetings and demonstrations for the suffrage amendment culminated in a great national parade in Washington, in 1913. Woodrow Wilson had just been inaugurated and the city was still crowded with visitors.

We had a tremendous parade with the thousands of women in line—working women, middle class women, society women wives of congressmen, women of all kinds—and a few brave men. Marshals on horseback pranced up and down. Beautiful Inez Milholland, the well known suffragette leader, was grand marshal, riding a white horse.

As we started marching, we were set upon by hundreds of thugs and ignorant men (and some women). People had come across the Potomac from Virginia and from other nearby places to break up our parade. The chief of police gave us no protection whatsoever and not a policeman was on duty along the line of parade. It was a cold day in March and the thugs tore off women's furs and coats and struck the women brutally, knocking some of them down.

That night on my way by street car to a protest mass meeting a few hoodlums, seeing my "Votes for Women" button, began to get ugly. I stood up in the middle of the crowded car and made a grandstand play. I said, "I have heard a great deal about the chivalry of Southern gentlemen and I appeal now to that chivalry. I have had enough of these insults—after what we have gone through today on the streets of Washington—just because the women want to take equal part with the men in their government. I am a mother with six sons and daughters and I protest against this treatment. Is there any Southern gentleman who will protect me in this public conveyance?"

An old gentleman, sitting with his wife and daughter, stood up, tipped his hat, and said, "Come sit with us. We will protect you." (As though I really needed "protection!") So I went over and sat with them and the hoodlums did not say another word.

8. Calumet and Ludlow—
Massacre of the Innocents

IN the fall of 1911, the Socialist Party in Schenectady, New York, had elected a Socialist mayor, Charles R. Lunn, a Congregational minister. In 1913, toward the end of his first term in office, I went to Schenectady to act as local organizer of the Socialist Party. Soon after my arrival, the General Electric shop, with 15,000 workers, who composed most of the citizenry of the town, went out on strike for the right to organize. The superintendent of this shop was a leading member of Mayor Lunn's church.

It was really a general strike. Everybody was out, molders, machinists, carpenters, etc. Because of the bitter cold, we could not hold open air meetings. The men met in their respective union halls, but the women workers—of whom there were some 2,000—had not been organized before, and had no place to go.

I went up to the Mayor's office, and told him I wanted to use his church so we could talk to the women. The Mayor sputtered: "What will the 'elders' say? The management of the factory will be furious!"

"You pledged yourself to stand by labor," I reminded him, "and we've got to have that church!"

We got the church, and it was there that we organized the girls for the picket lines. The police, left over from the old regime, beat up some of the girls on the picket line in the traditional manner. At once I took twenty-five men of the strike committee, husky machinists and molders, to see the Mayor.

"We do not need any policemen," we told him. "We are having perfectly orderly picket lines. If police are needed, why not make us deputies to take care of the scabs?"

He gave us all police badges and swore us in as policemen. Then we went back to the picket line. When the scabs arrived from Troy and Albany, we ordered them to leave. When they resisted, we arrested them, turned them over to the police commissioner who was a Socialist, too, and had them locked up until the strike was over. We organized the women into the Electrical Workers Union and got a contract for a union shop. In less than a week we had won the strike.

This shows how much even a little political power, weak as it was, meant to the workers in backing up their industrial organization. Lunn was defeated in the 1913 campaign for re-election, but was elected again as Mayor in 1915. Later he joined the Democratic Party and ran for Governor of New York on the Democratic ticket.

During my work in Schenectady, I became acquainted with Dr. Charles P. Steinmetz, the great electrical scientist and inventor. Steinmetz was an ardent Socialist, despite his big position and big salary with General Electric, and was appointed to the Board of Education at the time of Mayor Lunn's election. In 1915, Steinmetz was elected president of the Common Council.

One striking speech I heard him make was before a group of manufacturers, holding a national convention on industrial education. Those manufacturers with their industrial education experts were talking about how to "educate" the workers in their shops. And for what purpose? To teach the workers to be satisfied with low wages. One "expert" produced charts and figures to show how in his industry they proved to their workers that what they received in wages was actually more than the value of what they produced for the owners. Read correctly, the charts really showed how much the workers were robbed.

Dr. Steinmetz rose to speak. He was a hunchback, with a large, noble head set upon a deformed and twisted body. You could scarcely see his body as he stood behind the rostrum, just his great head.

"Gentlemen!" he said, "The youth who come into our shops do not need that type of education. They will get that type of education all too soon in your factories. What they need is real culture—culture of the mind, and culture of the body. Give your workers opportunities for real development, both mental and physical. Let them study while they are on the job, so they need not remain manual laborers, but may become technicians and engineers. Give them a chance to appreciate the beautiful things of life, too. . . ."

That was the first time I had ever heard anyone talk about education as they talk about it and practice it in the USSR today. His speech was shocking to the manufacturers who were interested only in making the workers more content with their lot. Steinmetz later became tremendously interested in the Russian Revolution, following its development closely, its cultural and technical progress and especially its electrification program, about which he corresponded personally with Lenin.

It was just before Christmas, 1913, when the General Electric workers won their strike. At that time a strike involving some 15,000 copper miners against the powerful Calumet and Hecla Mining Company of Michigan had been raging for five months. Stirring stories were being told about the militancy of the miners of Calumet. When the Schenectady workers asked me to take some money they had raised and to help the wives and children of the striking copper miners, I agreed at once.

The Michigan copper country is away up in the Northern Peninsula. The land had belonged for years to the state of Michigan, under the terms of the "St. Mary's Land Grant," made long ago. Some Yankees from Boston, among them the Page family, discovered that this land was rich in copper and went to Michigan, bought up judges and legislators and formed the St. Mary's Land Grant Company. The land was supposedly granted for the purpose of building the Portage Lake Canal, which by 1885 was found to be "only a worthless ditch, a complete fraud." But the rich copper lands that belonged to the people of Michigan had been sold by the dummy company to the Boston financiers, who organized the Calumet and Hecla Mining Company. At the time of the strike, the Calumet and Hecla stockholders were receiving 400 per cent dividends. The wages of the workers were unbelievably low, under a dollar a day. Mr. Watson, the ruthless manager, received a salary of $125,000 a year. When the miners presented their demands to Mr. Watson, he tore them up. The company organized deputies, called in the state police, and imported 1,700 Waddell-Mahon detectives who were deputized. Miners were killed and their women outraged. The bosses formed a Citizens' Alliance, to which the business men of the town and their wives belonged.

The miners were highly skilled. Among them were Russians, Bulgarians, Finns, as well as native American workers, and Cornish miners whom they called "Cousin Jacks." All were firmly united for their demands, which included recognition of the Western Federation of Miners, and the right to have two men work a claim. The claims were deep pits, 800 to 1000 feet deep. The men went down the slippery sides of these pits with their water drills, weighing 170 pounds, and called "widow makers." They had to work them up and down, holding them over their heads. The water coming from the drill added to the danger. Often workers fell down the slippery sides. The miners believed there would be less risk if two of them worked a claim together.

The homes of the miners were spotlessly clean but the houses were falling to pieces, and there was almost no protection from the bitter cold. The families owned little enough clothing even when the men were working, and now they were in rags.

I reported to strike headquarters as soon as I got off the train. The secretary told me that 800 women had organized an auxiliary of the Western Federation of Miners and were having a meeting. I went to their meeting hall and knocked on the door. A big fine looking Slav girl, about 24 or 25 years old answered. This was Annie Clemence, president of the ladies auxiliary. She looked at me, and seeing a strange face, wanted to know who I was before letting me in. I told her I had come from New York to see what I could do to help the women and children. She asked me if I had a "card," meaning a union card.

I took out both my Mine Workers' Union card, and my Socialist Party card. When she saw the red Socialist card, her face lighted up and she said, "I have one of those, too," and I noticed that she was wearing a big Socialist Party button.

She invited me into the hall, where the women were discussing what quantities of food and clothing were to be sent for distribution to the various mining camps. It was clear how desperate was the need for clothing. The women were making sure that everyone had his proper share and that no favorites were being played. Of all nationalities, they worked together beautifully.

One of the questions Annie Clemence raised at the meeting was about a Christmas entertainment for the strikers' children. She said the children must not be deprived of their Christmas because of the strike, and she was therefore trying to collect enough money for Christmas presents. Next day she went to the nearby towns of Houghton and Hancock and collected $58 for the strikers' children—a brave thing to do with the agents of the mine owners watching every move. With the money, Annie bought mittens, stockings, toys and candy.

I stayed in Calumet helping with the relief work. There was a campaign on for a Socialist governor in Michigan and I spoke in various Socialist halls, using the situation in Schenectady to illustrate what having a Socialist in office could mean.

Among the Finnish miners were many Socialists. They put their clubhouses at the disposal of the strikers. At that time there was implanted in my heart a feeling of deepest warmth and respect for the Finnish people. I noticed especially how much attention they paid to their children, teaching them to sing and to dance, no matter how poor they were. These Finnish social clubs were always putting on plays and concerts throughout the copper country.

However, the Christmas entertainment Annie Clemence had arranged for the children took place in the "Italian Hall," a big room up a long flight of stairs. The door from the stairs opened into the back of the hall facing the platform.

On Christmas eve the children gathered in the hall, where Annie had fixed up a Christmas tree. First the children sang, and then the presents were given out. A little tow-headed Finnish girl of about 13, with long braids down her back, sat down at the piano. She had started her piece when a man pushed the door open and shouted: "Fire!"

There was no fire. But at the cry the children started to rush out of the hall in terror. Annie and one of the mothers got up and said, "Don't be scared, children, there isn't any fire." We around the platform did not realize how many had gone through the door, as the room was still crowded. We tried to keep the entertainment going. The little girl kept on playing.

In about five minutes the door at the back of the room opened, and a man came into the room with a little limp figure in his arms. Another man followed, carrying another child. Then another, and another and another. They laid the little bodies in a row on the platform beneath the Christmas tree. The children were dead. Then they went back and got more little dead bodies and brought them in and placed them on the platform. There were seventy-three of them. I can hardly tell about it or think about it even today.

The people in the hall were deathly silent, frozen with horror. Then Annie screamed, "Are there any more children dead?" And one of the deputies said, "What's the matter with you. None of these children are yours, are they?"

She cried out, tears streaming down her face, "They are all mine—all my children."

What happened was this. In the panic a man with a child in his arms had fallen at the bottom of the stairs. There were two doors to the box entry, both opening outward. When the man fell, the child in his arms fell through one of the doors, out into the street. The deputies, who had been threatening to break up the entertainment, were standing outside of the door. They themselves had raised the cry of "Fire!" and knew what was happening. Someone, it was never known who, seeing the man sprawling on the threshold, quickly closed the door, and both doors were held shut from the outside, so that no one could get out. The children rushing out of the hall fell all in a heap on top of the man in the closed box of the stairway. The staircase was made an air-tight coffin pen by those who wanted to create panic and disaster in order to discredit the union. Afterwards I saw the marks of the children's nails in the plaster, where they had desperately scratched to get free, as they suffocated.

Then the deputies outside opened the door and carried the dead children upstairs.

They kept bringing the children up the stairs, into the hall, as the people rushed forward in agony and fear to look for their own. Priests arrived and began to pray over the dead. Then Annie went wild and started pummelling the priests and pushed them away from the children, because these same priests had been preaching against the strike. "Don't let those scab priests touch these children!" she cried. The deputies took her away and locked her up in the courthouse. Then they came for the bodies of the children, took them to the courthouse and kept them there all night, until they could get undertakers.

Moyer, president of the Western Federation of Miners, and other union officials from Denver had been expected that day. The mine owners had evidently planned to put the blame on the union officers to frame them. But they had not yet arrived. In almost every house there was a dead child. One Finnish family had lost three children. Some of the mothers had not attended the entertainment and did not know what had happened until late at night when they went out to look for the children who didn't come home. Next day the town was paralyzed with grief.

The Citizens' Alliance gave their women $1500 to give to the bereaved mothers for funeral expenses. They arrived at the Finnish woman's house just as they brought the three little bodies from the undertaker's. Annie was sitting with the half-crazed mother. The women from the Alliance said, "Here's $100 to bury your children with."

The mother straightened up, as though waking from a trance and said, "What you want—to buy my children? You want to pay for my children? I love my children like my soul but I would put them in the ground naked before I'd touch a penny of your blood money!"

They went from one house to another. Not a single man or woman touched a penny.

That night Charles Moyer arrived. He stayed at a hotel in Hancock, a nearby town. Another officer of the union, a young man, who was with him, told me what happened.

They were sitting in their hotel room planning how to prevent panic among the people at the funeral next day. They feared some of the parents might become frantic when they buried the children and that the soldiers might shoot them down. Martial law had been declared and none of the workers was allowed to carry arms.

Suddenly there was a pounding on the door. Moyer, a small man, about fifty years old, opened it. Twenty-five or so leading citizens of that neighborhood stood there, led by Peterman, lawyer for the mine owners, a big butcher of a man.

He shouted, "We want Moyer—where is Moyer?"

Moyer stepped out and said quietly, "I am Moyer. What do you want?"

Peterman said, "We have collected $1500 to bury the children of Calumet and no one will take it. You must make them take it."

"No," said Moyer. "I shall not make them take it. We have clothed our naked, we have fed our hungry, and we will bury our dead." Then he slammed the door on them. Quick as a flash, these "leading" citizens—lawyers, doctors, businessmen—opened the door again. One of them hit Moyer in the forehead with the butt of a pistol. Blood gushed over him. They struck the other union officer, cutting his face open. Moyer was shot in the back and dragged with his companion down the stairs and out of the hotel. Not a single man in the lobby lifted a finger to help them.

Some of the men shouted, "Throw them over the Portage Lake bridge." Another said: "No—we'll put them on the train and send them to Milwaukee." They dragged them, coatless and hat-less in the bitter cold, over the bridge to the railroad station, where James MacNaughton, president of Calumet and Hecla, threatened Moyer with hanging if he returned, and slapped him across the face. Then both union men were thrown onto the train.

The conductor, a good man and a good union member, gave them first aid, but they had no medical attention until they reached Milwaukee next day. The conductor wired Victor Berger to meet the train next morning with an ambulance and take them to the hospital.

Moyer returned as soon as the bullet was removed. The union afterwards sued these "leading" citizens of Calumet for brutal assault, but never got any satisfaction.

The day after the attack on Moyer the funeral was held. The procession was headed by Annie Clemence carrying a red flag. She said to me somberly, "This red flag is our only hope. If they do not let me carry it, there will be trouble." She did not know what I knew at that time—that a train had come in from North-ern Michigan full of armed iron miners, ready to protect their fellow workers.

The procession went first through the town, then across the hill through the snow. The fathers carried the little white coffins of their children on their shoulders. Never as long as I live can I forget that procession winding through the hills and woods with the seventy-three little white coffins—coffins of children killed by capitalist brutality and greed.

After the funeral, the miners appealed to Congressman Mac-Donald of Michigan to call for a federal investigation of the company's actions. Judge Hilton, the lawyer for the Western Federation of Miners, went with Congressman MacDonald to see President Wilson. Wilson appointed five Congressmen, two Republicans, one an Ohio mine owner, and three Democrats, to serve as the committee.

They set up a court of investigation. The court room, guarded by machine guns at the doors, was crowded every day with miners who came to see and hear as well as to testify. I sat at the press table and sent a weekly story to the Socialist press.

I heard Annie Clemence tell how one morning when she was collecting the workers to go on the picket line, and they were marching down the middle of a road carrying an American flag, they were met by another group coming from the Keweenaw mine, carrying another American flag. The state police attacked them and the Keweenaw miners' flag was cut into tatters by the soldiers bayonets. "I took my flag and held it out in front of me," Annie told the committee, "and said, 'Go ahead and shoot me if you want to—right through this flag—and then the workers will know what you do to your women and your flag in the copper country.' They did not have the nerve to shoot."

One day during the hearings, Congressman Taylor of the committee said to me, "You know, these men are talking about going down into the mine to look things over. I wouldn't risk my life going down there—I've got a family." "The miners go down every day, and they have families, too," I told him. He stayed behind when the others went down.

A Turkish-Armenian came a long way to testify at the hearings. The mine owners' lawyer asked him, "Why did you come here to testify?"

"I heard there was a federal government investigation here," he said, "and I made up my mind to come and tell my story and see what your government would do about it. If you do not pay any attention to my story, I'll know just what 'freedom' means in this country."

He was an American citizen living in Minneapolis, a skilled machinist, out of work. Copper company agents had told him skilled men were wanted in the copper country. They assured him there was no strike on, and made arrangements to meet him at the station.

When he got on the train he found it was full of working men. He and his friends sat there growing more and more suspicious that they were to be used as scabs. At the first station, they started toward the door. A man carrying a revolver growled at them, "Where are you going?" and blocked their way.

One of the men answered, "We are going for some sandwiches."

"No you aren't," the man with the revolver said. "You can't get out of this car."

They were kept under guard all the way, were received by a heavier guard and still under guard, were forced to go down into the Ahmeek mine, the first one open. They were given no money until after the first two weeks. They planned to leave after getting their pay, but were told that their wages were all owed to the company for fare, materials, etc. They were treated like prisoners all that time, and could not get back to their homes for nearly two months.

Hearing this story, the chairman of the committee said to me, "Do you know—it makes me feel ashamed of being an American."

Pat, former marshal of Ahmeek, testified: "Do you know what they did to me as soon as these things began to happen? They took away my gun—and I'm the marshal!"

The former marshal had become our friend. It happened this way. I was talking in a big Socialist hall in Calumet one night, on the election campaign, telling the miners how much better it would be for them if they had their own governors and their own mayors, when I saw Pat, listening with his eyes and ears wide open. This idea was a revelation to him. He decided that was just what he wanted. He came up to me after the meeting and asked me to come over to his town and speak. "I will have every man in town out to hear you," he said.

It was dangerous for me to go to Ahmeek. It was just about the time they were attempting to open the mine and the town was filled with deputies. Pat told me the exact time I was to come so they could meet me, but I miscalculated and there was no one to meet me except two deputies on horseback, who wheeled their horses around, one on each side of me, and rode right alongside me up the hill. I was boiling mad to have these two big deputies on horseback watching a little woman like me, and said, "Do you think I am afraid of you?"

I walked straight on up the hill. Suddenly I saw a big crowd of miners and their wives rushing toward me, screaming and shouting. Finally, I made out one woman's words: "You said you would come and talk to us women today and Pat won't let us come to the meeting! He says there is only room for the men!" Pat had told them I could talk to the women after the election. Now I must talk to voters! He finally prevailed and chased all the women home, since the meeting-place was, indeed, not big enough for all.

Peterman, the mine owners' lawyer, frequently referred to the strike as a "red strike" or a "strike run by the Socialist Party," using the same red-baiting tactics against the union as the reactionaries use against unions today. The commission wired for Victor Berger to come and testify under oath as to whether this was a Socialist strike or not. When he took the witness stand, Petermann did everything possible to confuse him. Angered by Petermann's provocative questions, Berger sometimes got his words twisted, and at such times, Casey, the Congressman from Pennsylvania, would say to him, "This is what you mean, isn't it, Mr. Berger?" and put very plainly and simply what Victor Berger wanted to say.

Walking back to the hotel where all of us from outside Calumet were staying, I said to Casey, "How did you learn our formulas, 'Comrade' Casey?" He explained laughingly, "I've worked long enough in Pennsylvania with Jim Maurer (who was a Socialist legislator there) to know them well!"

By a trick, Hilton, the miners' lawyer, managed to get the Christmas tragedy into the record. He walked up to the chairman and said, "Mr. Chairman, at this point I wish to know how far you are going into the investigation of the disaster which occurred on December 24th, at 4 o'clock in the afternoon, when the children were gathered for a Christmas party, and . . . ." Keeping right on he got the whole story into the record.

After the investigation, the printed reports of which were somehow never available to us, the strike continued. In order to publicize it and to raise money for the strikers, I took Annie Clemence on a tour with me, through the mid-Western cities.

We had a big send-off in Calumet. The mothers and fathers whose children had been killed came to the train. The South Slav society presented Annie with a nice black suit, and a black velvet hat, as big around as a cartwheel, with a row of little pink feathers around the crown. I persuaded her to save the hat until she got back and wear a neat little black hat I had bought for her in Chicago.

The first night in Chicago Annie spoke to a teamsters' union of about 2500 members. I warned her beforehand, "Annie, talk to these men just like you talk to your fellow union members in Calumet; but whatever you do, don't say anything about 'scab priests.' These men are mostly Catholics." Annie, a Catholic herself, said, "I will try not to, Mother, but I can't help it. It makes me so mad when I think of the priests trying to make the men scab." She had no more than started, when she sailed into the "scab priests." The men just laughed.

While we were in Chicago, we were entertained by William Bross Lloyd in his beautiful mansion near Lake Michigan. "Are you still alive?" was his greeting. "I thought you would be teaching the devil how to manage hell by this time!" His big house, lined with books, was always open to me and the strikers I brought there. Annie was astonished that these people with servants and such a magnificent house should be concerned about her. Mr. Lloyd was worried about her going out alone for fear some of the agents of the copper company might do her harm. One day, however, she was gone the whole afternoon. Mr. Lloyd sent scouts out to hunt for her. Suddenly I had an inspiration as to where she might be. Earlier in the day Mr. Lloyd had taken us out to a restaurant, and found the place was struck. Seeing the girls picketing rather lackadaisically, Annie walked right up to them and said, "Girls, that's not the way to picket. Make a noise. Call out 'Strike on! Strike on!' Ask the people not to go in!"

We rushed down to the restaurant and sure enough there was big Annie, leading the picket line, shouting lustily to the passersby.

After we left Chicago, I kept Annie touring with me for two months. Annie received a lot of attention, especially from reporters. But before long she began to get homesick for her husband since she had never been away before.

I found out, too, that she was pregnant, and had been, in the midst of all those struggles. So I sent her back home.

Annie was one of the most truly heroic women I have ever met. She had a vivid, arresting personality, impressing even our enemies. Several years later I was talking for the Socialist Party in Chicago when right in the middle of a meeting, Annie came running up the aisle shouting, "Oh, Mother, Mother, Mother!" and threw her arms around me. It turned out that her husband had not been very good to her and her little girl had lost her arm in an automobile accident. Annie had come to Chicago and was working in a factory to support herself and her daughter. Since then I have tried vainly to find her again.

As for the Calumet strike, the miners were finally starved out. During the eight-month struggle the union had spent $271,000 for relief, with little help from the A. F. of L. Many of the miners' demands, including the eight-hour day, had been granted, but they did not get union recognition. Only in the last couple of years have they been able to start organizing again.

In the spring of 1914, I went out to Colorado for the Socialist Party to work among the miners, then waging a desperate struggle against the terrible working and living conditions, and for the right to organize. The principal company in that section was the Rockefeller-controlled Colorado Fuel and Iron Company. Trinidad, where its offices and stores were located, was in a real state of war. Machine guns and searchlights were mounted on top of the company's building in the center of the town.

I went directly to the home of old John Barnhouse, a Socialist, and a teacher and leader of the miners. He was now seventy-five, with a long white beard and looked like a patriarch. Unable to get out among the miners as he used to, they came to tell him their problems and ask his advice. In the big dining room of his home, lined with books, he would sit with the miners, their wives and sons and daughters around him. Now his home was head-quarters for the strike leaders. It was early spring and still cold. The miners, evicted from their company-owned houses, were living in tents at Ludlow.

The woman who helped John Barnhouse's daughter keep house was a miner's wife and very militant. On April 18, while I was at the house, a committee of miners' wives from Ludlow came to see her. In great agitation, they piled out of the mule-drawn cart that had brought them. They were all very worried about their children. The tent colony was in an open field, surrounded on three sides by railroad bridges, where state soldiers were stationed watching every movement. Now and then they took a pot shot at a worker standing guard. One day a little boy went out to get a drink and was shot at by the soldiers. The women were terribly afraid some of their children would be killed.

After much discussion, the miners' wives decided to dig a cave inside the biggest tent and put all the children there at night. The women dug the hard earth with their short shovels all that day and the next. The following night they put thirteen children and one pregnant woman inside the cave for the night. The cave was so deep that a tall man could stand up in it and be out of sight.

That night the soldiers waited until all the miners were asleep. They stole around the colony and soaked the bottoms of the tents with kerosene. Then they applied a match and there was a great burst of flame. The miners and their wives came running out of their tents, but there was a roaring wall of fire between them and the thirteen children and the pregnant woman in the cave. As they climbed out of the cave and before they could fight their way out of the blazing tent, the soldiers on the bridges started firing their Gatling guns. All the children who had been placed for safety in the cave were killed—not by the fire, but by the bullets of the soldiers.

The men and women who escaped had no place to go with the few quilts and belongings they had saved, except the fence corners of the charred tent colony. There they huddled that night, and for months afterward many of them had no other place to live.

Coming so soon after Calumet, the murder of these children seemed too much to bear. I shall never forget the despair and agony on the parents' faces on the awful day of the funeral when the thirteen little children, victims not only of John D. Rockefeller, but of the government of the state of Colorado, were buried.

We organized hundreds of women in the state of Colorado to protest, and the day before the funeral, these women, rich and poor, camped on Governor Ammons' lawn. They told him they would sit there until he sent a telegram to President Wilson, demanding federal troops to protect the women and children.

The Governor, loath to act, since it was from his own National Guard that the women and children had to be protected, held out until 8 o'clock that night before sending off that telegram.

With a number of miners' wives, I went back to Trinidad. In Ludlow feeling was running high. The state soldiers stayed in the background but the people did not trust them. Men from Trinidad and other camps went to Ludlow to protect the people there, but martial law had been declared and the miners had no guns with which to defend themselves.

The women drove over to the community near Trinidad, where the miners had little patches of land they cultivated, and collected bags of potatoes from them. Then the women stowed the sacks of potatoes in their old cart and drove away up to Walsenburg, Colorado, to sell the potatoes to the miners in Walsenburg. When they came back there were guns under the empty sacks.

We had a big supper prepared for them in Trinidad. Miners from Ludlow were there, fathers of the murdered children. As they went out after supper, the women quietly put a gun in the hand of each man.

The federal troops had not yet arrived. That very night, not knowing they could now defend themselves, the state soldiers attacked these miners living in fence corners with their families. There ensued a historic working class battle, called the "Battle of the Red-necks," because the miners tied red handkerchiefs around their necks so they would not shoot each other. The outraged miners drove their persecutors away.

But the strike was defeated, the union broken up, many of the men driven out of the camps, the rest put under the yoke of the newly devised Rockefeller company union (which only a few weeks before this was written was declared illegal by the National Labor Relations Board). Travelling over the same route some years later, I still found a few of my old miner friends who fought in that battle. The miners wanted very badly to have a meeting for me but they were only permitted to meet in Ludlow on the anniversary of the slaughter of the children. While I waited for that date to come around, a mass meeting was arranged for me at Trinidad. Some of my old friends among the miners walked twenty miles to get there.

The union could not meet openly. The night before the memorial meeting I attended an "underground" union meeting at Delagna, nine miles from Ludlow, to make plans for the next day's memorial to be held at Ludlow, at which they expected me to speak. I warned them:

"The old labor leaders who are coming from Iowa may not want me to speak. You know I am a Bolshevik." This was after the Russian Revolution had taken place and I knew what to expect from some of the officials of the miners' union.

The men said quietly: "We are the union here. If we say you speak, you speak!"

Next day we walked nine miles to the memorial service. There at the place where the children were killed, the U.M.W.A. had erected a stone monument which still stands. On it are the figures of a miner and his wife, with a little child lying at their feet. The inscription reads:

"Erected by the United Mine Workers of America, to the memory of the men, women, and little children who died in freedom's cause, April 20, 1914."

Two union leaders came from state headquarters in Iowa, one of the few times they had appeared in that section. One of them asked me what I was going to talk about. I looked at the faces of these poverty-stricken people who had come from their little shacks and said, "There is one thing sure. I am not going to talk about the dead children. I am going to talk about the children of today, children living in houses not fit for animals to live in. . . ."

"Well," he said, "we will let you talk fifteen minutes."

"I can say a good deal in fifteen minutes!" I replied.

I can see them yet, sitting there, the miners and their families all bunched together; old Mexican women with their children in their arms, who had walked miles in the cool April weather to come to the meeting; and just below us, the cave where the children were killed, walled up with concrete as a perpetual monument to their memory.

I made the most of my fifteen minutes. I talked about what I knew of their daily worries and needs, and how they must build a strong union to win decent conditions. Then one of those old labor leaders got up and started to make a very conservative and quite meaningless speech. Those big women with their kids just turned their backs and waddled off down the road. One of them said out loud as she went, "We like that little woman. She Bolshevik. She understand us."

The speaker turned around to me in distress: "I don't know what to do. I can't hold these people!"

"Talk about their needs today," I told him. "Talk about where they live and how they live and how to get together. What good does it do just to tell them to organize, without telling them how?"

But he was saved further embarrassment. A terrific sandstorm came up suddenly and everybody had to run.

The Socialist Party organization in Trinidad became a strong center from which came a number of charter members of the Communist Party. John Barnhouse's daughter, Grace Marions, was nominated on the first Communist ticket for Governor of Colorado.

Today the Colorado coal diggers are well organized under the banner of the United Mine Workers and their battle-scarred history has forged strong fighters for the C.I.O.

From Colorado I returned to work in Ohio and most of the winter of 1914-1915 was spent among the miners. There was a strike at that time in Southern Illinois and Ohio which involved 40,000 miners in Eastern Ohio, too. The Southern Ohio miners had had a very good contract but the mine owners threatened to take it away from them. Eastern Ohio miners struck not only for benefits of their own, but to get the contract of the Southern Ohio miners ratified. They wanted a state-wide uniform contract.

It was a well-fought strike, though Jock Moore, a well-known Democrat, and Ohio president of the United Mine Workers of America, seemed to be chiefly concerned with pushing into power a young man who had worked in the mines near Columbus. The man was William Green, who had been active politically, was elected to the State Senate of Ohio, and later became National Secretary of the U.M.W.A. when William B. Wilson was appointed Secretary of Labor by President Wilson. There was nothing unusual about this young man except his inordinate lust for place and power. He stood out among the miners mainly because of his apple-cheeked complexion. Most of the miners were sallow and thin.

I worked with the relief committee, made up of the priest, an active Socialist and a Democrat—a real "united front" committee, which managed to distribute our scant supplies to the best advantage. It was my function to tour the neighboring areas, raising money.

I wrote the story of the strike for *Pearson's Magazine,* describing camps like Wheeling Creek and others along the river, where the shacks were owned by the company, and the miners had to trade at company stores. The cost of materials needed for work in the mines, powder and drills and tools, was taken out of their wages. Most of the houses were built on piles with no foundation, and were hard to keep warm, especially as carpets were almost unknown. The only toilets were outdoor privies, almost under the windows of the houses. The whole water supply in many of the camps was a pump. Often I have seen women running out to the pump in the freezing cold, to wash their potatoes, or struggling back to their cabins with pails of water for their washing. The water had a bad taste, and health of the children was constantly threatened. I was instrumental in getting the reporters from Cleveland and other Ohio cities to expose these conditions, and the mine owners patched up the houses a little—and raised the rent.

We found families with eight and ten children, none of them able to go to school for lack of clothes. In Wheeling Creek we found a woman and five children huddled around an old stove, two small boys actually leaning against it for warmth. The wind was blowing through great cracks in the unplastered walls. A little barefoot girl, in a thin cotton dress, was running around the cold floor. The mother couldn't speak English, but we managed to coax one of the little boys to talk with us. "Did you have any breakfast?" I asked. He shook his head, and pointed to the bare table and closet. The father had grown desperate and had gone away looking for work. The mother, not hearing from him, had settled down into helpless despair. We roused her from her stupor of misery by telling her that the miners' relief committee would soon send her food and clothing.

Walking over the fields and hills we came to the home of Peter Krehill, who had gone out the night before to pick up coal along the railroad to warm his wife and three babies. He had been struck by a train and instantly killed. As I looked at the beautiful face of this dead soldier, and heard the bitter sobs of his young wife, I found myself saying to her, "Oh, don't you see he's found peace; he's out of the war." "Is death then the only way out?" the widow asked. I pulled myself together and said, "No, dear; but some hard living will have to be endured before we can bring freedom and peace to all the miners of Ohio."

Later, to get the viewpoint of the mine operators, I dressed up very nicely and went to see the president of their association, who had a big office in Columbus. Thinking I was a respectable reporter for one of the big magazines, he was only too glad to give me his side of the story. After he got off his line of "comfortable houses for the miners," I asked him to tell me truthfully whether he thought it was right for men who did such useful work as coal-mining to live in the kind of homes I had seen. He answered:

"Street-car men and other workers live in better homes because they demand them. When these miners demand them they will get them."

"But that is just what they are doing now!"

"In competition with Pittsburgh and other coal fields of course we can't give them their demands; why, do you know, one of our deals of 1,700,000 tons of coal gave us a margin of only a little more than 4 cents per ton."

"Then," I answered, "perhaps you are beginning to realize that the business of managing this great natural resource, the foundation of all industry, is growing beyond the power of private coal companies to administer in the interest of human happiness?" That ended the interview.

The miners held out firmly, and in the spring, after a long hard winter, a state-wide contract was won.

9. The War and the Post-War Repression

THE World War had begun. Workers whose strong hands had built the roads and factories and made all the world's goods, farmers whose sweat and toil had made the earth productive, were being driven to destroy the fruits of their toil, to slaughter each other in the ferocious imperialist conflict for markets and colonies.

During two and a half years of war, American capitalism grew fat on sales of munitions to the warring nations, made big loans to the Allies, and grabbed markets, making the most of the weakening of its capitalist rivals. A wave of anti-war sentiment swept the country. President Wilson was re-elected to the tune of "He kept us out of war," only to betray the people a few months later when possibility of German victory endangered Morgan's war loans and American imperialist positions. On April 6, 1917, America entered the war. The great masses of the workers were not for the war, and showed no eagerness to volunteer. A compulsory draft was soon imposed. We saw the shameful spectacle of the reactionary A. F. of L. leaders acting as recruiting agents, promising not to conduct strikes or to attempt to organize the unorganized "for the duration." The people were soon engulfed in a wave of war hysteria, the hymns of hate against Germany began, the persecution of pacifists, Socialists, anyone who raised a voice against the war. Workers were driven by slogans of "100 per cent production for war" and "give till it hurts," enforced deductions from their wages for liberty bonds, and so on.

The differences between the left wingers and right wingers of the Socialist Party sharpened with America's entrance into the World War. Because of his revolutionary attitude Debs was the recognized spokesman of the militant rank and file membership. On the platform and in action he always identified himself with the policies of the left wingers and frequently found himself in conflict with the official leaders of the party. Debs and other left wingers went to prison for their stand against war. But the right wing leaders became more and more passive and in many cases came out for the war. It became clearer every day that the leaders of the American Socialist Party were deserting the interests of the workers, following the example of the Social-Democrats abroad who had turned against the working class, voted for military appropriations and were defending the right of their capitalist governments to rob and oppress not only their own, but other peoples.

In 1917, I spent many months organizing for the United Cloth Hat and Cap Makers' Union, one of the oldest unions in America. I started in New York where we organized 30,000 millinery workers, and also carried on organizing work in New England cities, St. Louis and Philadelphia. From the start we had an industrial union, taking in the blockers, sizers, the women who did straw hat sewing and those who worked on hand-made hats. The latter were the most skilled, and the hardest to organize. I was arrested many times, and on one occasion after a bitter fight on a picket line, I was fingerprinted. In another strike there were 160 arrests. But I organized many shops and won many closed shop contracts with the Hat Makers' Association. Often today I meet children and grandchildren of girls I led back to their machines after victorious strikes. Max Zuckerman, then the president of the union, has long since gone to the hat-makers' heaven, but Zaritsky, their president, today plays a reactionary role.

When the "war convention" of the Socialist Party took place

in St. Louis, April 7 to 14, 1917, I was in the midst of a seven-months strike in that city, organizing a shop making trench caps for soldiers, and attended the convention between strike meetings. After a hot discussion, all except a minority came out against the war, and the anti-war resolution was backed by the preponderant majority of the party when submitted to a referendum. Many of the Socialists opposed the war on purely pacifist grounds, not correctly understanding its imperialist nature. The Socialist leaders failed to carry out a militant struggle against the war. John Spargo, Charles Edward Russell, William English Walling and others left the party and did war work. But others, myself among them, felt we must immediately organize the workers against this slaughter, and many of the rank and file members of the party fought courageously against the war.

The news of the March Revolution in Russia had a profound effect on the Socialist Party. We all rejoiced at the news of the overthrow of the Tsar. But as the real facts seeped through, as Russia remained in the imperialist war and the bright promises of peace, land and bread for the masses failed to materialize, we of the left wing saw that the complete victory of the Revolution was not yet. A sharp division came about between those who continued to support the bourgeois Provisional Government and those who supported Lenin and the Bolsheviks in their fight for the transition from bourgeois-democratic revolution to socialist revolution. During this struggle the Bolshevik Party was engaged in the tremendous task of winning over the majority of the working class and the support of millions of peasants for the final overthrow of the bourgeoisie and transfer of power to the Soviets.

Then, in November, 1917, the Bolshevik Revolution flashed its message of hope to the world. In a sixth of the world the workers had power! The forces of life and progress had prevailed over the forces of death and destruction. Word of the Socialist Revolution brought new life and hope to the oppressed everywhere. It brought new courage and inspiration to all who made the workers' cause their own. It brought what had seemed a distant, shining ideal into the realm of practical, living reality.

Difficult as it was to get authentic news of what was happening, the great blazing truth of the October Revolution shone out from all the distorted news reports. The weak and temporizing Kerensky regime was no more. The Bolsheviks were in power; the dictatorship of the proletariat was established. The workers' and farmers' government called on the world to stop fighting and make a just peace. The land and all its resources, the factories, the mines, the railroads, the banks, belonged to the people. All means of production were in the workers' own hands, and no man could profit from another's labor. All races were declared free and equal. Women's emancipation was complete, for the first time in history. As we got up in the morning, as we went to bed at night, as we went about our day-to-day struggles, we thought: "In Russia they are already building a socialist society!"

But while some of us rejoiced at that thought, there were others who drew back from it in alarm. This was not what the petty bourgeois leaders of the Socialist Party wanted. They did not want to see the end of capitalism, only its reform, leading to a soft seat in the City Council or Congress at the end of the road. They greeted the news of the Revolution with dismay and hatred. It was discussed in committees of the party and by the membership as a whole. All who were real Marxists and sincere Socialists supported the Bolsheviks. I myself was a Bolshevik from the very beginning. After the Revolution, wherever I went, I upheld the policies of Lenin and the Russian Communists, urging the Socialist Party to adopt more militant tactics.

A state convention of the New York Socialist Party was held to nominate candidates for the forthcoming state elections. I had just given up my full-time union work in order to be state organizer for the party in New York State. But I continued to help the unions, though with little encouragement from the New York bureaucracy who were not too pleased when party functionaries gave much time to union work. "You are spending too much time on strikes!" they complained, "and not enough doing Socialist work." "This *is* Socialist work," I told them.

The delegates from the unions called for my nomination as

lieutenant governor on the Socialist Party ticket. Judge Jacob Panken, who had campaigned many times for the legislature in one of the assembly districts, advised that someone far more conservative should be selected. He urged me not to accept. My answer was: "I shall stand anyway because the union workers nominated me, and they must want me. Besides, at this critical time, I don't want to see conservatives running."

Those of us who carried on the campaign had a pretty tough time during those lurid days when all who were against the war were persecuted. Often we received buckets of cold water from tenement house windows and soft tomatoes from those who called us names and reviled us.

In the midst of my campaign, I was sent to upstate New York. The state committee of the Socialist Party wanted me to straighten out matters in Oneida where the party members were bitterly taking sides on the "wet" or "dry" question. A machinist from Utica told me he was tired of the squabble over the wet and dry question, in the midst of war time. "Why do you waste your time with these people," he asked me, "when there is a big strike on in Utica? Why not come back to Utica after your meeting here and lead the women out of the Savage Arms shop, tomorrow morning?" The next day I was leading a strike in the Savage Arms shop. The men had been receiving $1.08 an hour and the women 17 cents an hour for assembling, and the women were demanding equal pay for equal work.

I spoke at large strike meetings held every afternoon in a big theatre. The War Board came into the strike, and seeing the strength and unity of the workers agreed to their demands. The captain who represented the War Board was amazed at the discipline of the strikers.

The government clamped down mercilessly on all expression of anti-war feeling. In June 1917, the Espionage Act had been passed, imposing heavy penalties on any action that might be construed as interfering with mobilization of military and naval forces, followed the next May by the Sedition Act, making any criticism of the Administration illegal. Local agencies and self-appointed vigilante groups carried on witch-hunting campaigns. My meetings swarmed with policemen and plain-clothesmen waiting to pounce on me.

On June 16, 1918, Debs made a speech in Canton, Ohio, which was an impassioned attack on the war as well as a defense of Charles E. Ruthenberg and Alfred Wagenknecht, already in prison for their opposition to the war. In the heart of the steel region, Debs declared the war was not being fought for democracy, but for the profits of the steel trust. The great warm heart of Debs was full of abhorrence of the very idea of war. He said, "When I think of a cold, glittering steel bayonet being plunged in the white quivering flesh of a human being, I recoil with horror. I have often wondered whether I could take the life of my fellow men, even to save my own." But he made it clear that his opposition to this war was not on mere pacifist grounds but because he understood its predatory nature. Elsewhere he said, "I am opposed to every war but one; I am for that war with heart and soul and that is the world-wide war of social revolution." And he ended his speech at Canton:

"The world of capitalism is setting; the sun of socialism is rising. It is our duty to build the new nation and the free republic. We need industrial and social builders. We Socialists are the builders of the beautiful world that is to be.... In due time the hour will strike and this great cause triumphant—the greatest in history—will proclaim the emancipation of the working class and the emancipation of all mankind."

Debs was arrested. At his trial on September 12, addressing the court and the people, Debs uttered these beautiful and unforgettable words:

"Years ago I recognized my kinship with all living beings, and I made up my mind that I was not one bit better than the meanest of the earth. I said then, I say now, that while there is a lower class, I am in it; while there is a criminal element, I am of it; while there is a soul in prison, I am not free."

With the darkness of prison days looming ahead of him, he cried out his belief that the time had come "for a better form of government, an improved system, a higher social order, a nobler humanity and a grander civilization." The coming of the new society, he told his jailers, could no more be prevented than the coming of dawn on the morrow.

For these noble utterances, Debs, who was then sixty-five years old, was sentenced to ten years.

I gave up the organizing work which had kept me largely in New York City, and went out on the road speaking at Socialist Party meetings to raise money for an appeal for Debs.

The comrades in Springfield, Massachusetts, had been given two weeks notice that I was coming. I found two scared party members at headquarters, an old Russian-Jewish comrade, and a young American. No meeting had been prepared. I was pleading with them, trying to get their courage up, when a redheaded Irishman rushed up the stairs. He had just heard I was in town.

"Why do you sit here and talk to these two mummies?" he shouted. "Why don't you come with me? There is a big strike on at the Smith and Wesson Works and thousands of men and women are gathered in Hibernian Hall."

He literally dragged me down the steps and rushed me to the mass meeting. There the people cheered me and asked me to lead the picket line, because a great many of the strikers were women. They were striking for the same thing as the workers at Utica— equal pay for equal work. The men realized what it would mean to the whole machinists' union if the company was permitted to pay the women such low wages. There were very few scabs.

Evenings I went off to fill my speaking dates for Debs defense meetings in nearby towns and was on hand for the picket line at 6:30 every morning. Again, as in Utica, the War Board came in and was compelled to agree to the workers' demands.

The Socialists in Springfield insisted it was impossible to hold any open air meetings for Debs because of the war hysteria. But Dan Donovan, a machinist, and I conducted a big strike mass meeting right in front of the post office. Crowds came and we had no police interference. The same thing happened the next week in Lynn, where the workers in a war materials shop had just won a strike and where for the first time the local electrical workers were organized. The workers held mass meetings every day in the park, but the Socialists would not hold a meeting for Debs.

At the "victory" meeting in Lynn, thousands of people had gathered to hear the leaders of the Electrical Workers' Union. Seeing me there, the workers picked me up and carried me on their shoulders to the platform. They knew very well that I was a Socialist organizer and why I had come there and were eager to have me speak to them about Debs.

This whole experience in Massachusetts was typical of what was happening in the S. P. throughout the country. The Socialist leaders had absolutely failed the working class, not only by refusing to take part in anti-war actions but also by failing to lead the workers in their economic struggles.

The response I always got from the rank and file indicated how the workers would have welcomed vigorous Socialist leadership. As for James F. Carey, state secretary of the Socialist Party in Massachusetts, I felt he was secretly *for the war*. It was very clear that he was avoiding me, as well as actually shirking his duties as state secretary. I found him practically hiding out in his own home in a city where a meeting had been scheduled but not held. He lived in a house with a little balcony jutting out over the doorway. I rang the bell but no one answered. I was about to go away when I heard voices on the balcony. I walked out into the street and saw Carey sitting there. I stood in the middle of the street and proceeded to tell him what I thought of him in a loud voice, so the neighbors could hear. I denounced him as a coward and said the reason he was doing nothing was that he was really supporting the war, and had betrayed the workers.

I received an official invitation from the Machinists' Union of Bridgeport, Connecticut, to be their speaker on the following Labor Day along with their international president, William Johnston. He had recently returned from France where he had been sent by President Wilson, and was for the war with all the fervor of a "hundred percenter."

The machinists of Bridgeport had been demanding equal pay for equal work for women workers, and the day before Labor Day they had gone out on strike for this as well as for higher wages and for the right to organize. Mr. Johnston had guaranteed President Wilson that his union would deliver 100 per cent production. He was horrified, therefore, to see the workers with banners bearing such slogans as, "Down with the manufacturers," picturing them as hogs feeding on war profits.

"We can't have a strike!" Johnston cried.

"Look here, Brother Johnston," I said to him, "if you don't talk to the workers about the strike and show your sympathy, they won't listen to you. They are just full of strike now because of the War Board's decision in Springfield. They expect a similar decision from the War Board here."

However, when he got up to speak, he only talked about "loyalty" and "our great president, Mr. Wilson" until he was red in the face. Not a hand applauded. When I spoke about the success of the Springfield strike, the audience was enthusiastic.

That night the Mayor and the president of the Central Labor Council gave a big dinner to the officials and speakers of the celebration. Mr. Johnston announced he was going to telegraph President Wilson that he had called off the strike.

A member of the War Board leaned over and whispered to me: "Not one man, nor 400 men could stop that strike!" And when he got up to speak he said just that. He said the men had not received one wage increase that whole summer, although they worked harder and faster than ever before. He said the strike was obviously a mass strike, that no one man instigated it and no one man could stop it.

Johnston did telegraph President Wilson, who wired the men to call off the strike. But the workers ignored the command. Mr. Johnston, enraged, revoked the charter of this very big local.

Returning to New York, I transferred my membership in the union to the Micrometer Lodge of the Brooklyn Navy Yard. This

lodge, too, came into conflict with Mr. Johnston, and once
when he came to speak, the men gave him a very angry reception, and he revoked the charter of this lodge, too.

The warmth and power that radiated from Debs continued to
exert an influence on those around Debs in prison, and to reach
beyond the prison walls.

Because of overcrowding in the Federal prison at Atlanta, Debs
was taken temporarily to Moundsville, where he was kept in a
little one-room cabin, with a door opening out into a typical
southern yard, full of trees. I went to visit him there, and when
I arrived Debs came to the door and put his arms around me as
he always did. I had made him a little brown muslin bag for
his personal belongings. I brought him books and grape juice
and little odds and ends I knew he would need, and he was
deeply grateful. He showered me with questions about the movement outside.

As we talked, Negro prisoners were sitting around under the
trees, practising on band instruments. Debs was like a father to all
the inmates of the prison. He knew all their first names, all their
life stories. Debs told me how fond he was of these Negro boys and
asked me to be sure on my way out to stop and tell them how fine
their music was. "They are such good boys," he said. "I'd like
them to get any happiness they can—it will mean a lot to them
to talk to you. . . ."

Debs seemed to be treated quite well at Moundsville. As I left
the warden asked me, "Does Mr. Debs seem to be well treated?"

"Yes, he seems to be," I answered.

Then to my surprise, the warden said, "Please do not tell the
public this, because if they think he is treated too well, he might
be removed." Before the week was up Debs was transferred to
Atlanta, Georgia, a very different kind of place.

Long afterward when I was in Atlanta, a comrade who had seen
Debs on the day of his release, told me about Debs' last hours
in the jail, revealing how deeply Debs felt his responsibility to
all human beings, wherever he was. He had said to the comrade,

THE POST-WAR REPRESSION   149

"These men love me, they trust me and depend on me, and I hate to leave them." As Debs sat in the warden's office, the warden's son, a lad of about seventeen, ran into the room, threw his arms around him and said, "Father, I can't bear to say good-bye to Mr. Debs. I want to go with him."

At the very last Debs turned to the comrade and said, "I still hate to leave these men. I am sorry to go." The warden had let every prisoner come to the front windows of the prison, and as the car drove away they all stood at the windows waving their hands, calling out, "Good-bye, Debs. Good-bye, Debs."

Men like Carey who were so chicken-hearted during the war have been forgotten. But Debs, who exclaimed: "I enter the prison doors a flaming revolutionist, my head erect, my spirit untamed, my soul unconquerable!"—Debs will be remembered by our children, and our children's children.

In the fall of 1918, both right and left wingers participated in a mass meeting in the old Madison Square Garden, New York City. A campaign of incitement and hatred was being directed against the Bolsheviks and the revolution by the newspapers. We knew that this incitement would make public speeches in support of the Russian Revolution difficult and dangerous, but were determined that there should be such speeches.

Socialists had been in the habit of waving both little red flags and American flags at their meetings. The day of this meeting, Mayor Hylan of New York City declared that red flags would be prohibited. But when I arrived at the hall, I beheld a sea of red. The men wore red neckties and red handkerchiefs protruded from their pockets; the women wore red blouses or dresses and red hats. I wore the brightest scarlet blouse I could find.

We had expected trouble and were therefore not completely taken by surprise to find an array of young soldiers lined up back of the speakers' stand.

Julius Gerber, city organizer of the Socialist Party, said to me, "Comrade, we are having you speak immediately. Turn around and speak to the soldiers. They intend to start a riot and push us

over the platform into the pit. Tell them to fight for democracy
at home!"

When I stood up my scarlet blouse flamed like a red banner and
the house rocked with applause. I turned my back on the audience
and addressed the soldiers behind me. I pleaded with them that as
they believed in and fought for democracy abroad, they must
stand for democracy in America. And then I went on to talk
about the Russian Revolution. In the midst of my talk, about
fifty policemen also came up on the platform. It was under these
circumstances we had to carry on our meeting.

Many of the audience were brutally attacked by rioters as they
left the hall. That same night, a young Russian-Jewish dentist and
his girl, who had not attended the meeting, were set upon by a
mob, many blocks away from the meeting, simply because it was
thought they looked like Russians.

A little over a year later, I was chairman at a meeting on the
Soviet Union in the New Star Casino. I remember so vividly the
message John Reed brought to us. He had come to the meeting
from a sick bed, and was so weak he had to lean against me. "I
cannot stop!" he insisted, when I urged him to sit down, seeing
how ill he was. "I was there! I saw it! I must tell them about it!"

He told us about the "ten days that shook the world," about the
great Lenin, and the courageous Soviet workers, and the new
life they were building. He spoke of the terrible persecution of the
first workers' state by all the so-called Christian countries, which
were trying by every means to keep socialism from succeeding,
and our own country's part in armed intervention.

Not long after that, John Reed returned again to Russia. He died
there of typhus, on October 17, 1920, and was buried under the
Kremlin wall, honored and beloved by both Soviet and American
workers.

The reactionary attitude of the Socialist Party leaders toward
the World War made it difficult to work with them, and I turned
my attention to those who were fighting against the war. The
federal prisons were filled with "conscientious objectors," I.W.W.'s

and others. At one time we had 150 class war prisoners in Leavenworth and elsewhere, as well as hundreds of appeal cases to be taken to the Supreme Court.

There were several defense organizations. A People's Council organized by liberals, to work for the termination of the war and a just peace, had a section composed of union men and women engaged in defense activities. The I.W.W. had its own defense organization. A group of us in New York, representing different unions, formed the Workers' Defense Union for the defense of political and anti-war prisoners. Elizabeth Gurley Flynn was secretary and organizer, Fred Biedenkapp treasurer, and I, national field organizer. In this capacity I visited almost every state and federal prison in the country during 1918 and 1919.

I always cooperated with other defense organizations and was also a member of a legal committee, composed largely of lawyers; and of a league of parents and relatives of conscientious objectors led by Norman Thomas then (1918-1919) editing *The World of Tomorrow*. A pacifist during the World War, he had recently become a member of the Socialist Party.

I often visited among others Bill Haywood, Ralph Chaplin, Charles Ashleigh, Harrison George, Alexander Cornish, all of them sentenced to from ten to twenty years. On one occasion I helped a group of I.W.W.'s and other political prisoners win a hunger strike at Leavenworth county jail. I carried the prisoners' demands to the sheriff, telling him he would be responsible for their death if he didn't give them better food. The sheriff gave in. He had to. We had found out that the federal government allowed 79 cents a day for food and he spent about 13 cents.

Kate Richards O'Hare was arrested and served 14 months of a five-year sentence for an anti-war speech in which she said women should refuse to breed sons to fertilize the soil. I visited her in the Missouri State Penitentiary at Jefferson City, and found she had to sew a daily quota of heavy duck overalls for the prisoners. The number was beyond her strength and one good old Negro woman helped her to make up this stint.

Heartbreaking as was my work for the prisoners, I owe to

it some of the richest experiences and friendships of my life. It was a privilege to meet these courageous men and women.

One of the saddest cases was that of Perley Dow, nephew of a chief justice of New Hampshire. He was ill with tuberculosis and his wife was taking him to a sanatorium in Colorado. At a stop-over in Denver, he read an account of some chauvinistic utterance of President Wilson. Perley Dow wrote an article saying the President should be impeached for such statements. He was arrested and taken to prison in such a weakened condition that he had to be propped up on the seat of the train. His wife went with him to the state prison at Canyon City, Colorado, and lived in town to be near him, taking in sewing to make a livelihood.

After Perley Dow had been in prison a year, growing weaker all the time, pressure from the Workers' Defense Union and other organizations resulted in getting him paroled. But the authorities still would not let him out. I went all the way to Colorado, taking the necessary papers to the sheriff for his release. About a week later, we did get him out. He died within two months.

In that same prison were Louise Olivereau, who had written a book against conscription, and Flora Foreman, an Oregon school teacher who in a private conversation had advised a young girl not to marry a soldier who was home on leave—advice given not because he was a soldier but because of his weak character. She was arrested almost immediately on the complaint of the girl, and given a three years' sentence. One day I went to visit these two girls to tell them of our efforts to get them out. I carried with me a big bunch of spring flowers. But the sheriff growled, "They don't want to see anybody," and would not even let me leave the flowers for them. We later succeeded in getting them released.

Among the conscientious objectors in Leavenworth, was Norman Thomas' brother, Evan, and a young man named Erling Lunde, son of a rich Swedish manufacturer of Chicago who was very helpful to me in the C. O. cases. One day the elder Mr. Lunde asked me to find out whether his son was living or dead. A note written on a piece of toilet paper had come to him from Leavenworth through a released "regular" prisoner, saying that Erling was in the hospital ill with scarlet fever and had not been heard from in a long time.

Erling Lunde's wife was Laura Hughes, a pacifist friend of mine from Canada. Although her father was an ardent advocate of conscription, and her uncle was Sir Samuel Hughes, war minister of Canada, Laura Hughes was drawn to the labor movement and she had worked with me in Toronto. I was therefore doubly interested in finding out what had become of Erling Lunde. I went to Fort Leavenworth and told the warden that I was the aunt of Laura Hughes, who wanted news of her husband. He came back and reported that he had inquired at the hospital but could find no trace of him. Convinced that young Lunde was dead, I demanded to see Evan Thomas.

They brought Evan in, looking thinner than any human being I had ever seen. I gasped, "Oh, Evan, what has happened to you?" He told me he had gone on a hunger strike because they had taken a group of Mennonites underground to a punishment cell and put them on bread and water. One of these Mennonite men died from the treatment he received.

Evan assured me Erling Lunde was living, and I went right back to Chicago and informed Mr. Lunde.

From Chicago I went to New York and gave Norman Thomas news of his brother. He aroused the people in Baltimore, where his brother lived, to protest, and we in New York gave wide publicity to the matter. The following week, I called a meeting in the Rand School of all the relatives of the boys in Leavenworth. The afternoon of the meeting, Norman Thomas phoned asking me to guess who was in town. I said, "I suppose your mother," and he said, "Yes, and she's got Evan with her. Our campaign got him out."

Caroline Lowe was a wonderful person, a capable lawyer and a devoted Socialist. She was attorney for the United Mine Workers in Pittsburgh, Kansas and for the I.W.W. during the war days.

I helped her in the Wichita case, one of the most flagrant. These I.W.W. boys were not agitating against the war; they were simply organizing, and for this they were hounded and persecuted. One night, in September, 1917, a group, including Ed Boyd, the secretary, a sensitive, middle-aged man, were sitting in the Wichita headquarters. Suddenly about twenty-five hooded men broke in, grabbed them, took them out in the woods, stripped them and poured hot tar and feathers over them, and left them there hoping they would die.

One of them managed to crawl to a farmhouse. They were almost afraid to go in because of the hatred that had been stirred up against them. The rich farmers were particularly savage because the I.W.W. had organized a powerful agricultural workers' union to keep wages up. But it happened that this farmer was very sympathetic. He came out with gallon cans of linseed oil which he poured over their tortured bodies, took them to his house, got them clothes and kept them for about ten days. Returning to their homes, all were immediately arrested and locked up in the Wichita jail, one of the worst I have ever seen. The cells were angular cubicles, shaped like pie-cuts, rotating around a piston in the center, keeping the prisoners exposed through the grating and in continual motion. The guard was able to stand still and watch them as they moved. All sense of human dignity was murdered in that place.

On my first visit there, with Caroline Lowe, one of the boys warned us: "Don't stand near the walls anywhere, they are alive with bugs." One of the men in that prison went insane. Another died.

It was our job to expose conditions in that jail as quickly as we could. We aroused so much mass pressure on the county authorities that at last they were compelled to tear that jail down.

During my tours for the war prisoners I went back to New York periodically to report to the organization and consult with Elizabeth Gurley Flynn and others in this work. So began my long years of association with that fighting daughter of a long line of fighting Irish ancestors. At sixteen she was already active in the I.W.W., and Joe Hill put her in a Wobbly song, "The Rebel Girl." While she did not join with us in the early days of the Communist Party, she worked with us closely. Finally, after an interlude of ten years of illness in Portland, Oregon, she came back to New York and joined the Party, and is today one of our finest speakers, and one of the most honored and beloved members of our National Executive Committee. The story of Elizabeth's life is interwoven with many of the great labor struggles of this country. Workers everywhere know her lovely ringing voice and glowing spirit and great fighting heart. Calumet—Passaic—Paterson—Lawrence—all these places knew her on the picket line and the platform. Today, bearing a heavy burden of sorrow from the sudden death of her only son, Fred, she fights on for a world in which mothers will not have to lose their sons needlessly in battles for their masters.

The armistice in November, 1918, brought only temporary relief from persecution. Wild with joy that the war had ended, the people thought the lightless nights and wheatless days, the lack of coal, the high prices, and the terrible restrictions on liberty would be ended now. But though the weight of the knowledge of that continuous senseless slaughter in the trenches of Europe was lifted from all our hearts, for the masses of the people there were new privations. The workers faced growing unemployment and a new drive against their living standards. The continued existence of the Soviet Republic, the revolutionary ferment stirred up by the war among the masses in Europe, the rising class consciousness of American workers, filled the masters with fear for their cracking system. There was no restoration of liberties; the attack grew fiercer, the anti-red hysteria more frenzied. With most of our war-time prisoners still in jail, a new series of raids and arrests began. One day in late June, I was going out of the Workers' Defense office in the Rand School Building, when I ran into about fifty fat men piling in. They began to push me back: "You get back in that building. Nobody can leave."

The men were agents of the "Lusk Committee," appointed to

investigate Bolshevism in New York State, making a raid on the
Rand School, national center for the various educational activities of the Socialist Party, where a number of labor organizations
had offices. The raiders, led by that arch red-baiter Archibald
Stevenson, of the Republican Union League Club, forgot all
about me and began searching the rooms. I went flying upstairs
to Elizabeth. We had numerous lists of contributors to the Workers' Defense, which we did not want to fall into their hands. I
gathered up all the account books, lists, records, letters, etc., into
a big market basket, which I carried down the back stairway into
the cellar. I asked our janitor, a loyal Socialist, to hide the basket
in the ashes where he could get it again.

I went back upstairs, but the Workers' Defense office happened
to be the only room the raiders didn't enter. They were busy
trying to open the school safe. George Strobell, the manager of
the building, a faithful Socialist, refused to give up the key. "You
have no warrant authorizing me to open the safe or give you the
key," he said. "I am the manager and intend to remain the manager." He was a quiet little man, but very firm. He calmly walked
out the back door with the key in his pocket and went home.

That night the state police stood guard over the safe. We also
had three guards to see what they took if they got it open.

In two days the Lusk Committee returned with a safe-cracker.
They blew the safe open, but our lawyer, S. John Block, was
there and counted and noted everything they took.

The Lusk Committee succeeded in getting the board of directors of the Rand School indicted and the school fined. Under the
wartime espionage act, the American Socialist Society, which
owned the Rand School, and Scott Nearing, as author of an anti-
war pamphlet, *The Great Madness,* had previously been indicted
in April, 1918. The A.S.S. was found guilty in February, 1919,
but Scott Nearing was acquitted.

After the trial we asked one of the jurymen why they had
found Scott Nearing innocent. He answered that they had all enjoyed the pamphlet, which had been read aloud in court, and felt
that it told the truth.

The Senate Overman Committee in Washington, investigating Bolshevism, and the Lusk Committee in New York functioned in the same un-American manner in those days as does the Dies Committee today. They used the same illegal methods to get "evidence." Then as now a procession of unsavory witnesses were permitted to spread their lies and slander on the record and to libel decent American citizens, while the press had a Roman holiday.

10. The Communist Party is Born

SINCE work for the political prisoners began to center on the prisoners at the Leavenworth federal prison, it seemed advisable for me to go west to live. I went there in the summer of 1919 and in addition to the other work, I helped out on the *Workers' World,* an excellent paper started by the left wingers of Kansas City, for which Earl Browder was writing most of the editorials. I was appointed Socialist organizer in Kansas City, Missouri.

Earl Browder with his two brothers, Waldo and Bill, and four other young men had been sentenced to Leavenworth Penitentiary for two years, charged with printing leaflets against conscription. About the time I arrived in Kansas City, the three Browder boys and their bondsmen were notified that their appeal had been denied and they must begin serving their sentences in Leavenworth Penitentiary. The prosecution hunted everywhere for their printing press. But it was in a deep backyard pit dug by Browder's father, a good old militant Socialist.

The seven boys surrendered to the authorities, and the wife of one of the men and myself accompanied them and the U. S. Marshal and the deputy to the prison. We went on the interurban trolley that runs from Kansas City, Missouri, to Leavenworth, the boys all wearing their Debs buttons conspicuously. When we got to Leavenworth, the boys gave me their purses and personal trinkets to keep for them. I remember to this day my spasm of anger when the marshal declared he was "delivering up seven prisoners to the government."

I stayed on in Kansas City working for the paper. I visited the seven boys and the other Leavenworth prisoners every Saturday, bringing them news and literature. Earl Browder always wanted books and news of the movement: he wanted every detail of the fight against the interventionists in the Soviet Union, of the great steel strike then going on, of developments within the party.

I toured for the *Workers' World* through Missouri, Nebraska and Kansas. Everywhere I encountered the sharp cleavage among the Socialists on the Russian Revolution and the war. I was highly gratified when all three states where I had been working sent left wing delegates to the Chicago convention in 1919 when the left wingers split from the Socialist Party. I was elected a delegate, but since Earl Browder was still in prison, I had to remain and help hold the paper together, and Gertrude Harmon was named in my place.

The left wing of the Socialist Party, prior to the convention, had elected twelve out of fifteen members of the National Executive Committee, and was supported by the majority of the party. But the election was repudiated by the right wing, who went so far as to suspend seven language federations and the whole Michigan party organization, pledged to the left wing program. They even called in the police to help run the left wing delegates out of the convention. The differences between the reformist and the revolutionary wings were too great to be reconciled in a united organization. The right wing had supported the war-time course of the Second International, whose leaders were everywhere helping their governments to carry on imperialist warfare. Their class collaboration policies had inevitably led them into the camp of capitalism, and the capitalist class made the most of their assistance. The right wingers had sabotaged the St. Louis anti-war resolution, had compromised on the question of America's entry into the war, and opposed the Russian Revolution.

Since the earlier splits the left wing group had learned much. Syndicalist tendencies had been outgrown. The Russian Revolution had taught us the theory and tactics of real revolutionary struggle. The formation of the Communist International in March, 1919, as the answer to the bankruptcy of the Second International, gave world leadership to the revolutionary groups everywhere who were adopting as their guide the principles of Leninism—that is to say, the principles of Marx applied to the era of imperialism.

The time had come to form a new, truly American revolutionary party. On August 31, 1919, the expelled left wingers formed the Communist Labor Party. On the following day another group, which had refused to attend the convention altogether, formed the Communist Party. These two parties were basically in agreement and sixteen months later (December, 1921) they merged, with other elements who left the Socialist Party. C. E. Ruthenberg was elected General Secretary, and took active leadership on his release from jail.

After the delegates brought back the news, I called a meeting of the Kansas City membership to consider reorganizing as the Communist Labor Party there. The meeting was held in early September, and with no opposition whatever our whole group became charter members of our Communist Party at that time. Earl Browder, then in prison, at once signified his intention of signing the charter. Bill Browder signed several weeks after he got out of prison. The day I became a charter member of the Party is one I shall remember and be proud of all my life. I was now fifty-seven years old, and a whole new vista of glorious living opened before me. I knew that all my development, all my strivings to bring about a better society, on this day laid a course I could finally subscribe to with all my heart and mind. I felt that our new Party, firmly rooted in American soil, would be capable of leading the workers to final victory because of its faith in the workers themselves. I have never changed my mind about this and never will. My years in the Communist Party have been years of closest association with the workers and farmers of our country, years of great privilege, because I have learned far more from the workers than I have ever taught them. The fullness and richness of my life I owe to them and to my work in the Party.

Our new Party was subjected to immediate persecution everywhere. Before long an injunction was issued against the *Workers' World,* the paper was raided and one of the editors arrested. The raiders literally smashed everything to bits.

Some of our political prisoners were now coming out, and with their help we started building our Party. We began to organize systematically in districts and states; we held study courses, started a youth movement, and above all, tried to get the Party members to take more interest in union work. This was a tough job because of an incorrect attitude then current that to belong to what the S.L.P. used to call the "pure and simple" unions of the A. F. of L. was compromising with the labor fakers. But it was considered the duty of every Communist Party member to joint the union of his craft and where none existed to try to organize one. It has been the policy of the Communist Party from the beginning that its members should take part in organizations that represent the masses. While our Party understood this principle in theory, it was, in fact, isolated from the masses in those days, and was to go through a long period of struggle before it learned to merge theory and practice, and to take part in the every day struggles of the workers and farmers.

The militancy of the workers during this period, expressing itself in numerous strikes, especially the great steel strike of 1919, and the rise of our revolutionary party, were answered by increased persecution on the part of the "liberal" Wilson administration. On November 7, 1919, the Palmer raids began. Arrests and deportations of our members and sympathizers in the effort to strangle our Party forced it underground. While unquestionably the terrorist methods used against us made some sort of underground organization necessary, certain of our members developed romantic adventuristic tendencies. Some of our more timid members, refusing to lift up their heads and struggle, made the underground movement an excuse for hiding the face of the Party long after it was necessary.

I was made national organizer for the Eastern Division of the Communist Labor Party, and returned to the East. I campaigned for the Party everywhere. I went from town to town to hunt up people who might subscribe to our paper, *The Communist*. I used to have boxes of the papers sent to grocery stores and homes of sympathizers. We would pick up bundles in the middle of the night, and distribute them from house to house.

I settled in Boston, where Carl and Dick were going to school. All during the war my boys had fought against wearing the students' uniform for military training. Dick had been in Boston University over a year, and Carl was in his first year of college. Refused admittance to the last year of high school because he would not take military training, he had to go to preparatory school at night. He earned his tuition by working in a Y.M.C.A. restaurant used by soldiers passing through. Dick also worked his way through college.

The Palmer raids made my work difficult. Once when I came home I found the Palmer men had demanded to search my place. But they had no search warrant, and the landlady would not let them enter. On January 2, 1920, I went to speak in Worcester, Massachusetts, in a Finnish Hall, at a meeting for Jim Larkin, the Irish revolutionary leader, whom we were trying to get out of a New York prison on bail. Sidney Bloomfield, well-known in our Party today, was acting as chairman for the first time in his life. Although it was a defense meeting, he turned it into an organizing meeting for the Communist Labor Party as well. We had a batch of new literature on sale, telling the aims of our Party. I had just bought some and put it in my handbag.

Suddenly twelve big men came through the door and swept the literature off the table into boxes they were carrying. Sidney did not realize they were Palmer men, and went right on with his recruiting. I fairly hissed at him: "Shut up! We are raided!"

It was bitter cold and only the faithful had come. In addition to many American workers, there were Slavs and Finns in the audience. They were so good, so innocent, so honest that when the police asked if they were citizens, some said "No," although they did not have to answer at all.

I went down among the audience crying: "Do not answer any questions. This is not a court!" The Palmer men were beating up people right and left. There had been about sixty dollars in the collection. Just before Sidney was grabbed, he managed to whisper to me, "The money's under your coat on the seat." So I stood by the coat all the time. Every once in a while a Palmer man would grab me roughly and say "You are under arrest," then go off to beat up someone else. Then I thought to myself—"What a fool you are, to stand here waiting for them to come back and get you."

So I picked up my coat and the baskets under it and calmly made for the side door. As I walked out, the Finnish janitor crawled from under a table and asked me, "I am only the poor janitor, what shall I do?" "Hurry up and get out of here, or they will get you, too!" I advised him.

Fearful that Carl and Dick would be worrying, I returned to my hotel, called them on the phone and said I was detained, but did not say why. Then I tore up every shred of literature I had. There was no toilet in the room, where I could get rid of it, and I was afraid to go out in the hall. I tore it all into infinitesimal pieces and mixed them up in the wastebasket. I did not take off my clothes all that night, expecting them to come after me. The newspapers came out about 6 o'clock the next morning with big headlines, and a three column story quoting my speech—although I had made none. The paper said I would be arrested that morning.

As I went down in one elevator, the detectives went up in the other. I took a cab to the depot and waited in the ladies' room until the train pulled in.

Back in Boston, Carl and Dick too had spent the night destroying letters and papers. The house had been watched all night. We realized at once that I would have to go away. But where?

On that night of January 2, 1920, in more than thirty cities and towns of the United States, the Department of Justice, planning mass deportations of foreign born members of the Communist Labor and the Communist Parties, had raided lawful assemblages and arrested hundreds of men and women. Stool pigeons had helped get the meetings organized simultaneously. The approximate number of arrests officially reported was 2,500. Hundreds were held for deportation. The people they took from our meeting in Worcester were held for months in a terrible prison on an island near Boston.

At Dick's and Carl's urging, I went to New York and from there, on the advice of comrades, to Colorado. Carl and Dick sacrificed scholarships in Boston to come with me. I lived very quietly until after the winter was over. The two boys got jobs selling coffee, Carlie driving a mule team from store to store.. In the spring I returned East and the boys entered college—Dick, the Alliance Francaise, at Columbia, and Carl, the Columbia School of Journalism. Carl soon had a job as assistant telegraph editor on the *New York Tribune* to pay his way through Columbia. When, not long after, he was asked to work on the Party paper in Chicago, he went at once without hesitation, giving up both his job and the chance of completing his college course.

I went on a tour for the war prisoners and the new political prisoners arrested in the raids. Many of our leaders were held under heavy bail, and we were still appealing cases to the higher courts. One of our most important cases was that of Ruthenberg, who was serving a sentence in New York State under an antiquated criminal anarchy law exhumed for the purpose. Money for an appeal was urgently needed for his and other cases. From a large meeting in Kansas City, Missouri, where I raised $150, I went to Kansas City, Kansas, to speak to a meeting of the packing house workers. During the day I went out to see the boys in Leavenworth, and went right from the prison to the hall, still carrying the collection of the night before in a little Boston bag.

We took up a large collection which I put in my bag along with the money raised the previous night. As I finished speaking a tough looking customer came up, reached for the collection, and said, "You are under arrest."

"You have no right to arrest me," I cried. "You just dare to touch that bag and I will have *you* arrested for stealing." Just then the hall filled with policemen. They took me, the chairman, the women who had taken the collection, and several others—eleven men and five women in all—to the jail and would not let us call a lawyer or our friends. They put the women down in the basement of the prison, under the cells, in order to intimidate us. Gertrude Harmon, who was among us, was the wife of a local Socialist printer. She heard one of the guards say, "We will send the old man home and tell him his wife has gone home, too." Afraid some harm might come to her and that her husband would not hear about it, Gertrude suddenly began singing at the top of her lungs, first a song about "liberty," and then one about how "she lost her man." It had the desired effect. Her husband upstairs heard her and realized where we were. They let her and Mrs. O'Sullivan, the chairman, and their husbands, go home, so only three women were left. One, a young southern girl, had never been to any kind of a labor meeting before. The detectives took her aside and said, "What do you want to be with these people for? Don't you know who they are? Are you an I.W.W.?" "No, I never have been," she answered, "but I think I shall be one now."

The bed was so terribly dirty we sat up all night. In the morning, after we had been tried by a "kangaroo court," they took us to a real court with a judge and several prosecutors.

When I came out of the patrol wagon, a schoolteacher and a doctor friend of mine were waiting with liberty bonds. But they discovered these were not enough. I slipped my bag with the collection to the schoolteacher, after having held it in my hands all night.

In the court they read the criminal syndicalism law to us, and accused us of advocating the overthrow of the government by force and violence, of violating the law "by spoken and written word."

We pleaded "not guilty" and they held us under the outrageous bail of $28,000 and clapped us back into jail. We had had nothing to eat since the evening before. Around 5 o'clock an awful old matron brought us each a tin pan with a piece of leathery meat, gravy and potato. The girl beside me took one look at her plate and turned white as a sheet. There was a big roach swimming around in the gravy.

Just then there was a great commotion on the stairs. We heard the matron squawk as a burly red-haired Irishman pushed her aside, and came running up to our cell crying: "Mother, what in the world are you in here for?"

It was Tim McCreach, organizer of the meat cutters' union in Kansas City, Kansas. Tim arranged bail for us. He got the court clerk out of his home to accept the bonds of two well-to-do sympathizers. "Tomorrow you can help get bail for the boys," he assured me. Then he gave us a big supper and took us over to Kansas City, Missouri.

I telephoned Joe Shartz, a Dayton lawyer, with whom I had worked years before. He had promised me that he would defend me if I was ever arrested. At the trial next week, the chief witness was a regular gangster. He testified: "That woman said the Tsar was overthrown in Russia, the Kaiser was overthrown in Germany and we ought to have done it in this country."

"Where were you when you heard Mother Bloor?" asked Shartz.

"Out in the alley looking in through the window."

I was found "guilty," but the sentence was suspended, an appeal was made, and I was put under bail.

My tour for defense funds for Ruthenberg and the others took me to Portland, Oregon. While there I received the news that I had been elected a delegate to the Red International of Labor Unions, an organization of all progressive and radical unions of the world, which was having its first conference in Moscow. I knew I was on my way to see great and happy things.

11. Russia, My First Visit to Socialism

EARL BROWDER was very anxious to have William Z. Foster attend this R.I.L.U. congress in Russia, where he would see the great progress of the Russian workers since the Revolution, their heroic and intelligent building of a new society in spite of foreign intervention and famine, and rejoiced when Foster decided to go. At that time Foster was in the Brotherhood of Railway Carmen and a delegate to the Central Labor Union of Chicago. Since the defeat of the great 1919 steel strike which he had led, Foster had been struggling with the organization of the Trade Union Educational League, a left wing organization opposed to dual unionism, dedicated to the idea of developing a strong, progressive bloc within the old line unions. This policy had found powerful support in Lenin's pamphlet, *"Left Wing" Communism: An Infantile Disorder.*

Browder and myself went as T.U.E.L. delegates. Foster went as an observer. Bill Haywood, who joined the Communist Party early in 1921, headed an I.W.W. delegation. There were also delegates from the One Big Union of Toronto, the Detroit Federation of Labor and the Seattle Central Labor Council.

A group of us left together on a Scandinavian boat that landed us at Libau in Latvia. From there we took the train to Riga, then a center for all kinds of anti-Soviet groups and a dispatch point for anti-Soviet newspaper slanders. We were packed into a sort of freight car with our baggage piled all around us, and went overland across Latvia. We could see the ravages of the world war everywhere—smashed railroad cars, wrecked stations and bridges.

It took us two nights and three days to cross Latvia, normally a few hours trip. The train was full of Russian immigrants, who were then going back to their home country in such numbers that it was impossible to take care of them all in a country devastated by civil war and blockade. In our car there were over twenty people, including our six delegates, and a man and his wife who were our interpreters. The men fixed up a place for us to sleep so we would not have to lie on the floor. It was March and very cold, and they kept the window shut. The men smoked incessantly and one could scarcely breathe. Every once in a while, while everyone slept, I would take out pieces of wood that plugged cracks to let in a little air.

At the Soviet border everyone on the train suddenly seemed transformed. Going across Latvia no one talked to strangers. The minute we got over the border the tension ceased. The whole train blossomed out with red flags and scarves, which the passengers waved joyously from every window and door. We six R.I.L.U. delegates were met by an escort in Leningrad who accompanied us to Moscow.

The opening of the Congress was delayed because of the difficulties of the delegates from many countries in getting there. We used the time visiting factories and new Soviet institutions. Foster's interpreter told me he asked questions incessantly. Every night Foster would come back excited because of some wonderful new thing he had learned. Browder typed out the stories Foster and I told, as well as his own observations, and sent daily stories back to America. Before long Foster told us he was convinced by what he saw and read of the correctness of the Communist policies.

Our arrival coincided with the beginning of a new era for the workers' state. The days of war, intervention and blockade were over, leaving terrible ravages in their wake, and for the first time the leaders could concentrate on problems of peaceful economic development. About the time of our arrival, the Tenth Party Congress took place, adopting Lenin's wise and far-seeing New Economic Policy, replacing the rigid regime of War Communism that had been made necessary by the war and the blockade. Peasants had been grumbling at the requisition of their surplus food and the lack of commodities. The wheels of industry, which had gone down to about 15 per cent of pre-war production, were beginning to turn again. There was wreckage everywhere to be repaired, the population suffered from hunger and disease. Lenin saw that the country needed an economic breathing spell, just as earlier, when the Brest-Litovsk Treaty was signed with Germany, it had needed a relief from war. The NEP meant replacing grain requisitions by a tax in kind, so that the peasants could sell their remaining surplus as they wished. Lenin and the majority of the Party's Central Committee knew this would revive agriculture, increase circulation of goods, bring closer together the workers and peasants, and create a sound basis for building up industry. Although this temporary retreat would mean a certain revival of private trading, they felt strong enough to control this revival, using it only as long as necessary to create a solid economic foundation on the basis of which the final offensive against all remnants of capitalism could be launched.

We heard a good deal about the opposition to Lenin on the NEP, and on the question of the trade unions (Trotsky wanted to make them state organs, wiping out trade union democracy). But we saw that the Party had rallied around Lenin, and we had complete confidence that it was on the right path. We saw how the courageous Soviet workers gathered all their strength to defeat their enemies and to build a socialist society.

I was amazed and overjoyed at the atmosphere of freedom and ease I found in the factories. Workers *sang* at their looms and machines. The word we heard most on their lips when we asked them questions was "nasha"—ours. They controlled their own conditions of labor and life through their unions—all organized on the industrial principle. There were difficulties of course. Much machinery stood idle for lack of parts. The methods used seemed terribly primitive by American standards. But their first job was to rebuild after the years of war and civil strife. Then they would apply modern methods and technique. They were full of glorious plans.

In a clothing factory I saw many unused machines, and was told that the owner had fled taking vital parts of the machinery with him. I made a list of what was lacking and after my return to America gave it to the Amalgamated Clothing Workers, (whose leaders were more militant then than they are today) who saw that the needed parts were provided. What a reception I got at that factory on my next trip over!

One day a group of the delegates spoke at a big factory ten miles outside of Moscow, abandoned by the International Harvester Co. during the war, but now reopened and making plows. I was told, "Don't be nervous about the language—just talk as though you were at home." The man who interpreted for me spoke about twice as long as I did, and made a great hit on my behalf.

Despite their difficulties the Soviet people were already doing a great deal for children. At this factory they had built a beautiful day nursery and kindergarten. In a special workroom older women were making and mending clothes for the factory workers' children.

Slim as were the available rations the workers always managed to find food and refreshment for their foreign visitors, and we were often embarrassed by the lavishness of their hospitality.

This was in 1921, when they were still demobilizing the army and there was an untold amount of hard work to be done. Every Saturday the whole nation contributed a day's work and we visitors also volunteered. Earl Browder helped clean up the hotel yard as his *Subbotnik* (Saturday) duty.

Every day at three o'clock a comrade took me to some factory to speak. The workers listened eagerly to the "Americanka." Informing the workers on what was going on in the rest of the world was a big educational job and I was proud to have a small part in it.

The Russians had a great deal of respect for Americans, and especially for American technique. But there was also bitterness over America's part in armed intervention. Some of the Russian boys were wearing American army coats which, they told us wryly, came from Wrangel's army—and plenty of American rifles had been found among the counter-revolutionary armies, too.

I heard Gorky speak before a big union meeting. I could not understand what he said, but I could see that he was inspired by the crowd and the occasion, that he loved the workers deeply, and that they loved him. He looked as I thought he would, like a peasant. When I met him afterwards, he asked me about America, and whether we were still reading his books. I told him how much his *Mother* meant to me, and to many other Americans.

At this time, too, I made an enduring friendship with Arnold Lozovsky, a cultured and many-sided personality and a fine Bolshevik, who became head of the R.I.L.U., and who today is Assistant Commissar for Foreign Affairs of the U.S.S.R.

So we spent our time through March and April. Then came the First of May.

Early in the morning we were awakened by the sound of familiar songs in English. We rushed to the windows and saw eighty or more Russian-American workers who had come over to help build up Soviet industry. We sang back to them and they called to us to come down and join their parade.

We marched singing to the Moscow Soviet building. The chairman of the Moscow Soviet came to the window and we had an exchange of greetings. We returned to the hotel for a picnic lunch (all the waiters and hotel workers of course were off duty), and then made for Pushkin Square—a wide square with beautiful trees, opening into a great boulevard.

Huge crowds were surging to the square, and street cars decorated with red flags and green boughs came to the square bringing groups from unions and other organizations. Hitched to the cars were platforms carrying bands, trained animals, tumblers, and circus performers. Side shows, concerts, speeches, were going on everywhere. In the evening, visitors made five minute speeches before the curtains of the biggest Moscow theatres. I spoke at the Art Theatre.

Soon after, the historic first Congress of the Red International of Labor Unions opened. The formation of the R.I.L.U. had become necessary as a result of failure to represent the interests of the workers on the part of the Amsterdam Trade Union International, controlled by the leaders of the Second International. In addition to the Russian unions, left Socialist and syndicalist unions of various countries were represented, as well as organized minorities from other unions. A dozen or so syndicalist delegates from Spain, France and Italy were regular disrupters, attempting to turn the convention into an anarchist organization. Before the congress opened, Emma Goldman and Alexander Berkman, then in Moscow, asked the American delegation officially for guest tickets. We unanimously voted not to give them tickets, knowing they would join with the disrupters. But somehow they got into the congress, and although they had no right to a voice, they tried to organize an anti-Communist, anti-Soviet bloc. They egged on the syndicalists to propose censuring the Soviet Government for suppression of the Kronstadt revolt, engineered some months before by White Guards, Socialist-Revolutionaries and Mensheviks, with foreign aid. Voted down, Emma Goldman and Berkman tried to stage a riot. It is an established fact that at this time Goldman and Berkman were actively supporting the Anarchist bandit Makhno, who pillaged the peasants of the Ukraine and led an armed struggle against the Soviet Government.

Emma Goldman was given asylum in the U.S.S.R. after having been deported from the United States, but as an Anarchist she opposed the Soviet Government as she opposed all governments. When she abused Soviet hospitality by organizing counter-revolutionary groups, she forfeited her right of asylum, and was asked to leave the country.

The voting at the R.I.L.U. was based on the size of the countries represented, and their labor movements. Big countries like Germany, Russia, America and Great Britain had sixteen votes each.

No one could say that Russia, or a nearby country like Germany, influenced the voting. Since we had six regular delegates it was decided that five should have three votes each, and the remaining delegate one. One of our I.W.W. delegates gave us a lot of trouble, actively opposing all the decisions of the congress. Bill Haywood, however, and a strong I.W.W. minority supported the R.I.L.U. Already seriously ill with diabetes and with a twenty-year prison term for his anti-war activities hanging over him, Bill stayed on in Moscow, becoming head of the American Kuzbas Colony in Siberia in 1922. Later he worked with the International Red Aid to help class war prisoners in all the capitalist countries. He died in Moscow in 1928.

The issue at the congress which most affected the American delegates was that of dual unionism. Our policy of working within the A. F. of L. and independent unions won over the I.W.W. policy. The R.I.L.U. endorsed the T.U.E.L. as its American section. The congress also declared strongly for political action. The syndicalist idea of abolishing the state and turning the industries over to the trade unions met sharp defeat.

At the congress I first met Tom Mann, serving with him on the constitution committee. We have been warm friends ever since.

The significance of the R.I.L.U. congress was impressed upon the entire labor movement of the world. It encouraged labor unions everywhere to unite industrially. Each country at this congress prepared its own program, incorporating in it the call of the congress for industrial unionism.

All R.I.L.U. delegates were given tickets to the Third World Congress of the Communist International taking place at that time. It was held in the Palace of the Tsars, inside the Kremlin Walls. It was thrilling to walk up the wide staircase into the great Coronation Hall lined with magnificent paintings and look through the long windows opening out on the winding Moscow River. You could see the domes of the many Moscow churches, gold and silver and blue, with their glittering decorations. It was hard to believe it was not a dream. On the platform were Lenin and Clara Zetkin and many of the great comrades I had read about. There were delegates from China, Japan, Cuba, Mexico, Canada—every country of the world.

In the big dining room just outside the meeting hall were long tables set with tea, cake and sandwiches, served by girls with white dresses and red caps. The photographs and revolutionary mementos that then lined the walls have since been taken into Moscow's Museum of the Revolution, whose collection, I am proud to record, includes two pictures of me.

The second day of the Congress, I saw Lenin for the first time. A small man entered very quietly from a side door near the platform and sat down at a table behind a large group of palms, and immediately began making notes. "Lenin is here! Lenin is here!" the whisper began spreading; finally the delegates could restrain themselves no longer and rose and sang the "Internationale" in every language at once. Lenin, bent over his papers, paid no attention. When he got up to speak, they began it again and sang as loud as they could. He waited until they got through, looking thoughtfully out over the audience, then back at his notes, a little impatient to begin, and then started speaking directly and simply, without oratorical tricks or flourishes. There flowed from him a sense of compelling power, and of the most complete sincerity and selflessness I have ever seen.

After the meeting, Lenin walked down the big hall to shake hands with all of us. He was especially glad to see the Americans, and asked us many questions about things in America, and particularly, I remember, about American farmers.

A few days later Lenin defended the theses proposed by the Russian delegation against amendments offered by some of the delegations. The particular point at issue was the necessity first of creating a truly revolutionary party in each country, and then of winning over large masses. Some of the delegates were urging that the demand for large masses be dropped, arguing that victory was achieved in Russia even though the Party was very small. Lenin said that anyone who failed to understand the necessity of winning over the majority of the working class was lost to the

Communist movement. It was true that the Party itself in Russia was small at the time of the Revolution, he said, but the important thing to remember was that in addition to that, they had won over the majority of the Soviets of Workers' and Peasants' Deputies all over the country.

"We achieved victory in Russia," said Lenin, "not only because we had the majority of the working class on our side (during the elections in 1917 the overwhelming majority of the workers were for us and against the Mensheviks), but also half the army—immediately after we seized power—and nine-tenths of the masses of the peasantry—within the course of a few weeks—came over to our side."

Lenin proceeded to point out that the meaning of the term "masses" changes as the character of the struggle changes. There were times, he said, when the enlistment of several thousand really revolutionary workers by the side of Party members for some particular struggle meant the beginning of the process of winning the masses. But in a period when the revolution has been sufficiently prepared, a few thousand workers can no longer be called masses. "The term 'masses' then means the majority: not merely the majority of workers, but the majority of all the exploited."

Over and over again he reiterated that in order to achieve victory it was necessary to have the sympathy of the masses, of the majority of the exploited and the toiling rural population. Failure to understand and prepare for this, he explained, was the key to the weakness of the Party in many countries.

A deep impression was made on me by Lenin's insistence that we should always be ready to recognize our mistakes and learn from them how best to organize the struggle. He concluded with the words:

"We must not conceal our mistakes from the enemy. Whoever is afraid of talking openly about mistakes is not a revolutionary. If, however, we openly say to the workers: 'Yes, we have made mistakes,' it will prevent us from repeating those mistakes in the future, and we shall be better able to choose the proper time. If, during the struggle itself we shall have the masses—not only the majority of the workers, but the majority of all the exploited and oppressed—on our side, then victory will certainly be ours."

The women at the Congress, including Clara Zetkin and Alexandra Kollontai, organized a Communist Women's Conference. As the only woman from America, I represented America on the presidium. We held our conference in Sverdlov Hall, a smaller building in the Kremlin in an upper floor of which Lenin, his wife and his sister had a simple little apartment. Tremendous emotion swept the hall when a group of Mohammedan women delegates took off their veils for the first time there before us, and faced the world as free human beings. I reported on the condition of the 8,000,000 women at work in American industry, and I can remember how shocked the delegates were to learn of the extent of child labor in a developed country like ours.

It was a great privilege to work so closely with these wonderful women of our movement. Clara Zetkin, one of the outstanding members of the German Party, all her life long devoted herself especially to work among women. She was known throughout the world for her great fight against the World War. She had been a friend of Engels, and Lenin was very fond of her, and loved to talk with her. She was a fine orator, and spoke with a strong resonant voice. Though she suffered from a heart ailment, she never spared herself. I have seen her talk until she dropped unconscious. At such times her son, who was always with her, would revive her, and then she would continue. The last time I saw her was in 1929. She was already beginning to fail. She was sitting outside the door of a committee meeting, resting, and I can remember her telling me she wished that she still had the strength I had. In the last popular election in Germany before Hitler became dictator, she was elected to the Reichstag on the Communist ticket, and, as the oldest member, opened the session. Weak and frail as she was at that time, she made a powerful attack on Nazi brutality, appealing to the German people to unite against fascism. The year I was seventy, she was seventy-five, and she sent me birthday greetings. She spent her last months in the Soviet Union, where she died in June 1933.

I was very much impressed too with the brilliant and handsome Alexandra Kollontai, who had been active in the woman's movement even in pre-revolutionary days. She had been for a time People's Commissar of Social Welfare. When I first met her, she was one of the leaders of the Workers' Opposition, taking the line that the interests of the trade unions were opposed to those of the Soviet state and the Party. Lenin, to whom she was deeply devoted, convinced her of the fallacy of her position, and she abandoned her oppositionist stand, becoming a loyal supporter of the Party's position. She became Minister Plenipotentiary to Norway, the first woman ambassador in the world, was for a time ambassador to Mexico and is today Soviet Ambassador to Sweden.

One of the greatest privileges of all was meeting Nadezhda Krupskaya, Lenin's wife, one of the most selflessly devoted human beings I have ever known. She always worked closely with Lenin, helping him in all his problems, and was technical secretary of the Party's Central Committee during their days of exile, a task which involved the handling of voluminous correspondence under conspiratorial conditions, and the most exacting labor with codes. Originally a teacher, her greatest interest was always in education, and her early work in the revolutionary movement had been organizing workers' study circles. As Vice Commissar of Education, she was in charge of adult education in the U.S.S.R. She told me of the immense problem of overcoming the illiteracy inherited from the tsarist regime. On my later visits she always sent for me to ask me for ideas from America which might be useful to the Soviet educational system.

Toward the end of our visit we began to get reports of really desperate famine conditions in many sections of the country. Famine was an old story in Russia. Under the regime of the tsars, it was expected every few years. There had been terrible famines in 1891, 1906 and 1911. And then, before the young Soviet republic could organize crop production as it has now done so effectively, the partial crop failure of 1920 was followed in the summer of 1921 by one of the worst droughts in history and a complete crop failure in the main grain regions. Over thousands of miles not a stalk of wheat or rye grew to maturity. Thousands were dying of starvation, thousands were migrating to cities that could not help them.

When I was leaving Moscow to return to America, our old comrade Boris Reinstein, then doing educational work in Moscow, saw me off at the train. Reinstein had been a member of the Socialist Labor Party in the United States but had come to Russia at the time of the Revolution in 1917. He was one of the chief translators at the congresses I had attended. As we said good-bye I said to him, "Boris, you have conquered the enemies on the outside of the Soviet Union and some of the enemies inside the Soviet Union. Can you conquer famine?"

He answered, "We organized our Red Army from untrained peasant boys. They won the revolution. We have demobilized them now and sent them back to the factories, fields and workshops to build our Soviet economy." Then he said with tears of emotion running down his face, "Don't worry, they will do it. Nothing can break the Soviet Union."

12. Reaction's Roman Holiday

AFTER I returned to America in the fall of 1921, I started to raise money for famine relief, in a campaign carried on by the Friends of Soviet Russia who were at the same time pressing for recognition of the Soviet Republic. While I was campaigning in Detroit, I came down with pneumonia, and was in the hospital eight weeks. Helen and the boys came out to be with me. I was taken sick just before a mass meeting, and in my delirium kept raving about getting to the meeting on time. In the crisis, while the nurse's back was turned, I threw off the bed covers and my family were horrified to find me staggering down the hall declaring I must get to the meeting. It had taken place several days previously.

The Party sent me out to California to recuperate. Dick went along to look after me, entering the University of California. Three weeks after my arrival in California, I already felt well enough to go back to work. At the end of December, the Workers' Party was organized as the open expression of the Communist Party, driven underground by the "red raiders," and I became the first organizer of the Workers' Party in Los Angeles.

The Workers' Party was actually the American Communists' first united organization. With us joined the "Workers' Council Group," the last detachment of the left wing remaining with the old Socialist Party, the I.W.W., and most important of all, the trade union groups led by William Z. Foster, who now became one of our Party's leaders.

The California district of the Workers' Party in those days also took in Arizona, Utah and Nevada. Within a few months we had nearly 1,000 members of the Workers' Party in this region, a good basis for the growth of the Communist Party when it finally came out all the way above ground in April, 1923.

The Socialist Party, now that the last militant group had left its ranks, was greatly weakened. Debs, while not in agreement with the Socialist Party leadership in many things, had run as its candidate from prison in 1920 and received nearly a million votes (919,799). To the committee which notified him of his nomination he had said: "There is a tendency in the party to become a party of politicians instead of a party of the workers. That policy must be checked." And he declared his hearty support of the Russian Revolution, without reservations. But when he came out of prison, sixty-eight years old, and in broken health, he permitted the Socialist leaders to use him as a figurehead and failed to take the step that would have been the logical fulfillment of his life as a great revolutionist.

The Socialists were increasingly hostile to the Soviet Republic. When I first came back from my trip to Russia one of the Socialist Party leaders I met asked me for an interview. "Why yes," I told him. "I give interviews to the capitalist papers, why not to you?" I went up to the office, and there were Abe Cahan, George Goebel, Charlie Erwin and others, and all began attacking me at once. How could I support Lenin? How could I defend the "Soviets' lack of democracy"? Abe Cahan hinted that I was really too old to know what it was all about anyway. "Let's see," he said, "How many years is it now that you have been around agitating and organizing strikes?"

"Just about as long as you have, Abe Cahan," I flashed back. "It seems to me I remember that once when I was in the Socialist Party I had a birthday, and when we compared notes, we turned out to be the same age. So I guess that makes us both 59 today, which I for one don't consider too old to keep on fighting for what I believe in!"

Abe Cahan had left Russia as a boy to escape tsarist persecution. But instead of hailing the success of his Russian brothers, he had turned against them and not only would not listen to my reports of their achievements, but himself became one of the most vicious of anti-Soviet slanderers, vying with Hearst in publishing articles by renegades and reactionaries in his paper *The Forward*.

In June, 1922, I happened to be in Southern Illinois when the miners of the state went out on strike. I had been making speeches on the Russian Revolution among the miners and raising money. I was in Ziegler, Illinois, when suddenly word came that they were trying to open a big strip mine at Herrin, about 100 miles away. The United Mine Workers had Illinois 100 per cent organized. Until that time there had been no scabs in the Illinois mines.

We got the news in Ziegler that the scabs who were trying to work the strip mine at Herrin had been employed by a strike-breaker who had also been active in the Calumet strike, and was known and hated all over the mining regions. He had gotten thugs from several big cities to come to this little coal camp to break the strike. As soon as the miners heard this, camp after camp mobilized.

The men from Ziegler stopped in every mining camp along the way, picked up more men, and marched on to Herrin, determined to save the strike at all costs. When they got to Herrin they were greeted warmly. Long tables were set in the street, where supper was ready for them. The mayor and the sheriff of the town had been miners themselves. The miners were told to go on and drive the thugs out. The men slept at Herrin that night, and started out fresh the next morning to the strip mine.

When they arrived they found the superintendent had rallied his foremen in a two-story office building. They were on the second floor porch while the heavily armed thugs were barricaded behind a wall of solid earth that had been scooped up by a steam shovel.

The union men elected a committee of five trusted miners, with a young miner whose father was well known all over the state as chairman. He led the committee towards the office carrying a white handkerchief on a stick.

The young man began to read the demands, the main one being that every scab should be over the state border inside of two hours. As the young man read, the foremen and the thugs shouted and hooted. Baffled, he turned to consult his committee, and as he turned, the men on the porch fired down into the committee and the young man fell dead.

In a spontaneous outburst of rank-and-file workers to defend their own people, the miners began shooting with a few old rusty guns they had gathered up. In two seconds, the superintendent had paid for the boy's life. Then the miners turned their attention to the scabs, who were paralyzed with fright. They were told to get out of the state. Some ran away. Those who did not were shot down. No one in the county would take care of the remains of the dead scabs. These were not ordinary working men who become scabs through weakness. They were thugs and hired murderers.

The strike leaders were arrested and tried. Public opinion put the blame for the shootings squarely on the mine superintendent. At the first trial, the jury could not agree. They could not get a jury willing to hang those fellows. The second trial also resulted in a hung jury. The men were freed. A state-wide contract was won, and it was years before thugs were again employed.

One reason the Herrin strikers had so much protection was because the town of Herrin was one of the most strongly organized union towns in the state. Not only the miners but machinists, electricians, carpenters, bricklayers, everybody belonged to a union. No one would wear a garment without a union label.

The California membership elected me as a delegate to a national convention of the Workers' Party to be held in Chicago in the summer of 1922. The great national strike of 400,000 railroad shopmen was then in full swing, and on my way I made stopovers wherever I could be useful to the strikers. One night, in Salt Lake City, I went out to the picket line with the strike captain and saw the strikers pull a very clever trick. A lot of scabs were working at the round house, under police guard. The strikers prepared a dummy and took it to one of the entrances. As the scabs started coming out after work the strikers started pummeling the dummy around. All the police rushed down to that gate. This gave the strikers a chance to grab the scabs coming out of the other gates, pile them into cars, and take them fifty miles out into the desert and leave them there. No violence was done to anything but the dummy, but it was much harder to get scabs after that. One of my brothers, a manufacturer of medical supplies, was living in Salt Lake City then. He told me most of the businessmen in the town were sympathetic to the strikers because they hated the railroads. They had organized a commissary department, and helped feed the strikers. My brother drove me around in his car and went out with me to the picket line.

In St. Louis, I met Bill Foster, and we spoke together at a strike meeting of the railroad shop men. When we took our seats on the platform, we saw about a dozen policemen in front of us looking very tough. I made it my special business to address them in a sympathetic manner, telling them I was sorry they had to work overtime, that some day when I had more time I might return and organize them into a policemen's union. When the collection was taken, some of these cops contributed.

In Minneapolis, we had tremendous meetings. The T.U.E.L., of which Foster was national secretary, played an important role in this strike. Their call for a general strike of all workers to smash the Daugherty federal injunction was endorsed in 200 railroad centers. This strike might indeed have been won had all of the railroad workers come out. But their leaders betrayed them. Grabie, president of the Maintenance of Way workers, ignored their strike vote, and kept them at work. The strike was finally broken by a separate settlement with the Baltimore and Ohio railroad which involved acceptance of the B. & O. Plan.

When I finally reached Chicago, I was informed that I was elected as a delegate representing both the Kansas and California state party organizations to the "underground" convention of the Communist Party at Bridgman, Michigan. The convention was raided when its whereabouts were revealed by a stool pigeon, Francis E. Morrow. Eighteen of our people were arrested on the spot, but I managed to get away with some of the others before the Red Squad arrived. Thirty-two of us were indicted for violating the criminal syndicalism law of Michigan.

While I was staying with comrades in Chicago, the Chicago *Tribune* came out with the announcement that Ella Reeve Bloor was in town, and "they expected to get her before night." The next morning I got up early, went to the grocery store, bought a little lunch, and, without any baggage, took a trolley to Galesburg, Illinois. There I bought a nurse's outfit, a suitcase, a long coat and a sailor hat, and went to St. Louis to the home of a good comrade there who was ill with cancer. I knew he was planning to go to Vienna to have an operation, and my idea was to go along as his nurse.

The comrade in St. Louis was very ill and could not travel. But he was in close touch with all that had happened. "You must get out of St. Louis at once," he told me. "They raided the Workers' Party office yesterday and they are after everybody."

A girl comrade went with me to the railroad station and bought me a ticket to New York. I stayed out of sight until the train came along. Arriving in New York at midnight, I went right to Helen's studio where Carl was also staying.

Carl exclaimed, "I thought you were arrested long ago from the telegrams we have been getting in the *Tribune* office from Chicago."

The next morning Carl went out to get something for breakfast. When he came back he said, "Mom, you will have to get out of here quick. There are two dicks watching the house."

The detectives hung around all day, but some of the comrades arranged to get me away. About seven o'clock, a woman comrade, who was about my size, came in, and gave me her hat and coat to put on. I went downstairs where another comrade was waiting for me with a taxicab. We drove for hours, or so it seemed, then changed cabs and finally went to a comrade's apartment, where I stayed for two weeks.

Four months after the Bridgman convention, in December 1922, the Workers' Party met in a national convention in New York City, united all elements, and adopted a constructive program. This convention authorized the central executive committee to take all necessary steps to protect foreign-born workers, and to develop an energetic campaign against the imperialism of the United States in all its manifestations. A special resolution on the Negro question called for complete legal, economic, and social equality. This convention called for the liberation of all class war prisoners and recognition of the Soviet Republic by the United States.

I went to Russia in September, 1922, as a delegate from the Central Labor Council of Minneapolis to the Second Red International Labor Union Congress. This was a large convention, made up of all kinds of unions, a real united front, achieved despite Samuel Gompers' threat to take away the charters of the unions that sent delegates. There were delegates present from the Central Labor Councils of Seattle and Detroit, showing the effect of the first congress on the trade unions of America.

The change in Russia since the year before was amazing. In spite of the terrible burden of famine that had been piled on top of all their other difficulties, and the armed intervention that had continued until the fall of 1922 when the Japanese were finally driven out of the Soviet Far East—there was already a strong sense of revival and growth. The gaping sidewalks were repaired, panes were in the broken windows, stuffed with paper and rags the year before. Houses were repainted and new construction was going on. Stores and restaurants were operating. Theatres and operas were flourishing—although that, of course, had been true even in the darkest days. Everyone was working, building, study-ing. Though food from abroad had saved many lives in the famine districts, no help for economic reconstruction had come, instead, the rest of the world had striven to prevent the existence and growth of the socialist state.

The economic revival was of course due to the unity and will of the Soviet people, directed by the Party leaders. The New Eco-nomic Policy worked out as Lenin had foreseen. He had been opposed by ultra-leftist elements, who saw the NEP as a renunci-ation of the gains of the Revolution; and by rightist elements who, never having had faith in the working class, had never believed in the possibility of building socialism, and so wanted to see much more far-reaching concessions to private capital. Now, a year and a half later, the results proved how correct Lenin was.

At the Fourth Congress of the Communist International which was held at that time, Lenin reported that the peasants had not only overcome the famine, but had paid their food tax to the government with practically no measures of coercion. Such up-risings as had occurred up to 1921 had ceased; the peasants were now satisfied. Lenin stressed over and over again that the peas-antry was a decisive factor in Russia. Lenin also reported a general revival in light industry and great improvements in the conditions of the Petrograd and Moscow workers. The situation in heavy industry, however, remained grave, although some improvement could be seen. "In order to put heavy industry in good condition," he said, "many years of work will be required" and he urged great economy in all things to provide a basis for heavy industry, on which all industry depended and the country's independence itself.

Lenin had been seriously ill from after effects of the wounds he had received in August, 1918, when the Socialist-Revolutionary Dora Kaplan had tried to assassinate him; but he spoke strongly and clearly, and we all rejoiced that he could be with us again.

During this period in Moscow I met many young Americans who had come over to help in famine relief and reconstruction work. Not only the Russians themselves, but groups from other countries had done heroic work in the famine regions in distributing food and clothing and helping to establish homes for the orphans of the civil war and famine. Hoover's organization, the American Relief Administration, had helped save many lives. Hoover himself had no love for the Soviet Union, and had formerly tried to use relief activities to overthrow the Bolsheviks. But the conditions under which their work was accepted by the Soviet Government made further such attempts impossible. Associated with this organization were many fine young people. Of special importance was the work of the American Quakers, whose American Friends' Service Committee had raised a lot of money and sent over a group of people to distribute food and clothing, many of whom we met in Moscow. One of the first Americans to go down into the famine district was Anna Louise Strong, who ever since has spent most of her time in the Soviet Union and through her writing and lecturing has contributed so much toward greater understanding of the Soviet Union in America.

Some American trade unions and the American Friends of Soviet Russia had raised large sums of money. One of their special contributions was the tractor unit headed by my son Hal. He was at a party Anna Louise and I gave in our rooms, to which we invited a lot of Americans as well as Russian friends. Hal was shy at first meeting all these strangers, but before long, almost everyone in the room had gathered around Hal, firing questions at him about Soviet farming conditions and the practical technical help he was giving; and his clear intelligent answers and the accounts of his experiences kept them absorbed all evening.

One night after a group of us had been to hear a beautiful performance of the opera "Carmen," I was walking along the hotel corridor to my room when I heard someone shouting, "Where is Comrade Bloor?", and running along the hall toward me I saw my great friend Santeri Nuorteva, whom I had known in America, where he had been the first Soviet representative, and Martin Anderson Nexö, the great Danish writer, their arms full of big loaves of steaming brown bread. They had just gotten these loaves right out of the bakery oven, and would I please make some coffee for them—they knew I had a "primus" in my room. We sat there talking almost the whole night.

Nexö was such a simple and natural person, he could never endure to have any special attention paid to him because of his fame. I have never known a jollier, better natured person. His great novel, *Pelle the Conqueror,* had long been one of my favorites, with its wit and warmth and great human understanding. I asked him whether he had actually seen the "arks" described in Pelle, great tenement houses overflowing with poverty-stricken human beings. "Yes, I have seen them," he said, "my dear comrade, how can anyone escape seeing them? There are too many such arks in the world—we must try to get rid of them everywhere as they are doing here." Nexö's books were very widely read in Russia. He was dumbfounded when he arrived there to find large royalties waiting for him in the bank. He turned over all the money at once to a Children's Home in Samara.

After my return to the United States, in the early spring of 1923, the seventeen of us who had been indicted went down to St. Joseph, Michigan, the day Foster's trial opened and told an astonished magistrate we wanted to give ourselves up and plead "not guilty."

We secured the necessary bail, and that left us free to attend Foster's trial, the first to come up on the false charge of "assembling with persons who advocated the overthrow of the government." The detectives, who had been looking for us everywhere, were infuriated to see us walk calmly in and take our seats. During the interrogation of the jurors, we noticed a nice looking Swedish woman among them. Foster said to me, "I am afraid of that woman; her husband is a leading business man here; she has sons in the army, and she is apparently conservative." But all our challenges had been used up. So she was accepted as a juror. It turned out that this Swedish woman hung the jury. She did not believe Foster guilty. "The evidence shows he is a good man," she declared. "Everything he said and did showed he worked for humanity." Foster was discharged on bail.

When Ruthenberg was tried on the same charge, he took advantage of the opportunity to make a strong statement on the meaning of socialism. Ruthenberg made it clear that Communists do not stand for force and violence, but they know that when the capitalist class senses that the majority of workers and farmers decide to secure relief from exploitation, "the capitalists, in the final struggle, will resort to force to protect their privileged position and maintain their power to exploit the workers and farmers. . . ."

Despite his magnificent refutation of the charges, Ruthenberg was found guilty and sentenced to from five to ten years in prison. The case was appealed to the United States Supreme Court, and was still pending when his death in 1927 removed him from their jurisdiction.

After the Foster and Ruthenberg trials, I went all over the country, among the miners of Indiana and Illinois especially, who were working at that time, and raised nearly $30,000 for the defense of the Bridgman victims, among the miners' locals.

There had to be a legislative act to take the Bridgman case off the docket of the state of Michigan. This was finally accomplished through the devoted efforts of our lawyer, who after eleven years succeeded in having all the cases dismissed.

During this period I served as national organizer of the International Labor Defense. One of our major cases then was the Centralia case. The persecution of the I.W.W. had been intense throughout the West, and the Lumbermen's Association attempted to smash the I.W.W. in Washington, where they were very strong. At a Red Cross parade in April, 1918, a raving mob had demolished the I.W.W. headquarters, placed ropes around the necks of the loggers, some of whom were dumped into jail, some carried across the county line.

On Armistice Day, November 11, 1919, the I.W.W. boys were dedicating a new hall. Outside, the American Legion and other patriots were holding a parade. At a pre-arranged signal the paraders suddenly swept toward the I.W.W. headquarters, smashed the door in, some of them entering with ropes in their hands. The I.W.W. boys had legal advice that it was quite lawful to defend their hall against attack. Bullets from within halted the mob, killing two of the raiders and wounding several. The raiders forced their way in, seized all the workers there but Wesley Everest, who managed to break through the door and head for the river. Everest had fought courageously in the World War, and was said to have won more medals than the celebrated Sergeant York. He had come back to help the lumber workers get better conditions. Now he was running toward the river for his life, the bullets of the mob whistling around him. The river was too deep to ford, so seeing his position was hopeless Everest offered to surrender to any lawful authority. They paid no attention, but rushed on, firing as they came. Then he started shooting back, and with his last bullet, shot Dale Hubbard, nephew of the chief plotter against the I.W.W.'s. The mob tortured Everest, and threw him into jail. That night the lights of the city were suddenly extinguished, and an unresisted mob broke into the jail and dragged Everest out. They took him to the Chealis River, and as the city lights came on again, hung him from the bridge. He did not die at once, so they hauled him back, and flung him over a second time. The automobile lights showed unspeakable mutilations on his body. They riddled him with bullets, then cut the body loose to fall in the river. It was later hauled out and taken back to the jail and exhibited to Everest's fellow workers.

In the reign of terror that followed, over a thousand were arrested, some for having newspapers giving a true account of these events. Union halls were closed down, labor papers suppressed. A group seized at the Centralia hall were tried at Montesano, with the cards stacked against them. Of the eleven men tried, Eugene Barnett, John Lamb, Britt Smith, Bert Bland, Commodore Bland, Roy Becker and John McInerny were found guilty of second degree murder and, despite a jury recommendation of clemency, given the maximum sentence of from 25 to 40 years in Walla Walla prison. Two were acquitted. Nineteen-year-old Loren had been driven insane by torture. A "labor jury" representing

A. F. of L. unions in the state attended the trial and adjudged the men not guilty. Five of the regular jurymen later signed affidavits that the sentence was unjust. The I.L.D. and other labor organizations fought vigorously in their defense. Their freedom was finally won ten years later.

The Seattle branch of the I.L.D., which I was working with during 1923 and 1924, did everything it could to help them. Hearing the keeper was giving everything we sent them to the regular criminals—to the thieves and murderers—I went down and interviewed him and raised a big fuss. We finally got better conditions for them. Our lawyer Elmer Smith, who lived in Centralia, became so deeply involved in the case that they went after him, too. He was arrested on the charge of being an "accessory."

In later years, Elmer Smith joined our movement. He died not long ago.

Learning that the Centralia victims were cold in Walla Walla, which was way up in the mountains, Charlotte Todes, then living in Seattle writing her book *Labor and Lumber,* and I canvassed Seattle. For the fourteen men in jail whom we were looking after, we got two suits of heavy underwear apiece, lumber jackets and long woolen stockings and mittens. I brought the box to the prison but the warden refused to let the men have the things. I insisted on seeing the boys anyway, and was taken into the reception room and one by one they came in the door. When I told them their friends had sent them underwear but that the warden would not let them have it, they said, "Mother, we will tell you what to do. You are going to Chicago. Why not take it to the Illinois mine strikers as a gift from us?"

I carried the huge box to Illinois and the miners, who had been on strike for a long time, were deeply appreciative of this wonderful gift direct from the boys in prison.

I often visited Tom Mooney when I was on the Coast and organized a big Mooney conference in San Francisco, attended by many trade unions. Each time I visited Mooney, I took four or five young people with me. One would send in a request for John

B. McNamara, another for Matthew Schmidt, etc. Then I would ask for Tom Mooney and we would all sit together along the line and talk together. We had many wonderful conferences there. Mooney was nearly always cheerful but I used to fear sometimes when I saw his pallor that he would never come out alive. I feel very happy now that he is well and useful and free.

13. Hitch-hiker, Sixty-three Years Old

EARLY in 1923, the Workers' Party was already functioning as a political party and by the end of the year we were all the way above ground, as the Communist Party. The Party had gone a long way in getting rid of its sectarianism. The affiliation with it of the T.U.E.L. forces led by Foster had brought the Party into mass actions. A big drive was on for industrial unionism, for a labor party, and for recognition of Soviet Russia. Militant elements in the unions had organized into the "Conference for Progressive Political Action," and so formed a basis for our first united front work. Large masses of workers began to rally behind the T.U.E.L., and the prospects for a real Labor Party looked bright.

But now we faced new difficulties. The year 1923 marked the beginning of the "Coolidge prosperity" period. The United States was pulling out of its post-war depression, and cashing in on captured new markets. Transformed from a debtor to a creditor nation, we were exporting huge quantities of capital. Industry was booming, and the owners started on the maddest scramble for profits in history, at the expense, as always, of the workers. The workers were tricked into accepting speed-up and rationalization plans by bonus and welfare systems, profit-sharing and so on. A new school of economists preached a gospel of high wages, with which the workers were gradually to buy themselves into partnership with the bosses. A lot of Socialists fell for this sort of thing. Actually, of course, real wages advanced very little dur-

193

ing this period, those of unskilled workers hardly at all. But the illusions of prosperity dangled before the workers sapped their militancy, and union morale fell very low.

This class collaboration policy just suited the A. F. of L. leadership. At their 1923 convention in Portland the A. F. of L. enthusiastically endorsed the Baltimore and Ohio R.R. plan whereby the unions, in return for recognition, carried out the owners' plans of speed-up, reducing production costs and even getting rid of undesirable workers and suspending union rules. In the growing corruption of the trade union bureaucracy, gangster methods were used to get rid of the militant opposition. The Labor Party movement eventually fizzled out in the fiasco of the LaFollette Progressive Party.

All this combined slowed down the work of the T.U.E.L. and it became somewhat isolated from the masses. Our Party, too, found itself in an isolated position. It now had the additional handicap of the fierce factional struggle which sapped its strength from 1923 to 1929. But through these years of struggle a strong core of real leadership was developing and the membership as a whole was getting a deeper grasp both of revolutionary theory and of the practical problems of the American movement.

Since the possibility of mass action was limited during this period I devoted my energies, in addition to the defense work, to trying to spread knowledge of our movement, through our Party paper, the *Daily Worker,* established the year before. I thought it would be a good idea for me to go by train from coast to coast, stopping off and getting subscriptions for the paper on the way. But the Party did not have the funds.

Therefore, I volunteered, in the summer of 1925, to hitch-hike across the country, from California to New York, having bundles of the paper sent me for distribution at each stop. I guaranteed that the Party would not have to pay anything for transportation, only for meals and lodging. I felt that if I could do this at my age (I was now 63) it might be an example to some of the younger comrades to save train fares for the Party.

My plan was accepted. A comrade drove me out to the edge

of Berkeley, California, where I stood by the roadside carrying only a brief-case. On the side of it was painted "From Coast to Coast for the *Daily Worker*." I must say I felt a little shaky and wondered what was ahead.

A man in a big car who gave me a lift to the Vallejo Ferry, looked me over and asked "Where are you bound?" "New York," I told him. He kept on staring and finally remarked: "Well, it takes all kinds of people to make the world, and I guess you are one of them."

I made Sacramento by 9 o'clock at night and got a room in a hotel. The next morning I got a ride from Sacramento to the foot of the Sierra Nevada mountains, the highest range in California. The mountain passes had only just been opened for travel, and there were still icy stretches of road. I saw a middle-aged man driving along, and learning that he was going over the Truckee Pass all the way to Reno, I got in. We climbed up and up into the high Sierra Nevadas, looking down thousands of feet to the tree tops below.

At Reno I went right to the post office and to my amazement found a card from my son Dick, whom I had left behind in Berkeley. It said, "I am at the Y.M.C.A. and have arranged a meeting for you there."

Understanding how much the success of this trip meant to me, he had taken a train ahead to Reno, knowing it to be a hard nut to crack. There was only a skeleton of a Party organization there. Some workers and farmers came to the meeting—a small group who had been consistent Socialists and later became Communists. I got some subscriptions to the *Daily Worker,* and later did some house to house canvassing, as I did everywhere.

The next morning, Dick said "good-bye" looking rather sad to leave his "little old mother" heading toward the lonely desert. I had been warned only to take a lift going the entire way across, and not to fall in with some prospector who might dump me in the middle of the desert. Luckily an agricultural agent came along who drove me to a nice little town where a comrade had arranged a meeting for me in a medicine show tent right on the edge of the desert. I got a number of subs there and travelled on across the Nevada desert, stopping wherever there was a little oasis and town, often having to wait nearly all day for a ride.

Barren and desolate, Nevada seemed all the lonelier because of the remnants of past grandeur in some of the deserted little mining towns, where fortunes had once been made over night from mines now abandoned, and where just a few stranded people remained.

At a little oasis near where the "Covered Wagon" had been filmed, the only place to stay was a cabin in the desert with a little restaurant attached, where a young couple lived—the man had tuberculosis. I waited there all that afternoon, and all night, but no car came by. Then, as they asked a high price for meals, I determined to start out into the desert the next morning, looking back for landmarks in order not to lose my way. After I had gone several miles, I came to a little house with children playing in the yard, and a forlorn looking woman leaning over the gate. She looked me all over. I must have appeared strange indeed to her—a white-haired woman in high boots and breeches, carrying a brief case.

She asked me what I was doing. I told her "I am going from coast to coast for a labor paper." And as she looked puzzled, I went on, "You see, I am working for the labor movement..."

"Oh," she interrupted, "don't do that. There is too much labor in the world already."

She was the wife of a smelter worker near Ely, Nevada, where it was impossible to bring up children because of the poisonous smelter fumes. So they had built this little place in the desert and her husband came to see her once in two or three months when he could get away.

I really felt scared when I left that little house behind. It was astonishing how far I could see when I looked into the broad expanse ahead of me—where an unbroken sea of gray sage and golden rabbit brush swept on for miles and miles to the foot of the next mountain range. I learned to love my trips across the deserts more than almost all the other experiences of my trips.

But I love the Southern deserts best—there is something warm about the yellow Arizona desert soil, while the Nevada desert is lonesome and terrifying, for all its lovely colors.

At last a young man came along, driving an old Chevrolet. He cheerfully offered me a ride and told me that he had been all the way to California looking for a job as carpenter. Arriving in California, he found a telegram from his home town in Utah that a new courthouse was being built there and a job was waiting for him. So he had turned right around and was retracing his route. He drove me all day and that night I stopped at a hotel. The next morning he called for me and took me as far as his home town in Utah.

By a succession of such lifts, I reached Salt Lake City, where the comrades had arranged a nice meeting for me, and where I saw my capitalist brother whom I had not seen since the 1922 railroad strike. He was horrified that I was hitch-hiking. When I left his home, his wife drove me forty miles on my way. I got rides with all kinds of people, canvassing and holding meetings at every stop. I always tried, when possible, to ride with workers who stop for hitch-hikers more readily than people in swanky cars. At one point I got a lift in an old Model T Ford. I told the two men in it who, in their blue shirts, appeared to be railroad workers, that I was always especially glad to ride with workers. But I couldn't get them interested in what I was doing. After hearing a little of their conversation, I soon gathered that they were bootleggers and had a cargo aboard, and I made an excuse to get out at the next town.

Going to Rock Springs, Wyoming, after crossing the Continental Divide from Utah, we went through the Alkali Desert, where the air is heavy with the alkali dust that gets in your throat and it is impossible to get water fit to drink. Riding with a man and his daughter, I noticed that he did not seem to be able to judge distances well, nor to avoid bad spots in the road. We had some terrific bumps and several narrow escapes. When they left me, the daughter asked me: "Don't you think father drives very well, considering he only has one eye?"

At Rock Springs the next night we had a mass meeting of the miners at their union hall. I always got a warm welcome from the miners because I could show them my union card in the United Mine Workers of America. The following morning a Finnish comrade took me about thirty miles over the hills and mountains on my way to Colorado. There the Denver comrades had put up a *Daily Worker* booth at a big fair held by the Central Labor Council, and were eagerly awaiting me. I stood in front of the booth in my hitch-hiking costume, and sold many papers.

The rest of my route included stop-overs in Kansas City, Mo., Chicago, Dayton and other points in Ohio, then Pittsburgh and Philadelphia, winding up in New York.

I came back with a new knowledge of our country and its people, a new determination to work with all my strength so that this great and beautiful land of ours might one day belong to the people themselves. I had seen so many lonely and poor and dispossessed living bereft in the midst of untold riches. Coolidge "prosperity" was now in full swing, and many industries were booming. But new machinery and rationalization systems were filling the roads with people passing back and forth looking for jobs. On this trip I got to know the great, rich fellowship of the open road, and experienced the great kindness of people everywhere to hitch-hikers. I found thousands of people all over the country hungry for the message the *Daily Worker* brought them.

I arrived in New York on the day that the S.S. *Majestic,* with a load of scabs, was coming into port, during a marine workers' strike, and the Party and the *Daily Worker* offices were humming with excitement. All the people who could be mustered were going down with banners to meet the ship when it came in. I joined the group leaving from the office, still wearing my hiking clothes. Morris Hillquit was arriving on that ship. We carried a banner greeting him: "Morris Hillquit, why did you come back on a scab ship?" The Socialists, there to meet him, were horrified when they saw our banners, and smuggled Hillquit out by a side door of the pier. The police came but did not arrest us because we just stood outside the dock entrance singing solidarity songs at the top of our lungs so the sailors would hear us. Many marine workers joined in this picketing.

After the demonstration, I went back and reported on my trip. The *Daily Worker* office was delighted with the large number of subscriptions I had secured on the road.

Soon after this, all over the country, there was a stir among the radical textile workers' organizations to organize the industry. Of its million workers only about five per cent were organized in the North, and none in the South. The industry was in a state of depression due to over-production. There was much unemployment and wages were very low. The principal union of the textile workers was the A. F. of L. United Textile Workers' Union, but there were also several independent organizations. The union leadership had fallen in with the current class collaboration program and, instead of trying to organize the unorganized workers, actually helped the employers in their speed-up schemes. There was a lot of militancy among the rank and file, where the T. U. E. L. had been doing good work. It now proposed a united front among the various unions to prepare the way for amalgamation, and to organize the unorganized. It set up united front committees in the mills, which were merged into a "United Front Committee of Textile Workers," to carry on organizational work.

I went to Lawrence to organize such a United Front Committee. I found the workers there, who were of many different nationalities, very militant indeed, and we succeeded in organizing large numbers of them. The American Woolen Company, where a militant group of Franco-Belgian workers were employed, was determined not to have its workers organized, but we flooded the whole mill with propaganda and got a lot of members.

Although it was winter, I held many successful open-air meetings in front of the mills. Every day I went to the entrance, spread newspapers out on the snow and talked to the workers as they came out. We also had meetings in halls, and finally the whole town was stirred up by the organization spirit.

A Passaic textile workers' paper, edited by Margaret Larkin and for which that fine labor journalist, Mary Heaton Vorse, wrote, kept the organizers and workers in the various textile regions in touch with each other. George Siskind, who had come to help me, always went with me to the American Woolen Co. mills to distribute the paper to the workers coming out. As soon as they spied us coming, the workers came rushing over us like a wave, they were so eager for the papers.

When the mill owners saw we meant business they organized company unions. In the Pacific Mill we encountered a particularly tough proposition. The 600 workers we had organized there exerted a strong influence on the others, but this was partially counteracted by the fact that trained, skilled spies, imported by the mill owners from the Thiel detective agency, had managed to get into official positions in our union. We discovered that the president of our union was a member of the company union and was acting as a spy.

Finally, with the help of Johnny Ballam who had been in Lawrence before organizing textile workers, we worked out a plan to revise the constitution of the United Front Committee prohibiting any company union member from being an official of our organization.

This new provision was fought bitterly, but a large majority of the workers were with us. The show-down meeting was held in our hall, rented by officials who also belonged to the company union, although the chairs and equipment belonged to us. Our first test of strength was on the nominations for chairman. Having been elected some weeks before by the union as their organizer, I was no longer an "outsider." There were two nominations, a Thiel man put up by the company union men in our organization, and I. The opposition tried to break up the meeting. Expecting trouble, we had husky men posted beside Johnny, the secretary of the union, and myself. The adoption of the constitution went smoothly enough until we came to the provision that no member of the company union could hold office. Then there was a general uproar. When the new constitution was adopted by a very large majority vote, the stool pigeons and company union men, realizing that they had no more power in our union, all got up and went down the stairs, threatening to come back and take our hall from us.

An Italian hall in another part of the city offered us the use of their hall and offices, so we hastily removed all our furniture and supplies and the company union was left with an empty hall.

Meanwhile, the big Passaic strike involving over 15,000 workers was on. In January, 1926, the U. F. C. members had been discharged by the Botany Mills for presenting demands for rescinding a five per cent wage cut, time-and-a-half for overtime and no discrimination against union workers. The other workers in that mill struck, and the strike spread to other mills. The workers carried on the strike with great heroism and unity against the bosses' efforts to break it through the courts, the police, and all kinds of terrorism.

This was the first mass strike under Communist leadership. Alfred Wagenknecht organized an extensive relief set-up. While the A. F. of L. leadership was hostile, a number of their locals cooperated very well. Bakers' Union men took turns each week baking bread for the strikers. Every morning early, their trucks could be seen going over the ferry from New York to Passaic, filled with bread for the strikers.

A big national relief campaign was started and I was assigned the task of raising funds. Since most of the weavers were women one of our jobs was to organize groups of women sympathizers. I cooperated with Elizabeth Gurley Flynn and other women organizers in organizing the care of the 1,000 or so strikers' children who had to be provided with sandwiches and milk every day.

I took strikers with me on tours to Buffalo, Cleveland, Cincinnati, and other large cities, and raised thousands of dollars for the strikers and to keep the children fed. In Passaic itself, in spite of the police persecution, we managed to hold many large meetings in a big roofless enclosure back of a beer garden. I spoke there to as many as 11,000 people at a time. Even newspaper men were maltreated by the police—films were destroyed, reporters beaten up. But we succeeded in getting a good seven-reel motion picture taken, with actual photographs of tear gas bombing by the police, which I showed in several cities, arousing a lot of public sympathy for the strike.

When after six months the bosses were unable to break the strike, they tried the maneuver of offering to deal with the strikers if they would get rid of the Communist leadership and join the U. T. W. The workers decided to call the bosses' bluff, since they did not wish to block a settlement. Strike leaders who were Party members were withdrawn, and the workers affiliated with the U. T. W. The employers then refused to deal with the U. T. W., and the strike continued under Party leadership, as the U. T. W. did nothing.

In December, after eleven months of struggle, the Botany Mills accepted the union demands, restored the wage cut, agreed not to discriminate against union members and to recognize the grievance committee, and the other mills soon followed. The victory was only partial, because the U. T. W. leadership failed to follow up the strike with any organizational campaign. But the strike strengthened the resistance of textile workers everywhere, and developed in Passaic a strong corps of revolutionary workers with a new conception of the meaning of the class struggle politically as well as industrially.

Following the settlement of the Passaic strike, I was working in California for the I. L. D. on cases of class-war prisoners, arrested in demonstrations of the unemployed before courthouses asking for food; and of agricultural workers from a flareup of spontaneous strikes. Then, on April 9, 1927, the news was flashed across the world that Sacco and Vanzetti had been sentenced to death.

Nicola Sacco and Bartolomeo Vanzetti were two Italian immigrants who, like many others, had followed a dream to America—

a dream of freer and more spacious life for themselves and for their fellow-men. Both had arrived in America in 1908, although they did not meet for several years. Both had found bitter disillusionment in the "land of the free," where wages were low and jobs scarce and indignities heaped on "dago" laborers. But they were young and vigorous and earnest, and they both sought the answer to the inequalities and injustices they found in place of the freedom they sought. They became part of a loosely knit organization of Italian immigrants grouped around the anarchist Luigi Galleani. Sacco had become a skilled shoe worker and took part in the workers' struggles for better conditions. He married Rosina, a pretty North Italian girl, and they named their first child Dante. Vanzetti had finally found work in a cordage factory in Plymouth. More studious than Sacco, and with no family to look after, he did an immense amount of reading, and spoke and wrote for the labor movement. His health having been undermined by long years of work under unbearable conditions, in the spring of 1919 he bought out the equipment of a fish peddler so he could work in the open air. Not long after occurred the wave of red raids and deportations I have described in another chapter. Galleani was deported with many of his followers.

To Sacco's bungalow, where he tended his garden after the long day's work, came Vanzetti and their other friends to discuss the tragic fate of many of their comrades. When the Department of Justice attempt to force confessions about a bomb plot from two innocent Italians ended in Andrea Salsedo's death plunge from a Park Row building, and Robert Elia's hasty deportation, the Italian colony decided to hold a protest meeting at which Vanzetti was to speak. They arranged with a friend, Mike Boda, to use his dilapidated car to take their books and literature to a safe place.

Meantime there had been a wave of unsolved payroll robberies in that part of Massachusetts, and Chief of Police Michael Stewart needed to make an arrest for the sake of his reputation. Boda, under suspicion as a radical, was chosen as victim. Stewart asked the garage owner to report when Boda called for his car. When

Sacco and Vanzetti came to get the car they fell into the trap prepared for Boda. Already marked themselves as radicals, they served Stewart's purpose equally well and were charged with the murder of a paymaster and his guard at Bridgewater, Massachusetts, in the theft of a $15,000 pay-roll.

In Vanzetti's case a previous pay-roll robbery charge was trumped up against him, so that he came to trial as a convicted thief. Both men had air-tight alibis. Defense witnesses proved that Vanzetti was selling eels at the time of both crimes, far from the place where they were committed. Sacco had the testimony of an official of the Italian Consulate to prove that he was in Boston that day. But Judge Thayer, disregarding this evidence, practically instructed the jury to accept the case framed up by the prosecution, which the defense was not permitted to show was false, and these two fine workers, who hated violence and loved their fellow-men, were sentenced to die.

For seven long years these two innocent men had been in jail, while one appeal after another for a new trial was denied by Judge Thayer. Through all those years a steady mass protest had swelled throughout the world at the unjust verdict. The I. L. D. worked steadily to prove them innocent. We felt that Sacco and Vanzetti meetings should be held all over the country in a last effort to save their lives. I decided on another hitch-hike, because there wasn't enough money to send me across the country in any other way.

14. Sacco-Vanzetti

THIS hitch-hike for Sacco and Vanzetti was over different terri-
tory, in part, from the first one. I left San Francisco early in the
spring of 1927, went southward through the orange country, stopping at Los Angeles and other southern cities.

Just outside of Los Angeles I got a ride from a well-fed looking
man in a big car. I told him I was working for a newspaper and
was on my way to New York.

He informed me he was the president of the Chamber of
Commerce of Azuza, California. I began to rave about California's
climate and its wonderful orange groves. Finally he said. "You are
a very good talker. Have you a contract with your people?"

"Oh, yes, I have a contract." I did not tell him it was a contract
for life. He offered me fifty dollars a week to lecture for the local
Chambers of Commerce about the climate and the crops.

Crossing the Yuma Desert, one of the hottest in the country,
I got a ride with a poor man in an open Ford truck. The water
we carried with us was almost at the boiling point, so I got some
oranges and gave the driver a slice every little while. He had a
little pet dog which he kept in his shade all the time so it would
not get overheated. But I sweltered.

But the desert was beautiful, and I loved the bright golden days
and clear starry nights in Arizona. The Painted Desert, not far
from the Grand Canyon, is usually considered the most beautiful,
but I preferred the desert between Phoenix and Tucson where

the giant cacti stand like sentinels with arms outstretched, and the ground is carpeted with flowers. One of the greatest compensations for my hard organizing work was sleeping out in the desert under the stars.

In Phoenix I learned that the American Legion had succeeded in getting the permit for our meeting in the park revoked. But we held the meeting anyway nearby. I renewed many old acquaintances, meeting many charter members of the Party whom I had recruited six years before when I was district organizer of California. There was rising indignation everywhere over the case of Sacco and Vanzetti.

From Prescott, Arizona, where I arrived flat broke and went hungry till evening when funds arrived, a good-natured looking German farmer gave me a lift to Flagstaff. He was going to the copper mines of Jerome, Arizona, to see if he could get a job for the summer.

We drove on for fifty miles through the most beautiful mountain scenery I had ever seen, to the foot of a terrible mountain road which seemed to go straight up. An old native at the foot of the mountain said it used to be the road up to Flagstaff, but that nobody used it any more. The owner of the car asked whether I wanted to go back over the fifty miles we had come or keep on going. I told him to go ahead.

I shall never forget that ride. The driver of the car was so overwhelmed with the beauty of it that he kept stopping the car when it was practically perpendicular, and getting out to look at the scenery.

After the hair-raising drive to the top I thought going down would be simple. We had about forty miles of driving through lovely forest, and all went merrily until we struck a muddy stretch and went in up to the hub. After hard but fruitless work in which I joined, a Standard Oil truck came along and pulled us out. At Flagstaff, I stayed all night at a tourist camp, and the next morning the friendly farmer came for me to take me further.

Chummy as we had become I may say I was somewhat surprised to receive a proposal of marriage from him the next day.

He explained that he was a widower, and that after he and his son had earned some money during the summer, they were going back to Oregon to start an apple orchard. He had noticed that I was pretty husky, and thought I would be a real help on the farm. But I told him, too, that I had a contract with my people.

The time set for the execution of Sacco and Vanzetti was drawing near. Along my route I tried to arrange joint actions with the Socialists, but they were very backward about demonstrating. They depended too much on the courts, not enough on mass public pressure. However, general indignation was growing, and my big open air meetings often provided the occasion for really spontaneous expressions of protest.

Philadelphia was the last stop on my hitch-hike tour for Sacco and Vanzetti and I arrived on the outskirts on August 17, 1927. With the one nickel left in my purse, I telephoned to the International Labor Defense office, and some comrades came in a car to meet me. I asked them at once to lend me some money to get home to Arden to see my children. It was practically a year since I had seen them.

"Oh, you can't go home!" they exclaimed. "We will give you money to go to a hotel and wash up but you have to go right on to Washington to speak at the courthouse there at a last big rally for Sacco and Vanzetti." The execution was scheduled for the following Monday and all the big cities were having protest rallies.

I told the comrades I had no clothes but my hiking outfit. "Never mind," they said. "Get some clothes from your daughter in Washington. You simply must go."

The Playhouse, at which the Washington meeting took place, was packed. A lawyer, Mr. Morningstar, Harvey O'Connor and myself were the speakers. The emotional intensity of the meeting can scarcely be described. Feeling was running very high and there was a desperate desire to do something to prevent the execution. Mr. Morningstar talked in a very bitter and revolutionary manner. "What has our country come to that such things can happen!" he cried. "If this execution takes place, the workers may well revolt." At this meeting I was the most conservative speaker!

The next morning I took the train back to Philadelphia thinking of course that I could now go to see my children. But there I was told I must stay and speak at a big mass meeting in Philadelphia on Sunday afternoon.

Then came a telegram from the national office of the I. L. D. asking me to represent them in Boston on Monday, help organize pickets around the State House and in every way try to influence the governor to grant a reprieve to Sacco and Vanzetti.

I took the train that night, arriving in Boston early in the morning of that shameful Monday. The city looked as though it were under a war-time siege. Armed men guarded every public building and patrolled the crowded streets. There was tremendous tension throughout the city. Thousands of people gathered on Boston Common discussing the case. Many storekeepers had closed their shutters; many workers went on a protest strike.

I felt as I walked along the street, seeing these manifestations of protest, "It's too late, brothers. It's too late. This should have been done long ago."

When I arrived at Paine Memorial Hall, writers, artists, teachers, workers of all kinds, from every state in the union, were offering their services to picket the state house. Besides the regular counsel, lawyers like John Finerty of the Attorney General's office in Washington, Francis Fisher Kane of Philadelphia, Arthur Garfield Hays of New York, and others stayed with Governor Fuller pleading with him until the last minute. Simultaneously committees of women, accompanied by Vanzetti's sister who had come from Italy, visited the governor's wife and mother, pleading with them to use their influence to get a reprieve.

We organized the pickets at the State House in such a way that leaders in union and other organizations would lead the picket line. They carried placards "Justice Is Dead Today in Massachusetts," "Justice Is Crucified Today." All day long the death watch continued. The police ordered the pickets to keep moving and said that each line could picket for only seven minutes. Each group kept on until they were stopped by the police. In addition to the hundreds of policemen, on foot and mounted, there were hordes of private detectives and imported professional dicks.

One came up to me shouting at the top of his lungs, "I know you. I saw you in the Ohio miners' strikes. I saw you in Calumet, Michigan. I know you." I called back, "I know you, too. I was in those strikes helping the workers. You were beating and killing strikers. I saw you!"

The police began arresting people right and left and toward evening, we had 160 arrests on our hands, among them, that of Grace Hutchins, the first Bostonian to be hauled in. We sent people around to collect money and for $25 each we bailed them out. One woman gave us bail money for four people, one of whom turned out to be her own daughter who she had not known was in Boston.

I went down to the State House with one of the last groups of pickets. As each four at the head of the line were arrested, we put four more in. I remained in back, knowing I would have to lead the last picket line. Our turn came at last. I started off with my banner followed by the local secretary of the I. L. D., Harry Cantor, and two others. We were promptly arrested and taken to the Joy Street Jail. We finally were released at about 7 o'clock and tried to arrange a meeting. All the auditoriums in town were refused us. The only place we could secure was a small building in a congested workers' section, containing two small halls, one above the other. Everyone who had come to help rushed to the hall. The speakers first addressed the crowd downstairs and then went upstairs. Thousands of people gathered around the building. The open space in front soon became so jammed with people that it was almost impossible for them to stand. They were surrounded by armed men who grew more insolent and threatening as night came on.

As the time drew near for the execution the crowd increased, the people became almost hysterical and we were afraid some of them would be provoked to violence. One of the defense lawyers of Boston came to me and suggested: "Mother, if you will stand at the window and talk to them, the whole meeting can stand at your back and those outside can feel they are part of this meeting. Try to hold them together so they will feel they are doing something—so they feel they are in the meeting." I stood up in the window with a crowd in back of me and a crowd in front of me and spoke to them slowly:

"We stand in the shadow of death tonight. Let us try to think the thoughts Sacco and Vanzetti are thinking now. Let us try to act as they would have us act. Let us stand united without regard to nationality, creed, or color." Just then an armed thug called out "You'd better go back to Russia where you came from," and a tall woman in the crowd called out, "She can't go back to Russia. She's an American. Her ancestors took part in the Boston Tea Party." The workers took up the cry, "She can't go anywhere else. She belongs here with us. She's an American."

Immediately after that, a secret service man and a policeman rushed up the stairs and placed me under arrest. One of the young men in the hall grabbed hold of me and said, "Mother, we won't let you go to jail." I said, "Don't you know, comrade, that if I don't go, there will be trouble? That's what they want—don't play into their hands. We must prevent a riot at all costs."

My arm was black and blue where the secret service man grabbed it. He was very nervous, afraid of trouble. The policemen were nervous too. "Don't worry, boys," I reassured them, "I won't let the crowd hurt you." When I got to the bottom of the stairs, the crowd surged towards the door. A man in front had a knife open in his hand. He said to the police, "Don't you dare hurt Mother Bloor." "I am all right, boys," I said. "Don't make a disturbance. Go down and picket the jail where Sacco and Vanzetti are." I thought if they went to the Charlestown Street jail, Sacco and Vanzetti would at least know we were working for them until the last minute. They did go down and were beaten up unmercifully. Some were thrown into the same jail where later in the evening Sacco and Vanzetti were executed. I was taken to a jail near the meeting hall. Fifteen policemen sat around me as though I were a very dangerous person indeed and began to lecture me. Before they gathered around me they had sent in a riot call to disperse the meeting where I had been speaking.

One old gray-haired sergeant said, "You were inciting those people. Don't you know there would have been a riot if you had kept on?" I explained that on the contrary I had prevented a riot. Then my old friend, Dan Donovan, the machinist, came down with $100 to bail me out. "I know you are tired," he said, "but please come right up to the office of the defense committee. The Italian friends of Sacco and Vanzetti are just about at the breaking point."

I went to the office and found them all crying bitterly. Standing in their midst was a beautiful, gentle little woman, the wife of a Harvard professor, Mrs. Jacques. She had taught Sacco to speak English. She was talking to them very quietly. As I came in she was saying: "Nicola Sacco, I shall never see the green grass again, I shall never see the flowers, but I shall think of you who loved them so."

Then she broke down and I took up the thread and talked to them, trying to comfort them and calm them.

The telephone bell rang sharply twice. That was the prearranged signal from the newspaper men that they were executed.

There was a terrible scene then, as these comrades and friends of Sacco and Vanzetti shouted and cried and threw themselves on the floor.

In the morning we all went into court to be tried, 160 of us. Our lawyer was Arthur Garfield Hays, who gave his services freely and made a gallant fight for freedom then, though today, alas, he is more concerned with the rights of Henry Ford and those who oppose all that Sacco and Vanzetti stood for.

He suggested that some of us plead "not guilty" so that a test case could be made. For the rest it would be much better to pay the fine now and let them go. Since they were from all over the country it would be difficult to keep track of them in order to follow through their appeals. The seven selected for the test case were Edna St. Vincent Millay, Katherine Huntington, whose ancestor signed the Declaration of Independence, John Dos Passos, John Howard Lawson, William Patterson, a Negro lawyer practising in Boston, Ellen Hayes, Professor of Astronomy at Wellesley, and myself.

We were placed under bail to appear in court at the following term in October. As we were about to leave the courtroom a beefy-faced policeman called out "That Bloor woman has another charge—inciting to riot." So they brought me back and entered bail against me for that. Later the two charges were combined in one and I was tried with the others during the winter. The judge ordered several postponements, though most of us had to come long distances to be tried. Finally in January we had a trial which lasted a week, with a pompous red-baiter of a prosecutor. We had a pretty good jury and were found not guilty. This verdict six months after the execution is a significant commentary on what the people of Boston felt about the whole shameful episode.

After the execution, a committee of fifty was formed to arrange suitable funeral services, not only in Boston, but also in New York—to do honor to these crucified workers. Included were representatives of the garment workers' unions, newspaper organizations, defense organizations, many well known writers and professional men. The bodies of Sacco and Vanzetti lay in state for a week in a humble undertaker's room in a working class neighborhood of Boston, so that thousands of workers could view their faces, and remember them forever. People journeyed long distances to pay them tribute. The faces of these men, as they lay there in state, seemed to express a feeling of absolute peace after their long suffering. As long as I live, I shall never forget the classic head and features of Vanzetti.

At the funeral, at least 150,000 people paraded eight miles behind the open limousines, filled with flowers, in which the bodies of these two martyrs of labor were carried to the crematorium. I walked with the Italian needle trades workers, girls of a union I had organized in Boston. At points along the road mounted state police reined in their horses ahead of us and backed them into us. Just ahead of me I saw a young Italian girl being kicked by a horse. As I helped pull her away the horse kicked back at me, his hoof landing on the same side where my arm was already black and blue from the pinching of the secret service man, so my whole side was sore. But I kept on with the procession.

I realized by the actions of the police that they were not going to let us get into the grounds of the crematorium. I left the procession, took a taxi to the crematorium where I met a good old-time fighter by the name of O'Brien, who had the same idea I had. We were determined that the workers should be represented at the crematorium. We both had bands on our arms, one of which I have on my table as I write. It says, "Remember, Justice Crucified, August 22, 1927." The police around the crematorium asked us: "Are you on the pall-bearers' committee?" We said we were and walked into the crematorium with the pall-bearers and stood side by side as they brought in the bodies, and Mary Donovan, secretary of the defense committee, read a brief statement.

Mrs. Sacco and Vanzetti's sister remained in their autos outside. O'Brien and I stood behind the coffins as they were lowered into the cremation chamber, both of us feeling that at the very last moment, we were representing the workers.

It had been arranged by the funeral committee that the ashes should be taken charge of that night by the undertaker and that a committee composed of Mrs. Jessica Henderson, who had aided Sacco and Vanzetti throughout the seven years of their imprisonment, Powers Hapgood and myself should take them the following morning to New York where a big demonstration was being planned.

Mrs. Henderson and I stayed together that night and early in the morning called the undertaker to arrange about getting the ashes, but got no answer. We went to the undertaker's parlor but could not get in, nor find anyone who could tell us anything. We were up against a blank wall. It would be impossible to hold up the demonstration in New York, so it was decided that I go on ahead by train with Powers Hapgood, while Mrs. Henderson would bring Mrs. Sacco by car.

Mrs. Henderson went immediately to the home of Mrs. Sacco, who was in a dazed condition and stepped right into the car, not bothering to put on a hat or get any of her things together. Mrs. Henderson called at the defense office in a last attempt to get the ashes, but they were still not there. She saw two death masks there, made by William Gropper. She took them in the car with her.

I arrived at Grand Central Station towards evening, and went straight to Union Square. Thousands upon thousands of workers, come to do honor to Sacco and Vanzetti, had been standing there for hours. Speaking was already going on, and the crowd was tense and emotional waiting for the ashes which they had been told were coming. There were no microphones at that time, so stands had been erected at different points throughout the square. On housetops machine guns were placed, and police stood on patrol. I knew that the presence of Mrs. Sacco would make the crowd feel that everything possible had been done to bring the Boston and New York workers together in their sorrow, but I did not know what to tell them because I was not sure yet myself that she would get there in time.

They asked me to speak, and I was wondering how I could keep the crowd patient when I saw Mrs. Henderson's car. I almost fainted with relief when Mrs. Sacco stepped out. I took her hand and we walked up to the railing of the platform. When the crowd saw us, and realized that the frail, hatless little woman in a black dress was Mrs. Sacco, a great moaning sigh of grief went up from the thousands of people gathered there. The Italians struck up the solemn strains of their revolutionary funeral anthem. Former Anarchist friends of Sacco's and Vanzetti's, men of all shades of political belief, Italian workers and workers of other nationalities, all sang together, dirges, songs of rebellion, songs of solidarity and hope. The long agony of the workers' struggle went into their singing, and it swelled into a mighty cry of protest that filled Union Square, and flung a message far beyond to the ears of the murderers of these two noble sons of the people. Then there was silence.

I put my hand on Mrs. Sacco's arm and said:

"This is the bravest woman in the world today. She has come to be a part of you, to sorrow with you."

She could not utter a word, she was so broken. But she stood there courageously before all those people.

Then Mrs. Henderson put the two death masks in the center of the banks of flowers that had been piled on the platform, speeches were made all over the square, speeches full of grief and anger and passionate determination to carry the banner of freedom still higher, and again the stirring sound of revolutionary songs filled the square. That great meeting in Union Square was one of the most moving and inspiring events in my life. The finest thing about it was the tremendous sense of solidarity this common grief had given to all the people there, the feeling that Sacco and Vanzetti belonged to the working class of the world and had bequeathed to workers everywhere a sense of unity to strengthen them in their future struggles.

All over this country, all over the world, demonstrations were being held that day and night to protest the murder and to honor the memory of Sacco and Vanzetti. In Soviet Russia whole issues of the leading papers were devoted to the case. In many European cities Americans were hardly able to go out on the streets, because of the anger of the workers toward America. A friend of mine then in Italy told me a taxi driver wouldn't take her in. "You Americans killed Sacco and Vanzetti," he told her, "I don't want you in my taxi."

After the Union Square meeting, the masks were taken to a workers' hall in New York and there for a week they were wreathed with flowers, Young Communist Leaguers and others standing honor guard.

The case of Sacco and Vanzetti can never be closed until we have achieved the full freedom for all the workers of the world, for which they so deeply longed and so courageously fought.

15. The Fight for Industrial Unions

FOLLOWING the struggle for the freedom of Sacco and Vanzetti and its tragic ending, I turned to the struggles of the miners.

Because of over-development during the war, followed by cut-
throat competition among the operators, increasing mechanization
and the increasing use of oil and water power as fuel, the coal
industry was in a tremendously depressed state all through the
Coolidge era. Mass unemployment, steady lowering of wages and
worsening of working conditions were the rule. The Lewis administration was very conservative at that time, and many of the
officials of the U.M.W.A. were more concerned with current
union-management co-operation schemes than with building a
strong union. Militant elements were being expelled. The union
was actually falling apart in many districts. The Trade Union
Educational League developed a large following among the more
progressive miners and created a national Save-the-Union Committee, with the purpose of carrying on a vigorous organization
campaign, uniting the anthracite and bituminous miners for
joint struggle, and electing progressive officials. Operating on a
broad united front basis, the Save-the-Union Committee had
strong rank and file support, but could not make much headway
against the bureaucratic machine. All its proposals were voted
down at the convention late in 1926.

On April 1, 1927, with the expiration of the Jacksonville agreement, (an agreement providing that union wages in the northern

fields should be maintained at the 1920 scale), the union was practically locked out of all the unionized bituminous fields in the north. Lewis called a bituminous strike, but authorized temporary agreements in a number of districts.

For a whole year, during the strike, the Party and the T.U.E.L. battled for more united action. During the latter part of 1927 I went to help strengthen the strike forces in Pennsylvania. The strike was bitterly fought by the mine owners and blocked by the reactionary union leaders. The state police, sent in by Governor Fisher (himself a mine owner) and the coal and iron police, a uniformed force maintained by the mine owners, drove the people out of their houses into the snow. We managed to build barracks for the miners to live in, but in some cases too late, and many women and children died of exposure. On our way to meetings we were set upon over and over again, pulled out of our cars, and dumped on the road with all our literature.

One day, going with Powers Hapgood and Tony Minerich to a strike meeting about fifty miles from Pittsburgh, attackers chased us all the way to the meeting. On the platform sat two professors from Pittsburgh University who had come down to investigate infringements of civil rights. They had stenographers with them. We entered the hall, the state police on horseback at our heels, one of them riding straight into the hall. This frightened the professors out of their wits, and they started dictating madly to their stenographers. We were so used to it that we did not pay much attention. The owner of the hall grabbed the horses and told the police to get off his property, which they finally did, and then the meeting proceeded.

Rumors and reports came to us continually from Colorado of the progress of a strike out there. Some of the miners were I.W.W.'s, some, U.M.W.A. men; but they were united in striking against the terrible conditions of the mines. In Walsenburg, near the scene of the old Ludlow strikes, the police terror was especially ferocious. Nine miners were killed in the Columbine mine by police and thugs.

In Trinidad lived a miner's daughter named Milka Sablich,

who worked in a laundry. Amazed to discover that men actually had to be coaxed to go on the picket line, she volunteered and thereafter was seen everywhere at strike meetings and on picket lines. She had red gold hair and a fiery tongue, and soon they were calling her "Flaming Milka." She was dragged around by the horses of the state police, she was thrown into jail, but she kept right on.

The fame of "Flaming Milka" spread and we asked her to come East and tour with me to raise money for the strike and link up our struggle with that in Colorado. Emery, an I.W.W. from Colorado, came along with her and the three of us held rousing meetings.

At one meeting where she was asking for funds she overheard a woman saying: "That girl's got a silk dress on—how dare she ask for money for the strikers?" Flaming Milka flashed back: "I earned this dress by washing clothes in a laundry. Every penny we collect from you goes to the miners—don't be afraid of that. And I'll have you know that miners' children like pretty things as well as anyone else! I have a right to wear this silk dress."

Despite terror and hunger and neglect of the strike by union officials, many miners in the key districts were still standing firm a year after the strike began. On April 1, 1928, the Save-the-Union Committee held a big national conference in Pittsburgh attended by 1,125 delegates representing some 100,000 miners. The conference decided to extend the strike further into Western Pennsylvania and West Virginia and the anthracite districts.

At this convention there were many reports of great opposition to the Save-the-Union Committee by the leadership in every local union of the United Mine Workers of America, although in most cases the members of the committee were in the majority. So many of these reports came from Illinois that I was asked to go there to investigate matters on the spot.

Bill Foster was one of the most active organizers of the "Save-the-Union" movement. In the 1919 steel strike I had seen his fine generalship and now again I had cause to admire his great organizing gifts, his ability to plan and carry through a tremendous campaign, his great proletarian courage and, most of all, his complete trust in the workers—the real secret of his success with them.

Right after the Save-the-Union Committee conference a revival of picketing brought 19,000 unorganized miners of Fayette and Westmoreland into the strike. But the sabotage of the U.M.W.A. leadership proved too big a handicap. The strike was formally over when the union signed a separate agreement in Illinois. The bituminous coal fields were now for the most part open shop, a terrible defeat for organized labor, wiping out the achievements of years.

At the Save-the-Union Conference there had been strong sentiment for the formation of an independent movement, but the Communist Party and T.U.E.L. elements had opposed this move, because we felt labor unity was all-important. The disastrous end of the strike, however, the absolute failure of the U.M.W.A. to take steps toward organizing the unorganized, compelled us to consider the problem of launching an independent union, at least temporarily. The call for a new fighting union was issued in June, and at a convention in Pittsburgh in September, 1928, the National Miners' Union was organized.

Twenty-five delegates were sent from Indiana, where I was then working. We did not have enough money to go by train or stay at hotels, so we patched up five old Fords, piled five delegates into each car and drove through Indiana and over the hills of Pennsylvania to Pittsburgh.

There we found a war going on between the old leadership and the new young strong union. Hearing that they would try to capture our hall, our weary miners from Illinois and Indiana who had just arrived, slept on the hard boards of the hall all night to protect it.

The next morning we had about 150 people in the hall, with about 750 delegates still on the way. The reactionary elements paraded around the hall preventing anybody from going in. When they themselves tried to enter, we kept them out. The police came and dispersed us. In the afternoon we all went to the outskirts of

Pittsburgh to a Ukrainian Hall. One hundred and fifty of the delegates were missing, having been arrested as they tried to enter. So there were two conventions—one in the jail and one in the Ukrainian Hall. As a member of the National Executive Committee, I participated in all the sessions in the Ukrainian Hall and had to stay there all night and sleep on the hard floor myself. Only one other woman, a delegate from Wheeling, West Virginia, was with me in this convention.

The next day, the pickets who had attacked our other meeting found out where we were and tried to force their way in; the county sheriff would not let them into the hall nor let us go on with our meeting. But we had already elected our National Committee for the year, and our officers and our main business had been accomplished.

We had succeeded in organizing a militant industrial union based squarely on a class struggle program, which later led a number of successful local strikes against wage cuts, and finally in 1931 led a strike in Western Pennsylvania, Eastern Ohio and Northern West Virginia involving 42,000 miners. But when conditions were again ripe for a united union when the U.M.W.A. revived during the strike wave of 1933, the National Miners' Union threw their strength behind the U.M.W.A. and became an important factor in its re-establishment. Today the U.M.W.A. is a fighting union within the C.I.O.

I went back to Indiana to organize locals of the new union. The old union had gradually disappeared. Wages were down to almost nothing. The introduction of the "loader and conveyor," a new machine which loaded the coal and carried it to the cars automatically, had thrown hundreds of miners out of work. In the Panhandle mine down in Southern Indiana, for example, the number of workers had been reduced from 500 to 38. To my organizing meetings I always summoned wives and sisters and daughters along with the miners themselves. With them on our side half the battle was won. Clinton, where I held one of my first organizing meetings, was the home of one of the vice presidents of the United Mine Workers. While all the rest of the town was barren, he lived in a model house, with flowers around it. This was symbolic of the gap between the leadership and the rank-and-file. From him and other old-line leaders and from the Ku Klux Klan came the opposition to my organizing efforts. More than one fiery cross burned on hill sides near our meetings; more than one meeting was broken up, our members set upon by thugs. But the rank and file were with us, and we built strong N.M.U. locals all through Indiana.

The textile industry, like coal, remained in a depressed state all through the Coolidge era. I have already described the passivity of the A. F. of L. United Textile Workers' Union even after the Passaic strike. In 1928, the New Bedford strike, involving 25,000 textile workers, gave rise to the independent National Textile Workers' Union.

Strikes flared up all through the South during 1927. The N. T. W. U. concentrated on the struggle in Gastonia, North Carolina. The A. F. of L., suddenly alarmed at the success of the new union, started to organize the South. But following their "no strike" policy, they crushed the spontaneous strike movement and encouraged the speed-up which the workers themselves were so desperately fighting.

The N. T. W. U. efforts in Gastonia, where the strike centered in the Loray Mill of Manville Jenckes Co., were met with a wave of terror. Organizers were beaten up and arrested, loading the International Labor Defense with cases. We gave to this fight a large number of our Party forces.

My son, Carl, then editor of the *Labor Defender,* went down to Gastonia with some Y. C. L.'ers and representatives of other organizations. Carl and one of the textile organizers were taken for a ride one night and after a beating and threats were dumped into jail. Our organizers could not go out without running the risk of beating and arrest. Women comrades suffered especially from the horribly primitive arrangements in the jail.

The Workers' International Relief, led by Alfred Wagenknecht, had come down to Gastonia at the beginning of the strike with relief stores and food supplies and set up a strikers' camp. The mill owners and their thugs came one night, just after the arrival of fresh supplies, and spilled the bags of flour over the railroad tracks, poured kerosene on the food, broke up the camp and demolished the Union Hall.

The undaunted strikers, however, collected enough money to build a new union hall. Since no company would deliver the lumber, the boys had to carry it on their shoulders, board by board. Hearing rumors that the thugs were planning new raids, the strikers held a solemn meeting at which they decided to protect their new union hall and food supplies, as they had every right to do. They organized a guard of thirteen strikers who went on duty every night, each with a rifle on his shoulder.

On the following Friday, the day relief was distributed, the police and deputized gangsters staged another and more vicious armed attack on the union hall.

The sentry, a slight young fellow, attempted to halt the thugs, telling them: "You cannot get into this place unless you have a warrant!" Jeering, they shot him in the arm. As he fell the other guards came to the rescue. Shots were fired on both sides and chief of police Aderholt, leading the attack, was wounded. He died in a few days. Altogether seventy strikers were arrested and charged with murder. It is well to remember that from then on the strikers were able to feed their people unmolested.

The trials were outrageous examples of the injustice meted out to organized workers in the South. Through the efforts of the lawyers furnished by the International Labor Defense and through public support, the majority of the workers were released. At the final trial in September, the number of defendants was cut to seven, and the charge to second degree murder. Found guilty, savage sentences of from 17 to 20 years were meted out to four Northern organizers while the three Southerners received sentences ranging from 5 to 15 years.

In this strike, Ella May Wiggins, who had worked for nine years in the mills, a widowed mother of five children, was very active. A skilled weaver, she had never received more than $9.00

a week in all her long years in the mill. The average was $5.00 a week for women spinners. Ella May composed songs to cheer the strikers, some of them funny and some of them sad.

On the night of September 14, 1927, a group of strikers were driving to a nearby town to try to organize a smaller mill with Ella May sitting in the truck singing her songs. Suddenly a shot rang out and Ella May's voice was stilled forever. The murderer was identified as a tool of the Gastonia police chief.

I toured the West to raise money for the defense of the Gastonia strikers. On my way back at the end of 1929, I attended an I.L.D. convention in Pittsburgh. This convention was memorable among other things for the vigorous fight made by J. Louis Engdahl, our National Secretary, against the discrimination practiced by the Pittsburgh hotels against the Negro delegates.

We had engaged rooms for all the delegates in the Monongahela Hotel. When we arrived late at night with twenty-five Negro delegates, the manager of the hotel made a great fuss and said that while they could stay there that night, they must all get out immediately the next morning.

Next morning, we voted that the whole convention should adjourn to the hotel in an orderly fashion. We marched to the hotel carrying banners emphasizing "no discrimination." We filed into the lobby, which by that time was filled with newspapermen, policemen, and curious crowds. Engdahl mounted a chair in the lobby and, speaking loudly enough to be heard in the street, too, he explained why we had come there. Then he called upon other speakers. Bob Dunn was there, Bill Dunne, Robert Minor, Negroes from the North and the South, whites from all over. I called attention to the fact that in this same hotel there was a room with a placque in it which said that Lincoln once slept there. I suggested that it would be appropriate if that room at least were open to the Negro delegates.

At the convention it was decided that I should go South where William Green's emissaries were telling the workers he was going to organize them. I was to follow with the message that if workers were to be organized something more had to be done than just talking about it.

Since I felt it would be impossible to raise travel expenses in the South, I sent telegrams to sympathizers, and finally received, besides some small contributions, a substantial one of $500 from a Socialist woman friend in California. This enabled me to make the trip without calling on our hard pressed people in the South.

I arrived in Gastonia during the trials of the murderer of Ella May Wiggins, and of some of our own people.

At the trial of Ella May Wiggins' murderer, the cruelty of the capitalist class and their tools was brought home to me sharply as I saw her orphaned children sitting there with her relatives. It recalled the Ludlow murders, the slaughter of the children of Calumet, and the murder of Fannie Sellins. The capitalist class shoots down mothers and children. It stops at nothing, no matter how monstrous, to prevent the organization of the workers.

It was fortunate that I had received the money I started out with, for when I arrived in Charlotte, N. C., I found that all the strikers who were out on bail and many organizers of the union and the I. L. D. were attempting to run a co-operative establishment without any funds. By the time I arrived they were all very hungry people, and I bought groceries to feed them. Then I found their union hall hadn't any wires for electricity, so my fund paid for wiring the hall. Other textile districts, too, were in desperate straits. A call came from a town 135 miles from Charlotte, asking us to help organize a mill at Lumberton, N. C. The workers had gone on strike and had applied to the union in Charlotte for relief. We sent a man down to help these people and he took Oliver with him, one of the Gastonia strikers, a very gifted boy of about seventeen, who had learned that the Lumberton strike had arisen because of the hard conditions of the young workers —boys and girls being worked 12 to 16 hours a day.

Caudle, the man who called on us for help, had been hunted and persecuted ever since the strike started. About midnight, after sending our two men there, we received a telephone call from a man at Charlotte saying that Oliver had been carried off and thrown into the swamps. Towards morning, we received a call from Oliver himself. He had managed to crawl out of the swamp. The next day, his brother and some others went and got him. That same night, Caudle's house was attacked. For his attempt to defend himself, his wife and his home from the mob, he was arrested, and charged with carrying firearms illegally.

We were asked to bring Oliver down to testify against the mob. When the same mob had taken him, he had heard them say they were going to kill Caudle, and his testimony would make it clear that Caudle had carried a gun in self defense. We did not know whether it was safe for Oliver to go or not, and discussed it pro and con all night. It was finally decided that if I went along, my gray hair might protect him. With us went a whole carload of former Gastonia strikers. When we got to the courtroom Oliver pointed to a man sitting there and said: "There's the leader of the mob that threw me in the swamp." They didn't let Oliver testify and Caudle was found guilty. I offered his wife money from the I. L. D. to bail her husband out while we appealed the case. She said she wanted to appeal the case but he would be safer in jail than home.

While I was talking to her, the mob grabbed Oliver again, as he was going down the front steps to the car. They beat his head against a stone monument in front of the courthouse. Our men struggled to get him away from the mob. I grabbed one of the leaders by the coat collar and asked him if he knew this was America. He turned to me, snarling, "I'll show you about America." But we finally got Oliver away and started the 135-mile trip back. Some of the cars started after us. But we got away.

The organization of the new unions through the efforts of the T. U. E. L. in mining and textiles had been followed by the organization of an industrial union in the needle trades in January, 1929. This trend marked a change in the policy of the T. U. E. L. which had previously taken a strong stand against dual unionism. At the T. U. E. L. conference in August-September 1929, the new policy was upheld and the name of the organization was changed to Trade Union Unity League. The T. U. U. L. was to function through three groups: (1) national industrial unions organized on the basis of "one shop, one industry, one union"; (2) industrial leagues, loosely organized groupings not yet strong enough to be full-fledged unions; (3) trade union minority groups—national industrial sections working inside the conservative unions. At the same time, the conference warned sharply against a general system of dual unionism. New unions were to be formed only where the A. F. of L. unions were in a hopeless state, or did not exist at all. Its main task was the organization of the unorganized into industrial unions, and at the same time the organization of the revolutionary workers within the reformist unions.

The T. U. U. L. determined to pay special attention to work in the South, and to the special problems of the Negro workers. In Charlotte, N. C., before I went further South, I was asked by the T. U. U. L. to go with some of their organizers, one of them a Negro, to organize the workers in tobacco shops in Winston-Salem, N. C. That town, with its brick walled factories, is like a huge prison. Wages at that time were the lowest received by any workers in the South—the lowest paid being the Negro women, the next lowest, the white women, then the Negro men, then the white men. We were naive enough to believe we could organize a union there at that time, of white and Negro men and women together. However, we did succeed in having a meeting where Negro and white workers told their grievances and we gave them some pointers on how to go about organizing.

From North Carolina, I went through the South, and westward through Arizona, Texas, Southern California and up the coast, back to my old post in Seattle, where I continued my work for the I. L. D., with Seattle as my headquarters that winter.

Hoover, the great humanitarian and engineer, elected in 1928 on promises of "a chicken in every pot and a car in every garage" was soon instead to give his name to the "Hoovervilles." The dizzy structure of false prosperity reared through the bull market years crashed to bits in October, 1929. This was only the outward dramatization of a world-wide process of stagnation and decay long under way in the capitalist system. Capitalism could produce ever greater quantities of goods, but could not provide the masses with the means to buy back the products of their own toil. The result was "over-production"—although the masses of the people had to do without the essentials of living.

Wages were slashed on all sides, unemployment mounted. The class collaboration policy had weakened the labor movement disastrously during the Coolidge era, and now the old line trade union leaders adopted a policy of retreat and surrender. Within two weeks after the crash, the A. F. of L. and Railroad Brotherhood officials at a White House conference with employers pledged themselves not to strike and not to seek wage advances during the economic crisis, while the employers were to keep wages at existing levels. The employers made no pretense of keeping their part of the bargain, but the conservative trade unions did their "patriotic" duty and kept strikes at a minimum. Nor did the dwindling Socialist Party offer any leadership whatever in the crisis. The Socialist vote in 1928 was cut a little more than a fourth of its vote in 1920, its membership had dropped precipitously, its influence in the trade unions was negligible.

But while trade union and Socialist Party leaders retreated in confusion, our Party, basically united at last and cleansed of hostile elements, now became a factor of growing importance in workers' struggles.

The Soviet Union, entering on its period of socialist construction under the first five-year plan, had been hampered by its internal enemies. Trotsky and his followers over-estimated the strength of capitalism and, not believing that socialism could succeed in one country alone, actually fought against its success. Bukharin and his group, on the other hand, underestimated the strength of capitalism, and supported the continued existence of capitalist elements within the socialist state. These and other groups, working sometimes separately but eventually in combination, followed a road that led to terrorist acts, counter-revolutionary attempts, and traitorous plots with foreign powers. These groups found their counterpart in disruptive groups in other countries. In 1928 our Party rid itself of the Trotskyite elements (later to be taken in by the Socialists and spewed out again). Lovestone, who represented the Bukharinist ideology, predicted new triumphs of American capitalism in the Hoover regime. The falseness of his theory was soon exposed, the trickery by which he had gained temporary leadership of the Party unbared, and he was defeated in the Central Committee. His plotting to seize Party property and regain his position led to his expulsion with more than two hundred of his personal followers.

Immeasurably strengthened in unity and political clarity, our Party during the next few years, under the leadership of Earl Browder as General Secretary and William Z. Foster as Chairman, became a powerful force in working class struggles of America.

Following the 1929 crisis our Party saw that the two most immediate and important problems of the workers were unemployment and the organization of the unorganized workers into industrial unions. We were in the forefront of both these mass movements.

It was through the initiative and organizing force of our Party that huge demonstrations of the unemployed took place in American cities early in 1930. A million and a quarter people took part, and unemployment was burned into the consciousness of the politicians as an issue that must be faced. With our help councils of unemployed were organized in various localities; in July, 1930, the first National Conference of Unemployed Councils met as the central body for the organization of relief struggles all over the country. The Unemployed Councils stimulated nation-wide mass pressure for relief and organized the 1931 and 1932 "Hunger Marches" to Washington, besides local demonstrations. The efforts to unite all unemployed organizations throughout the country were finally successful in 1936 when the National Unemployment League, dominated by the Socialists, and other smaller groups, merged with the Unemployed Councils to form the Workers' Alliance.

The Party also set in motion a mass demand for unemployment insurance. There is no doubt that the mass pressure developed through the work of the Unemployed Councils, with the constant participation and help of the Party, pointed the way to those measures of security and relief later gotten under the New Deal.

16. Farmers Take a Holiday

IN Seattle I received a telegram from the Central Committee of the Party asking me to take charge of the Party's 1932 election campaign, in North and South Dakota.

Andrew Omholt was the Party's candidate for Congressman and Pat Barrett for Governor. I went into the campaign with all the zeal I possessed. Our campaign brought the program of the Communist Party to many of these farmers for the first time. We made full use of the North Dakota law providing that each party could post bulletins at every crossroad, with five word slogans for each party. Our slogan was very direct: "Communist Party—Workers, Farmers, Unite."

Along with the miners and textile workers, the farmers were a depressed section of the population all through the boom years. In the decade between 1920 and 1930, there was a crisis of "over production" (with millions starving), farm prices falling below the cost of production, and the number of farms decreasing by 150,466. During the year ending March 1, 1930, 20.8 out of every 1000 farms were lost through forced sales, foreclosures or bankruptcy. Hoover refused effective farm aid. His makeshift Agricultural Marketing Act was administered by a Farm Board made up of bankers, and prices continued to drop. The Party's practical proposals for farm relief started many of the farmers thinking along new lines.

The Party was first to advance the demand for a sharp cut in the unreasonable spread between the low prices paid to the farmer and the high prices paid by the consumer. Other important proposals by the Party were support for these demands: "No more foreclosures. No evictions. No deficiency judgments. The farm family holds the first mortgage!" The Party also advocated cash relief for those in distress through no fault of their own, and close cooperation between the farmers and organized labor.

This campaign in North Dakota is personally memorable to me because of my marriage to that pioneer North Dakota farmer and good Communist, Andrew Omholt. He was district organizer of North and South Dakota and Montana, and we campaigned together, visiting towns as far as 700 miles from the headquarters in Minot, North Dakota.

After the election campaign was over, we helped organize the farmers into the United Farmers' League, an organization which paved the way for the great Farm Holiday movement. The Hoover depression had hit with particular severity the farmer on the dry plains of the Dakotas and the Great Lakes region of cut-over timber lands ruined by the lumber barons. The United Farmers' League appeared in this region to fight for the homes, equipment and livestock of thousands of farmers who had exhausted their resources.

Once, in Frederick, we were called on by a farmer named Lutio who was about to be evicted by the bank from the family home where he had brought up seven children. The U.F.L. got together about seventy cars and drove down there. We told the sheriff and the banker they couldn't evict the Lutio family. The banker gave ten days' grace; then the new tenant would move in. We told him the Lutios would make room for the new tenant, but would keep on living there too. They had no place to go and no money. A week later I was asked to come down again, to explain to some 60 or 70 new people who had joined the U.F.L., as a result of our visit, how they should function. We held a big meeting before the cooperative gasoline station. The banker's seventeen-year-old son rounded up hoodlums to break up the meeting. They catcalled and booed me. But we had mobilized a group of powerful young Finns, and I announced, "You can stay here all night, but we're going to have this meeting." Presently the hoodlums disappeared. A big Finnish woman whispered to me, "They've gone to get the fire engine and hose." But I wasn't worried. I had seen our husky Finns detach themselves from the crowd and follow them. When the hoodlums reappeared with the fire engine and hose, there was a tug of war; somehow the hose got slit, and it was the hoodlums who got the wetting. We had our meeting, and the Lutios were not evicted.

In 1931, the first of four successive years of drought, there was a severe grasshopper plague in the Dakotas. The Red Cross workers sent out from eastern cities to administer relief had very little understanding of the farmers and their needs. If a farmer drove up to the relief station in a battered old Ford, the Red Cross worker would say, "You can't have any relief if you can afford to drive here in a car." "But I had to drive twenty miles to get here," would be the answer. "Why didn't you use a horse?" "My horses are dead in the fields."

One very helpful action at that time was the following: North Dakota farmers took truckloads of lignite coal, very plentiful all over North and South Dakota, to exchange for hay. But when farmers in Red River Valley sent word to the United Farmers' League that they had a lot of potatoes, and if the men dug them we could have them to distribute, the Red Cross refused to let us ship the potatoes we dug where we knew they were needed. However, our strong organization finally prevailed and directed the farmers to meet the carloads of potatoes wherever they were sent.

During the 1932 Presidential campaign which resulted in Roosevelt's election and in which Foster and Ford were the Party candidates, the big militant milk strike then going on in Iowa came up for discussion at a meeting of the Central Committee of the Party in New York. With crops a little better, prices for farm products had reached a record low. Strikes, which the farmers called "holidays," by which they meant a moratorium for evictions and foreclosures, were sweeping the farm areas, with Iowa as the storm center. Feeling that something must be done by our Party in recognition of the importance of the milk strike, I suggested that Hal should be sent out with me to Iowa to encourage the farmers. Milo Reno, president of the Farmers' Holiday Association, had called the governors of seven states together in Sioux City, Iowa, to discuss moratoriums for farm debts. We feared his purpose was to break the strike, so successfully carried on by the farmers, and in which they had the cooperation of the workers of nearby cities, since the farmers gave the milk to the children of the unemployed instead of throwing it out when they stopped trucks trying to make deliveries to the big trusts.

We wired Hal to come to Des Moines, and met him there. After holding a big meeting in Des Moines, Hal, Rob Hall, who had joined us, and I drafted a set of resolutions for the Sioux City conference, dealing with such problems as the low price of milk at the milk sheds, and the spread between that and the price paid by the consumer; and a call for a convention of real dirt farmers in Washington to carry their problems direct to their congressmen. The meeting of governors was to take place in Sioux City next day and we were determined to get the ear of those farmers coming to town to tell the governors what they wanted.

We got up early the next morning and drove all day to Sioux City, some two hundred miles away. The papers featured statements by Milo Reno that the strike was over, which we knew was not true, because the pickets were as lively as ever on the roads, and no milk was passing through. The governors had arrived and had put up at the largest hotel. A few days before, a county sheriff, near Sioux City, deputized over a hundred men to stop the pickets by force. But instead of the deputies stopping the unarmed pickets, it was the pickets who, with bare hands, took charge of the deputies, disarmed them, removed their coats, and sent them back in their shirt sleeves to Sioux City.

About 10 o'clock in the morning Hal, Rob Hall, and I drove out to the park where 10,000 farmers were already assembled. Towards noon the number swelled to about 15,000. They were milling around, apparently with no plans or leadership. I went up to one keen-looking farmer and asked, "Where are your leaders? You are Holiday members, aren't you?" "Yes, we are Holiday members, but I don't know whether or not we have any leaders. If we have, they must be up with the governors in the hotel." His tone was sarcastic. "Well," I said, "I am national organizer of the United Farmers' League of North Dakota, and have brought greetings from North Dakota. They are willing to cooperate in this strike in every way." The farmer's eyes popped. "Woman, can you speak?"

"A little."

He just took me by the shoulders and lifted me up on a table and said, "Shoot!"

In about a minute the farmers were around me in a solid mass, and I talked as I had never talked before. I told them not to listen to the governors' instructions to stop their fight just as they were gaining the victory, but to seize this opportunity to tell the governors their needs. They wanted me to go on and on and finally asked me to lead their parade.

That parade was something to remember. A cowboy band led it, followed by farm boys on horseback, and after them the prize truck. In it stood forty men, straight and proud, representing picket line Number 20—which had never let a truck go by. Behind Number 20 came the marching farmers. I was hoisted up on top of the truck cab. Perched up there precariously as we rode through the streets of Sioux City, I kept waving to the crowds with one hand, and trying to hold on with the other. I had often felt ready to die for the miners, but this time I was sure I was about to die for the farmers! The parade had a thunderous reception. Workers lining the streets shouted: "Boys, we are with you. We'll help you, and you help us!" We halted before the governors' hotel, and the farmers called out, "Come on, governors, send out your soldiers, we are ready." We could see them peeping out from behind the curtains and knew they were good and scared of these farmers.

Before the meeting had disbanded at the park, I had said, "Why not hold a meeting right in the hotel, draft resolutions to the governors, and tell them in an organized fashion what you want and why you want to continue the strike?" So now they marched right into the hotel auditorium, elected a chairman, and passed all the resolutions unanimously. The meeting ended with a call to the convention in Washington, and election of a committee to present the resolutions to the governors. The governors at first contemptuously refused to see the committee and didn't give in until about 9 o'clock. Late that night the newsboys ran through the streets shouting, "Extra! Extra! The farmers have the governors on the spot!" The resolutions, printed in the papers, made a great stir. The next day the farmers went on with their strike. We went out to their picket lines in the middle of the day. The women brought cooked dinners to the men, setting tables right by the roadside. We were invited to eat with them. Every time a milk truck came along, the men stopped eating, made the truck driver turn around and go back, and then returned to their dinners. They asked me to stand on the table and talk.

That night we visited another picket line. Here they had cleared a big space at a cross-roads, erected a temporary platform draped with flags, and wanted me to talk. Having no leadership from their own organization they were hungry for encouragement. As a farmer's wife from North Dakota, they accepted me as one of their own.

This was followed in Iowa by the period of the "penny sales," when the militancy of the organized farmers kept them on the land until they got their moratorium. At sheriff's sales, the farmers gathered, bid ten cents for a cow, ten cents for a plow, ten cents for the house, etc., allowing no other bids. Having bought the farmer's property, they gave it back to him again.

In Lamar, Iowa, thirty miles from Sioux City, a well liked farmer was behind in his interest payments to an insurance company. The company lawyer came with the judgment note enabling the insurance company to put in a bid for the farm and take it over in case the farmers did not bid. The news went around like lightning. Two truckloads of Unemployed Council members joined the thousands of farmers assembled at the court house.

They told the sheriff that he would not be able to sell the man out. "I must," he said, "or I will lose my job." Then they went to the lawyer and asked, "Have you got a judgment note?" "Yes," he told them. "You are not going to use it to bid with," they said. "I must," he cried, "or I will lose my job." The farmers took him out of the court house and stood him under a tree, and asked, "Will you write a telegram to your company and tell them to withdraw the note?" He said, "No, I can't do it." One old farmer said, "Get the rope." They didn't intend to use the rope, but they had one handy, threw it over the limb of the tree and repeated: "Will you send the telegram?" "Give me a paper and pencil!" He wrote: "Withdraw the note. My neck is in danger."

Another method the farmers used successfully to prevent evictions was the "silent protest." In Sioux City, the farmers packed the court room every month on the day set for the public sale of foreclosed farms and small homes. As he read each item on his list, the county treasurer would pause for bids. But the farmers there to save their neighbors' farms would just stand silently with grim smiles on their faces, and no bids would be made. Once a man ventured to bid, and the farmers quietly closed in on him and heaved him out with their shoulders, hardly moving, just pushing him along until he went through the door. Groups of unemployed workers came too to stand there with the farmers in case they were needed. At the end of December, the county treasurer said in disgust, "I've done my duty, but there's not a bid in the lot of you. The sales will be postponed until spring." The farmers never failed to appear to make their silent protest. It was the most convincing demonstration I ever saw of the power of solid, persistent organization.

Even after the moratorium law on farm debts was passed in Iowa, the judges kept on selling farms illegally. The farmers gathered in protest, were met by troops and some terrible fights occurred. One judge at Lamar who ignored the moratorium bill was taught a lesson by the farmers who took him out of his office one day and made him walk a mile in his B.V.D.'s.

I never saw anything like the militancy of those farmers. They were wonderful. Only on one occasion a few of them threatened to get out of hand. The National Guardsmen sent to Lamar were just high school boys—some of them farmers' sons. The night after their entry into Lamar, we heard a tramping up the stairs, and a bunch of hot-headed farmers came into our office saying, "How many men can you give us? What arms have you got?"

"Wait a minute, boys," I said. "We haven't any guns, you know."

"We can't stand having those young boys come and interfere with our rights—we're going to do something about it."

We made them sit down and talk it over. We told them we were preparing leaflets calling on Milo Reno to organize a big meeting of the Holiday Association in Des Moines, and rallies before the court houses in various counties to protest to the Governor against violations of the law and sending in the National Guard. We got them to see this was a better way than to go out and start a fight.

Within a week soldiers had raided our office, taken away baskets full of our papers, thrown our people into jail, arrested and held incommunicado a harmless old man who was distributing our leaflets. Andy and I were away at the time. They had planned to arrest us for inciting to riot when, as a matter of fact, it was we who had stopped a riot!

By the end of 1932 our work among the farmers had broadened out to such an extent that we were able to hold a highly successful Farmers' Emergency Relief Conference in Washington in December, 1932.

My son Hal was asked to help call such a conference by the Farm Holiday Committee in Sioux City. Some Nebraska Holiday members carried the news of the proposed conference back to their officers and it was enthusiastically supported. The call was quickly endorsed by Pennsylvania, New England and Alabama farm organizations, and became a real national conference. Working with Hal on the conference preparations were Lem Harris, Rob Hall, Otto Anstrom, and other active, intelligent young men who were familiar with the problems of the farmers.

Two hundred and forty-eight delegates from twenty-six states, representing thirty-three organizations and unorganized farmers attended the conference. It took place at the same time as the big march of the unemployed to Washington. The unemployed were being held outside the city by Hoover's police, and some were getting pneumonia and dying of exposure. The farmers' protests to their Congressmen were an important factor in finally getting the unemployed marchers into the city. The farmers themselves were treated courteously by their Congressmen, and even given a police escort into the city.

The farmer delegates visited their Congressmen, then came back and reported to the conference. One after another was told, after hearty handshakes, "I'm all for you, boys, but there's nothing we can do here." It was a good education for them. Twelve of us who were delegates from North Dakota were taken to lunch by Senators Nye and Frazier and Congressman Sinclair. When we got back the others jokingly accused us of having been bought. "Don't worry," we told them. "It was only a fifty-cent lunch!"

Delegations called upon the President and the Vice-President. The delegation to Vice-President Curtis included a Negro. Before being admitted, their pockets were flipped by a guard. Then they were lined up single file to shake hands. Curtis refused to shake the Negro's hand. The farmer who followed after him didn't put out his hand. Instead he said:

"Mr. Curtis, if you won't shake hands with our Negro delegate, I guess I don't want to shake your hand."

A plainclothesman hustled him off saying, "You ought to have your block knocked off."

One of the high points of that convention was the arrival of the sharecroppers' delegation from the South. They arrived a day late. Many of the farmers were living in tourist cabins down on the Potomac, only some of which were heated. The white farmers rushed to offer their heated cabins to the Negro delegates from the South, who they thought would suffer from the cold. The sharecroppers got a tremendous ovation at the convention. An Alabama sharecropper reported on the desperate conditions in his state, telling about the extreme poverty and the struggle for even the most elementary rights. A tactless delegate asked, "Tell us about the terror in the South," whereupon the speaker, who had lived for months under its shadow and was now near exhaustion from a sleepless and foodless journey, collapsed. We had to protect these sharecropper delegates from any publicity whatsoever, as their very lives were endangered by their attendance.

The conference raised demands for a moratorium on farm debts, and mapped out a program for militant action to improve farm conditions, including a struggle to prevent foreclosures, evictions and loss of farm property.

The convention voted to organize the Farmers' National Committee for Action, and to publish a weekly paper. The F.N.C.A. was a broad, united front movement taking in all kinds of farm organizations. I was asked to superintend the organization of the committee in five states—Montana, North and South Dakota, Iowa and Nebraska. Moving my headquarters to Sioux City, Iowa, I took up my work as secretary of the Farmers' Committee in these five states, Andy becoming organizer for the Sioux City district.

Following the Washington conference similar conferences and mass demonstrations took place in Nebraska, South Dakota, Iowa, and elsewhere. We who were on the Farmers' National Committee of Action Executive Committee attended Farmers' Holiday and Farmers' Union State Conventions as delegates. One memorable occasion was at the State Agricultural Fair grounds in Lincoln, Nebraska. Several of us had been made fraternal delegates—among others Lem Harris who had become national secretary of the F.N.C.A. He had just returned from a visit to the U.S.S.R. and had secured from Julien Bryan, well known lecturer, his motion picture of collective farms. The Washington Conference had received these pictures enthusiastically, and Lem took it for granted the Nebraska farmers would be interested. But the backward element there tore down the screen. Next morning a man whom I knew was no farmer but a postman and a notorious Republican politician proposed a resolution condemning "that man" for bringing pictures of the Soviet Union to the conference. He shouted, "The farmers of Nebraska don't want to see, hear or know anything about Russia!" He was quickly seconded and the chairman was about to ask for discussion. Seeing the resolution about to be stampeded through, I climbed up on a table and cried at the top of my lungs, "Wait a minute, brothers, before you do anything like this. Don't you realize that at this very moment the President and Congress are considering recognition of the Soviet Union and all over our country people are advocating this move? What will they think of you farmers of Nebraska if you pass a resolution like this?" They stopped to think, because these men had voted for Roosevelt and were opposed to Hoover and his Farm Board. "And where does this resolution come from?" I went on. "From a farmer? No! From a Hoover postmaster!" I got applause and the vote, too.

The main thing we urged at these conferences was legislation to protect farmers from foreclosures. In Iowa the Lieutenant Governor pledged such legislation to the farmers who crowded in at a joint session of the House and Senate, with other farmers singing outside. At the conference at Pierre, South Dakota, farmers marched into the Capitol and presented their demands right on the floor.

In November, 1933, we held the second big F.N.C.A. conference in Chicago, heard reports of the success of the penny sales from many sections, and organized national legal defense work for farmers. The conference went even further than the Washington Conference by raising the demand for cancellation of secured farm debts of small and middle farmers, along with the stand against forced sales and auctions of impoverished families. It called for cash relief for destitute farm families, lowered taxes, measures to increase farmers' purchasing power, and abolition of oppression of Negroes. Here, with agricultural worker delegates present, we first brought vigorously to the fore the problems of agricultural workers. Our idea was to break down the antagonism between small farm owners and the agricultural workers. We made a special point of bringing the workers and farmers together at this convention, as in all our work. To drive home the point of workers' and farmers' unity, we wound up the convention by hiring a large auditorium for our final session, where thousands of Chicago workers cheered the farm delegates. The central section was reserved for the 702 farmer delegates from thirty-six different states. That meeting was a real demonstration of solidarity.

Next year, 1933-34, I was in Nebraska, bringing a message of encouragement and hope to these farmers triply stricken by drought, the dust storms that went with it, and low prices for farm products. It always seemed to me the farm women were the greatest sufferers. The choking, dust-filled air burns throat and eyes. It seeps inexorably into the houses, which have often been thrown out of plumb by high winds, leaving gaping chinks. Food, bed-clothing, furniture are all covered with a thick deposit, making it impossible to keep homes clean and tidy in the manner that these brave farm women would wish. Even their small and indispensable vegetable gardens are lost. Many a farm woman has carefully watered her small vegetable garden every evening in the hope of raising a few fresh vegetables only to have a hot dry wind blow a sand-blast which slithers the leaves and stops the growth of the plants. The combination of calamities to which these families were subjected would seem overwhelming, and yet they were in no sense beaten. We organized large groups of Nebraska farmers and found them just as militant as the farmers of Iowa.

17. Fighting Fascism Abroad— and At Home

AT the time of Roosevelt's inauguration in 1933 every bank in the country was closed, industry was paralyzed, hundreds of thousands of farmers had lost their farms, the farmers' purchasing power was only 41 per cent of pre-war, and 17,000,000 unemployed were pounding the pavements and highways of our rich country. The New Deal was backed by finance capital to prop up the tottering capitalist system.

The Agricultural Adjustment Administration was organized to restore farm prices by limiting farm production, by plowing under cotton, slaughtering pigs, and holding productive lands idle, while millions went hungry and ragged. While the AAA program of cash benefits brought some relief to the small farmers, the lion's share went to the landlords and banks. Moreover, the destruction of food and fiber was hardly a rational solution.

My work among the miners, textile workers and farmers illustrates, I think, the extent to which our Party was learning to work within the labor movement for the immediate, concrete needs of the workers, farmers and middle class people. I have shown how the passivity—even worse, the sabotage—of the reactionary trade union leaders and their no-strike policy made it necessary for us (for a certain period) to support organization of independent unions. Practically all the important strikes between 1929 and 1933 were carried on by the T.U.U.L. unions.

The quarter of a million workers who participated developed a militancy and strength later to stand them in good stead.

The mild economic revival set in motion by Roosevelt's policies, and the legalization of the right of collective bargaining, brought a new situation. Thousands of workers began to strike against the starvation minimum wages set by the N.R.A. codes. While the National Labor Board established in August 1933 had as its main purpose the killing of the strike movement, while employers resorted on the one hand to the encouragement of company unionism, and on the other to violent suppression of strikes, the workers took section 7-a seriously, determined to get everything they possibly could out of the New Deal. The end of 1933 found strikes raging in coal, steel, copper, automobiles, textiles, the needle trades and other industries, involving altogether 812,000 strikers, almost three and a half times as many as in 1932. In these strikes the unemployed, in spite of their own destitution, refused to become strike-breakers.

In this country, reaction sought through Roosevelt to breathe life into the dying capitalist system by giving it a semblance of liberalism. In Europe, finance capitalism, facing an even more intense crisis, could maintain itself in power in many countries only by open, terrorist dictatorship of its most chauvinistic elements. Scarcely recovered from the first world war, a new era of wars for the imperialist redivision of the world had begun in 1931 with the Japanese seizure of Manchuria—an era reaching its horrible climax as I write.

In Germany, where the crisis hit hardest, the treachery of the Social-Democrats paved the way for National Socialism. The rise of Hitler and the unrestricted aggressive nationalism in foreign politics which is an integral part of fascist dictatorship, brought close the day of mass slaughter imperialism could not avoid. We Communists knew that every minute war could be delayed meant more time to build the strength and unity of the workers everywhere. We gave our support to every peace movement with a realistic anti-war policy.

The most effective anti-war organization at this time was the American League Against War and Fascism (later to become the American League For Peace and Democracy) founded at an anti-war congress attended by over 2,000 delegates representing many organizations, September 29-October 1, 1933.

A number of delegates from abroad attended this congress, among them Tom Mann of England and Henri Barbusse of France, representing the World Committee Against War and Fascism. Tom Mann received a wonderful reception at the pier, marine workers carrying him on their shoulders to a waiting crowd outside. A shameful attempt was made to detain the great author and humanitarian Barbusse on the same charge of "moral turpitude" used against Maxim Gorky years before, because a woman secretary traveled with him. Quickly organized pressure on Washington brought his release within a few hours and the warmth of the reception he received at the great mass meeting at Mecca Temple made up in part for official boorishness.

Just as this historic congress ended, reports reached us of an instance of fascist terror occurring right in our own country. In a big steel strike in Ambridge, Pennsylvania, an orgy of violence had been unleashed against the strikers.

Since 1919, it had been almost impossible to organize the steel workers. Because of the passivity of the A. F. of L. union, the Steel and Metal Workers Industrial Union was organized and in the fall of 1933 launched a number of strikes. The U. S. Steel and other companies in Ambridge were determined no union should exist there. But the workers were swarming into the new union, of which Pat Cush, veteran of the Homestead strike, was president, and between 5,000 and 6,000 joined the strike. The day the strike started the whole town of Ambridge was filled with deputy sheriffs and thugs brought in and paid by the bosses, supplied with tear gas, clubs and guns. They immediately attempted to terrorize the unarmed strikers as they picketed peacefully. But the sturdy steel worker pickets only became more militant.

Union headquarters in Pittsburgh sent men to help. As they entered the town they were set upon and chased out, local and state police cooperating with the thugs. By the second day bands of murderers were roaming the streets of Ambridge like wild beasts, breaking into the steel workers' homes, rushing picket lines, beating up strikers and their sympathizers, and firing wildly. By the end of the day two strikers lay wounded with dumdum bullets. That night men, women and children gathered around huge bonfires to call for increased picketing. The women showed a wonderful spirit, refusing to be terrorized. By the next day the gang of deputy sheriffs and thugs swelled to many hundreds. From the Jones and Laughlin plant across the river at Aliquippa, they marched on Ambridge, and the bosses at the Spang Chalfant Mills attempted to run in truckloads of scabs. The mayor held strike leaders at headquarters, trying to bully them into withdrawing their picket lines, and when that failed, arresting one on a trumped up charge. The union office was raided and other arrests were made.

As the pickets at the mill drove back the scabs, the mob of deputies led by the local sheriff went into action. First they used tear gas, then clubs, then rifles. When the smoke lifted Adam Pietraszeski, a former mill worker and Party member helping the strikers, lay dead, and fifty strikers were wounded.

When the details of the massacre reached us, I asked to go down there to pay tribute to this martyred comrade. Our Party leaders did not want to expose me to danger, but realized how important it was to have the Party leadership represented there. Learning that the union planned to hold a mass funeral in the local Polish Hall, it was agreed that I should go. On the morning of the funeral I was met at Pittsburgh by Dave Doran, then organizer of the Pittsburgh Y.C.L. He had managed to get into the town of Ambridge the day before to help and encourage the strikers and their wives. The terror had not abated. Toward the close of the day he was driven out of town.

I set off immediately for Ambridge with Pat Cush in a car driven by a comrade. The roads leading to Ambridge were filled with thousands of miners and steel workers from the Ohio, Monongahela and Allegheny valleys, coming to attend the funeral.

Every entrance to the town was guarded by machine guns and heavily armed deputies. Fire engines and trucks blocked all approaches. At the outskirts of Ambridge we met thousands of workers who had been driven back. The roads were littered with overturned trucks and cars; women were being driven along the road on foot. I said to Pat: "Let the comrade take his car back before it is wrecked. Suppose you go on and try to get in on foot. I'll turn up my coat collar and try to get in. Don't know me."

With an old coat and hat worn for the occasion, I looked like a dumb old grandmother toddling along. I walked right past the thugs into the town. The killers were everywhere, hands on the triggers of their guns. Most of the townspeople were huddled in their houses; here and there I caught a glimpse of a terror-stricken face at a window. When I reached Polish Hall I walked past the doorway to get the lay of the land. Immediately two Polish comrades fell in behind me, and pretending to be talking to each other warned me that the Polish Hall had been occupied by the deputies, and that I must keep on going until I reached the house of the murdered comrade.

Pietraszeski's house was on the edge of the town, and around it thousands of workers were massed. I arrived as they were carrying the coffin out of the house. A worker got up to speak, but was immediately arrested. The policemen started laying about with their clubs, and a woman screamed, "They are going to shoot again!" Just then an old time Jewish comrade whom I had known for years grabbed hold of me and said: "Do you want to be killed too? Get right into my car and cover yourself up. There will be no funeral here. You will have to speak at the grave." We got hold of Pat and took him along, and by a miracle dodged the police.

We reached the cemetery just in time to hear a Ukrainian workers' chorus singing a beautiful funeral hymn. The wife and family of the murdered worker were standing at the grave, the coffin resting on boards across it. Hundreds of workers had managed to reach the grave. As the singing ended, I started for the grave. Suddenly there was a sharp dig in my side. I looked up in surprise at a tall gray-haired man who had been standing beside me during the singing, with head bared. I had taken him for one of the mourners. To my amazement he was poking a sawed off shotgun in my side. I kept right on walking with the gun digging into my side. As I reached the grave and raised my hand, ready to speak, I got a terrific dig. I thought surely the gun would go off. But I had come there to speak and nobody would stop me. I can still remember what I said:

"Friends, I represent here today the workers of America who protest against the cruel murder of this strike sympathizer, killed because of his determination to help organize the workers. I also represent here today the workers of France through Henri Barbusse, who came to this country on a mission of peace and was greeted with the news of the war being waged against the workers here. He asked me to add his protest against the outrageous attack of the steel trust on these peaceful, innocent workers. I also represent here today the workers of Great Britain through their great leader Tom Mann who is now in New York, and who asked me to add the protest of the British workers. And, above all, I represent the political party of which this man was a member, the largest political party in the world today, the party that in Russia was responsible for freeing the workers and farmers, for freeing 170,000,000 people from tsarist slavery. In the name of the Communist Party of America I protest this murder and honor the name of this martyred hero...."

I felt sure those would be my last words on earth, as that man was still holding the gun against me, standing closer and closer, grim as death itself. But somehow or other I didn't feel frightened. I knew I was doing my duty to the working class, and that was the only thing that mattered. Pat Cush, who stood on the other side of me, was unaware of the presence of the gun. He stepped forward when I finished and spoke of the aims of the union. Then the comrade who had brought us hustled us back into his car again and we drove quickly away. As I looked back, I saw a large crowd of deputies moving menacingly toward the grave—just too late to carry out the attack on us they were obviously contemplating.

The gun episode had happened so quietly I thought it was no use mentioning it to any of the comrades. But the next morning when I went into the union office I found all the boys bending over a picture in the morning paper. "Mother," they exclaimed, "why didn't you tell us there was a gun in your side?"

The picture showed me addressing the crowd at the grave, and alongside of me, big as life, my gray-haired friend sticking his gun into me. The paper was the *Pittsburgh Gazette,* an organ of the steel trust. That first edition was hastily withdrawn from the stands and we were not able to procure a copy of the original photograph.

We saw to it that these events were well publicized through our press and at numerous meetings. So outraged was public opinion by the Ambridge massacre that in February, 1934, Gifford Pinchot, then Governor of Pennsylvania, appointed an investigating commission. The commission recommended legislation to abolish private police. Such legislation was later passed in Pennsylvania.

In July 1936 I was invited to Ambridge again, this time to celebrate my birthday—a wonderful contrast to my previous visit. A beautiful picnic was arranged by the Party and union members in a park within the city limits. Representatives of the Communist Party and labor officials made speeches. A huge birthday cake was presented to me, there was singing and dancing and everybody had a wonderful time. Nobody interfered with us. What had brought this change? What miracle had taken place? The miracle was the organization of the C.I.O. in steel, the miracle which has transformed the towns of Farrell, Aliquippa, McKeesport, and Sharon in Pennsylvania, and many others. Now, three years later, not only union meetings, but Communist meetings, demonstrations, workers' meetings of all kinds could be held openly. The union has not only strengthened the power of the workers in these towns, but gives inspiration to all the workers in steel and coal in that vicinity.

After his return to France, Barbusse wrote me asking me to organize a delegation of women from America to an International Women's Conference Against War and Fascism, in Paris. I concentrated first on getting farm delegates, and held meetings in Nebraska to arouse the farm people against fascism and the approaching war to such an extent that they would send a woman delegate to Paris. My efforts evoked the hostility of officials in the towns where I spoke—especially the county sheriff in Grand Island, who came up to me after a big meeting furiously angry, saying: "Why do you come here talking against war? War is a good thing. We will have more jobs if there is a war."

One evening I attended a meeting of the Unemployed Council in Grand Island to interest them in an anti-war conference to elect a delegate to Paris. At this meeting Carl Wiklund, a farmer from Loup City, requested support for a spontaneous strike of forty-seven women on a large poultry farm. Chickens were shipped here by the carload, many dying on the way. The girls were compelled to pluck the rotting carcasses, their fingers often becoming infected, and they had to spend a lot on doctors' fees.

The Farmers' Holiday Association had arranged to hold a mass meeting in support of the women's demands in the courthouse yard the following day. I agreed to speak, so I was driven there the next day. With me was a young Negro woman, secretary of our Anti-War Committee. Her husband, Floyd Booth, was organizer of the Unemployed Council of Grand Island. A large crowd from the Unemployed Council of Grand Island went along in a truck.

Frank McDonald, County Chairman of the Farmers' Holiday Association, was chairman. Everything was peaceful and quiet. One of the strikers read the demands. A committee of twenty-five was elected from the crowd to present them to the farm manager. The meeting awaited the committee's return quietly, and presently they brought back the report that some of the demands on sanitary requirements had been granted, but the demand for higher wages was refused.

Just after the report was read, a prominent farmer took the platform and said, "These members of the Unemployed Council have been here nearly all day, and have had nothing to eat. It seems to me that we should take up a collection to buy them some food."

A chorus of assent greeted the proposal and hats were passed around.

At that moment a note was handed to me on which were scrawled the words, "All people from Grand Island must be out of this place by 5 o'clock." It was five o'clock then. As I handed the note to the chairman, the meeting was set upon by a crowd of thugs including the town's "leading citizens," armed with blackjacks, and with deadly weapons peculiar to the locality called "saps," hollowed lead-filled broomsticks.

Bert Sell, one of our leading farmers from a nearby district, who had been among the speakers, had his skull broken by one of these "saps." They tramped on him after he fell and injured him so that he never recovered. His four sons defended him valiantly and were in turn attacked by the gangsters.

Floyd Booth was chased by a gang crying, "Get the Nigger! Get the Nigger!" Members of the Unemployed Council managed to get him away from the mob.

A big brute had Harry Smith, the Loup City Unemployed Council organizer (who later fought with the Loyalists in Spain), on the ground, beating him with a blackjack in each hand. It looked as though it was all up for Harry when a little farmer jumped on the thug's back and Harry managed to get away.

We got the unconscious Bert Sell to the hospital. Then I took the young Negro woman back with me to Grand Island.

The next evening about seven o'clock, before Andy returned from his work, the sheriff came stamping up the stairs and into my room accompanied by a regular gangster, and said threateningly, "It's time for you to get out of this county. You can't interfere with my business any longer." I sat there silently, feeling sure they were going to "take me for a ride." Just then, two members of the Unemployed Council arrived asking to see Andy.

I managed to whisper, "Don't leave. Stay here with me." In a few minutes the Grand Island Chief of Police joined our little gathering. He said I would have to come along. I asked him to let me see his warrant, but he said it was just for "investigation." As I still refused to budge, he and the other two drew their guns. They pushed me down the stairs. The two Unemployed Council members crowded into the police car with me. At the City Hall they threw me into a cell where I found Mrs. Booth, who had been held there since morning. She told me that Floyd had been put in a cell downstairs. She warned me against lying on the bed which had been occupied by a syphilitic prostitute all afternoon.

Meantime the men from the Unemployed Council went to find Andy, who came back with them. But the warden would not let anyone see me, and next morning would not let me telephone. About three o'clock that afternoon the Sheriff and Chief of Police took Floyd Booth, his wife, and me in a car over to Loup City, fifty miles away, to be arraigned.

There the District Attorney charged us with brutally attacking thirty men—the leaders of the gang that attacked us! Seven farmers had already been charged with the same offense. The authorities had the crust to include the dying farmer and his sons in the indictment. The seven farmers had secured bail, and one of them told me that a good old Socialist farmer was ready to put up bail for me. I asked him if there was bail for Floyd Booth and his wife, too, and they told me the farmers were too poor because of the terrible drought to raise any more. I felt I could not accept the bail and leave the two Negro comrades in jail, in an atmosphere so dangerously charged with bitter hate of Negroes.

The temperature was 110 in the shade. After we pleaded "not guilty" we were taken back to the jail in Grand Island, where the young woman and I were placed in a garret cell under the copper roof, the hottest place I have ever seen in my life. Floyd was held downstairs in the same jail.

The sheriff finally permitted me to wire to the noted I.L.D. lawyer, my good friend David Bentall.

After eleven days in this hell-hole, Floyd and his wife were allowed to go home to attend the funeral of Floyd's father who had died while he was in jail. As the trial was the next day, they took them right from the funeral to the courthouse. As soon as I was able to telephone to my husband that they had been released, he immediately secured the bail money, came back to Grand Island, woke up the sheriff and made him execute a bail bond. I was free to leave the jail with him after ten o'clock the night before the trial. I never appreciated fresh air so much.

The trial lasted a week, before a jury made up of the worst elements of the county. The prosecution challenged any farmer who belonged to any kind of organization—except a church— and as a farmer who isn't a member of some kind of organization doesn't amount to much, only the riff-raff were left to form the jury.

This frame-up ended with a sentence of 30 days and $100.00 fine and costs—$350.00. Since Nebraska has an intermediary court between the district court where we were tried and the State court, we had to go through another trial within a few weeks with the same results except that young Mrs. Booth was let go. We appealed to the state supreme court. Bail was secured for all of us. Since the state supreme court held no session until the following fall, we went about our work.

I held a successful anti-war conference in Grand Island, where a young farmer's wife, Maggie Pritchau, was elected delegate to Paris.

Then I went east to organize our delegation. Altogether I secured fifty-two women delegates, among them wives of miners, farmers and sharecroppers, workers, social workers, middle class women who hated war, and representatives of religious organizations. There was a Socialist woman from Milwaukee, Jessica Henderson of Boston, who had worked on the Sacco-Vanzetti case, and Ida, a trade union girl from Detroit. Polish Mary, youngest member of our delegation, came from the Chicago stockyards, bringing with her the signatures of 15,000 Polish women recording their hatred of war and fascism. A representative from the

Federation of Finnish Women bore a banner to be presented to the international conference. The four Negro women delegates were: Capitola Tasker, Alabama sharecropper, tall and graceful, the life of the whole delegation; Lulia Jackson elected by the Pennsylvania miners; a woman who represented the mothers of the Scottsboro boys; and Mabel Byrd, a brilliant young honor graduate of the University of Washington, who had had a position with the International Labor Office in Geneva. At the meeting we held in New York just before we left she was elected secretary of our delegation and I was made chairman. Many of the women had never crossed the ocean before. As I was the only one not seasick, I had quite a job cheering up the others. We held meetings telling the other passengers our purpose, and our principles. The French purser, when we asked permission to hold a meeting, said: "Ah—peace, it is very beautiful, peace. But, er—ladies, I must ask you, please to speak only about peace, but fascism—you must say nothing about that." So we avoided the term, but made our ideas quite clear.

We received an enthusiastic reception on our arrival. The Socialist delegate, Capitola Tasker, and myself, were elected on the executive committee of the conference. Mabel Byrd, the young colored woman who was the secretary of our delegation, was elected one of the conference secretaries.

The conference, which was held in August, 1934, united women from all over the world in a great protest against the rising menace of fascism and the oncoming war. Over forty nations and all races and creeds were represented, making a varied array of tongues and costumes. Mrs. Harry Pollitt led a delegation of seventy-five from England. There were women from Austria and from Germany—refugees from the concentration camps of fascism, who risked their lives to come. A high point of the conference was the entrance, after we had gathered together for our opening session, of ten delegates from the Soviet Union. They were a beautiful group and everyone was inspired by the presence of these women absolutely free from the limitations the rest of the women of the world suffered under capitalism.

I was asked to make the opening speech after the president's report. I quaked—for once in my life it seemed to me I could not possibly get up in front of a vast throng of people, but, of course, I could not refuse. When I got up to speak I was determined to make them understand how much it meant that these remarkable women from all over the world, united by one great desire for peace in the world, had come together. Deeply moved myself, I realized how much I expressed the emotion of all when women from many countries came up and hugged me, women from Holland, from South Africa, from the Far East, some of whom hadn't understood my words, but had understood the message they carried.

An amazing and enthusiastic unity was established in the sessions that followed in preparedness to fight the common enemy, imperialist capitalism, breeder of fascism and war.

We had appointed to the resolutions committee the Negro woman from the miners' union. I walked into the committee room one day just as they were reading the English translation of the anti-war manifesto that was to express the ideas of the whole conference. One of the pacifist delegates was saying:

"I think there is too much about fighting in that manifesto. It says fight against war, fight for peace—fight, fight, fight. . . . We are women, we are mothers—we don't want to fight. We know that even when our children are bad we are nice to them, and we win them by love, not by fighting them—"

Then Lulia Jackson, the little Negro miner's wife, stood up.

"Ladies," she said, "it has just been said that we must not fight, that we must be gentle and kind to our enemies, to those who are for war. I can't agree with that. Everyone knows the cause of war—it is capitalism. We can't just give these bad capitalists their supper and put them to bed the way we do with our children. We must fight them."

Everyone laughed and applauded, even the pacifist. Assured that our resolutions committee was in good hands, I went back to my place on the platform.

The strong anti-war manifesto presented at the close of the conference, which included the determination to fight for the peace policy of the Soviet Union, was adopted unanimously.

This was an exciting time in France. Less than two weeks before the Socialist and Communist Parties had concluded their united front pact. A broad anti-fascist People's Front was developing. There was great public approval of our conference, and we were feted everywhere. The Communist mayor and city council of one of the Paris suburbs invited us to spend a day in their beautiful park. There were physical culture displays and dances by children, and music and singing all day long. Women from each delegation greeted the vast audience, which included thousands of French people and groups of tourists. Capitola stood up straight and proud and told them about fascism in our own South, about lynching, about the terror the sharecroppers were meeting in their efforts to organize for a better life. She finished by singing the sharecroppers' song, adapted to the occasion. Her rich voice rang out:

> "Like a tree that's standing by the water,
> We shall not be moved—
> We're against war and fascism,
> We shall not be moved."

On the boat going home Capitola said to me:

"Mother, when I get back to Alabama and go out to that cotton patch back of our little old shack, I'll stand there thinking to myself, 'Capitola, did you really go over there to Paris and see all those wonderful women and hear all those great talks, or was it just a dream that you were ever there?' And if it turns out that it really wasn't a dream, why Mother, I'm just going to broadcast all over Alabama all that I've learned over here, and tell them how women from all over the world are fighting to stop the kind of terror we have in the South, and to stop war!"

During the 1936 election campaign for Browder and Ford we drove through the town where Capitola lived. Had our carload of white people stopped there it would have made the local authorities feel sure Capitola must be a red. It was a real tragedy to me not to stop.

About a month after I returned from the Paris Conference I received a summons from the state supreme court of Nebraska to appear at once in Loup City to serve my sentence. They had turned down our appeal.

There was wide public protest that I had to serve a sentence at my age on such a raw frame-up. Members of the National Committee of the Party went with me to Pennsylvania station, where a large number of my friends were congregated. Women from many organizations brought me flowers and greeted me with tenderness and sadness. At the top of the stairs I made a brief speech of farewell, telling them that I would be back to work with them harder than ever—no Nebraska jail could dampen my spirits.

At Philadelphia another group of comrades waited at the station to say good-by, and bring me flowers. In Omaha where I had to change for a local to Loup City, still another large crowd of friends and comrades met me, some accompanying me to Loup City. The seven farmers had already begun their terms in Loup City jail, and I was informed that since there was no jail for women prisoners in the county, the Loup City sheriff would take me back to Omaha the next day. This sheriff then in office was one of the very thugs who had raided the meeting. He had been elected since my trial. I didn't feel very comfortable about driving 200 miles alone with him.

At Omaha there was an argument between the Loup City sheriff and the Omaha sheriff, who didn't want me because he was afraid there would be demonstrations around the jail. He assured me that I would receive no special privileges. And I certainly didn't. Most of my mail was taken away from me, the letters I wrote were censored; the food set before me in a rusty tin pan was not fit for a stray cat.

The matron handed me a uniform that was stiff as a board. She ordered: "You will put this on." "No," I said, "I won't put that thing on. I shall wear my own clothes." In the cell she led me into, privacy was impossible. There were ten women there. The cots were in little open cubicles each containing a toilet and cold running water. There was a shower which for sanitary reasons I preferred not to use. I commandeered a clean bucket to catch the warm water from the shower, which, turned upside down, I could sit on. The other girls sat on a wooden bench which served as a table at meal time. Each of us had our own tin bowl and pewter spoon. I asked the matron if she would buy me some fruit. She said I could only buy things at the commissary which offered snuff, smoking tobacco, or cigarettes. I used the money given to me for prison comforts to buy Copenhagen snuff for a young Finnish girl, and Bull Durham tobacco for Beulah, a Negro woman who became my friend.

The first night I was sitting disconsolately on my inverted bucket, when I heard a queer sound which seemed to come from the baseboard of the cell. Looking down I saw a ventilator connected with the cell next to us and a colored woman's face peering through. "Mother Bloor, is you there?" she was asking. "Yes," I said, "I am Mother Bloor. Who are you?"

"I am Beulah."

"Beulah, what did you come to this place for?"

"Mother, I done got the beatenest husband. He threw me in the Missouri River." It seemed that Beulah and her husband both got drunk and had fallen into the river, and now they were both in jail.

Then to my astonishment Beulah asked: "Mother Bloor, do you know Kate O'Hare?"

I laughed and said, "Yes, Beulah, I know her well. Where did you know her?" "I knew her in Missouri," she said. "Where is she now?"

"Oh," I said, "I guess I know where that was. It was in Jefferson City, wasn't it?"

"Yes, ma'am," said Beulah, "that's where it was." "Well, Beulah, I saw her in that prison, and she told me about you. You used to help her make the heavy overalls she worked on. She was very grateful to you for it."

Beulah was delighted that I should have heard about this and to hear that Kate Richards O'Hare was out of prison.

Beulah's sentence was short and as she was leaving I begged her, "Beulah, do try not to get in this place again. It isn't fit for humans." She said, "Mother, I sure don't want to come back here any more. But those policemen have it in for me." Inside of three days I heard the girls call out—"Here comes Beulah back again." Drunk again! She had led a parade of children through the streets singing at the top of her lungs. It was too much for the Omaha police to see anyone so happy, so they brought her back.

Most of the girls and women there were quite young and all of them dope fiends or alcoholics. One good-looking girl only 19 years old told me she loathed her business of prostitution, but felt hopeless about ever escaping from it. That tragic group was one of the most horrible indictments of our system I had ever seen.

I became friends with the girls—playing cards with them—using my spare underclothes and some pillow cases that were sent me to make things for them, as they had only the rough prison suits to wear day and night.

One day a visitor came from New York. He had been literally pounding at the gates for an entire week and was one of the very few that were allowed to see me. It was my dear old friend and comrade, Paul Crosbie, who had visited the governor and done everything he could to get me out. He had heard that I had no butter, so he had carefully wrapped up some for me, and slipped it to me when the matron turned her back for a minute. Visitors were allowed only once a week.

The seven farmers and I were released about the same time, neither they nor I wanting to get out until we were sure we would all be out. On my way home through Chicago, with a few hours to spare, I went to a defense meeting for Angelo Herndon. They were very pleased to see me, and wanted me to speak. I had been so starved that I ate too much dinner that night and had a terrible case of indigestion. That, added to the weakening through the horrible jail conditions, nearly finished me and I thought I would die as I awaited my turn at the meeting. I don't believe I ever told Angelo what an effort I made to speak for him that night. But speak I did, in spite of the pain.

Angelo Herndon was known from one end of the country to the other for his beautiful character. Two years before, at the age of nineteen, he had organized an unemployment council in Atlanta, Georgia, and led a demonstration of Negro and white workers together to demand relief. For this he had been convicted under a state law dating back to 1861 of "attempting to incite to insurrection," and in January, 1933, had been sentenced to twenty years on the chain gang by an all white jury. After serving seven months, he was now free on bail of $15,000 (raised in less than a month in small amounts, from people all over the country). Later the United States Supreme Court refused to review his case on a technicality, and he had to go back and serve more time before he was finally freed by a decision of the U. S. Supreme Court in April 1937. While the main fight for his release was carried on through the I.L.D., there was a broad Joint Committee to Aid the Herndon Defense, including Socialists, I.W.W.'s, Negro organizations, etc. Over a million petition signatures were obtained and the results showed the efficacy of united mass pressure.

I shall never forget the day Angelo was freed. As I was walking to our office a girl came running toward me shouting joyously, "Angelo Herndon is free!" A little further on I saw some boys running toward Broadway shouting: "Angelo Herndon is free, Angelo Herndon is free!" All along the street were groups of our people who took up the cry, "Angelo Herndon is free!" A few days later Pennsylvania station was packed with men, women and children, white people and Negroes, greeting Angelo as he came in from the South, welcoming him to freedom.

Ever since then Angelo has been working in every possible way to call attention to the oppression of his own people and of the white workers too. We are fortunate indeed in having Angelo in our movement, and not only Angelo, but many other outstanding Negro leaders. There is Ben Davis, Jr., who graduated with high honors from Harvard and has since given himself wholly to our cause. As I write he has just come back from a tremendous tilt with the powers-that-be in Washington over the anti-lynch bill. I could go on indefinitely naming our great Negro comrades such as James Ford, whose nomination for the Vice-Presidency of the United States I had the great honor of presenting to the National Convention of the Party four years ago, William Patterson, Henry Winston, and many others I am proud to be associated with. Among the women, too, are many brilliant, fine and devoted comrades.

From the Herndon meeting in Chicago, I was escorted to my train. In Pennsylvania Station in New York the following afternoon I was joyfully welcomed back by the same big crowd of relatives, friends, and comrades that had seen me off a month before.

I picked up my work where I had left off. It was decided that my husband and I should live in the East. We organized a local headquarters in Philadelphia of the Farmers' National Committee for Action. My husband and I frequently toured Pennsylvania farm sections. My son Hal, then living near Washington, worked with us actively.

Next spring, 1935, I made an automobile tour through the country. Our plan was to visit our farmer friends in the Middle West and then go on to the Southwest, stopping for two weeks at Commonwealth College of Arkansas, where I was scheduled to give a lecture course. My husband and I started out one lovely day in June loaded down with blankets, camping materials, dishes, etc. My granddaughter, Herta Ware, was with us.

Our first stop was Pittsburgh, where we had several meetings in my old fighting ground. Then on to Chicago, through the Northwest. On warm nights we spread our blankets on the ground and slept in the open. Often we cooked our meals on the camp stove. Along the way mass picnics and meetings were arranged for us. We finally arrived in Houston, Texas, where the state organizer had arranged a series of meetings in the oil region. Conditions were bad in Texas where one of our organizers had recently been beaten to death in jail. I had a wonderful surprise in Texas, meeting my son Dick who had driven all the way from California to have a visit with me.

In Dallas we had very successful meetings, although it was hot August weather. Finally the day came for Dick to go back to California. It seemed as if he could not leave me. We said good-bye five or six times that morning and, finally, after he had started, he came back. The next morning we went to the telegraph office and found a wire telling us that my beloved oldest son, Harold Ware, had been fatally hurt in an automobile accident near Harrisburg, Pa. The wire said not to come until I had received later news, that they would telegraph every hour.

I cancelled my dates for that night in Texas, and we spent the time waiting in the car in front of the telegraph office. Hal was so dear to all three of us, waiting was the hardest thing of all. Next morning we heard that he had passed away without regaining consciousness. Here we were, with all our belongings, sitting in front of the telegraph office, not knowing where to go or what to do—with the greatest grief of our lives. I did exactly what I thought he would want me to do. I went straight on to Commonwealth, where he had wanted me to go, knowing that they would receive me, not only for my own sake, but for his sake, with kindly tenderness.

When we arrived, we found literally hundreds of telegrams from Hal's friends and my friends who knew how dear he was to me. After two days I opened my classes on farm problems. This work probably saved my spiritual life. Although it was very hard, I went through with it. The two weeks' course I gave in Commonwealth has not only been repeated in later years, but I find by meeting the students in various places that it was well worth while.

At this period there was an effort to make Commonwealth a real united front school for farmer and worker students of all political leanings. There were Communists, Socialists and unfortunately, one or two Trotskyites. Lucien Koch was then director, and Charlotte Moskowitz, whom we all called "Chucky," the devoted executive secretary. Both of them had been there for nine years, doing heroic pioneer work. Joe Jones, one of our best proletarian artists, was there, painting a mural. The miners portrayed in that huge mural were so life-like they seemed to breathe; its lynching scenes so realistic your blood ran cold. It pictured the life of the sharecropper, the fields of cotton spread out before the window of a miserable shack, a vista of labor, fear and futility to the woman lying on her cot. It was a powerful representation of the life of the sharecroppers and the miners, of the terrible oppression of the Negroes of Arkansas, and a terrific indictment of our system. On finishing it, Joe said, "I want to give this painting to the people of Arkansas. It belongs to them and they must protect it. The time may come when our enemies will want to burn down these buildings, and we want the farmers here to know what this mural means. We will hold a meeting, and you will speak, Mother, and I will present it to them."

Students went through the whole area announcing the meeting. Some of the farmers walked eight miles to the meeting; some people came from the town of Mena ten miles away. One sharecropper was heard to say wonderingly to another as he opened the door of the dining room, and saw the painting before him: "Why that's us, ain't it!" Joe's beautiful speech brought tears to everyone's eyes.

One Sunday, while I was sitting on the porch of my little cabin in Commonwealth, a committee of mountain folk came to see me. They had walked eight miles down the mountain to ask me to speak the following Wednesday at their Huey Long Club. I promised to go, and one old man with them said, "Sister, you will have to open with prayer because our president is a preacher and he will ask you to open with prayer. Can you pray?" I said, "Oh, yes. I can pray."

Most of the students went along with me to the meeting, and at the appointed time we were at the church. The old man who had invited me got up and announced: "I don't know what the trouble is, but our preacher didn't come. I suppose he was afraid of a 'contraversity.' But old lady Bloor is here, and she will talk to you. But first I want all the gals in the room to come up front and sing." "Chucky" went up to their old melodeon and played. Our girls stood up with the women of the mountains, and what did they sing first but: "Just Like a Tree—Standing by the Water—We shall not be moved—Jesus Saves, Jesus Saves, Jesus Saves." Our girls sang along with them and when the hill folk finished our girls kept right on with our own version which the hill people sang lustily too. Fortunately the preacher arrived in time to do the praying. In my speech I didn't praise their hero Huey Long. I told them that no one man could help them, that they must help themselves. I told them they must have their own organizations—they were part of this government and they must bring pressure on the government to secure a decent life for themselves.

Afterwards we urged the people of Mena to help the hill people, who were close to starvation, to organize a Workers' Alliance to demand state and county relief from the government. This brought results. On my second trip there I went up to this same place again. Only a year had passed. With me was the theatrical director of the New Theatre League from New York who had her guitar with her, and played and sang folk songs and songs of our movement in an open air meeting under the trees. The chairman of the meeting was the president of the local Southern Tenant Farmers' Union of that mountain. They were now all members of the county Workers' Alliance and had secured many benefits the winter before. Not even the ghost of Huey Long was present.

We came back from that trip through Washington. It was a sad homecoming. A number of my son Harold's associates in the farm work met me at my daughter Helen's house in Washington, and they were like bereaved children without him. Wherever I go I see young men and women who have come into the movement through him, especially in the farm lands of the Northwest and the South, and his pioneer work is bringing forth great fruit, through the many people he inspired.

18. Hal Ware—
Pioneer of Collective Farming

MY son Hal made such an important contribution both to the development of our work among farmers in America and to the upbuilding of the Soviet Union through his agricultural work there, that I would like to digress at this point to write about his work.

Hal was my oldest son, but the third in the family, Grace and Helen being older. As a boy he loved the outdoors, was full of restless, eager vitality and bold curiosity. He had a startlingly vivid imagination, and an urge and talent for organizing that continued and marked his whole life. More than ordinarily shy, he forgot his shyness when engaged in one of his organizing ventures, and a flow of colorful, stirring talk would come from him, so persuasive that those who heard him were completely carried away. He grew slim and tall, and when we moved to Arden was captain of the baseball team and a leader in tennis and other games. He missed a lot of school because of his siege of tuberculosis, but he read a lot and was always able to make up two or three years of ordinary schooling in a few months of intensive study. His interest in socialism began as early as I can remember.

When we lived in Arden, and later, when I was away on my trips, he often had the responsibility of looking after his three younger brothers—Buzz, Dick and Carl. He disciplined them—

and organized them so that they did the cooking and household chores—more than I was able to make them do!

Hal's interest in agriculture began early. He started raising truck in a small garden in Arden, and sold it around the countryside. His keen sense of beauty showed in the way he fixed up his boxes of vegetables to sell, arranging them artistically in green boxes.

He first planned to study forestry. He used to tell me his dreams of a life in the open, alone on the hillside, a sea of green tree tops below him. While taking the entrance exams for Pennsylvania State College he found that the forestry course would take four years, while there was a fine two-year agricultural course. Beginning to feel, too, that he did not want to live away from people, but among them, he chose agriculture. His interest in economics and politics developed intensely at this time, and while at college he wrote me constantly for the latest news of the socialist movement. We were always very close to one another, and no matter how many months or years we were apart, we could always pick up just where we had left off.

Hal worked his farm during the summer to meet his college expenses. Finishing his course at twenty-one he came back to Arden to farm. From his truck garden, Hal branched out into the mushroom business. He started with a small mushroom house, often staying up all night keeping the oil stove going to maintain the temperature. The mushroom business grew, and he got Tony, a young Italian, to help him. Then he bought an orchard. Whatever Hal organized, he had to build into something larger, and when it was going successfully, went on to something bigger still. "I always want to see what's beyond that next hill, Mom," he used to say. He was beginning to feel confined in Arden, and was already planning work among farmers, organizing them for socialism. But he felt he must first master every detail of farming, so that he could work among farmers as one who understood their problems and spoke their language.

The new age of mechanization had come to the farm and Hal realized he had to know the problems of large scale industrialized farming as well as those of a garden plot before he could offer the farmers solutions to their problems. Every step Hal took now was carefully directed toward his later work. He applied himself intelligently and devotedly to preparation for leadership in the farm movement.

Hal, aware that his father had set aside a sum of money for each of his children after his death, asked for his share now, at the moment of his life when it would mean most. So Mr. Ware helped him to buy a grain and dairy farm in Westchester County. There Hal, with a big herd of cows which he milked himself, a tractor and other farm machinery, organized and ran an up-to-date farm. He was the first to introduce the gasoline tractor in that locality. He patched up two old hand cultivators, fitted them to a tractor, and got immediate results. Neighboring farmers, who at first thought he was a crank, were soon following his example.

While Hal did a splendid job of running his farm, he never lost sight of his larger purpose. He read economics and scientific agriculture, studied Marx, and kept constantly abreast of the latest developments in the socialist movement. His first vote was cast for Debs. His interest was always with the left wing of the Socialists, and when the Communist Party was formed, he became a charter member. He went right to the Party with the problems of the farmers. But the Party was not yet in a position to launch a farm program on the scale he visualized.

As soon as the Russian Revolution occurred, Hal read everything he could lay his hands on about Russian agriculture, realizing that under a socialist government the farmers for the first time in history would have a chance to work out a fundamental solution for their problems and that their experiences would be of the utmost importance to us here in America.

About that time Lenin, needing material about farmers in America and unable to find it, wrote to the Party in his clear, blunt manner, asking: "Have you no farmers in America?" Hal was asked what he could do about making a report. He said he would have to make an extensive survey of the country. But that was impossible as there were no funds. Hal said, "Give me five dollars and I'll beat my way across the country."

He knew the time had come for him to go directly into Party work. He was a farmer himself, and a good one. He knew the problems from all angles because war conditions had driven him close to bankruptcy. What he needed now to fill out his experience was just what this broad survey offered. He gave up the farm and moved with his family to New York to familiarize himself with general Party problems.

Then, in a pair of brown over-alls, with only a toothbrush and five dollars in his pocket, Hal started off on a six-months' trip studying the migratory farm workers by becoming one of them. He followed the harvest through the South to the Middle West and then to the Northwest, and back again through the wheat fields of Minnesota and Wisconsin. He hoboed all the way, working where he could, bumming his way when he couldn't get work, his keen eyes and ears absorbing information.

The trip was adventurous as well as rewarding in experience and knowledge. Once, through inexperience, Hal failed to cover his head riding through a snow tunnel in the mountains of the Northwest on top of a freight car. The monoxide fumes overpowered him, but by a miracle one of his buddies, feeling the unconscious body rolling off the top of the train, reached out and grabbed him as he was slipping over the edge. Rounding a slow curve Hal was able to drop off. He fell asleep, and it was dark when he woke. Alone in the mountains, he was hunting for a way down, when he heard a cry of human agony. He followed the sound until he found a trail which led to a lonely cabin. Frantic screams froze him with horror. He had no weapon but a stick which he had instinctively picked up. Shouting to an imaginary companion, "Wait here a minute, Buddy," he entered and called out, but was answered only by groans. In the room beyond, moonlight showed a woman writhing in agony on the bed.

It took Hal some time to find a lamp and matches, and then the full gravity of the situation burst on him. Before him was a young girl giving birth. Hal knew he mustn't lose his head.

Quickly he made a fire and put water on, meanwhile reconstructing mentally every detail of the scene when he had watched the delivery of one of his own children. He sterilized a pair of scissors, delivered the baby, cut the umbilical cord, turned the baby upside down, spanked it as he had seen the doctor do and was relieved when a lusty yell came. Presently the infant was wrapped in a blanket and resting in its mother's arms. The mother smiled wanly, and then nearly knocked Hal over by remarking, "Oh, Doctor, it was lucky you arrived in time!"

The husband, it appeared, had gone to fetch a doctor, but had miscalculated on the time of the baby's arrival.

When Hal returned he prepared a detailed survey on migratory workers, types of agriculture and conditions of the farmers of America, and a map showing distribution of types of farms, farm incomes and so on, in different sections of the country. The survey and map were sent to Lenin. When I was in Moscow in 1921, Lenin wrote me a pencilled note praising this work. That precious note was sacrificed on one of the occasions when my papers were destroyed.

Hal next had four months valuable experience of reorganizing the horticultural work on the big mechanized farm of the Loyal Order of Moose at Mooseheart, Illinois, and spent some time working among the farmers of North Dakota.

Back in New York Hal was called in to advise on agricultural purchases for Russian famine relief. Through the initiative of the Friends of Soviet Russia, the American Federated Russian Famine Relief Committee had been formed as a clearing house for the relief funds raised by trade unions. There was $75,000, collected in the United States in their treasury with which they proposed to purchase food supplies. Hal saw the problem in bigger terms than immediate relief. He said, "Why not put the money into tractors and seed, grow food on the spot and at the same time help the government's program of teaching the Russian peasants modern agriculture which will keep them from ever having famines again?" The idea was accepted. Practical farmers being needed as teachers, Hal went to North Dakota and picked out nine husky "sod-busters." They left their plows to go for expenses only—knowing that was better than they could do on a North Dakota farm. While Hal exaggerated the hardships, he made it sound like a glorious adventure, which indeed it was.

Next Hal collected twenty carloads of the latest type American farm machinery, a supply of Canadian rye seed, two passenger automobiles, tents and equipment for his men.

Hal wanted to take his tractors to the great steppe grain lands in Saratov or Tambov region, but tractors were little known in Soviet Russia in those days—and some of the Commissariat of Agriculture officials, not understanding the significance of the work as Lenin did, assigned them to rough rolling country near Perm. As Hal later found out, there was more to this than ignorance. Even then the wreckers were at work, trying to prevent the building of socialism. But Hal was not daunted. His carloads of machinery were shipped to the nearest railroad station—about sixty miles from the farm. The roads were terrible, scores of bridges had to be repaired or built before they could get the tractors to their destination. Peasants along the way crossed themselves as the "devil machines" appeared, women and children ran screaming from them, and priests drew circles around them, warning that their use was going against the will of God. But the Americans explained their mission patiently through interpreters, and presently crowds of peasants were out building the bridges for them and peasant boys were mounted on the seats of the tractors, showing a quick skill at handling the machines.

Finally the odd procession arrived at the state farm in Toikino where they were to work, in time for the spring planting. Hal drew most of his workers from the surrounding villages, and within a few weeks forty young Russian peasants were themselves driving tractors on seven hour shifts, while the American workers taught and supervised for fourteen hours a day. The work had a double purpose—to produce as much grain as possible on the spot, and to win the countryside to new methods of farming.

Farmers came from miles around begging that the tractors be sent to help them plow their land, (Kolchak's armies and the famine had swept this district clean of horses). Hal, seizing the opportunity to make a demonstration, would take his tractor and plow the peasant's narrow strip of land to the end of the plot. Then he would get off hopelessly, indicating that he could not turn the tractor around in such a narrow place. "These new machines are too large for your small strips," he would say. "I guess it just won't work." But the peasants had seen the long furrow of brown earth turned up so swiftly by the tractor's shining blades. No horse-drawn plow ever went so deep. So the peasants put their heads together. "Why not throw all our strips together in one big piece, and then he can turn his tractor around and plow them all at once?" And for thousands of peasants in Perm that summer this meant the beginning of collective farming.

Among the local officials there were bureaucrats and wreckers who did not want this venture to succeed, and sent complaints to Moscow. An interpreter, one of Trotsky's henchmen, tried to sow disruption among the Americans and suspicion of them in the countryside. Hal discovered that he was deliberately distorting and misinterpreting his requests and instructions, so that urgently needed shipments of gasoline and supplies did not reach them on time, and the work was hampered in many ways. Lenin, unknown to Hal, sent his own investigator to the farm, who reported that what these Americans were doing fitted in exactly with the Bolshevik program of transforming the primitive, individualistic and unproductive farming of the past into collectivized modern agriculture. Lenin instructed that the fullest possible co-operation be given to the American group. And in the Moscow *Pravda* of October 24, 1922, Lenin published a letter to Hal about his work (V. I. Lenin, *Collected Works,* Vol. XXVII, page 308, Russian Edition) in which he said, in part:

".... You have accomplished successes which must be recognized as quite exceptional ... I hasten to express my deep appreciation, with the request to publish it in the organ of your society and if

Ella Reeve Bloor speaking at the Sacco and Vanzetti memorial meeting at Union Square, New York, in 1927

Harold Ware (1890-1935)

possible in the general press of the United States of America. . . .

"I again express to you deep thanks in the name of our republic and request you to keep in mind that not a single kind of help has been for us so timely and important as the help shown by you."

By winter, Hal figured the work they had come for was finished. They had gathered in a big harvest, put 4,000 acres under winter wheat, taught dozens of young Russian peasants how to operate tractors, and started the peasants of Perm on the road to collectivization which was to prove the solution of Russia's farm problem. So they presented their tractors and machinery to the state farm, leaving that fine North Dakota farmer, Otto Anstrom, to help look after the machinery during the winter, and pass on more of his knowledge and skill to the Russians.

Otto lived with the peasants all that winter and told me afterward it was one of the happiest years of his life. I was in Moscow when the other farmers were on their way home. The whole city turned out to greet them. When I asked how they liked the work, they said it was far better to work for this wonderful, growing, young country than back in North Dakota as poor farmers fast losing their land, with agriculture in a decadent state and with no constructive plans to fight drought.

Now Hal visualized a more permanent set-up, a model farm and training school to work out and demonstrate large scale farming methods best adapted to Russian conditions. A group of American specialists would start the farm and train a Russian staff. Hal saw that the future of Soviet agriculture was in mechanized, co-operative production. Since this offered an immense market for American agricultural machinery, his first plan was to get American companies to provide the machinery on credit and send over skilled men to operate and demonstrate it. The Soviet Government gladly offered co-operation. Hal went back to talk to the farm machinery concerns. He interested some of the largest firms in his proposal. But when it came to financing, the higher ups in the companies refused credit. Absence of diplomatic relations between the two countries, and of normal trade relations, made them fear to put any substantial money into the scheme. Even Hal's persuasiveness could not overcome the years of hostile propaganda and the tales of instability of the Soviet regime.

One of Hal's special missions on his trip back to America was to bring a letter and an autographed photograph from Lenin to Steinmetz. On February 16, 1922, Steinmetz wrote to Lenin expressing his interest in the plans of the young Soviet Republic and offered to help with information and advice. Steinmetz, as a lifelong Socialist, was deeply thrilled at the coming of the new socialist order in Russia. As a scientist he was even more thrilled at the tremendous vistas opened up through Lenin's bold and farseeing electrification program, the first of the great Soviet plans, which laid the basis for the complete transformation of the country from a backward agrarian state to a modern industrial nation. Lenin answered immediately:

Dear Mr. Steinmetz:

I heartily thank you for your friendly letter of February 16, 1922. ... I see that you have been led to your sympathy with the U.S.S.R. on the one hand through your social and political views. And on the other hand you, as a representative of electrical science in one of the most technically advanced countries in the world, have become convinced of the necessity and inevitability of replacing capitalism by a new social system which would establish planned regulation of the national economy and guarantee the well-being of the mass of the people on the basis of electrification in all countries. In all countries of the world there is growing— more slowly than might be desired, but irresistibly and steadily— the number of representatives of science, technique, and art, who are convinced of the necessity of replacing capitalism by a different social and economic system, and who are not repelled or frightened by the "terrible difficulties" of the struggle of Soviet Russia against the whole capitalist world, but who rather are led by these difficulties to an understanding of the inevitability of the struggle and of the necessity of doing everything in their power to help the new to prevail over the old.

I wish especially to thank you for your offer to help Russia with information and advice. Since the absence of official and legally established relations between the Soviet Union and the United States greatly complicates both for us and for you the practical realization of your proposal, I am taking the liberty of publishing both your letter and my answer in the hope that thus many people living in America or in countries connected by trade treaties both with the United States and with Russia will assist you (with information, translations from Russian into English, etc.) to carry out your intention of helping the Soviet Republic.

With warmest greetings,
LENIN.

The letter did not reach Steinmetz until Hal brought him the original copy on his return to the United States late in 1922. Hal made a special trip to Schenectady to deliver the letter and photograph. Steinmetz's secretary met him at the door and said:

"No one can see Dr. Steinmetz today. He is having a conference with all the vice-presidents."

Hal said in his quiet way, "Please take a note to Dr. Steinmetz —it is important." Tearing a page from his notebook he wrote: "I have just come from Moscow, with a personal message from Lenin. I will wait until you are free."

In five seconds the door was flung open, and Steinmetz himself rushed out, his arms outflung, saying, "Come in, come in, come in!" He hustled Hal into his private office, ordering his startled secretary over his shoulder, "Don't let anyone in!"

He bombarded Hal with questions about Lenin, about education, about science, about the electrification program, about the organization of industry, about agriculture. Time went on, and one by one the vice-presidents opened the door and peered in. "Get out of here!" Steinmetz growled at them, and went on asking questions and listening eagerly to what Hal told him. Finally he said:

"Young man, do you realize what Russia has been doing? In this short time they have developed a standardized, planned electrification program for the whole country. There's nothing like it anywhere. It's wonderful what they have done. I would give anything to go over there myself and work with them."

He wrote a letter to Lenin for Hal to take back personally on his next trip. Steinmetz intended to accept Lenin's invitation to visit Russia as a consultant. But the difficulties due to lack of normal relations prevented his making the arrangements as quickly as he had hoped, and within a year he died. It has always seemed to me especially tragic that the meeting of those two great men, Lenin and Steinmetz, could not have come about.

When Hal found he could not realize his plan through the machinery companies, he sought other means, for not only did Hal have within him the boundless energy of his pioneer ancestors, but an indomitable will which refused to accept defeat. Convinced that enough money could be raised from individuals to finance the plan, he made another quick trip to Moscow armed with new proposals, which the Soviet Government accepted, offering to turn over a huge tract of land to a Mixed Russian-American Company.

The next two years Hal spent organizing his project back in America, raising money, visiting machinery companies and studying their products, securing samples for demonstration purposes, and selecting a group of experts able to handle all phases of farm work, and willing to pull up stakes in America and take their families with them. For since it was a several years' job, Hal knew that for the venture to be successful, normal family life had to be made possible.

The Russian Reconstruction Farms, Inc., organized by Hal, got together a group of twenty-five Americans, farmers, mechanics, technicians, social workers. They were able to raise in funds, and in credit, the necessary $150,000. The Soviet Government turned over to the company 15,432 acres of farm land in the North Caucasus with good grain fields, vineyards, farm buildings, houses, a flour mill, cattle—but a negligible amount of farm machinery.

Hal and the other Americans brought their families over, and dug in, Americans and Russians working together.

This farm introduced the best types of modern farm machinery to the Soviet Union, made the peasants in the district machine conscious, worked out efficient methods of farming vast tracts of land. By the application of modern methods, by early and deep plowing, they were able, despite an unusually hot and dry summer, and a destructive locust plague, to produce a yield more than a third above what had ever been known in that district. They tested out various types of machinery, and demonstrated that the popular light Fordson tractor was not suited to the Russian steppes, which needed heavier, more durable machines. They introduced the first combine (harvester-thresher) into Russia. They showed how work could be done in the fields in three shifts and how, during the busy season, even the night need not be lost, by rigging up a dynamo in the field to supply light when time meant saving the crop. They introduced "houses on wheels" and modern field kitchen service so the workers could camp comfortably in the fields during the rush season. They built up a well equipped central repair shop, organized traveling field repair crews, and taught their tractor drivers not merely to drive their machines, but to keep them in good condition.

The work was followed closely in Moscow and Hal was called to help work out a plan for the mechanization of agriculture. As a consultant he helped build up a network of scientifically managed state farms all over the country.

When the question arose of training directors for the state farms, Hal advised that instead of sending them to America to learn large scale farming methods under very different conditions than those under which they would have to apply them, American agricultural experts be brought over to teach the Soviet agricultural specialists on their own ground. The plan was accepted.

Hal was commissioned to select them and comb America for the best types of tractors and a full complement of modern farming machinery and general equipment. On his return to the Soviet Union after a year in America, Zernograd, the great state farm at Verblud, near Rostov, was organized, becoming Experimental Demonstration Farm No. 2. Hal was made production manager, and assistant to the Soviet director, with a group of American specialists to advise and teach in the various departments. The big demonstration farm and school has been one of the most important single factors in the development of the present Soviet system of state and collective farms. It was in Zernograd that Hal first demonstrated the advantages of large caterpillar tractors over all others for Russian conditions. Today the bulk of Soviet tractor production is of that type. All the American types of machinery imported for that work are now being made in Soviet factories, in many cases the American models having been improved upon. Today Zernograd is a thriving agricultural city.

When Zernograd was firmly established, Hal was sent to state farms throughout the country to report on their condition. He traveled widely, especially in Kazakstan, where he acted as consultant on the spot and later presented a full report and recommendations.

On my last visit to the Soviet Union in 1937, Andy and I visited the big model farm and school at Verblud. A group of American and English delegates to the Twentieth Anniversary Celebration of the Revolution went with us, and officials from Rostov. We started out in a long procession of automobiles and were met on the road by cars carrying leaders of the state farm. At Verblud we were taken, first, into the office where the director of the farm and the secretary of the Communist Party awaited us. Both made speeches of greeting and I was asked to answer for the group. I told the story which I have just recorded here, of the first pilgrimage of that American boy to Russia, which ended in the organization of their state farm. Then I gave them a picture of Hal which they put in their Lenin Corner, the most honored spot in any Soviet institution.

As we left the office a large committee of young boys and girls came running after me from the big agricultural college there. They told me a big audience was waiting for me in the auditorium. The word had spread that Harold Ware's mother was to be there. All the students knew Hal's name because of the scholarships that had been established there in his memory and they gave me a wonderful reception.

Hal gave ten years of his life to the work in Soviet Russia. When it was clear that the cause of mechanized farming was won in the U.S.S.R., and that the Russian farmers, already collectivized, no longer needed him as much as the American farmers did, he came back to take charge of the Party's agrarian work here. The farm activities I have described in other chapters, in which I took part, were developed and expanded under his inspiration and leadership.

19. Our 1936 Presidential Campaign

I have come to the year 1936, when Franklin D. Roosevelt was elected to his second term. My main activity that year was campaigning for the Communist candidates for President, Earl Browder, and his running mate, James Ford, and against the reactionary Republican candidates, Alfred M. Landon and Col. Frank Knox, representing the forces of incipient American fascism. But before I write about my part in that campaign, I want to look back a little over national and world developments during the first Roosevelt administration.

I have already spoken of the great strikes of 1933 and our part in them. In 1934, the struggles took on greater scope and militancy. That was the year of the Pacific marine workers strike, the great San Francisco general strike, and the national textile strike.

These struggles were for the most part conducted under the banner of the A. F. of L., and the T.U.U.L., the Party playing a strong role. The A. F. of L. leaders were terrified at the influx of new workers, fearing to lose their bureaucratic control. William Green and his craft union supporters deliberately refrained from any real effort to organize unorganized workers, and sabotaged spontaneous efforts of the workers in the mass production industries to organize, by splitting them up into splinter craft groups. But the growing militancy of the masses was crystallyzing into a progressive wing in the A. F. of L. and weakening the hold of the reactionaries. It became clear that the place for all revolutionary workers was now within its ranks. Accordingly the independent unions began merging with the A. F. of L. The T.U.U.L. was formally liquidated in March, 1935. Meantime John L. Lewis had come to the fore as the leader of the industrial union advocates. At the 1935 A. F. of L. convention the proposal of Lewis and his supporters to inaugurate a militant organizing campaign along industrial lines was voted down. Numbering about 40 per cent of the A. F. of L., they then formed the Committee for Industrial Organization, and a year later were expelled from the A. F. of L.

Our Party wholeheartedly supported the C.I.O. program for completing the organization of the mass production industries on an industrial basis. At the same time, we worked for labor unity, on a basis which would admit the C.I.O. industrial unions into the A. F. of L. intact and assure the continuance of C.I.O. policies by a united labor movement.

In a few short months after its formation the C.I.O. established strong and militant organizations in the big mass production industries. The first great victory was won by the rubber workers after a sit-down strike in Akron against Goodyear. The sit-down idea spread to the auto workers, who improved the tactic by co-ordinating activities inside the factory with picket lines outside. General Motors, never challenged before, gave way to the demands of the workers, and sit-downs followed in other automobile concerns. Then the drive in steel began. The C.I.O. worked within the company unions organized by the steel corporations during the early N.R.A. days. When these company unions went over to the C.I.O. en masse, the C.I.O. gave notice that if recognition were not granted there would be a strike, which, Lewis warned, would be supported by his coal miners. The United States Steel Corporation yielded, and the C.I.O. chalked up the greatest victory in American labor history.

Important realignments taking place on a world scale during this period inevitably had their repercussions in this country.

Hitler's brutal and bloody regime had come to power with the help of Great Britain, which knew that the resistance of the German working class had to be broken before Germany could be used for an attack on the Soviet Union from the West, while Japan attacked from the East—a plan never abandoned since the days of intervention. Hitler was further assisted with British gold and British influence as a counter-balance to France, grown too strong on the continent for England's liking. With the full support of the British Tory government, Hitler tore up one clause after another of the Versailles Treaty, repudiating obligations as quickly as he made them. Japan launched a series of aggressions against China, and Italy brutally subjugated Ethiopia. The year 1936 saw the beginning of Italian and German aggression against the democratically elected government of Spain, assisted by the shameful "non-intervention policy" of England, France and the United States, the Soviet Union alone aiding the defenders of Spanish democracy.

Only the Soviet Union pursued a steadfast policy of peace. At each crucial point it made peace proposals based on a realistic appraisal of the immediate world situation, which evoked warm response among the peoples but were consistently rejected by the ruling classes of the imperialistic countries. The Soviet Union pursues this policy of peace because it has eliminated the capitalists and their drive for profits. It has no need to dominate markets as the outlet for surplus goods and exported capital and therefore no need of colonies or subject territories. It needs peace for socialist construction.

Had the imperialist nations supported the Soviet proposals for collective security, had France later honored her pledges to Czechoslovakia as the U.S.S.R. was ready to do, how different would be the European picture now! Today, as I write, France lies prostrate under the heel of Hitler, where her reactionary leaders pushed her the day they turned Czechoslovakia over to Hitler and with it the magnificent defenses that might have saved France.

Since early 1933 our American Party had made numerous proposals for working class unity. While Socialists and Communists joined together in local election campaigns, in defense, unemployment and other activities, the Socialist leadership consistently rejected any general united front with the Communist Party, refused Communist proposals for joint tickets in the national elections and for co-operation in building a farmer-labor party. The old guard broke away to form the reactionary Social-Democratic Federation and the Socialist Party, under the leadership of Norman Thomas, turned away from the daily struggles of the workers and isolated itself completely from the masses. It signed its own death warrant by admitting to its ranks the Trotskyites, long before expelled by the Communist Party. The Trotskyites, with the avowed purpose of splitting any movement where they could gain a foothold, mouthed slogans about world revolution, while sabotaging any policy advancing the interests of the workers, serving fascism by helping to keep the working class divided.

Only the Communists saw that fascism had to be fought on both a national and a world scale, and flashed ceaseless warnings that it could only be defeated by the united efforts of the people's forces everywhere. Only the Communists called for a united struggle at the precise moment in history when the advance of the fascist movement could have been blocked. Our united front policy found us working closely with the youth, the Negroes, and people's peace groups, and co-operating with religious organizations on questions of immediate concern to the workers. Under Browder's guidance, the Party embodied the revolutionary traditions and the democratic strivings of the masses of the American people, and increasing numbers of workers, farmers and intellectuals were drawn to us.

Our Party had correctly appraised the meaning of the New Deal when it was inaugurated, regarding it with suspicion, perceiving that it was only a prop for a dying system, pointing out the fascist danger lurking in the N.I.R.A., with its lavish aid to finance capital, its bolstering up of the monopolies. We exposed the incongruity of the A.A.A. program for limiting production and destroying farm surpluses while millions went hungry and ragged. But we called upon the workers and farmers to make the most of every concession offered them under the New Deal, and aided in all the day to day struggles to bring relief to unemployed workers and destitute farmers and to organize ever growing numbers of workers into unions of their own choosing.

The organized pressure of the masses wrested more concessions from the New Deal than it was ever intended to give them and as soon as finance capital felt that the immediate danger of the collapse of its system had passed, it organized to throw overboard the progressive aspects of the New Deal. The mid-term elections in 1934 saw the formation of a coalition of finance capital against the President under the banner of the American Liberty League. The reactionaries of both parties rallied to the attack—Hearst and Al Smith, the Morgans and the du Ponts. But the outright reactionary appeal failed, the Democrats increased their majority in Congress in 1934 while big votes went to such movements as Upton Sinclair's EPIC party and the Townsend Pension Plan. The election results were less an endorsement than a mandate to Roosevelt further to develop a program to satisfy the burning needs of the people. Roosevelt, above all an astute politician, understood that having lost reactionary support, his only hope of re-election was to heed this mandate.

Big Business turned more and more toward the methods of fascism as the only means left them to crush the growing militancy of the workers and secure their profits, pushing forward such dangerous demagogues as Father Coughlin and Huey Long, at the same time they continued their open attack on Roosevelt. Then the nine old men in the Supreme Court went into action, declaring unconstitutional all the major legislative measures of the New Deal. They threw out successively the N.I.R.A., the Railroad Retirement Act, the A.A.A., the Guffey Coal Act and state minimum wage laws. Roosevelt rushed the Wagner Labor Relations Bill and other measures through Congress, to salvage what he could of the New Deal.

The months that followed showed more intense mobilization

of the forces of incipient fascism with the big capitalists opposing Roosevelt nationally and uniting behind Alfred M. Landon. Governor of Kansas and Col. Frank Knox, publisher of the Chicago *Daily News* as Republican candidates. Landon, supported by Hearst, Morgan, the du Ponts, Mellon and the most reactionary circles of Wall Street, was demagogically labelled a "safe and sane liberal." In a maneuver to draw votes away from Roosevelt, the Union Party was formed, with Lemke, posing as the friend of the farmers, as its candidate, supported by Coughlin and Huey Long's successor, Gerald K. Smith. We Communists knew that victory of these reactionary forces would give a boost to world fascism, bringing closer the danger of war.

At the Ninth National Convention of the Party held in June, 1936, we nominated Earl Browder for President and James W. Ford for Vice-President.

In a masterful report to the convention Earl Browder stated that because of the direct and immediate danger of fascism and war, the main issue of the 1936 election was not between socialism and capitalism, but between democracy and fascism. Browder said:

"... Workers are interested, it is not a matter of indifference to them as to which of two bourgeois parties shall hold power, when one of them is reactionary, desires to wipe out democratic rights and social legislation, while the other to some degree defends these progressive measures achieved under capitalism. Thus we clearly and sharply differentiate between Landon and Roosevelt, declare that Landon is the chief enemy, direct our main fire against him, do everything possible to shift masses away from voting for him even though we cannot win their votes for the Communist Party, even though the result is that they vote for Roosevelt. This is not the policy of the 'lesser evil' which led the German workers to disaster; we specifically and constantly warn against any reliance upon Roosevelt, we criticize his surrenders to reaction and the many points in which he fully agrees with reaction; we accept no responsibility for Roosevelt."

It was decided that a nation-wide campaign for our Party candidates should be made during the summer months with Earl Browder, James Ford and myself as the main speakers. Alexander Trachtenberg was the manager of this campaign, the biggest one ever undertaken by our Party. My itinerary took me across the country and back, through the Northwestern farm territories. A car was secured for the trip, and after celebrating my seventy-fourth birthday with the family in Arden, we set forth on July 9th, my husband at the wheel. With us were two of my granddaughters, Judy Ware, Hal's daughter, and Joan Ware, Buzz's daughter, both in their last year of high school.

We started in a heat wave and returned in a blinding snow storm, covering 15,000 miles. Too much of a strain, really, for one driver, and quite a strain for a speaker too, as no matter how tired and dusty one happened to be at the end of a long hot ride across the desert, meetings arranged with so much enthusiasm by the local comrades everywhere must be given the best you have. The girls were a great help organizing the local young people to help them usher, take collections and sell literature.

In California we held twenty meetings in ten days, getting a warm response to our call for a united front against reaction. Upton Sinclair's EPIC movement had proven a good training ground, its remnants being far to the left of the New Deal. The people of Hollywood were especially active in the struggle against fascism. But while there was a lot of support for the united front work in California it also had to face the offensive of the reactionaries.

While Earl Browder was jailed on a vagrancy charge in Terre Haute, Indiana, and attacked by terrorists in Florida, we had no serious police trouble, although we heard a great deal of the local repressive activities of reactionary groups everywhere we went. The only public attack upon us was made by the K.K.K. of Spokane, who burned a fiery cross on a high hill. But the audience knew nothing of the incident until they read about it next day in the papers.

In Oregon and Washington we found strong support of our

united front program in their Commonwealth Federations, which supported Roosevelt, but advocated a more progressive platform. The trip was used for recruiting as well as campaigning and almost every meeting brought us a large quota of new members.

Returning through Montana, we held a fine meeting at the United Mine Workers Hall in Butte. Bill Andrews, Comrade Frederickson and Pat, the well-known *Daily Worker* supporter, all helped to make our stay in Butte pleasant. My granddaughters were impressed with the grim ugliness of Butte, surrounded by bare, grey, empty fields—with the poverty of the place, and the "escapes" from this poverty—the gambling dives, open vice, dog races, horse races—every sort of gambling device imaginable. The Party had hard going in Butte, on account of the extreme poverty and the pressure of the Anaconda Copper Co., but with the strong organization of the United Mine Workers, and the growth of other progressive forces, Butte today is on the way toward building a strong Party organization.

From Butte and Great Falls, we went on to Minneapolis, stronghold of the Farmer-Labor Party, where many fine election mass meetings had been arranged for us; then we struck down into the farm regions. At Unity, Wisconsin, a wonderful meeting was arranged by the Party unit composed entirely of farmers. The young chairman made one of the best recruiting speeches I have heard. We found that the farmers we reached with our campaign message of militant defense of American democracy as a means to continue the struggle for better conditions, welcomed and understood our Party as an organization deep-rooted in American soil, carrying on the sturdy American tradition of freedom and democracy.

The secretary of the local Party unit and his wife, Mr. and Mrs. Frank Hardrath, did an amazing piece of organizational work, although both of them were busy with a farm of many acres, eighteen cows to milk and a large family of children and a big house to take care of. They had considerable opposition from local reactionaries. Both of them had gone from farm to farm, explaining the Communist program, calling on the farmers to come to the meeting, and leaving literature. Mrs. Hardrath had recruited members of her own family. She proudly introduced me to her mother, a new recruit to the Party.

Many times when I have felt overburdened I have thought of Mrs. Hardrath helping her husband with the milking, then preparing a big company supper for the speaker, her husband, her two grandchildren and neighborhood friends. I shall always remember her calmness and poise.

In Chicago I had to give a national broadcast for the Party, compressing a message for the women and the farmers of the country into fifteen minutes.

The next evening was the closing night of the campaign— marked by a tremendous mass meeting, 25,000 people packing the Chicago stadium. An honor guard of over a hundred young people escorted Ford and myself to the platform where Bill Foster waited to greet us. After the speeches, and a program of music, the chairman, Morris Childs, announced that we were about to hear the voice of our candidate for President, Earl Browder, radioed from a similar meeting in New York.

Browder's voice came to us firm and near, stirring the people to mighty applause, a fitting climax to the most brilliant campaign our Party had conducted. He declared that through its campaign the Party had opened the way for a firm alliance of all progressives, trade union and farmers' organizations. Summarizing what the campaign had accomplished, he said:

"In this campaign America has seen the real face of the Communist Party. America has seen the Communists as front-line fighters in defense of the people's material interests and their democratic rights. America has seen how false are the charges against us, that we are bogey men eating babies for breakfast, enemies of the family, the church, democracy and all things valued by men and women. America has seen how it was the Communist Party, small as it still is, that already performed a vital service for the whole population in clarifying the issues of this campaign, and keeping those issues clear amidst a fog of lies,

Ella Reeve Bloor and Earl Browder at a meeting in Chicago in 1936

The late Edwin Markham and Ella Reeve Bloor at her seventy-fifth anniversary celebration in Staten Island, N. Y., in 1937

slanders and misrepresentations. America has seen the Communist Party as the most consistent fighter for democracy, for the enforcement of the democratic provisions of our Constitution, for the defense of our flag and revival of its glorious revolutionary traditions."

The frenzy of the reactionaries' campaign against Roosevelt pushed him into a more progressive position than before, climaxed by his "We have just begun to fight" speech at Madison Square Garden on the eve of the election. He was elected by a landslide of 27,750,000 votes.

The winter and spring 1936-37 saw a vigorous recruiting campaign by our Party, in which I participated by a speaking tour reaching the mid-West. Our Party grew, strengthened its relations with the farmers and lower middle classes, participated in the great organizing campaign of the C.I.O. as well as working within the A. F. of L. In co-operation with the militant rank and file and with the progressive leaders in both camps of labor, our trade union forces worked toward the creation of a great united labor movement. We increased our work among Negroes, women, youth, the unemployed, the peace forces of the country, seeking to bring into being a great democratic front of all progressive elements. We ceaselessly exposed the splitting tactics of the Trotskyite and Lovestoneite enemies of the people. We supported all progressive legislation. At the same time we intensified the education of our Party members and organized wide study of the teachings of Marx, Engels, Lenin and Stalin, and of American history and revolutionary traditions.

20. The First Socialist Nation on Its Twentieth Birthday

IN September, 1937, my husband and I sailed to attend the Twentieth Anniversary Celebration of the Russian Revolution.

We stayed a week in London where we met many old comrades, among them Harry Pollitt and Tom Mann. Charlotte Haldane, wife of the well-known scientist, invited me to attend a big meeting at Shoreditch Hall, a historic meeting place in the East End, to greet soldiers on leave of absence from fighting with Loyalist forces in Spain.

The boys from Spain gave me a wonderful greeting. They were a part of the International Brigade, and gave me news of our fine American boys in the Brigade. The meeting was one of the high points of our trip.

Since then, because of the criminal non-intervention policy in which our government participated, and our shameful neutrality act keeping arms from the legally constituted democratic People's Government of Spain, the fight in Spain had been lost—but only temporarily. The influences that flowed out of the Spanish struggle have left their mark on our movement all over the world, and the lessons learned in that struggle will contribute toward the final victory of the people.

Our Party gave 1,800 of its own members to the fight in Spain, and a thousand did not come back. The influence of those who gave their lives and those who came back to fight reaction at home is at work in the youth of America today. Men like John

Day, organizing among the Missouri lead miners, the beloved Steve Nelson, fighting now against American fascists, Robert Raven, blinded in battle, but still carrying on, Johnny Gates, Milton Wolfe, and others all over the country, are fighting the battle better here because of their experiences in Spain. The memories of those who died renews the courage of those who remain: heroes like Dave Doran; Joe Dallett, whose words the Ohio steel workers cherish still; Tantilla, the Finnish giant, whom Minnesota farmers remember well. And we must not forget our older comrades like Julius Rosenthal, dying on a soldier's cot in Spain, insisting that the doctors attend the younger men first, because they had more years to give to the struggle. The memory of Milton Herndon is a flame of light in our hearts as is the living Angelo today. In Philadelphia, we remember Wickman, devoted worker for the defense of political prisoners, and others. Their comrades, like Sterling Rochester, carry on the fight today. Just the other day I stood beside him at a meeting in Philadelphia, when he led the singing of the Internationale, with that wonderful voice of his that led the boys in their songs of struggle under Spanish skies.

I cherish among my dearest possessions letters I received from the boys over there, some funny, some sad, all full of courage. One group called itself the "Mother Bloor Battalion." A machine gun was named after me, and when the boys took the "Mother Bloor" machine gun out to fight the fascists they always shouted and waved their flag. When the Spanish boys would ask what was so special about that machine gun, our boys would say, "Mother Bloor led the miners and the farmers in their struggles, and she is leading them here too." Then the Spanish boys would say, "Ah, yes, we understand, American Pasionaria!", and they would cheer too. That made me very proud.

Our boys who came back from Spain do not feel that their struggles there were futile. They are inspired by the supreme courage of the Spanish people, who are still working for democracy, still believing in it with all their souls, striving to unite again their forces for the struggle they know must come, the final struggle that must in the end be victorious.

On the Soviet boat to Leningrad, we felt as if we had really reached home, so thoughtful of our comfort was the Soviet crew. There were young women sailors as well as young men. They proudly showed us their Lenin corner on the boat and their treasures. Most of them were studying mathematics and nautical sciences in evening classes.

When we reached Moscow we were met at the train. One of the famous Soviet-made ZIS cars awaited us at the station. In the afternoon, just after our arrival, different groups came to greet me. First of all, the editor and others from the magazine *Rabotnitza* (*The Working Woman*) came bringing bouquets of beautiful flowers; then a group of old-timers, people who had been through the tsarist terror, asking me to speak at their club. Then came an old bearded peasant with a huge basket of white chrysanthemums from the Krupskaya collective farm near Moscow, with greetings from the members of the collective.

They had barely left the room when my old comrade and friend, Andre Marty, arrived. Andre Marty, former Communist Deputy, is known and beloved by the revolutionary movement throughout the world for his glorious action in 1918 when, in the French Black Sea Fleet, he led an insurrection of sailors, who refused to bombard Soviet Odessa. Marty wasn't satisfied with my room. He said it wasn't big enough. (He must have seen the crowds of people coming out of it.) He insisted that I let him make arrangements to move me to a new hotel, and rushed off to attend to this.

The new apartment was far more beautiful than any place I had ever dreamed of living in. Its windows overlooked the spires of the churches and towers of the Red Square and the Kremlin. Huge ruby stars had just been erected on the towers of the Kremlin wall and their clear, glowing red could be seen from all parts of the city at night.

On stands erected in the little parks everywhere, and in front of the Opera House, musicians played, and the people danced in the streets. All through the last days of October and through November this went on. Physical culture exhibitions were held, and crowds thronged the streets almost all night. Excursions drove in from the villages, in open trucks, bringing their own bands, driving from one street to another to see the decorations, singing beautiful revolutionary and folk songs, always singing. There were also groups from the Caucasus and Central Asia in colorful costumes.

Early on the morning of November 7 we proceeded to the Red Square, where visitors from every country of the world gathered. On the balcony of Lenin's tomb we were thrilled to see Stalin, Molotov, Kalinin, and the other great Soviet leaders.

Then, with a great blare of music, the Red Army swept through the arches into the Red Square, starting the glorious parade which lasted all day.

The parade was led by Voroshilov, mounted on a beautiful, prancing horse, followed by a cavalry troop on magnificent horses stepping high, in time with the music. Dismounting opposite Lenin's tomb, Voroshilov threw the reins to his attendant and walked over to join Stalin and the others. After the soldiers, thundered the great engines of war, tanks of new types; anti-aircraft guns; armed motorcycles; whole battalions of trained police dogs. Above, endless squadrons of airplanes flew in perfect formation. Some of the foreign military attaches out in front looked glum, especially the Japanese.

Then came the armed workers, rank on rank of them, filling the square with an ever-flowing sea of marchers with their red banners streaming over them. Many of the banners bore slogans about Spain. "Hail to Pasionaria!" "Greetings to the Brave Loyalists of Spain!" Standing next to the Spanish delegates, we cheered ourselves hoarse, and brought return cheers from the marchers, and the square resounded with mighty shouts of comradeship.

The Soviet trade unions were wonderful hosts and did everything possible to help us get whatever information we desired. Two-week trips through the country were arranged by them for the visitors, with our choice of itineraries. At Kiev, our first stop, a large welcoming committee awaited us, including a large number of women from the textile factories. A nice-looking young Ukrainian Jewish woman who spoke very good English acted as our interpreter. She asked us where we wanted to go. I told her we wanted to see the schools and the children in the nurseries. "Well," she said, "before you see the new things and the higher culture we have here, I suggest that you see the old things, the old culture. I will show you the old tenth century church and the old monasteries where the monks used to live." We didn't care much about monks, but we were game. The old church seemed to me an ugly structure. Inside there were quantities of gold, gold on the ikons, gold on the altar, gold everywhere. Behind the altar were papery, old dried-up mummies, with bright colored silken shoes on their feet. Our guide told us that the old church people brought shoes for the mummies, and sometimes nice new dresses, too!

Our guide then asked us if we wanted to see the bones. We didn't care so much about the bones, either, but were willing to see everything, and followed her down into the catacombs beneath the church, where there were acres of bones, some leg bones with chains still on them.

We were glad to get out of the dead past and into the sunlight of that wonderful city of Kiev, and walked along the wide bright avenue toward the "Children's Palace of Culture." Here children who show special talent for music or painting or dancing came every day from their regular schools to take lessons with special teachers. We saw room after room full of beautiful, gifted children of workers and the air was sweet with the sound of their laughter and music. Looking into their faces and into the faces of their teachers, contrasting what we saw here with the musty relics of the old religion, I felt these people had discovered a new religion, a religion of love, certainly not in opposition to Christianity, for is not the Christian religion founded on the teachings of Christ—"Love is the fulfilling of the law"? There are no underprivileged children in the Soviet Union, and there are beautiful institutions like this everywhere. That evening we saw an opera in this building presented by an amateur group of young people good enough to be professionals.

At Rostov-on-the-Don we were met by a committee which included the chairman of the City Soviet, and the director of the exquisite new Gorky Theatre. The director, who had one of the most sensitive, beautiful faces I have ever seen, told us of his desire to make the Gorky Theatre like the Moscow Art Theatre, where he had spent most of his life. He told us he had a group of a hundred talented people from whom he could select the cast for any play he produced. We saw here a comedy, "Ivan Ivanovitch," so well acted that we needed no interpreter.

After visiting the huge Rostov combine factory, we went on to Kislovodsk, where we stayed at a beautiful mountain health resort. Before leaving Kislovodsk, we were given a concert of folk songs and dances and music by native talent of the Caucasus mountains. During the intermission, a man came running across the hall to me crying out, "Aren't you Mother Bloor? Do you remember when we belonged to the same machinists' union in Brooklyn?" "Sure," I said, "the old Micrometer Lodge. They took away our charter because we were too radical. How long have you been here?" "Seven years—I live in Leningrad, but I come here for my month's vacation every year." "Aren't you going back?" "Why should I? There I would only be on the W.P.A. I am over 50 years old. Here I am teaching other men how to work, my wife is doing interesting work, both of my sons are college graduates—that could never have happened in the United States. I think I'll stay here!"

In Moscow we rode often in the beautiful subway. The first visit to the subway made a lasting impression on all of us. It was such a startling contrast to the dingy subways of New York and London. One Englishman said it was "like walking through an art gallery." I was told that in one of the stations where they have the highest escalator in the world, peasant women coming to Moscow for the first time go up and down for hours just for a thrill. Every station has its own special design and color scheme. One is in pastel shades, another in oriental marble flecked with gold, another in deep red tones. All around are sculptures and murals to delight the eye. The lighting is in itself a work of art. Some of the stations with their vaulted ceilings, their noble pillars and the soft radiance of their indirect lighting, are like cathedrals. The trains come in so softly you hardly hear them. So spotlessly clean are the floors that when a foreigner, unaware of local customs, unwittingly drops a cigarette butt some angry Soviet citizen is sure to protest that this is the people's subway, and must be kept clean. It is a joy to be where nothing is too good for the working class.

Another high point was the trip down the Moscow-Volga Canal, recently completed, which connects the Volga with the Moscow River, making the Soviet capital a port as well as railway center. It was a tremendous engineering project. Not only was it necessary to dam up the water and change its course, but a fantastic amount of water is pumped upward as high as a fifteen-story building. Eight hydroelectric stations were built along the route whose surplus power is used to work these pumps. A whole new "Moscow sea" appeared when the canal was completed, and Moscow now has an unlimited water supply.

The story of the builders of this canal is in itself an epic, comparable to that of the Baltic-White Sea Canal. A large part of the work was done by former criminals—thieves, embezzlers, killers, many of whom had never done a stroke of work in their lives. Many of them were former hobo boys from the wonderful self-governing colony of "Bolshevo," given a chance through this project to win their final freedom. The grand scale of the undertaking itself, the chance to learn skilled work and to become again honored members of society, the wise way in which they were handled—for none of them were forced to work—won all these former criminals to a complete break with their past. Over 22,000 workers were graduated from the schools connected with the project, and over 18,000 who began as ordinary laborers graduated from courses as skilled workers, hundreds becoming engineers. Practically all of the former prisoners received full amnesty.

Our boat had fine staterooms and a handsome dining saloon. The canal shores were landscaped, the landing stations were architecturally very beautiful, and the locks were adorned with statuary. The Moscow river port itself has been made a new resort for the people of Moscow, with parks, rest homes and water sport stations on its shores.

At the town of Kalinin, the chairman of the Regional Soviet told us: "We had a great meeting here yesterday. Thousands of people from all over the district nominated our deputy to the Supreme Council of Nationalities—a woman, Maria Petrova. She is the chairman of the City Soviet. This is her town, you know, so she must show it to you."

He telephoned her, and Maria Petrova, a beautiful, motherly looking woman of thirty-seven, a former textile worker, appeared. She showed us the newly finished theaters, large modern apartment houses, maternity hospitals, a new surgical hospital, and all kinds of institutions to help worker-mothers; material and cultural improvements everywhere. She told me she had a nursing baby six months old, one child of kindergarten age and one in the seventh grade.

That day was "free day" in the Soviet Union, and we apologized for encroaching upon her free time.

"I work in my free time by taking walks; I go to market places, to parks and all over town to see what is needed. I get ideas," she said smilingly.

Only in the Soviet Union can women enjoy to the full their right to motherhood, as well as pursuing whatever career they choose. Thus Maria Petrova, the head of the Kalinin Soviet, the mayor of the town as we would call her in America, like thousands of other mothers in the Soviet Union, has her own rich family life, at the same time fulfilling her responsibility to the people of the city of 200,000 over which she presides. We found everywhere we went that women had developed into respected leaders, winning more and more responsible positions each year.

During the First and Second Five-Year Plans over four and a half million women were drawn into industry. The Soviet professional women are now an important factor in the country. Before the Revolution there were in Russia only two thousand women physicians, and I was told on this trip there were 40,000 women physicians now.

Hundreds of women have been elected deputies to the Council of the Union and the Council of Nationalities. Chernyek, a woman Stakhanovite from the Sverdlov factory, expressed what their new life meant to Soviet women:

"Who knows a more radiant life than ours? Our youth is most brave and gifted. It is our aviators who soar the skies, our musicians who charm the world with their playing. We know that whatever field we choose we shall always be able to apply our knowledge and strength."

This supreme confidence and sense of responsibility are characteristic of all these women leaders.

You cannot travel in the Soviet Union without being overwhelmed by avalanches of statistics of thrilling progress. Nothing goes backward in the USSR—everything goes forward. What I have wanted to convey in these brief impressions is the sense of fulfillment and joy in their work we found in all the people we met, the wonderful spirit of comradeship and warmth with which we were greeted everywhere, which was but an extension of what the people feel for each other in this great land where "the institution of the dear love of comrades" has become a reality. And above all the joy it was to me, who had lived so long among the workers and farmers who knew only degradation and hardship, to be at last where labor is the most honored calling, to see the workers enjoying to the full all the fruits of their own toil, all the good things of the earth.

What socialism has accomplished in the face of gigantic obstacles and world-wide hostility seems almost incredible. Russia to begin with had been far behind the other countries in development. Her primitive agriculture provided a feeble foundation for a large scale industry dependent almost entirely on foreign capital. Civil war, intervention, blockade and famine sapped her strength long after the other nations had made peace. Beginning with less than nothing—because they had to restore before they could begin building anew—the Soviet people reared a modern industrial state, first in Europe in industrial production, second in the world.

And all this was possible because with the means of production in their own hands, the Soviet workers had developed a system of socialist planned economy, drawing all able-bodied people into the process of production, making possible rapid and steady accumulation of socialist capital and a simultaneous extension of consumption.

Along with increased production, there has been constant improvement in material and cultural conditions. Wages doubled during the Second Five Year Plan and steadily increase. The system of social insurance (a tax on industry, not on wages) covers illness, accident, old age, motherhood. The finest public health system in the world concentrates on keeping the people healthy. The labor unions administer a constantly improving system of labor protection. Vacations with pay, sanitarium care for those who need it, even special diets as prescribed by the doctor in the factory dining room—all these things are routine. Workers' clubs—"palaces of culture"—adjoin every plant, with all conceivable facilities for entertainment, sport and education.

For the children, day nurseries and kindergartens provide the best possible care, so that all women may combine maternity with any work they want to do. Education has long been compulsory and universal, with an ever-expanding university attendance. Courses of every kind are open to everyone who wishes to acquire greater skill or learn a new profession. No one need keep on doing "dirty work" or an uncongenial job. Any factory worker may become an engineer or an artist through facilities at his own place of work.

One of the greatest causes for rejoicing on the twentieth anniversary of the revolution was the wiping out of the nest of traitors in the treason trials of 1936 and 1937. The capitalist and Social-Democratic press and our fair weather liberal friends had set up an unprecedented howl about the trials, insisting that the confessions of widespread wrecking and espionage, of murders committed and planned, of conspiracies to dismember the Soviet State and open its gates to the enemy, were faked. Today, with the exposure of treachery in the governments and the armies of one capitalist country after another, history has made further argument unnecessary. No single factor was more effective in checking Chamberlain's and Daladier's plans for Hitler to march eastward than the elimination of these enemies of the Soviet people.

The adoption of the Stalinist Constitution at the Eighth Congress of Soviets in December, 1936, marked the complete victory of the socialist system in all spheres of the national economy. The new constitution codified into law the right of all to work; the right to rest and leisure; the right to maintenance in old age or sickness or loss of working capacity; the right to education. It proclaimed the equal partnership of men and women in all things, the equal rights of all peoples.

These provisions of the Soviet Constitution are not a promise for tomorrow, but a concrete expression of the reality of today. They mark the achievement of what Marxists call the first phase of communism—socialism. The fundamental principle of this phase is summed up in the formula "From each according to his abilities; to each according to his deeds." This formula recognizes the fact that social wealth has not yet reached the stage where it is possible for everyone to take out of the common fund everything required. When the higher phase of full communism is achieved, the formula will be "From each according to his abilities; to each according to his needs."

A year after the adoption of this constitution, we had the joy of seeing the progress already made toward this higher phase. We witnessed the great people's celebrations that took place following the first elections under the new constitution, on December 12, 1937, when 91,000,000 Soviet citizens elected their candidates to the Supreme Soviet on the basis of universal, direct and equal suffrage and the secret ballot.

Any organization of the Soviet people—trade unions, youth, cooperatives and cultural societies—have the right to put forward their candidates, and the Communist Party supports non-party candidates as well as its own. The elections are the culmination of a continuous democratic process whereby all the people, day by day, participate directly in the solution of all the problems which affect their lives. The nominations are not the result of high pressure campaigns, the outcome of which is determined by the amount of money thrown into the campaign, demagogic trickery, or outright corruption. The nominations, in which all the voters participate, are in a sense more important than the elections themselves. In the nominating meetings many names are brought forward. Every prospective nominee has the right to speak fully and freely, and is expected to answer innumerable questions which any voter has the right to ask. Each candidate's record is examined carefully. And since these candidates come directly from the people themselves, who have watched them in their day to day activities, even the nominating meetings are but the result of previous experience, and their results in no way depend on last minute deals or maneuvers. Because the people's interests are truly united, they come naturally to a unanimous decision as to who is best fitted to represent them. The deputies, once elected, maintain the closest possible connections with their constituents, and if they fail to carry out the people's will, they can be recalled at any time by a majority of their electors.

Among the deputies are no corporation lawyers, no professional politicians manipulated by big business for their own ends. Instead there are true sons of the Soviet people—working class leaders, miners, aviators, mechanics, farmers, Red Army men, doctors, scientists, teachers, artists and writers. Among the 1,143 deputies elected to the Supreme Soviet in the 1937 elections, 283 were non-Party people, and 184 were women—by far the largest number of women deputies that has ever participated in the parliament of any land.

Reporting on the new Constitution to the Eighth All-Union Congress of Soviets, Stalin had said:

"The complete victory of the socialist system in all spheres of the national economy is now a fact. This means that exploitation of man by man is abolished—while the socialist ownership of the implements and means of production is established as the unshakable basis of our Soviet society.

"As a result of all these changes in the national economy of the U.S.S.R., we have now a new socialist economy, knowing neither crises nor unemployment, neither poverty nor ruin, and giving to the citizens every possibility to lead prosperous and cultural lives. . . ."

Fifteen years before I had heard Lenin planning these things we now saw transformed into shining reality. I can never adequately express the gratitude I feel to have seen personally during my own life the fulfillment, in the Soviet Union, of man's brightest dreams, of those things I had been working for all my life. What a great joy and privilege it has been to have seen and talked with Lenin, the great leader of the Revolution, who foresaw and outlined in such detail the course that must be pursued to insure the complete victory of socialism; and now to witness the work of Stalin, the great builder, who has followed so surely the course charted by Lenin, and in turn charts the way to a still brighter future for all mankind.

The great plan outlined by Lenin has reached magnificent fulfillment in the great new industries and projects of the Stalinist Five-Year Plans. Lenin's concern for the farmers has come to fruition in the collective farms which have transformed both the countryside and the farmer. In factories, mines and farms, in schools and theaters, in the flowering of the many Soviet nationalities, the great beginnings started under Lenin's leadership have been reared into a beautiful new structure under Stalin. And the secret of Stalin's leadership, as was that of Lenin's too, has been his constant closeness to the Soviet people, his trust in them, their trust in him. "Leaders come and leaders go," said Stalin, "but the people remain. Only the people are immortal."

During our visit we learned that a new translation by K. I. Chukovsky of Walt Whitman's poems, recently issued by the State Publishing House for Belles Lettres in Leningrad, had been sold in many thousands of copies, and that Whitman was greatly loved in the Soviet Union. An introduction, called "The Poet of American Democracy," which was translated for me, recalled that in 1905, the first translation of *Leaves of Grass* had been confiscated and destroyed by the Tsar's police. Chukovsky was accused of subversive activity for the translation of "Pioneers! O Pioneers" and prosecuted by a Moscow Court. In 1913 public lectures on Whitman were prohibited in a number of Russian cities. But in spite of this suppression, the fame of Whitman spread because, as Chukovsky observed, the tenor of his poetry "made him welcome in a country where an uprising was maturing." In 1918, one of the first books published in the new Soviet Republic was a volume of Whitman.

It was through the new volume that I was first introduced to these lines written by Walt Whitman in 1881:

"You Russians and Americans! Our countries so distant, so unlike at first glance—such a difference in social and political conditions . . . and yet in certain features, and vastest ones, so resembling each other. The variety of stock elements and tongues, to be resolutely fused in a common identity and union at all hazards . . . the grand expanse of territorial limits and boundaries —the unformed and nebulous state of many things, not yet permanently settled, but agreed on all hands to be the preparations of an infinitely greater future . . . the deathless aspirations at the inmost center of each great community, so vehement, so mysterious, so abysmic—are certainly features you Russians and we Americans possess in common.

"As my dearest dream is for an internationality of poems and poets, binding the lands of the earth closer than all treaties and diplomacy—as the purpose beneath the rest in my book is such hearty comradeship, for individuals to begin with, and for all nations of the earth as a result—how happy I should be to get the hearing and emotional contact of the great Russian peoples."

How Whitman would rejoice, were he alive today, in the "internationality of poems and poets" already achieved over a sixth of the earth. How much more vigorously today would he press for closer understanding, for closer relations between the American and Soviet peoples as a step toward the fulfillment of his dearest dream—comradeship for all nations of the earth.

21. New Beginnings

THERE is still so much I should like to write about, so many great struggles, so many occasions rich with the comradeship of friends from everywhere.

Only three years ago, hundreds of them celebrated my seventy-fifth birthday in Staten Island, where I was born. Elizabeth Gurley Flynn was chairman of the celebration itself, and Anna Damon chairman of the arrangements committee. There was such a crush of people that the sturdy marine worker guards around the flower-garlanded platform had to announce that only people who came from far away could come up to greet me. But when I turned to welcome comrades supposedly from Seattle or Los Angeles, I saw instead dear, familiar faces from Brownsville and the Bronx. Hundreds came from far away, too. Edwin Markham was there in his heavy beaver hat (although it was a sweltering July day), bringing a poem written especially for the occasion. My dear friend Henry George Weiss wrote me a beautiful poem, as he always does. There were wonderful messages from Tom Mann, Harry Pollitt, Tim Buck, Andre Marty, Lozovsky, Lenin's widow, Nadiezhda Krupskaya, and from other leaders of our brother parties. There were greetings from all the members of our National Committee and Party workers all over the country, from leaders and rank and file members of women's, Negro and youth organizations. Tom Mooney wrote recalling our first meeting twenty-nine years before on the Debs "Red Special." Senators and Congressmen, artists, writers, poets, yes, even old-time Socialist friends, and a host of workers and farmers remembered my birthday. These messages warmed my heart not so much as a personal tribute, but as tributes to the cause from which my life is inseparable. Best of all, news of new recruits for the Party, pledges for intensified Party work, came as birthday gifts to me.

And now, as I write this final chapter, I have just celebrated my seventy-eighth birthday at our farm in Pennsylvania. A home of my own at last, after all these years of wandering! The many friends all over the country who have shared their homes with me must not think me ungrateful for saying this, for indeed I have many homes. But it means a great deal to us now to have a permanent place, where we can take care of our family and friends.

The farm has a special loveliness when the apple trees are in blossom, when "lilacs in the dooryard bloom" and the meadows are full of wild daffodils. But it is beautiful in all seasons. When the daffodils go, the purple fleurs-de-lis come, and after them the fields flame with tiger lilies, then daisies and clover, golden-rod and asters, and the blazing beauty of autumn. Woods and fields are full of birds at all seasons and in the heavy snows of last winter the pheasants came around the house like domestic fowl.

We have three cows, a heifer and a brood of chickens. The picture of the farm would not be complete if I did not mention our seven cats and our dog Buck. King of our cat colony is Benny, who goes wherever I go on the farm. When Andy starts from the house with his shiny milk pail, the cats form a line after him. They sit around patiently while he milks, waiting for the ration he never fails to give them.

At the farm we have a platform in a lovely grove of trees where we have lectures, motion pictures and pageants for our farm community. We have won a real place there, due to Andy's fine management of the formerly neglected thousand-apple-tree orchard which now bears beautiful fruit.

But when I write of our life on the farm, let no one think that I have any idea of *retiring* there. I always find plenty of work to do at home in the intervals beween speaking and organizing trips. As chairman of the Party in Pennsylvania and as Party candidate for Congress from our district, I am kept busy in my own state as well as with national work.

I should rather die than give up my active work with the Party —to give it up *would* be death. I have been so much a part of the Party that I cannot conceive of living in any sense without it. The clear voice of our Party is needed today as never before to give leadership to the struggles of the workers and farmers, and to bring about unity between them and between Negroes and whites, between men and women, and among all anti-fascist forces.

I do not minimize what our Party has done toward bringing about true equality, admitting no discrimination of race, color or creed in our ranks. But I have often felt, earlier indeed, more than today, that there has been some hesitancy in giving women full equal responsibility with men. As for myself, I have no complaints. I have been honored with great responsibilities. But the power of all our women must be used to the full—especially today! We women must take our place consciously by the side of men, dropping any sense of inferiority. We must speak up without waiting to be asked, *and we must have something to say.* We must use every ounce of strength that is in us to build a new world in which there will be no wars.

We have a great tradition to uphold, we women of America today, the tradition of those great pioneer women who helped build our country. Our Party is the inheritor of the traditions of all the struggles for women's rights throughout history. The finest type of progressive womanhood, working with devotion and courage for the rights not only of women but of labor, of the Negro people, of all oppressed humanity, is to be found today within our Party.

Women like Anita Whitney, a charter member of the Party and Party chairman of the State of California. Born in a conservative and wealthy family, Anita has never wavered in her loyalty to the workers, and, young today in her seventies, is one of our most vigorous and effective workers. Women like Caro Lloyd Strobell, sister of Henry Demarest Lloyd, and bright-eyed and witty as ever at eighty-one. Women like Rose Wortis, who also came into the Party in the early days and has been constantly active in trade union work; radiant Rose Pastor Stokes, who died of cancer caused by a blow from a policeman's club. And above all, our working women, our farm women, the Mrs. Jimmie Higgins' who are always ready to take their places on picket lines or lick stamps or distribute leaflets or sweep floors, the thousands of women without whom our Party could not exist. Although I have mentioned in previous chapters the name of my co-worker and dearest friend and comrade, Elizabeth Gurley Flynn, I feel that she belongs in this category of pioneers—especially because of her work during the first World War for the political prisoners. Although she was much younger than I in years, her experience and executive ability were always of the greatest help and inspiration to me during those dark days.

Nor can we forget the thousands of women in our movement throughout the world, faced with more difficult conditions than we, carrying on the struggle in the midst of terror and war. And guiding us all with her keen intelligence and great flaming spirit, that beloved leader of the Spanish workers, Dolores Ibarruri— La Pasionaria—who kindled new courage in all of us with her great rallying cry to the people of democratic Spain—"Better die standing than live on bended knees!"

I am by no means closing my life story. I expect to *live* that for years to come. As I read over the chapters of this book, I feel that it is after all not adequate in expressing to the reader the real "me." How can I describe the deep emotions I have experienced during all these years, in the crises that come in every mother's life—and especially a mother who goes into the battles of the workers. How can I make others feel and understand the homesickness of such a mother, even when the children are grown, the conflict in one's soul between the love of home and peace, and the responsibility of going out among the masses with the message that I have felt I must take to them. But the choice I made was not a sacrifice. It has been a privilege and joy. My greatest longing and desire is to retain my health and strength so that I may continue to work.

I have not mentioned all my dear friends and co-workers. It would take a larger book than this to bring before the readers of my story the wonderful characters who have gone along the road with me, and others I have met in passing; great names, long friendships, loves and comradeships of men and women. Men and women like Barbusse of France, Clara Zetkin of Germany, Elizabeth Gurley Flynn, Ruthenberg, Debs, Browder, Foster, Ford and thousands of others, thousands of farmers, miners, workers everywhere and their children who have been close to me always along the march—all these have been the comrades of my rich and joyous life.

To my own children, to my comrades, to my husband, to my beloved friends everywhere, I dedicate this book.

Postscript

FOUR more years have passed. Years so packed with joy and struggle and hard work, years of such epic world events, that only another book could begin to encompass them. That book will have to await my "retirement" from the active struggle which I hope is still a long way off. But my old friend Alexander Trachtenberg, who has done such wonderful work in publishing books from which we have all learned so much, and who made this book possible in the first place, has asked me to add a brief postscript for this new edition.

In 1941, I made another of those coast to coast tours through which every state and every city of our beloved country has become near and dear and familiar to me. This trip was in response to requests from many people who wanted me to make "personal appearances" in connection with the publication of the book, and I was happy to have this chance not only to bring the book and its message before many thousands of people but also, as I always do, to help boost our papers, the *Daily Worker* and the weekly *Worker,* and to recruit new members for the Party.

And then one bright day in June not long after my return from the trip, as the comrades from many Pennsylvania towns gathered at April Farms, the crashing news came over the radio that the German fascists had attacked the Soviet Union. That treacherous attack and the magnificent resistance to it of the whole Soviet people opened a new chapter in history.

The great Anglo-American-Soviet coalition came into being, as England and our own country both realized that the defense of the Soviet Union was also the defense of their own lands. The meaning of the Soviet-German non-aggression pact became clear as the Soviet armies and industries showed to what use the much needed breathing space had been put, and how indeed it had meant the salvation not only of the Soviet people but of people who loved freedom everywhere. Then, in December, came Pearl Harbor, and our country too abandoned what was left of its neutrality. With America also fully in the war, our alliance with the Soviet Union and all the United Nations was consummated.

From that time forward, along with all sections of the American people, the energies of our Party were wholly devoted to the winning of the war and the building of national unity. And so, when plans were considered for the celebration of my eightieth birthday in the summer of 1942, the only question, was how to make such a celebration a real contribution to the war effort. Anita Whitney was to be seventy-five years old on July 7, the day before my birthday, so it was decided to celebrate our birthdays jointly with nationwide win-the-war rallies.

The celebration really began for me with the great meeting in Madison Square Garden on July 2 to welcome home our dear leader, Earl Browder, released from his imprisonment for a passport technicality through the wisdom of President Roosevelt, who in his own words took this step "in the interests of national unity." There was a fine send-off meeting for me in Philadelphia, where the seamen gave me the slogan: "Mother—you keep'em smiling, we'll keep'em sailing!" Then off to the Coast to meet Anita, to share with her the joy of a great banquet to us both in San Francisco, and a series of inspiring meetings up and down the Coast—in Santa Barbara, San Diego, Los Angeles, Oakland, Sacramento, Portland, Seattle.

Then back across the country, stopping for meetings in Minneapolis, Madison, Milwaukee, Chicago, St. Louis, Kansas City, Detroit, Dayton, Cincinnati, Youngstown, Pittsburgh and many smaller places along the way. Seventy meetings, and seventy birthday cakes, from one end of the country to the other! Gifts poured in on Anita and myself, and a flood of personal tributes that sent new lifeblood coursing through these old veins. But the richest gift was the inspiration of seeing what the workers of America were doing for the war. Shipyard workers, steel workers, miners, farmers—among all the old friends and thousands of new ones, I found the same fighting spirit everywhere. And the women! Women like giants in the earth as they took on men's jobs, managed their children and households too, and courageously bore the sacrifices war made necessary. Of course, not all was well. Problems of child care were not getting enough attention, reactionary forces were trying to split the growing unity of our people, especially of Negroes and whites, and trying to spread defeatist doctrines. But the people all over the country were marching ahead united as never before. It was a special joy to feel the changing attitude toward Communists. Everywhere I found our Party people in the vanguard of those groups determined to weld an ever stronger unity among all the American people, putting their last ounce of energy into the war effort.

Back in New York the tour continued—twenty more meetings in all the five boroughs of New York—and a dozen more in upstate cities were to follow before I cut my last eightieth birthday cake!

I want especially to mention the wonderful co-operation and

enthusiasm of Mary Himoff, a good comrade from New York, who accompanied us on the trip, and contributed so much to its success.

The next year—1943—began with the glorious victory at Stalingrad that turned the tide of the war, and ended with another decisive victory—the concord of Teheran, that turned the tide of history. I had seen the first socialist state come into being and watched with dismay how the other nations of the world had tried to crush it. I had seen our own country, after the years of reaction and depression, enter into a new period of democratic progress under President Roosevelt. And now, this supreme event, which meant an end of the division of the world into a socialist camp and a capitalist camp, and the promise of a world in which the socialist and capitalist democracies will work together to banish the evil of fascism and the scourge of war from the earth, and free the people everywhere from hunger and tyranny and fear.

This year has brought the fruition of the military agreements made at Teheran—D-Day—the armies of the Allies converging on Germany from the west and the south and the east; and victory within our grasp.

The agreement of Teheran, and the events that have followed, led our Party to take the historic step of disbanding as a political party and forming the Communist Political Association, as the best instrument through which we can make our contribution at this period to national unity, to speeding victory and to a peaceful and secure post-war world.

The war and the great democratic coalition it has brought into being have changed many things. Many of the things we Communists have always fought for are being achieved in the course of the war itself. Never again will the common people of Europe stand for the kind of reactionary governments and leadership that sold them out to Hitler.

Today in America, the overwhelming majority of the people are not ready for socialism, and so socialism is not the issue. We Communists know we can make our greatest contribution to the socialist cause by fighting in common with all the progressive forces in our country for full employment, for equality for all minority peoples, for the complete realization of American democracy, for co-operation with all the United Nations and above all with the great Soviet Union, for post-war stability.

Because of this we threw all our forces into the campaign for the re-election of President Roosevelt, along with the labor movement and its powerful new political arm, the C.I.O. Political Action Committee, the Independent League of Artists and Scientists, and the great mass of independent voters who understood how much was at stake in this election.

It was a great joy to me to be able to participate actively in the triumphant campaign to re-elect the Commander-in-Chief of our country.

Our Pennsylvania women did wonderful work in the registration campaign, in getting out the vote and at the polls on election day. One special gathering in Philadelphia should be noted. Two of our young wives of soldiers overseas co-operated in housekeeping, taking turns cooking, and in looking after both babies, releasing each other for organization and education work. They sent out seventy invitations to mothers with babies for a Saturday afternoon meeting to plan with me their election day activities. It rained that afternoon, but many of them came. What I enjoyed especially was a guessing game in which I was able to pick out the fathers (they are all my boys!) of almost every baby, by their striking likeness to their dads. Many election day plans were made at that meeting. A group of grandmothers promised to club together to take care of the babies so that the mothers could act as watchers and runners all election day. One trained nurse in the children's ward of a large hospital who had her day off on November 7, undertook to take care of five babies that day, releasing five mothers to vote, after she had cast her own vote. It is especially good to record that this year, the twenty-fifth anniversary of the winning of suffrage for women in America, the women of America used their votes so effectively in the interests of the people.

In closing this final chapter of my book I feel very strongly that I should mention not only the joys of my long life, but some of the sorrows that have shaken my soul. It is only natural that, having attained such an age, many of my closest friends have passed out of life in the last few years. I shall miss very much on my future visits to California the staunch friend Robert Whitaker, who has always been so friendly to me in the past thirty years. And the valiant soldier, writer and friend, Colonel Erskine Scott Wood, who wrote me this tribute which Sarah Bard Field, his wife, sent me:

To Mother Bloor

I saw a gray old oak that stood upon a hill
And bent and bowed before the storm;
The howling hurricane that wrenched its limbs
And whirled them to the ground.
But always it returned, erect, deep rooted
In the mother-breast, proud and unconquerable
And shook its windblown hair in happy laughter.
And I have seen it guard the lambs in March
That frisked and sucked, shaking their rapid tails;
Or, in the August heat, it dropped its cloak of shade
Upon cud-chewing cows that couched on folded knees
Or stood with dreamy eyes giving the milk of life
To bull-head calves that butted the soft udders.
O venerable oak, the great Mechanic, Time,
Has wrought your coat of silver mail.
The glory of the combat has increased your strength
And when you fall as every warrior must,
The lark shall sing your requiem,
The whispering grass shall soothe your lying down.

Only last year we lost the gay, faithful friend and comrade, Art Young, who "kept up with the procession," till the last moment of his life. The very night he died, last New Year's Eve, he mailed me a post card on which he wrote, "Dear Ella—It has been a long road but now I think we are getting somewhere." And then in a corner he put the word "Teheran," which means so much to us.

Of course there have been many others as the years have passed, such women as Caro Lloyd, who was an inspiration to all of us. Not only have I lost the companionship of some of my older friends but like all the people of America today I have suffered from the loss of many of my young friends who have given their lives in the service of our country.

And now, as I near the end of my first eighty-two years, the greatest joy of all is to witness the coming into its own of organized labor as the decisive factor in our national life. All sections of the American people are waking up to the fact that their own future well being and security are dependent not only on the goods produced by labor, but on the well being and security of the workers themselves. In other words, that prosperity, like peace, is indivisible! And the workers, by their willingness to forego the strike weapon and to give themselves unstintingly to the war effort on the battle field and on the home front, have certainly shown that they have no interests apart from the highest interests of the nation as a whole. The workers have grown in maturity and power, and they have demonstrated that they can be counted on to use that power not only to achieve the conditions of work and the standards of living that are their right but to advance the interests of all the people. And they know that the first job is to wipe fascism from the face of the earth.

Index